The Long Night

SHE TURNED ON HIM FIERCELY:—"GO BACK!"
SHE CRIED

The Long Night

By

Stanley J. Weyman

Author of
A Gentleman of France, Under the Red Robe
The House of the Wolf

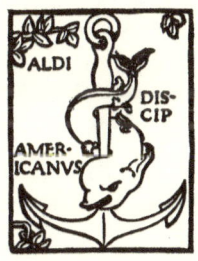

Illustrated by Solomon J. Solomon

WILDSIDE PRESS

CONTENTS

v

LIST OF ILLUSTRATIONS

The Long Night

CHAPTER I

A STUDENT OF THEOLOGY

THEY were about to shut the Porte St. Gervais, the north gate of Geneva. The sergeant of the gate had given his men the word to close; but at the last moment, shading his eyes from the low light of the sun, he happened to look along the dusty road which led to the Pays de Gex, and he bade the men wait. Afar off a traveller could be seen hurrying two donkeys toward the gate, with now a blow on this side, and now on that, and now a shrill cry. The sergeant knew him for Jehan Brosse, the bandy-legged tailor of the passage off the Corraterie, a sound burgher and a good man whom it were a shame to exclude. Jehan had gone out that morning to fetch his grapes from Möens; and the sergeant had pity on him.

He waited, therefore; and presently he was sorry that he had waited. Behind Jehan, a long way behind him, appeared a second wayfarer; a young man covered with dust who approached rapidly on long legs, a bundle jumping and bumping at his shoulders as he ran. The favour of the gate was not for such as he—a stranger; and the sergeant, anxious to bar, yet unwilling to shut out Jehan, watched his progress with disgust. As he feared, too, it turned out. Young legs caught up old ones: the stranger overtook Jehan, overtook the donkeys. A moment, and

3

he passed under the arch abreast of them, a broad smile
of acknowledgment on his heated face. He appeared to
think that the gate had been kept open out of kindness to
him.

And to be grateful. The war with Savoy—Italian
Savoy which, like an octopus, wreathed clutching arms
about the free city of Geneva—had come to an end some
months before. But a State so small that the frontier of
its inveterate enemy lies but two short leagues from its
gates, has need of watch and ward, and curfews and the
like, so that he was fortunate who found the gates of Geneva open after sunset in that year, 1602; and the stranger
seemed to know this.

As the great doors clanged together and two of the
watch wound up the creaking drawbridge, he turned to
the sergeant, the smile still on his face. "I feared that you
would shut me out!" he panted, still holding his sides. "I
would not have given much—for my chance of a bed a
minute ago."

The sergeant answered only by a grunt.

"If this good fellow had not been in front——"

This time the sergeant cut him short with an imperious
gesture, and the young man seeing that the guard also had
fallen stiffly into rank, turned to the tailor. He was overflowing with good nature: he must speak to someone. "If
you had not been in front," he began, "I——"

But the tailor also cut him short—frowning and laying
his finger to his lip and pointing mysteriously to the
ground. The stranger stooped to look more closely, but
saw nothing: and it was only when the others dropped
on their knees that he understood the hint and hastened to
follow the example. The soldiers bent their heads while

the sergeant recited a prayer for the safety of the city. He did this reverently, while the evening light—which fell grey between walls and sobered those who had that moment left the open sky and the open country—cast its solemn mantle about the party.

Such was the pious usage observed in that age at the opening and the closing of the gates of Geneva: nor had it yet sunk to a form. The nearness of the frontier and the shadow of those clutching arms, ever extended to smother the free State, gave a reality to the faith of those who opened and shut, and with arms in their hands looked back on ten years of constant warfare. Many a night during those ten years had Geneva gazed from her watch-towers on burning farms and smouldering homesteads; many a day seen the smoke of Chablais hamlets float a dark trail across her lake. What wonder if, when none knew what a night might bring forth, and the Fury of Antwerp was still a new tale in men's ears, the Genevese held Providence higher and His workings more near than men are prone to hold them in happier times?

Whether the stranger's reverent bearing during the prayer gained the sergeant's favour, or the sword tied to his bundle and the bulging corners of squat books which stuffed out the cloak gave a new notion of his condition, it is certain that the officer eyed him more kindly when all rose from their knees. "You can pass in now, young sir," he said nodding. "But another time remember, if you please, the earlier here the warmer welcome!"

"I will bear it in mind," the young man answered, smiling. "Perhaps you can tell me where I can get a night's lodging?"

"You come to study, perhaps?" The sergeant puffed

himself out as he spoke, for the fame of Geneva's college
and its great professor, Theodore Beza, was a source of
glory to all within the city walls. Learning, too, was a
thing in high repute in that day. The learned tongues still
lived and were passports opening all countries to scholars.
The names of Erasmus and Scaliger were still in the
mouths of men.

"Yes," the youth answered, "and I have the name of a
lodging in which I hope to place myself. But for to-night
it is late, and an inn were more convenient."

"Go then to the 'Bible and Hand,' " the sergeant answered. "It is a decent house, as are all in Geneva. If
you think to find here a roistering, drinking, swearing tavern, such as you'd find in Dijon——"

"I come to study, not to drink," the young man answered
eagerly.

"Well, the 'Bible in Hand,' then! It will answer your
purpose well. Cross the bridge and go straight on. It is
in the Bourg du Four."

The youth thanked him with a pleasant air, and turning
his back on the Gate proceeded briskly toward the heart
of the city. Though it was not Sunday the inhabitants were
pouring from the evening preaching as plentifully as if it
had been the first day of the week; and as he scanned their
grave and thoughtful faces—faces not seldom touched
with sternness or the scars of war—as he passed between
the gabled steep-roofed houses and marked their order and
cleanliness, as he saw above him and above them the great
towers of the Cathedral, the young man felt a youthful
fervour and an enthusiasm not to be comprehended in our
age.

To many of us the name and memory of Geneva stand

for anything but freedom. But to the Huguenot of that generation and day, the name of Geneva stood for freedom; for a fighting aggressive freedom, a full freedom in the State, a sober measured freedom in the Church. The city was the outpost, southward, of the Reformed religion and the Reformed learning; it sowed its ministers over half Europe, and where they went, they spread abroad not only its doctrines but its praise and its honour. If, even to the men of that day there appeared at times a something too stiff in its attitude, a something too near the Papal in its decrees, they knew with what foes and against what odds it fought, and how little consistent with the ferocity of that struggle were the compromises of life or the courtesies of the lists.

At any rate, in some such colours, framed in some such halo, Claude Mercier saw the Free City as he walked its narrow streets that evening, seeking the "Bible and Hand." In some such colours had his father, bred under Calvin to the Ministry, depicted it: and the young man, half French, half Vaudois, sought nothing better, set nothing higher, than to form a part of its life, and eventually to contribute to its fame. Good intentions and honest hopes tumbled over one another in his brain as he walked. The ardour of a new life, to be begun this day, possessed him. He saw all things through the pure atmosphere of his own happy nature: and if it remained to him to discover how Geneva would stand the test of a closer intimacy, at this moment, the youth took the city to his heart with no jot of misgiving. To follow in the steps of Theodore Beza, a Frenchman like himself and gently bred, to devote himself, in these surroundings, to the Bible and the Sword, and find in them salvation for himself and help for others—this seemed an end simple and sufficing: the end too, which all men in Geneva appeared to him to be pursuing that summer evening.

By-and-by a grave citizen, a psalm-book in his hand, directed him to the inn in the Bourg du Four; a tall house turning the carved ends of two steep gables to the street. On either side of the porch a long low casement suggested the comfort that was to be found within; nor was the pledge unfulfilled. In a trice the student found himself seated at a shining table before a simple meal and a flagon of cool white wine with a sprig of green floating on the surface. His companions were two merchants of Lyons, a vintner of Dijon, and a taciturn, soberly clad professor. The four elders talked gravely of the late war, of the prevalence of drunkenness in Zurich, of a sad case of witchcraft at Basle, and of the state of trade in Lausanne and the Pays de Vaud; while the student, listening with respect, contrasted the quietude of this house, looking on the grey evening street, with the bustle and chatter and buffoonery of the inns at which he had lain on his way from Chatillon. He was in a mood to appraise at the highest all about him, from the demure maid who served them to the cloaked burghers who from time to time passed the window wrapped in meditation. From a house hard by the sound of the evening psalms came to his ears. There are moods and places in which to be good seems of the easiest; to err, a thing well-nigh impossible.

The professor was the first to rise and retire; on which the two merchants drew up their seats to the table with an air of relief. The vintner looked after the retreating figure. "Of Lausanne, I should judge?" he said, with a jerk of the elbow.

"Probably," one of the others answered.

"Is he not of Geneva, then?" our student asked. He had listened with interest to the professor's talk and between whiles had wondered if it would be his lot to sit under him.

"No, or he would not be here!" one of the merchants replied, shrugging his shoulders.

"Why not, sir?"

"Why not?" The merchant fixed the questioner with eyes of surprise. "Don't you know, young man, that those who live in Geneva may not frequent Geneva taverns?"

"Indeed?" Mercier answered, somewhat startled. "Is that so?"

"It is very much so," the other returned with something of a sneer.

"And they do not!" quoth the vintner with a faint smile.

"Well, professors do not!" the merchant answered with a grimace. "I say nothing of others. Let the Venerable Company of Pastors see to it. It is their business."

At this point the host brought in lights. After closing the shutters he was in the act of retiring when a door near at hand—on the farther side of the passage if the sound could be trusted—flew open with a clatter. Its opening let out a burst of laughter, nor was that the worst: alas, above the laughter rang an oath—the ribald word of someone who had caught his foot in the step.

The landlord uttered an exclamation and went out hurriedly, closing the door behind him. A moment and his voice could be heard, scolding and persuading in the passage.

"Umph!" the vintner muttered, looking from one to the other with a humorous eye. "It seems to me that the Venerable Company of Pastors have not yet expelled the old Adam!"

Open flew the door and cut short the word. But it had been heard. "Pastors?" cried a raucous voice. "Passers and Flinchers is what I call them!" And a stout, heavy man, whose small pointed grey beard but emphasised the coarse virility of the face above it, appeared on the threshold, glaring at the four. "Pastors?" he repeated defiantly. "Passers and Flinchers, I say!"

"In Heaven's name, Messer Grio!" the landlord protested, hovering at his shoulder, "these are strangers——"

"Strangers? Ay, and flinchers, they too!" the intruder retorted, heedless of the remonstrance. And he lurched into the room, a bulky, reeling figure in stained green and tarnished lace. "Four flinchers! But I'll make them drink a cup with me or I'll prick their hides! Do you think we shed blood for you and are to be stinted of our liquor!"

"Messer Grio! Messer Grio!" the landlord cried, wringing his hands. "You will be my ruin!"

"No fear!"

"But I do fear!" the host retorted sharply, going so far as to lay a hand on his shoulder. "I do fear." Behind the man in green his boon-fellows flushed with drink had gathered, and were staring half curious, half in alarm into the room. The landlord turned and appealed to them. "For heaven's sake get him away quietly!" he muttered. "I shall lose my living if this be known. And you will suffer too! Gentlemen," he turned to the party at the table, "this is a quiet house, a quiet house in general, but——"

"Tut-tut!" said the vintner good-naturedly. "We'll drink a cup with the gentleman if he wishes it!"

"You'll drink or be pricked!" quoth Messer Grio; he

was one of those who grow offensive in their cups.   And while his friends laughed, he swished out a sword of huge length, and flourished it.   "Ca! Ca! Now let me see any man refuse his liquor!"

The landlord groaned, but thinking, it was plain, that soonest broken was soonest mended, he vanished, to return in a marvellously short space of time with four tall glasses and a flask of Neuchatel.   "'Tis good wine," he muttered anxiously.   "Good wine, gentlemen, I warrant you.   And Messer Grio here has served the State, so that some little indulgence——"

"What, art muttering?" cried the bully, who spoke French with an accent new and strange in the student's ears.   "Let be! Let be, I say! Let them drink, or be pricked!"

The merchants and the vintner took their glasses without demur: and, perhaps, though they shrugged their shoulders, were as willing as they looked.   The young man hesitated, took with a curling lip the glass which was presented to him, and then, a blush rising to his eyes, he pushed it from him.

"'Tis good wine," the landlord repeated.   "And no charge.   Drink, young sir, and——"

"I drink not on compulsion!" the student answered.

Messer Grio stared.   "What?" he roared.   "You——"

"I drink not upon compulsion," the young man repeated, and this time he spoke clearly and firmly.   "Had the gentleman asked me courteously to drink with him, that were another matter.   But——"

"Sho!" the vintner muttered, nudging him in pure kindness.   "Drink, man, and a fico for his courtesy so the wine be old!   When the drink is in, the sense is out, and," lowering his voice, "he'll let you blood to a certainty, if you will not humour him."

But the grinning faces in the doorway hardened the student in his resolution. "I drink not on compulsion," he repeated stubbornly. And he rose from his seat.

"You drink not?" Grio exclaimed. "You drink not? Then by the living——"

"For Heaven's sake!" the landlord cried, and threw himself between them. "Messer Grio! Gentlemen!"

But the bully, drunk and wilful, twitched him aside. "Under compulsion, eh!" he sneered. "You drink not under compulsion, don't you, my lad? Let me tell you," he continued with ferocity, "you will drink when I please, and where I please, and as often as I please, and as much as I please, you meal-worm! You half-weaned puppy! Take that glass, d'you hear, and say after me, Devil take——"

"Messer Grio!" the landlord protested.

"Devil take"—for a moment a hiccough gave him pause —"all flinchers! Take the glass, young man. That is well! I see you will come to it! Now say after me, Devil take——"

"That!" the student retorted, and flung the wine in the bully's face.

The landlord shrieked; the other guests rose hurriedly from their seats and got aside. Fortunately the wine blinded the man for a moment, and he recoiled, spitting curses and darting his sword hither and thither in impotent rage. By the time he had cleared his eyes the youth had got to his bundle, and, freeing his blade, placed himself in a posture of defence. His face was pale, but with the pallor of excitement rather than of fear; and the firm set of his mouth and the smouldering fire in his eyes as he confronted the drunken bravo, no less than the manner in which he handled his weapon, showed him as ready to pursue as he had been hardy to undertake the quarrel.

He gave proof of forethought, too. "Witness all, he drew first!" he cried; and his eyes quitting Grio for the briefest instant sought to meet the merchants' gaze. "I am on my defence. I call all here to witness that he has thrust this quarrel upon me!"

The landlord wrung his hands. "Oh dear, oh dear!" he cried. "In Heaven's name, gentlemen, put up! put up! Stop them! Will no one stop them!" And in despair, seeing no one move to arrest them, he made as if he would stand between them.

But the bully flourished his blade about his ears, and with a cry the goodman saved himself. "Out, skinker!" Grio cried grimly. "And you, say your prayers, puppy. Before you are five minutes older I will split you like a partridge though I cross the frontier for it. You have basted me with wine! I will baste you after another fashion! On guard! On guard, and——"

"*What is this?*"

The voice stayed Grio's tongue and checked his foot in the very instant of assault. The student, watching his blade and awaiting the attack, was surprised to see his point waver and drop. Was it a trick, he wondered? A stratagem? No, for a silence fell on the room, while those who held the floor hastened to efface themselves against the wall, as if they at any rate had nothing to do with the fracas. And next moment Grio shrugged his shoulders, and with a half-stifled curse stood back.

"What is this?"

The same question in the same tone. This time the student saw whose voice it was had stayed Grio's arm. Within the door a pace in front of two or three attendants, who had displaced the roisterers on the threshold, stood a spare dry-looking man of middle height, wearing his hat, and displaying a gold chain of office across the breast of his black velvet cloak. In age about sixty, he had nothing that at a first glance seemed to call for a second: his small pinched features, and the downward curl of the lip, which his moustache and clipped beard failed to hide, indicated a nature peevish and severe rather than powerful. On nearer observation, the restless eyes, keen and piercing, asserted themselves and redeemed the face from insignificance. When, as on this occasion, their glances were supported by the terrors of the State, it was not difficult to understand why Messer Blondel, the Syndic, though no great man to look at, had both weight with the masses, and a hold not to be denied over his colleagues in the Council.

No one took on himself to answer the question he had put, and in a voice, thin and querulous but with a lurking venom in its tone, "What is this?" the great man repeated, looking from one to another. "Are we in Geneva, or in Venice? Under the skirts of the scarlet woman, or where the magistrates bear not the sword in vain? Good Mr. Landlord, are these your professions? Your bailmen should sleep ill to-night, for they are likely to answer roundly for this! And whom have we sparking it here?" he continued. "Brawling and swearing and turning into a profligate's tavern a place that should be for the sober entertainment of travellers? Whom have we here—eh! Let me see them! Ah!"

"WHAT IS THIS?"
THE GREAT MAN
REPEATED,
LOOKING FROM
ONE TO ANOTHER

He paused rather suddenly, as his eyes met Grio's: and a little of his dignity fell from him with the pause. His manner underwent a subtle change from the judicial to the paternal. When he resumed, he wagged his head tolerantly, and a modicum of sorrow mingled with his anger. "Ah, Messer Grio! Messer Grio!" he said, "it is you, is it? For shame! For shame! This is sad, this is lamentable! Some indulgence, it is true"—he coughed—"may be due after late events, and to certain who have borne part in them. But this goes too far! Too far by a long way!"

"It was not I began it!" the bully muttered sullenly, a mixture of bravado and apology in his bearing. He sheathed his blade, and thrust the long scabbard behind him. "He threw a glass of wine in my face, Syndic, that is the truth. Is an old soldier who has shed blood for Geneva to swallow that, and give God thanks?"

The Syndic turned to the student, and licked his lips, his features more pinched than usual. "Are these your manners?" he said. "If so, they are not the manners of Geneva! Your name, young man, and your dwelling-place?"

"My name is Claude Mercier, last from Chatillon in Burgundy," the young man answered firmly. "For the rest, I did no otherwise than you, sir, must have done in my case!"

The magistrate snorted. "I!"

"Being treated as I was!" the young man protested. "He would have me drink whether I would or no! And in terms no man of honour could bear."

"Honour?" the Syndic retorted, and on the word exploded in great wrath. "Honour, say you? Then I know who is in fault. When men of your race talk of honour 'tis easy to saddle the horse. I will teach you that we know naught of honour in Geneva, but only of service! And naught of punctilios but much of modest behaviour! It is such hot blood as yours that is at the root of brawlings and disorders and such-like, to the scandal of the community: and to cool it I will commit you to the town gaol until to-morrow! Convey him thither," he continued, turning sharply to his followers, "and see him safely bestowed in the stocks. To-morrow I will hear if he be penitent, and perhaps, if he be in a cooler temper——"

But the young man, aghast at this sudden disgrace, could be silent no longer. "But, sir," he protested eloquently, "I had no choice. It was no quarrel of my beginning. I did but refuse to drink, and when he——"

"Silence, sirrah!" the Syndic cried, brutally cutting him short. "You will do well to be quiet!" And he was in the act of bidding his people bear their prisoner out without more ado when one of the merchants ventured to put in a word.

"May I say," he interposed timidly, "that until this happened, Messer Blondel, the young man's conduct was all that could be desired?"

"Are you of his company?"

"No, sir."

"Then best keep out of it!" the magistrate retorted sharply. "And you," to his followers, "did you hear me? Away with him!"

But as the men advanced to execute the order, the young man stepped forward. "One moment!" he said. "A moment only, sir. I caught the name of Blondel. Am I speaking to Messer Philibert Blondel?"

The Syndic nodded ungraciously. "Yes," he said. "I am he. What of it?"

"Only this, that I have a letter for him," the student answered, groping with trembling fingers in his pouch. "From my uncle, the Sieur de Beauvais of Nocle, by Dijon."

"The Sieur de Beauvais?"

"Yes."

"He is your uncle?"

"Yes."

"So! To be sure, I remember now," Blondel continued, nodding. "His name was Mercier. Certainly, it was. Well, give me the letter." His tone was still harsh, but it was not the same; and when he had broken the seal and read the letter—with a look half contemptuous, half uneasy—his brow cleared a little. "It were well young people knew better what became them," he cried, peevishly shrugging his shoulders. "It would save us all a great deal. However, for this time as you are a stranger and well credited, I find, you may go. But let it be a lesson to you, do you hear? Let it be a lesson to you, young man. Geneva," pompously, "is no place for brawling, and if you came hither for that, you will quickly find yourself between bars. See that you go to a fit lodging to-morrow, and do you, Mr. Landlord, have a care that he leaves you."

The young man's heart was full, but he had the wisdom to keep his temper and to say no more. The Syndic on his part was glad on second thoughts to be free from the matter. He was turning to go when it seemed to strike him that he owed something more to the bearer of the letter. He turned back. "Yes," he said, "I had forgotten. This week I am busy. But next week on some convenient day come to me, young sir, and I may be able to give you

a word of advice. In the forenoon will be best. Until
then—see to your behaviour!"

The young man bowed and waited, standing where he
was, until the bustle attending the Syndic's departure had
quite died away. Then he turned. "Now, Messer Grio,"
he said briskly, "for my part I am ready."

But Messer Grio had slipped away some minutes
before.

CHAPTER II

THE HOUSE ON THE RAMPARTS

THE affair at the inn which had threatened to turn out so unpleasantly for our hero, should have gone some way toward destroying the illusions with which he had entered Geneva. But faith is strong in the young, and hope stronger. The traditions of his boyhood and his fireside, and the stories, animate with affection for the cradle of the faith, to which he had listened at his father's knee, were not to be over-ridden by the shadow of an injustice, which, in the end, had not fallen. When the young man went abroad next morning and viewed the tall towers of St. Peter, of which his father had spoken—when, from those walls which had defied through so many months the daily and nightly threats of an ever-present enemy, he looked on the sites of conflicts still famous and on farmsteads but half risen from their ruins—when above all, he remembered for what those walls stood, and that here, on the borders of the blue lake, and within sight of the glittering peaks which charmed his eyes—if in any one place in Europe—the battle of knowledge and freedom had been fought, and the rule of the monk and the Inquisitor cast down, his old enthusiasm revived. He thirsted for fresh conflicts, for new occasions: and it is to be feared dreamt more of the sword than of the sacred Book, which he had come to study, and which, in Geneva, went hand in hand with it.

In the fervour of such thoughts and in the multitude of new interests which opened before him, he had well-nigh forgotten the Syndic's tyranny before he had walked a mile: nor might he have given a second thought to it but for the need which lay upon him of finding a new lodging before night. In pursuit of this he presently took his way to the Corraterie, a row of gabled houses, at the western end of the High Town, built within the ramparts, and enjoying over them a view of the open country, and the Jura. The houses ran for some distance parallel with the rampart, then retired inward and again came down to it; in this way enclosing a triangular open space or terrace. They formed of themselves an inner line of defence, pierced at the point farthest from the rampart by the Porte Tertasse: a gate it is true, which was often open even at night, for the wall in front of the Corraterie, though low on the town side, looked down from a great height on the ditch and the low meadows that fringed the Rhone. Trees planted along the rampart shaded this triangular space, and made it a favourite lounge from which the inhabitants of that quarter of the town could view the mountains and the sunset while tasting the freshness of the evening air.

A score of times had Claude Mercier listened to a description of this row of lofty houses dominating the ramparts. Now he saw it, and, charmed by the position and the aspect, he trembled lest he should fail to secure a lodging in the house which had sheltered his father's youth. Heedless of the suspicious glances shot at him by the watch at the Porte Tertasse, he consulted the rough plan which

his father had made for him—consulted it rather to assure
himself against error than because he felt doubt. The precaution taken, he made for a house a little to the right of
the Tertasse gate as one looks to the country. He mounted
by four steep steps to the door and knocked on it.

So quickly as to disconcert him it was opened. A lanky
youth about his own age bounced out. The lad wore a
cap and carried two or three books under his arm, much
as if he had been starting forth when the summons came.
The two gazed at one another a moment: then "Does
Madame Royaume live here?" Claude asked.

The other, who had light hair and light eyes, said curtly
that she did.

"Do you know if she has a vacant room?" Mercier
asked timidly.

"She will have one to-night!" the youth answered with
temper in his tone: and he dashed down the steps and went
off along the street without ceremony or explanation.
Viewed from behind he had a thin neck which agreed well
with a small retreating chin.

The door remained open, and after hesitating a moment
Claude tapped once and again with his foot; receiving no
answer he ventured over the threshold, and found himself
in the living-room of the house. It was cool, spacious, and
well-ordered, although in a corner the boarded-up stairs
leading to the higher floors bulked largely. On the left
of the entrance a wooden settle flanked a wide fireplace,
in front of which a small heavy table was placed. Another
table a little bigger stood in the middle of the room. Two
or three dark prints—one a portrait of Calvin—with a
framed copy of the Geneva catechism, and a small shelf of
books, took something from the plainness and added some-

thing to the comfort of the apartment, which boasted besides a couple of old oaken dressers highly polished and gleaming with long rows of pewter ware. Two doors stood opposite the entrance and appeared to lead—for one of them stood open—to a couple of closets: bedrooms they could hardly be called, yet in one of them Claude knew that his father had slept. And his heart warmed to it.

The house was still; the room was somewhat dark, the windows being low and long, strongly barred, and shaded by the trees, through the cool greenery of which the light filtered in. The young man stood a moment, and hearing no footstep or movement wondered what he should do. At length he ventured to the door of the staircase and, opening it, coughed. Still no one answered or came, and unwilling to intrude farther he turned about and waited on the hearth. In a corner behind the settle he noticed two half pikes and a long-handled sword; on the seat of the settle itself lay a thin folio bound in stained sheepskin. A log smouldered on the hearth, and below the great black pot which hung over it two or three pans and pipkins sat deep among the white ashes. Save for these there was no sign in the room of a woman's hand or use. And he wondered. Certainly the young man who had departed so hurriedly had said it was Madame Royaume's. There could be no mistake.

Well, he would go and come again. But even as he formed the resolution and turned toward the outer door —which he had left open—he heard a faint sound above, a step light but slow. It seemed to start from the uppermost floor of all, so long was it in descending; so long was it before, waiting on the hearth cap in hand, he saw a shadow darken the line below the staircase door. A sec-

ond later this opened and a young girl entered and closed
it behind her. She did not see him; unconscious of his
presence she crossed the floor and shut the outer door.

There was a something in her bearing which went to the
heart of the young man who saw her for the first time;
a depression, a dejection, so much at odds with her youth
and her slender grace, that it scarcely needed the sigh with
which she turned to draw him a pace nearer. At that
moment their eyes met. She, who had not known of his
presence, started with a low cry, and stared wide-eyed: he
began hurriedly to speak.

"I am the son of M. Gaston Mercier, of Chatillon," he
said, "who lodged here formerly. At least," he stammered, beginning to doubt, "if this be the house of Madame Royaume, he lodged here. A young man who met
me at the door said that Madame lived here, and had a .
room."

"He admitted you? The young man who went out?"

"Yes."

She gazed steadfastly at him a moment, as if she
doubted him or suspected some trick: then, "We have no
room," she said.

"But you will have one to-night," he answered.

"I do not know."

"But—but from what he said," Claude persisted doggedly, "he meant that his own room would be vacant, I
think."

"It may be," she answered ungraciously, the heaviness
which surprise had lifted for a moment settling on her
afresh. "But we shall take no new lodgers. Presently
you would go," with a cold smile, "as he goes to-day."

"My father lodged here three years," Claude answered,

raising his head proudly. "He did not go until he returned to France. I ask nothing better than to lodge where
my father lodged. Madame Royaume will know my
name. When she hears that I am the son of M. Gaston
Mercier, who often speaks of her——"

"He fell sick here, I think?" the girl said. She scanned
him anew with the first show of interest that had escaped
her. Yet reluctantly, it seemed; with a kind of aloofness
hard to explain.

"He had the plague in the year M. Chausse, the pastor
of St. Gervais, died of it," Claude answered eagerly.
"When it was so bad. And Madame nursed him and
saved his life. He often speaks of it and of Madame with
gratitude. If Madame Royaume would see me?"

"It is useless," she answered impatiently. "Quite useless, sir. I tell you we have no room. And—I wish you
good-morning." She turned from him with a curt gesture
of dismissal, and kneeling beside the embers began to occupy herself with the cooking pots; stirring one and tasting
another, and raising a third a little aslant at the level of
her eyes that she might peer into it the better. He lingered, watching her, expecting her to turn. But when she
had skimmed the last jar and set it back, and screwed it
down among the embers, she remained on her knees,
staring absently at a thin flame which had sprung up under the black pot. She had forgotten his presence, wholly
and utterly; forgotten him, as he judged, in thoughts
as deep and gloomy as the wide dark cavern of chimney
which yawned above her head and dwarfed the slight figure
kneeling Cinderella-like among the ashes.

Claude Mercier looked, and wondered, and at last
longed: longed to comfort, to cherish, to draw to himself

and shelter the budding womanhood before him, so fragile
now, so full of promise for the future. And quick as the
flame had sprung up under her breath, a magic flame
awoke in his heart, and burned high and hot. If he did,
not lodge here,

> *" The sky might fall, fish fly, and sheep pursue*
> *The tawny monarch of the Libyan strand! "*

But he would lodge here. He coughed.

She started and turned, and seeing him, seeing that he
had not gone, she rose with a frown. "What is it?" she
said. "For what are you waiting?"

"I have something in charge for Madame Royaume,"
he answered.

"I will give it her," she returned sharply. "Why did
you not say so at once?" And she held out her hand.

"No," he said hardily. "I have it in charge for her
hand only."

"I am her daughter."

He shook his head stubbornly.

What she would have done on that—her face was hard
and promised nothing—is uncertain. Fortunately for the
young man's hopes, a dull report as of a stick striking the
floor in some room above reached their ears; he saw the
girl's eyes flicker, alter, grow strangely soft. "Wait!"
she said imperiously; and stooping to take one of the pipkins from the fire, she poured its contents into a wooden
bowl which stood beside her on the table. She added a
horn-spoon and a pinch of salt, fetched a slice of coarse
bread from a cupboard in one of the dressers, and taking
all in skilled steady hands, hands childishly small, though

brown as nuts, she disappeared through the door of the staircase.

He waited, looking about the room, and at this, and at that, with a new interest. He took up the book which lay on the settle: it was a learned volume, part of the works of Paracelsus, having strange figures and diagrams inter-woven with the crabbed Latin text. A passage which he deciphered, abashed him by its profundity, and he laid the book down, and went from one to another of the black-framed engravings; from these to an oval piece in coarse Limoges enamel, which hung over the little shelf of books. At length he heard a step descending from the upper floors, and presently the girl appeared in the doorway.

"My mother will see you," she said, her tone as ungra-cious as her look. "But you will say nothing of lodging here, if it please you. Do you hear?" she added, her voice rising to a more imperious note.

He nodded.

She turned on the lowest step. "She is bed-ridden," she muttered hurriedly, as if she felt the need of explanation. "She is not to be disturbed with house matters, or who comes or goes. You understand that, do you?"

He nodded, with a mental reservation, and followed her up the confined staircase. Turning sharply at the head of the first flight he saw before him a long narrow passage, lighted by a window that looked to the back. On the left of this passage which led to a second set of stairs were two doors, one near the head of the lower flight, the other at the foot of the second. She led him past both—they were closed—and up the second stairs and into a room under the tiles, a room of good size but with a roof which sloped in unexpected places.

A woman lay there comely with the beauty of advancing years, though weak and frail if not ill; the woman of whom he had so often heard his father speak with gratitude and respect. It was neither of his father, however, nor of her, that Claude Mercier thought as he stood holding Madame Royaume's hand and looking down at her. For the girl who had gone before him into the room had passed to the other side of the bed, and the look which she and her mother exchanged as the daughter leant over the couch and their eyes met, the look of love and protection on one side, of love and confidence on the other—that look and the tone, wondrous and gentle, in which the girl, so curt and abrupt below, named him—these revealed a bond and an affection for which the life of his own family had furnished him with no precedent.

For his mother had had many children, and his father still lived. But these two, his heart told him as he held Madame Royaume's shrivelled hand in his, were alone. They had each but the other, and lived each in the other, in this room under the tiles with the deep-set dormer windows that looked across the Pays de Gex to the Jura. For how much that prospect of vale and mountain stood in their lives, how often they rose to it from the same bed, how often looked at it in sunshine and in shadow with the house still and quiet below them, he seemed to know—to guess. He had a swift mental vision of their lives, and then Madame Royaume's voice recalled him to himself.

"You are newly come to Geneva?" she said, gazing at him.

"I arrived yesterday."

"Yes, yes, of course," she answered. She spoke quickly and nervously. "Yes, you told me so." She turned to her daughter and laid her hand on hers as if she talked more easily so. "Your father, Monsieur Mercier," with an obvious effort, "is well, I hope?"

"Perfectly, and he begged me to convey his grateful re-membrances. Those of my mother also," the young man added warmly.

"Yes, he was a good man! I remember when he was ill, and M. Chausse—the pastor, you know"—the remi-niscence appeared to agitate her—"was ill also——"

The girl leant over her quickly. "Monsieur Mercier has brought something for you, mother," she said.

"Ah?"

"His grateful remembrances and this letter," Claude murmured with a blush. He knew that the letter con-tained no more than he had already said; compliments, and the hope that Madame Royaume might be able to receive the son as she had received the father.

"Ah!" Madame Royaume repeated, taking the letter with fingers that shook a little.

"You shall read it when Monsieur Mercier is gone," her daughter said. And with that she looked across at the young man. Her eyes commanded him to take his leave.

But he was resolute. "My father expresses the hope," he said, "that you will grant me the same privilege of liv-ing under your roof, Madame, which was so highly prized by him."

"Of course, of course," she answered eagerly, her eyes lighting up. "Anne—I am not myself, sir, able to overlook the house—you will see to—to this being done?"

"My dear mother, we have no room!" the girl replied;

and stooping, hid her face an instant while she whispered in her mother's ear. Then aloud, "We are so full, so—it goes so well," she continued gaily. "We never have any room. I am sure, sir"—and again she faced him across the bed—"it is a disappointment to my mother, but—it cannot be helped."

"Dear, dear, it is unfortunate!" Madame Royaume exclaimed; and then with a fond look at her daughter, "Anne manages so well!"

"Yet if there be a room at any time vacant?"

"You shall assuredly have it."

"But, mother dear," the girl cried, "M. Grio and M. Basterga are permanent—on the floor below. And Esau and Louis are now with us, and have but just entered on their course at college. And you know," she continued softly, "no one ever leaves your house before they are obliged to leave it, mother dear!"

The mother patted the daughter's hand. "No," she said proudly. "It is true. And we cannot turn anyone away. And yet," looking up at Anne, "the son of Messer Mercier? You do not think—do you think that we could put him——"

"A closet however small!" Claude cried.

"Unfortunately the room beyond this can only be entered through this one."

"It is out of the question!" the girl responded; and for the first time her tone rang a little hard. The next instant she seemed to repent of her petulance, for she stooped and kissed the thin face sunk in the pillow's softness. Then, rising, "I am sorry," she continued stiffly and decidedly. "But it is impossible!"

"Still—if a vacancy should occur?" he pleaded.

Her eyes met his defiantly. "We will inform you," she said.

"Thank you," he answered humbly. "Perhaps I am fatiguing your mother?"

"I think you are a little tired, dear," the girl said, stooping over her. "A little fatigues you."

Madame's cheeks were flushed; her eyes shone brightly, even feverishly. Claude saw this and, having pushed his plea and his suit as far as he dared, he hastened to take his leave. His thoughts had been busy with his chances all the time, his eyes with the woman's face; yet he bore away with him, a curiously vivid picture of the room, of the bow-pot blooming in the farther dormer, of the brass skillet beside the green boughs which filled the hearth, of the spinning wheel in the middle of the floor, and the great Bible on the linen chest beside the bed, of the sloping roof, and a queer triangular cupboard which filled one corner.

At the time, as he followed the girl downstairs, he thought of none of these things. He only asked himself what mystery lay in the bosom of this quiet house, and what he should say when he stood in the room below at bay before her. Of one thing he was still sure—sure, ay and surer, since he had seen her with her mother,

> "*The sky might fall, fish fly, and sheep pursue*
> *The tawny monarch of the Libyan strand!*"

but he lodged here. The mention of his adversary of last night, which had not escaped his ear, had only hardened him in his resolution. The room of Esau—or was it Louis' room—must be his! He must be Jacob the Supplanter.

She did not speak as she preceded him down the stairs,

and before they emerged one after the other into the living-room, which was still unoccupied, he had formed his
plan. When she moved toward the outer door to open it
he refused to follow, he stood still. "Pardon me," he said,
"would you mind giving me the name of the young man
who admitted me?"

"I do not see——"

"I only want his name."

"Esau Tissot."

"And his room—which was it?"

Grudgingly she pointed to the nearer of the two closets,
that of which the door stood open.

"That one?"

"Yes."

He stepped quickly into it, and surveyed it carefully.
Then he laid his cap on the low truckle-bed. "Very well,"
he said raising his voice and speaking through the open
door, "I will take it." And he came out again.

The girl's eyes sparkled. "If you think," she cried,
her temper showing in her face, "that that will do you any
good——"

"I don't think," he said, cutting her short, "I take it.
Your mother undertook that I should have the first vacant
room. Tissot resigned this room this morning. I take it.
I consider myself fortunate, most fortunate."

Her colour came and went. "If you were a boor," she
cried, "you could not behave worse!"

"Then I am a boor!"

"But you will find," she continued, "that you cannot
force your way into a house like this. You will find that
such things are not done in Geneva. I will have you put
out!"

"Why?" he asked, craftily resorting to argument. "When I ask only to remain and be quiet? Why, when you have, or to-night will have, an empty room? Why, when you lodged Tissot, will you not lodge me? In what am I worse than Tissot or Grio," he continued, "or—I forget the other's name? Have I the plague, or the falling sickness? Am I Papist or Arian? What have I done that I may not lie in Geneva, may not lie in your house? Tell me, give me a reason, show me the cause, and I will go."

Her anger had died down while he spoke and while she listened. In its place, the lowness of heart to which she had yielded when she thought herself alone before the hearth, showed in every line of her figure. "You do not know what you are doing," she said sadly. And she turned and looked through the casement. "You do not know what you are asking, or to what you are coming."

"Did Tissot know when he came?"

"You are not Tissot," she answered in a low tone, "and may fare worse."

"Or better," he answered gaily. "And at worst——"

"Worse or better you will repent it," she retorted. "You will repent it bitterly!"

"I may," he answered. "But at least you never shall."

She turned and looked at him at that; looked at him as if the curtain of apathy had fallen from her eyes and she saw him for the first time as he was, a young man, upright and not uncomely. She looked at him with her mind as well as her eyes, and seeing felt curiosity about him, pity for him—felt her own pulses stirred by his presence and his aspect. A faint colour, softer than the storm flag which had fluttered there a minute before, rose to her cheeks, her lips began to tremble. He feared that she

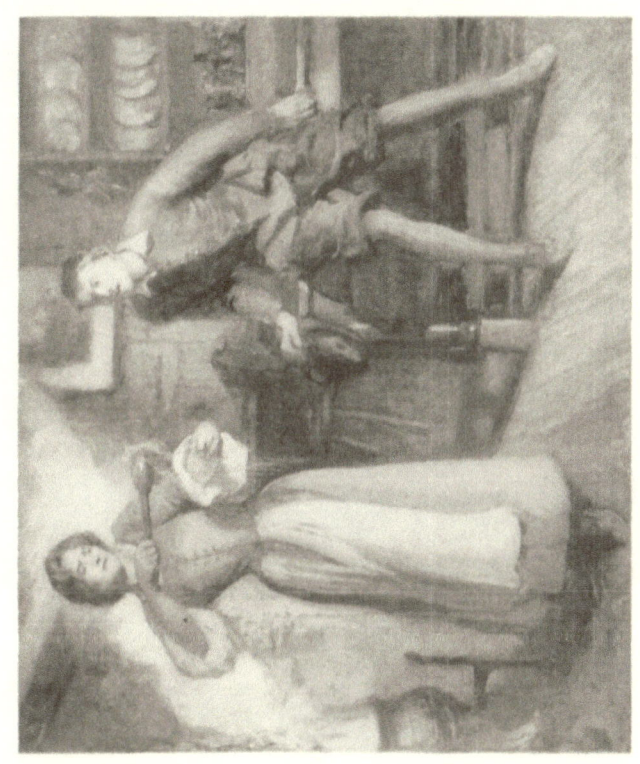

"DON'T," HE CRIED HOARSELY. "I WILL NOT BEAR IT! DON'T."

was going to weep, and "That is settled!" he said cheerfully. "Good!" and he went into the little room and
brought out his cap. "I lay last night at the 'Bible and
Hand,' and I must fetch my cloak and pack."

She stayed him by a gesture. "One moment," she said.
"You are determined to—to do this? To lodge here?"

"Firmly," he answered smiling.

"Then wait." She passed by him and, moving to the
fireplace, raised the lid of the great black pot. The broth
inside was boiling and bubbling to within an inch of the
lip, the steam rose from it in a fragrant cloud. She took
an iron spoon and looked at him, a new and strange look
in her eyes. "Stand where you are," she said, "and I will
try you, if you are fit to come to us or no. Stand, do you
hear!" she repeated, a note of excitation, almost of mockery, in her voice, "where you are whatever happens! You
understand?"

"Yes, I am to stand here, whatever happens," he answered, wondering. What was she going to do?

She was going to do a thing ouside the limits of his
imagination. She dipped the iron spoon in the pot and,
extending her left arm, deliberately allowed some drops of
the scalding liquor to fall on the bare flesh. He saw the
arm wince, saw red blisters spring out on the white skin,
he caught the sharp indraw of her breath; but he did not
move. Again she dipped the spoon, looking at him with
defiant eyes, and with the same deliberation she let the stuff
fall on the living flesh. This time the perspiration sprang
out on her brow, her face burned suddenly hot, her whole
frame shrank under the torture.

"Don't," he cried hoarsely. "I will not bear it! Don't!"
And he uttered a cry half-articulate, like a beast's.

"Stand there!" she said. And still he stood: stood, his hands clenched and his lips drawn back from his teeth, while she dipped the spoon again, and—though her arm shook now like an aspen and there were tears of pain in her eyes—let the dreadful stuff fall a third time.

She was white when she turned to him. "If you do it again," he cried furiously, "I will upset—the cursed pot."

"I have done," she said smiling faintly. "I am not very brave—after all!" And going to the dresser, her knees trembling under her, she poured out some water and drank it greedily. Then she turned to him, "Do you understand?" she said, with a long tense look. "Are you prepared? If you come here, you will see me suffer worse things, things a hundred times, a thousand times worse than that. You will see me suffer, and you will have to stand and see it. You will have to stand and suffer it. You will have to stand. If you cannot, do not come."

"I stood it," he answered doggedly. "But there are things flesh and blood cannot stand. There is a limit——"

"The limit I shall fix," she said proudly. "Not you."

"But you will fix it?"

"Perhaps. At any rate, that is the bargain. You may accept or refuse. You do not know where I stand, and I do. You must see and be blind, feel and be dumb, hear and make no answer, unless I speak—if you are to come here."

"But you will speak—sometime?"

"I do not know," she answered wearily, and her whole form wilting, she looked away from him. "I do not know. Go now, if you please, and remember!"

CHAPTER III

THE old town of Geneva, cramped for many generations within the narrow corselet of its walls, was not large; and it was still high noon when Mercier, after paying his reckoning at the "Bible and Hand," and collecting his possessions, found himself again in the Corraterie. A pleasant breeze stirred the leafy branches which shaded the ramparts, and he stood a moment, resting his burden on the breast-high wall, and gazing across the hazy landscape to the mountains, beyond which lay Chatillon and his home.

Yet it was not of his home he was thinking as he gazed; nor was it his mother's or his father's face that the dancing heat of mid-day mirrored for him as he dreamed. Oh, happy days of youth when an hour and a face change all, and a glance from shy eyes, or the pout of strange lips blinds to the world and the world's ambitions! Happy youth! But alas for the studies this youth had come so far to pursue, for the theology he had crossed those mountains to imbibe—at the pure source and fount of evangelical doctrine! Alas for the venerable Beza, pillar and pattern of the faith, whom he had thirsted to see, and the grave of Calvin, aim and end of his pilgrimage! All Geneva held but one face for him now, one presence, one

gracious personality. A scarlet blister on a round white
arm, the quiver of a girl's lip a-tremble on the verge of
tears—these and no longing for home, these and no
memory of father or mother or the days of childhood,
filled his heart to overflowing. He dreamed with his
eyes on the hills, but it was not

> " *Of Providence, foreknowledge, will and fate,*
> *Fixed fate, free will, foreknowledge absolute,*"

the things he had come to study; but of a woman's trouble
and the secret life of the house behind him, of which he
was about to form a part.

At length the call of a sentry at the Porte Tertasse
startled him from his thoughts. He roused himself, and
uncertain how long he had lingered he took up his cloak
and bag and, turning, hastened across the street to the door
at the head of the four steps. He found it on the latch,
and with a confident air, which belied his real feelings, he
pushed it open and presented himself.

For a moment he fancied that the room held only one
person, a young man who sat at the table in the middle of
the room and, surprised by the appearance of a stranger,
suspended his spoon in the air that he might the better gaze
at him. But when our hero had set down his bag behind
the door, and turned to salute the other, he discovered his
error; and despite himself he paused in the act of advancing, unable to hide his concern. At the table on the hearth,
staring at him in silence, sat two other men. And one of
the two was Grio.

Mercier paused we have said; he expected an outburst of anger if not an assault. But a second glance at

the old ruffian's face relieved him: a stare of vacant wonder
made it plain that Grio sober retained little of the doings
of Grio drunk. Nevertheless, the silent gaze of the three
—for no one greeted him—took Claude aback; and it was
but awkwardly and with embarrassment that he approached
the table, and prepared to add himself to the party. Something in their looks as well as their silence whispered him
unwelcome. He blushed painfully, and addressing the
young man at the larger table,

"I have taken Tissot's room," he said shyly. "This is
his seat, I suppose. May I take it?" And indicating an
empty bowl and spoon on the nearer side of the table, he
made as if he would sit down before them.

In place of answering, the young man looked from him
to the two on the hearth, and laughed—a foolish frightened laugh. The sound led Mercier's eyes in the same direction, and he took in for the first time the aspect of the
man who sat with Grio; a man of great height and bulk,
with a large plump face and small grey eyes. It struck
Mercier as he met the fixed stare of those eyes, that he
had entered, perhaps, with less ceremony than was becoming, and that he ought to make amends for it; and, in
the act of sitting down in the vacant seat, he turned and
bowed politely to the two at the other table.

"Tissotius timuit, jam peregrinus adest!" the big man
murmured in a voice at once silky and sonorous. And then
ignoring Mercier, but looking blandly at the young man
who sat facing him at the table. "What is this of Tissot?"
he continued. "Can it be," with a side glance at the new-
comer, "that we have lost our—I may not call him our
quintessence or alcahest—rather shall I say our baser ore,
that at the virgin touch of our philosophical stone blushed

into ruddy gold? And burned ever brighter and hotter in her presence! Tissot gone, and with him all those fair experiments! Is it possible?"

The young man's grin showed that he savoured a jest. But, "I know nothing," he muttered sheepishly. "'Tis new to me."

"Tissot gone!" the big man repeated in a tone humorously melancholy. "No more shall we

> *Upon his viler metal test our purest pure*
> *And see him transmutations three endure!*'

Tissot gone! And you, sir, come in his place. What change is here! A stranger, I believe?"

"In Geneva, yes," Claude answered, wondering and a little abashed. The man spoke with an air of power and weight.

"And a student, doubtless—in our Academia? Like our Tissot? Yes. It may be," he continued in the same smooth tones wherein ridicule and politeness appeared to be so nicely mingled that it was hard to say if he spoke in jest or earnest, "like him in other things! It may be that we have gained and not lost. And that qualities finer and more susceptible underlie an exterior more polished and an ease more complete——" he bowed, "than our poor Tissot could boast! But here is

> *Our stone angelical whereby*
> *All secret potencies to light are brought!*'

Doubtless," with a wave of the hand he indicated the girl who had that moment entered—"you have met before?"

"I could not otherwise," Claude answered coldly—he began to resent both the man and his manner—"have engaged the lodging." And he rose to take from the girl's hand the broth she was bringing. She, on her side, made no sign that she noticed a change; or, that it was no longer Tissot she served. She gave him what he needed, mechanically and without meeting his eyes. Then turning to the others, she waited on them after the same fashion. For a minute or two there was silence in the room.

A strange silence, Claude thought, listening and wondering: as strange and embarrassing as the talk of the man who shared with Grio the table by the fireplace: as strange as the atmosphere about them, which hung heavy, to his fancy, and oppressive, fraught with unintelligible railleries, with subtle jests and sneers. The girl went to and fro, from one to another, her face pale, her manner quiet. Had he not seen her earlier with another look in her eyes, had he not detected a sinister something underlying the big man's good-humour, he would have learned nothing from her; he would have fancied that all was as it should be in the house and in the company.

As it was he understood nothing. But he felt that a something was wrong, that a something overhung the party. Seated as he was he could not without turning see the faces of the two at the other table, nor watch the girl when she waited on them. But the suspicion of a smile which hovered on the lips of the young man who sat opposite—and whom he could see—kept him on his guard. Was a trick in preparation? Were they about to make him pay his footing? No, for they had had no notice of his coming. They could not have laid the mine. Then why that smile? And why—this silence?

On a sudden he caught the sound of a movement behind him, the swirl of a petticoat and the clang of a pewter plate as it fell noisily to the floor. His companion looked up swiftly, the smile on his face broadening to a snigger. And Claude turned too as quickly as he could and looked, his face hot, his mind suspecting a prank to be played on him; to his astonishment he discovered nothing to account for the laugh. The girl appeared to be bending over the embers on the hearth, the men to be engaged with their meal; and baffled and perplexed he turned again and, with ears burning, bent over his plate. He was glad when the stout man broke the silence for the second time.

"Agrippa," he said, "has this of amalgams. That whereas gold, silver, tin are valuable in themselves, they attain when mixed with mercury to a certain light and sparkling character, as who should say the bubbles on wine, or the light resistance of beauty, which in the one case and the other add to the charm. Such to our simple pleasures" —he continued with a rumble of deep laughter—"our simple pleasures which I must now also call our pleasures of the past, was our Tissot! Who, running fluid hither and thither, where resistance might be least of use, was as it were the ultimate sting of enjoyment. Is it possible that we have in our friend a new Tissot?"

The young man at the table giggled. "I did not know Tissot!" Claude replied sharply and with a burning face— they were certainly laughing at him. "And therefore I cannot say."

"Mercury, which completes the amalgam," the stout man muttered absently and as if to himself, "when heated sublimes over!" And then turning after a moment's silence to the girl, "What says our Quintessential stone to this?" he continued. "Her Tissot gone will she still work her wonders? Still of base Grios and the weak alloys red bridegrooms make? Still—kind Anne, your hand!"

Silence! Silence again. What were they doing? Claude, full of suspicion, turned slowly to see what it meant; turned to learn what it was on which the greedy eyes of his table-fellow were fixed so intently. And now he saw, more or less. The stout man and Grio had their heads together and their faces bent over the girl's hand, which the former held. On them, however, Claude scarcely bestowed a glance. It was the girl's face which caught and held his eyes, nay, made them burn. Had it blushed, had it showed white, he had borne the thing more lightly, he had understood it better. But her face showed dull and apathetic; as she stood looking down at the men, suffering them to do what they would with her hand, a strange passivity was its sole expression. When the big man (whose name Claude learned later was Basterga), after inspecting the palm, kissed it with mock passion, and so surrendered it to Grio, who also pressed his coarse old lips to it, while the young man beside Claude laughed—no change came over her. Released she turned again to the hearth, impassive. And Claude, his heart beating, recognised that this was the hundredth performance; that so far from being a new thing it was a thing so old as to be staled to her, moving her less, though there were insult and derision in every glance of the men's eyes, than it moved him.

And noting this he began in a dim way to understand. This was the thing which Tissot had not been able to bear; which in the end had driven the young man with the small chin from the house. This was the pleasantry to which his feeble resistance, his outbursts of anger, of jealousy, or of

protest had but added piquancy, the ultimate sting of pleasure to the jaded palate of the performers.   This was the
obsession under which she lay, the trial and persecution
which she had warned him he would find it hard to
witness.

Hard?   He believed her, trifling as was the thing he
had seen.   For behind it he had a glimpse of other and
worse things, and behind all of some shadowy brooding
mystery which compelled her to suffer and forbade her to
complain.   What that was he could not conceive, what
it could be he could not conceive: nor had he long to
consider the question.   He found the shifty eyes of his
table-fellow fixed upon him, and, though the moment his
own eyes met them they were averted, he fancied that they
sped a glance of intelligence to the table behind him, and
he hastened to curb, if not his feelings, at least the show
of them.   He had his warning.   It was not as Tissot he
must act if he would help her, but more warily, more patiently, biding her time, and letting the blow, when the
time came, precede the word.   Unwarned he had acted, it
is probable, as Tissot had acted, weakly and stormily:
warned, he had no excuse if he failed her.   Young as he
was he saw this.   The fault lay with him if he made the
position worse instead of better.

Whether, do what he would, his feelings made themselves known—for the shoulders can speak, and eloquently,
on occasion—or the reverse was the case, and his failure
to rise to the bait disappointed the tormentor, the big man
Basterga presently resumed the attack.

"Tissotius pereat, Tissotianus adest!" he muttered with
a sneer.   "But perhaps, young sir, Latinity is not one of
your subjects.   The tongue of the immortal Cicero——"

GRIO PRESSED

HIS COARSE LIPS

TO THE GIRL'S

HAND

"I speak it a little," Claude answered quietly. "It were foolish to approach the door of learning without the key."

"Oh, you are a wit, young sir! Well, with your wit and your Latinity can you construe this:

'Stultitiam expellas, furca tamen usque recurret
Tissotius periit terque quaterque redit!'"

"I think so," Claude replied gravely.

"Good, if it please you! And the meaning?"

"Tissot was a fool, and you are another!" the young man returned. "Will you now solve me one, reverend sir, with all submission?"

"Said and done!" the big man answered disdainfully.

"Nec volucres plumæ faciunt nec cuspis Achillem! Construe me that then if you will!"

Basterga shrugged his shoulders. "Fine feathers do not make fine birds," he said. "If you apply it to me," he continued with a contemptuous face—"I——"

"Oh, no, to your company," Claude answered. Self-control comes hardly to the young, and he had already forgotten his rôle. "Ask him what happened last night at the 'Bible and Hand,'" he continued, pointing to Grio, "and how he stands now with his friend the Syndic!"

"The Syndic?"

"The Syndic Blondel!"

The moment the words had passed his lips, Claude repented. He saw that he had struck a note more serious than he intended. The big man did not move, but over his fat face crept a watching expression; he was startled. His eyes, reduced almost to pin-points, seemed for an instant the eyes of a cat about to spring. The effect was

so plain indeed that it bewildered Claude: and so far diverted his attention from Grio, the real target, that when
the bully, who had listened stupidly to the exchange of wit,
proved by a brutal oath his comprehension of the reference
to himself, the young man scarcely heard him.

"The Syndic Blondel?" Basterga muttered after a
pregnant pause. "What know you of him, pray?"

Before the young man could answer, Grio broke in. "So
you have followed me here, have you?" he cried striking
his jug on the table and glaring across the board at the
offender. "You weren't content to escape last night it
seems. Now——"

"Enough!" Basterga muttered, the keen expression of
his face unchanged. "Softly! Softly! Where are we?
I don't understand. What is this? Last night——"

"I want not to rake up bygones if you will let them be,"
Claude answered with a sulky air half assumed. "It was
you who attacked me."

"You puppy!" Grio roared. "Do you think——"

"Enough!" Basterga said again: and his eyes leaving
the young man fixed themselves on his companion. "I begin to understand," he murmured, his voice low, but not
the less menacing for that, or for the cat-like purr in it.
"I begin to comprehend. This is one of your tricks, Messer
Grio. One of the clever tricks you play in your cups!
Some day you'll do that in them will—No!" repressing
the bully as he attempted to rise. "Have done now and
let us understand. The 'Bible and Hand,' eh? 'Twas
there, I suppose, you and this youth met, and——"

"Quarrelled," said Claude sullenly. "That is all."

"And you followed him hither?"

"No, I did not."

"No? Then how come you here?" Basterga asked, his eyes still watchful. "In this house, I mean? Eh? 'Tis not easy to find."

"My father lodged here," Claude vouchsafed. And he shrugged his shoulders, thinking that with that the matter was clear.

But Basterga continued to eye him with something that was not far removed from suspicion. "Oh," he said. "That is it, is it? Your father lodged here. And the Syndic—Blondel, was it you said? How comes he into it? Grio was prating of him, I suppose?" For an instant, while he waited the answer to the question, his eyes shrank again to pin-points.

"He came in and found us at sword-play," Claude answered. "Or just falling to it. And though the fault was not mine, he would have sent me to prison if I had not had a letter for him."

"Oh!" And then returning with a manifest effort to the tone and manner of a few minutes before.

> " *Impiger, Iracundus, Inexorabilis acer*
> *Jura neget sibi nata, nihil non arroget armis,*"

he hummed. "I doubt if such manners will be appreciated in Geneva, young man," and furtively he wiped his brow. "To old stagers like my friend here who has given his proofs of fidelity to the State, some indulgence is granted——"

"I see that," Claude answered with sarcasm.

"I am saying it. But you, if you will not be warned, will soon find or make the town too hot for you."

"He will find this house too hot for him!" growled his

companion, who had made more than one vain attempt to assert himself. "And that to-day! To-day! Perdition, I know him now," he continued, fixing his blood-shot eyes on the young man, "and if he crows here as he crowed last night, his comb shall be cut, and as well soon as late, for there will be no living with him! There, don't hold me, man! Let me at him!" And he tried to rise.

"Fool, have done!" Basterga replied, still restraining him, but only by the exertion of considerable force. And then in a lower tone but one partially audible, "Do you want to draw the eyes of all Geneva this way?" he continued. "Do you want the house marked and watched and every gossip's tongue wagging about it? You did harm enough last night, I'll answer, and well if no worse comes of it! Have done, I say, or I shall speak, you know to whom!"

"Why does he come here? Why does he follow me?" the sot complained.

"Cannot you hear that his father lodged here?"

"A lie!" Grio cried vehemently. "He is spying on us! First at the 'Bible and Hand' last night, and then here! It is you who are the fool, man. Let me go! Let me at him, I say!"

"I shall not!" the big man answered firmly. And he whispered in the other's ear something which Claude could not catch. Whatever it was it cooled Grio's rage. He ceased to struggle, nodded sulkily and sat back. He stretched out his hand, took a long draught, and having emptied his jug, "Here's Geneva!" he said, wiping his lips with the air of a man who had given a toast. "Only don't let him cross me! That is all. Where is the wench?"

"She has gone upstairs," Basterga answered with one

eye on Claude. He seemed to be unable to shake off a secret doubt of him.

"Then let her come down," Grio answered with a grin,
half drunken, half brutal, "and make her show sport.
Here, you there," to the young man who shared Claude's
table, "call her down and——"

"Sit still!" Basterga growled, and he trod—Claude was
almost sure of it—on the bully's foot. "It is too late, and
these young gentlemen should be at their themes. Theology, young sir," he turned to Claude with the slightest
shade of over-civility in his pompous tone, "like the pursuit of the Alcahest, which some call the Quintessence of
the Elements, allows no rival near its throne!"

"I attend my first lecture to-morrow," Claude answered
drily. And he kept his seat. His face was red and his
hand trembled. They would call her down for their sport,
would they! Not in his presence, nor again in his absence
if he could avoid it.

Grio struck the table. "Call her down!" he ordered in
a tone which betrayed the influence of his last draught.
"Do you hear!" And he looked fiercely at Louis Gentilis,
the young man who sat opposite Claude.

But Louis only looked at Basterga and grinned.

And Basterga it was plain was not in the mood to amuse
himself. Whatever the reason, the big man was no longer
at his ease in Mercier's company. Some unpleasant
thought, some suspicion, born of the incident at the "Bible
and Hand," continued to rankle in his mind, and, strive
as he would, betrayed its presence in the tone of his voice
and the glance of his eye. He was uneasy, nor could he
hide his uneasiness. To the look which Gentilis shot at
him he replied by one which imperatively bade the young

man keep his seat. And "Enough fooling for to-day,"
he said, and stealthily he repressed Grio's resistance.
"Enough! Enough! I see that the young gentleman
does not altogether understand our humours. He will
come to them in time, in time," his voice almost fawning,
"and see that we mean no harm. Did I understand," he
continued, addressing Claude directly, "that your father
knew Messer Blondel?"

"Who is now Syndic? My uncle did," Claude answered, rather curtly. He was more and more puzzled by
the change in Basterga's manner. Was the big man a
poltroon whom the bold front shown to Grio brought to
heel? Or was there something behind, some secret upon
which his words had unwittingly touched?

"He is a good man," Basterga said. "And of the first
in Geneva. His brother, too, who is Procureur-General.
Their father died for the State, and the sons, the Syndic in
particular, served with high honour in the late war. Savoy
has no stouter foe than Philibert Blondel, nor Geneva a
more devoted son." And he drank as if he drank a toast
to them.

Claude nodded.

"A man of great parts too. Probably you will wait on
him?"

"Next week. I was near waiting on him after another
fashion," Claude continued rather grimly. "Between him
and your friend there," with a glance at Grio, who had re-
lapsed into a moody glaring silence, "I was like to get more
gyves than justice."

The big man laughed. "Our friend here has served the
State," he remarked, "and does what another may not.
Come, Messer Grio," he continued, clapping him on the

shoulder, as he rose from his seat. "We have sat long enough. If the young ones will not stir, it becomes the old ones to set an example. Will you to my room and view the precipitation of which I told you?"

Grio gave a snarling assent, and got to his feet; and the party broke up with no more words. Claude took his cap and prepared to withdraw, well content with himself and the line he had taken. But he did not leave the house until his ears assured him that the two who had ascended the stairs together had actually repaired to Basterga's room on the first floor, and there shut themselves up.

CHAPTER IV

CÆSAR BASTERGA

HAD it been Claude Mercier's eye in place of his
ear which attended the two men to the upper room,
he would have remarked—perhaps with surprise,
since he had gained some knowledge of Grio's temper—
that in proportion as they mounted the staircase, the toper's
crest drooped, and his arrogance ebbed away; until at the
door of Basterga's chamber, it was but a sneaking and awkward man who crossed the threshold.

Nor was the reason far to seek. Whatever the stand-
point of the two men in public, their relations to one another in private were delivered up, stamped and sealed, in
that moment of entrance. While Basterga, leaving the
other to close the door, strode across the room to the window and stood gazing out, his very back stern and contemptuous, Grio fidgeted and frowned, waiting with ill-
concealed penitence, until the other chose to address him.
At length Basterga turned, and his gleaming eyes, his
moon-face pale with anger, withered his companion.

"Again! Again!" he growled—it seemed he dare not
lift his voice. "Will you never be satisfied until we are
broken on the wheel? You dog, you! The sooner you
are broken the better, were that all! Ay, and were that
all, I could watch the bar fall with pleasure! But do you

think I will see the fruit of years of planning, do you think
that I will see the reward of this brain—this! this, you
brainless idiot, who know not what a brain is—" and he
tapped his brow repeatedly with an earnestness almost gro-
tesque—"do you think that I will see this cast away, because you swill, swine that you are! Swill, and prate in
your cups!"

"'Fore God, I said nothing!" Grio whined. "I said
nothing! It was only that he would not drink and I——"

"Made him?"

"No, he would not, I say, and we were coming to blows.
And then——"

"He gave back, did he?"

"No, Messer Blondel came in."

Cæsar Basterga stretched out his huge arms. "Fool!
Fool! Fool!" he hissed, with a gesture of despair. "There
it is! And Blondel, who should have sent you to the whip-
ping-post, or out of Geneva, has to cloak you! And men
ask why, and what there is between our most upright Syndic, and a drunken, bragging——"

"Softly," Grio muttered with a flash of sullen resentment. "Softly, Messer Basterga! I——"

"A drunken, swilling, prating pig!" the other persisted.
"A broken soldier living on an hour of chance service?
Pooh, man," with contempt, "do not threaten me! Do
you think that I do not know you more than half craven?
The lad below there would cut your comb yet, did I suffer
it. But that is not the point. The point is that you must
needs advertise the world that you and the Syndic, who has
charge of the walls, are hail-fellows, and the world will ask
why! Or he must deal with you as you deserve and out
you go from Geneva!"

"Per Bacco! I am not the only soldier," Grio muttered, "who ruffles it here!"

"No! And is not that half our battle?" Basterga rejoined, gazing on him with massive scorn. "To make use of them and their grumbling, and their distaste for the Venerable Company of Pastors who rule us! Such men are our tools; but tools only, and senseless tools, for Geneva won for the Grand Duke, and what will they be the better, save in the way of a little more licence and a little more drink? But for you I had something better! Is the little farm in Piedmont not worth a month's abstinence? Is drink-money for your old age, when else you must starve or stab in the purlieus of Genoa, not worth one month's sobriety? But you must needs for the sake of a single night's debauch ruin me and get yourself broken on the wheel!"

Grio shrank under his eye. "There is no harm done," he muttered at last. "Nobody suspects what is between us."

"How do you know that?" came the retort. "What? You think it is natural Blondel should favour such as you?"

"It will not be the first time Geneva cloak has covered Genoa velvet!"

"Velvet!" Basterga repeated with a sneer. "Rags rather!" And then more quickly, "But that is not all, nor the half. Do you think Blondel, who is on the point, Blondel, who will and will not and on whom all must turn, Blondel the upright, the impeccable, the patriotic, without whom we can do nothing, and who, I tell you, hangs in the balance—do you think he likes it, blockhead? Or is the more inclined to trust his life with us when he sees us brawlers, toss-pots, common swillers? Do you think he on whom I am bringing to bear all the resources of this brain—this!"—and again the big man tapped his forehead with tragic earnestness—"and whom you could as much move to side with us as you could move yonder peak of the Jura from its base—do you think he will deem better of our part for this?"

"Well, no."

"No! No, a thousand times!"

"But I count drunk the same as sober for that!" Grio cried, plucking up spirit and speaking with a gleam of defiance in his eye. "For it is my opinion that you have no more chance of moving him than I have! And so to be plain you have it, Messer Basterga. For how are you going to move him? With what? Tell me that!"

"Ah!"

"With money?" Grio continued with a fluency which showed that he spoke on a subject to which he had given much thought. "He is rich and ten thousand crowns would not buy him. And the Grand Duke, much as he craves Geneva, will not spend over boldly."

"No, I shall not move him with money."

"With power and rank, then? Will the Grand Duke make him Governor of Geneva? No, for he dare not trust him. And less than that, what is it to Syndic Blondel, whose word to-day is all but law in Geneva?"

"No, nor with power," Basterga answered quietly.

"Is it with revenge, then? There are men I know who love revenge. But he is not of the south, and at such a risk revenge were dearly bought."

"No, nor with revenge," Basterga replied.

"A woman, then? For that is all that is left," Grio rejoined in triumph. Once he had spoken out, he had put himself on a level with his master; he had worsted him, or he was much mistaken. "Perhaps, from the way you have played with the little prude below, it is a woman. But they are plenty, even in Geneva, and he is rich and old."

"No, nor with a woman."

"Then with what?"

"With this!" Basterga replied. And for the third time, drawing himself up to his full height, he tapped his brow. "Do you doubt its power?"

For answer Grio shrugged his shoulders, his manner sullen and contemptuous.

"You do?"

"I don't see how it works, Messer Basterga," the veteran muttered. "I say not you have not good wits. You have, I grant it. But the best of wits must have their means and method. It is not by wishing and willing——"

"How know you that?"

"Eh?"

"How know you that?" Basterga repeated with sudden energy, and he shook a massive finger before the other's eyes. "But how know you anything," he continued with disdain, as he dropped the hand again, and turned on his heel, "dolt, imbecile, rudiment that you are? Ay, and blind to boot, for it was but the other day I worked a miracle before you, and you learned nothing from it."

"It is no question of miracles," the other muttered doggedly. "But of how you will persuade the Syndic Blondel to betray Geneva to Savoy!"

"Is it so? Then tell me this: the girl below who smacked your face a month back because you laid a hand upon her wrist, and who would have had you put to the door the same day—how did I tame her? Can you answer me that?"

Grio's face fell remarkably. "No, master," he said, nodding thoughtfully. "I grant it. I cannot. A wilder filly was never handled."

"So! And yet I tamed her. And she suffers you! She's sport for us within bounds. Yet do you think she likes it when you paw her hand or lay your dirty arm about her waist, or steal a kiss? Think you the blood mounts and ebbs for nothing? Or the tears rise and the lip trembles and the limbs shake for sheer pleasure? I tell you, if eyes could slay, you had breathed your last some weeks ago."

"I know," Grio answered, nodding thoughtfully. "I have wondered and wondered, ay, many a time, how you did it."

"Yet I did it? You grant that?"

"Yes."

"And you do not understand—with what?"

Grio shook his head.

"Then why mistrust me now, blockhead," the other retorted, "when I say that as I charmed her, I can charm Blondel? Ay, and more easily. You know not how I did the one, nor how I shall do the other," the big man continued. "But what of that?" And in a louder voice, and with a gusto which showed how genuine was his delight in the metre,

> " *Pauci quos æquus amavit*
> *Jupiter aut ardens evexit ad æthera virtus*
> *Dis geniti potuere,*"

he mouthed. "But that," he added, looking scornfully at his confederate, "is Greek to you!"

Grio's altered aspect, his crestfallen air owned the virtue of the argument if not of the citation; which he did not understand. He drew a deep breath. "Per Bacco," he said, "if you do do it, Messer Basterga——"

"I shall do it," Basterga retorted, "if you do not spoil all with your drunken tricks!"

Grio was silent a moment, sunk plainly in reflection. Presently his blood-shot eyes began to travel respectfully and even timidly over the objects about him. In truth, the room in which he found himself was worthy of inspection, for it was no common room, either in aspect or furnishing. It boasted, it is true, none of the weird properties, the skulls and corpse-lights, dead hands, and waxen masks with which the necromancer of that day sought to impress the vulgar mind. But in place of these a multitude of objects, quaint, curious, or valuable, filled that half of the room which was farther from the fire-hearth. On the wall, flanked by a lute and some odd-looking rubrical calendars, were three or four silver discs, engraved with the signs of the Zodiac; these were hung in such a position as to catch the light which entered through the heavily leaded casement. On the window-seat below them a pile of Plantins and Elzevirs threatened to bury a steel casket. On the table several rolls of vellum and papyrus, peeping from metal cylinders, leant against a row of brass-bound folios. A handsome fur covering masked the truckle-bed, but this, too, bore its share of books, as did two or three long trunks covered with stamped and gilded leather which stood against the wall and were so long that the ladies of the day had the credit of hiding their gallants in them. On stools lay more books, and yet more books, with a medley of other things: a silver flagon, and some weapons, a chessboard, an enamelled triptych and the like.

In a word, this half of the room wore the aspect of a

library, low-roofed and richly furnished. The other half, partly divided from it by a curtain, struck the eye differently. A stove of peculiar fashion, equipped with a powerful bellows, cumbered the hearth; and before this on a long table were ranged a profusion of phials and retorts, glass vessels of odd shapes, and earthen pots. Crucibles and alembics stood in the ashes before the stove, and on a side-board placed under the window were scattered a set of silver scales, a chemist's mask, and a number of similar objects. Cards bearing abstruse calculations hung everywhere on the walls; and over the fireplace, inscribed in gold and black letters, the Greek word "EUREKA" was conspicuous.

The existence of such a room in the quiet house in the Corraterie was little suspected by the neighbours, and if known would have struck them with amazement. To Grio its aspect was familiar: but in this case familiarity had not removed his awe of the unknown and the magical. He looked about him now, and after a pause,

"I suppose you do it—with these," he murmured, and with an almost imperceptible shiver he pointed to the crucibles.

"With those?" Basterga exclaimed, and had the other ascribed supernatural virtues to the cinders or the bellows he could not have thrown greater scorn into his words. "Do you think I ply this base mechanic art for aught but to profit by the ignorance of the vulgar? Or think by pots and pans and mixing vile substances to make this, which by nature is this, into that which by nature it is not! I, a scholar? A scholar? No, I tell you, there was never alchemist yet could transmute but one thing—poor into rich, rich into poor!"

"But," Grio murmured with a look and in a voice of disappointment, "is not that the true transmutation which a thousand have died seeking, and one here and there, it is rumoured has found? From lead to gold, Messer Basterga?"

"Ay, but the lead is the poor Alchemist, who gets gold from his patron by his trick. And the gold is the poor fool who finds him in his living, and being sucked, turns to lead! There you have your transmutation."

"Yet——"

"There is no yet!"

"But Agrippa," Grio persisted, "Cornelius Agrippa, who sojourned here in Geneva and of whom, master, you speak daily—was he not a learned man?"

"Ay, even as I am!" Cæsar Basterga answered, swelling visibly with pride. "But constrained, even as I am to ply the baser trade and stoop to that we see and touch and smell! Faugh! What lot more cursed than to quit the pure ether of Latinity for the lower region of matter? And in place of cultivating the 'literæ humaniores,' which is the true cultivation of the mind, and sets a man, mark you, on a level with princes, to stoop to handle virgin milk and dragon's blood, as they style their vile mixtures; or else grope in dead men's bodies for the thing which killed them. Which is a pure handicraft and chirurgeon, unworthy a scholar, who stoops of right to naught but the goose-quill!"

"And yet, master, by these same things——"

"Men grow rich," Basterga cried with a sneer, "and get power? Ay, and the bastard sits in the chair of the legitimate; and pure learning goes bare while the seekers after the Stone and the Elixir (who, in these days are descend-

ing to invent even lesser things and smaller advantages
that in the learned tongues have not so much as names)
grow in princes' favour and draw on their treasuries! But
what says Seneca? 'It is not the office of Philosophy to
teach men to use their hands. The object of her lessons
is to form the soul and the taste.' And Aldus Manucius,
vir doctissimus, magister noster," here he raised his hand
to his head as if he would uncover, "says also the same,
but in a Latinity more pure and translucent, as is his custom."

Grio scratched his head. The other's vehemence
whether he sneered or praised, flew high above his dull
understanding. He had his share of the reverence for
learning which marked the ignorant of that age: but to
what better end, he pondered stupidly, could learning be
directed than to the discovery of that which must make its
owner the most enviable of mortals, the master of wealth
and youth and pleasure! It was not to this, however, that
he directed his objection: the *argumentum ad hominem*
came more easily to him. "But you do this?" he said,
pointing to the paraphernalia about the stove.

"Ay," Basterga rejoined with vehemence. "And why,
my friend? Because the noble rewards and the considera-
tion which former times bestowed on learning are to-day
diverted to baser pursuits! Erasmus was the friend of
princes, and the correspondent of kings. Della Scala was
the companion of an Emperor, Morus, the Englishman,
was the right arm of a king. And I, Cæsar Basterga of
Padua, bred in the pure Latinity of our Master Manucius,
yield to none of these. Yet am I, if I would live, forced
to stoop 'ad vulgus captandum!' I must kneel that I may
rise! I must wade through the mire of this base pursuit

that I may reach the firm ground of wealth and learned
ease.   But think you that I am the dupe of the art where-
with I dupe others?   Or, that once I have my foot on firm
ground I will stoop again to the things of matter and sense.
No, by Hercules!" the big man continued, his eye kindling,
his form dilating.   "This scheme once successful, this feat
that should supply me for life, once performed, Cæsar
Basterga of Padua will know how to add, to those laurels
which he has already gained,

> ' *The bays of Scala and the wreath of More,*
> *Erasmus' palm and that which Lipsius wore.*' "

And in a kind of frenzy of enthusiasm the scholar fell to
pacing the floor, now and again mouthing hexameters, now
and again spurning with his foot a pot or an alembic
which had the ill luck to lie in his path.   Grio watched
him, and watching him, grew only more puzzled—and
more puzzled.   He could have understood a moral shrinking from the enterprise on which they were both embarked
—the betrayal of the city that gave them shelter.   He
could have understood—he had superstition enough—a
moral distaste for alchemy and those practices of the black
art which his mind connected with it.   But this superiority
of the scholar, this aloofness, not from the treachery, but
from the handicraft, was beyond him.   And for that reason it imposed on him the more.

Not the less, however, was he importunate to know
wherein Basterga trusted.   To rave of Scholarship and
Scaliger was one thing, to bring Blondel into the plot which
was to transfer Geneva to Savoy and strike the heaviest
blow at the Reformed that had been struck in that gen-

eration was another thing, and one remote. The Syndic was something discontented and inclined to intrigue; that was true, Grio knew it. But to parley with the Grand Duke's emissaries, and strive to get and give not, that was one thing; while, to betray the town and deliver it tied and bound into the hands of its Arch-Enemy was another, and a far more weighty matter. One, too, to which in Grio's judgment—and in the dark lanes of life he had seen and weighed many men—the magistrate would never be brought.

"Shall you need my aid with him?" he asked after a while, seeing the scholar still wrapt in thought. The question was not lacking in craft.

"Your aid? With whom?"

"With Messer Blondel."

"Pshaw, man," Basterga answered, rousing himself from his reverie. "I had forgotten him and was thinking of that villain Scioppius and his tract against Joseph Justus. Do you know," he continued with a snort of indignation, "that in his 'Hyperbolimæus,' not content with the statement that Joseph Justus left his laundress's bill at Louvain unpaid, he alleges that I—I, Cæsar Basterga of Padua—was broken on the wheel at Munster a year ago for the murder of a gentleman!"

Grio turned a shade paler. "If this business miscarry," he said, "the statement may prove within a year of the mark. Or nearer, at any rate, than may please us."

Basterga smiled disdainfully. "Think it not!" he answered, extending his arms and yawning with unaffected sincerity. "There was never scholar yet died on the wheel."

"No?"

"No, friend, no. Nor will, unless it be Scioppius, and he is unworthy of the name of scholar. No, we have our disease, and die of it, but it is not that. Nevertheless," he continued with magnanimity, "I will not deny that when Master Pert-Tongue downstairs put our names together so pat, it scared me. It scared me. For how many chances were there against such an accident? Or what room to think it an accident, when he spoke clearly with the *animus pugnandi?* No, I'll not deny he touched me home."

Grio nodded grimly. "I would we were rid of him!" he growled. "The young viper! I foresee danger from him."

"Possibly," Basterga replied. "Possibly. In that case measures must be taken. But I hope there may be no necessity. And now, I expect Messer Blondel in an hour, and have need, my friend, of thought and solitude before he comes. Knock at my door at eight this evening and I may have news for you."

"You don't think to resolve him to-night?" Grio muttered with a look of incredulity.

"It may be. I do not know. In the meantime silence, and keep sober!"

"Ay, ay!"

"But it is more than ay, ay!" Basterga retorted with irritation; with something of the temper, indeed, which he had betrayed at the beginning of the interview. "Scholars die otherwise, but many a broken soldier has come to the wheel! So do you have a care of it! If you do not——"

"I have said I will!" Grio cried sharply. "Enough scolding, master. I've a notion you'll find your own task a little beyond your hand. See if I am not right!" he added. And with this show of temper on his side also, he went out and shut the door loudly behind him.

Basterga stood a few moments in thought. At length

" Dimidium facti, qui bene cœpit, habet !"

he muttered. And shrugging his shoulders he looked about him, judging with an artistic eye the effect which the room would have on a stranger. Apparently, he was not perfectly content with it, for, stepping to one of the long trunks, he drew from it a gold chain, some medals, and a jewelled dagger, and flung these carelessly on a box in a corner. He set up the alembics and pipkins which he had overturned, and here and there he opened a black-lettered folio, discovered an inch or two of crabbed Hebrew, or the corner of an illuminated script. A cameo dropped in one place, a clay figure of Minerva set up in another, completed the picture.

His next proceeding was less intelligible. He unearthed from the pile of duodecimos on the window-seat the steel casket which has been mentioned. It was about twelve inches long and as many wide: and as deep as it was broad. Wrought in high relief on the front appeared an elaborate representation of Christ healing the sick; on each end, below a massive ring, appeared a similar design. The box had an appearance of strength out of proportion to its size: and was furnished with two locks, protected and partly hidden by tiny shields.

Basterga handling it gently polished it awhile with a cloth, and then bearing it to the inner end of the room he set it on a bracket beside the hearth. This place was evidently made for it, for on either side of the bracket hung a steel chain and padlock; with which, and the rings, the scholar proceeded to secure the casket to the wall. This done, he stepped back and contemplated the arrangement with a smile of contemptuous amusement.

"It is neither so large as the Horse of Troy," he murmured complacently, "nor so small as the Wafer that purchased Paris. It is neither so deep as hell, nor so high as heaven, nor so craftily fastened a wise man may not open it, nor so strong a fool may not smash it. But it may suffice. Messer Blondel is no Solomon, and may swallow this as well as another thing. In which event, Ave atque vale, Geneva! But here he comes. And now to cast the bait!"

CHAPTER V

THE ELIXIR VITÆ

AS the Syndic crossed the threshold of the scholar's room, he uncovered with an air of condescension that, do what he would, was not free from uneasiness. He had persuaded himself, he had been all the morning persuading himself, that any man might pay a visit to a learned scholar—why not? Moreover, that a magistrate in paying such a visit, was but in the performance of his duty, and might plume himself accordingly on the act.

Yet two things like worms in the bud would gnaw at his peace. The first was conscience; if the Syndic did not know he had reason to suspect that Basterga bore the Grand Duke's commission, and was in Geneva to further his master's ends. The second source of his uneasiness he did not acknowledge even to himself, and yet it was the more powerful: it was a suspicion—a strong suspicion, though he had met Basterga but twice—that in parleying with the scholar he was dealing with a man for whom he was no match, puff himself out as he might; and who secretly despised him.

Perhaps, the fact that the latter feeling ceased to vex him before he had been a minute in the room, was the best

testimony to Basterga's tact and management that could be
desired. Not that the scholar was either effusive or abject.
It was rather by a frank address which took equality for
granted, and by an easy assumption that the visit had no
importance, that he calmed Messer Blondel's nerves and
soothed his pride.

"If I do not the honour of my poor apartment so press-
ingly as some," he said presently, "it is out of no lack of
respect, Messer Syndic. But because, having had much
experience of visitors, I know that nothing fits them so well
as to be left at liberty, nothing irks them so much as to be
over-pressed. Here now I have some things that are
thought curious, even in Padua, but I do not know whether
they will interest you."

"Manuscripts?"

"Yes, manuscripts and the like. This," Basterga lifted
one from the table and placed it in his visitor's hands, "is
a facsimile, prepared with the utmost care, of the 'Codex
Vaticanus,' the most ancient manuscript of the New Tes-
tament. Of interest in Geneva, where by the hands of your
great printer, Stephens, M. de Beza has done so much to
advance the knowledge of the sacred text. But you are
looking at that chart?"

"Yes. What is it, if it please you?"

"It is a plan of the ancient city of Aurelia," Basterga replied, "which Cæsar, in the first book of his Commentaries
places in Switzerland, but which, some say, should be
rather in Savoy."

"Indeed, Aurelia!" the Syndic muttered, turning it
about. It was a plan beautifully and elaborately finished,
but, like most of the plans of that day, it was without
names. "Aurelia?"

"Yes, Aurelia."

"But I seem to—is this water?"

"Yes, a lake," Basterga replied, stooping with a faint smile to the plan.

"And this a river?"

"Yes."

"Aurelia? But—I seem to know the line of this wall, and these bastions. Why, it is—Messer Basterga," in a tone of surprise, not unmingled with anger—"you play with me! it is Geneva!"

Basterga permitted his smile to become more apparent. "Oh, no, Aurelia," he said lightly and almost jocosely. "Aurelia in Savoy, I assure you. Whatever it is, however, we have no need to take it to heart, Messer Blondel. Believe me, it comes from, and is not on its way to, the Grand Duke's library at Turin."

The Syndic showed his displeasure by putting the map from him.

"Your taste is rather for other things," Basterga continued, affecting to misunderstand the act. "This illuminated manuscript, now, may interest you? It is in characters which are probably strange to you?"

"Is it Hebrew?" the Syndic muttered stiffly, his temper still asserting itself.

"No, it is in the ancient Arabic character; that into which the works of Aristotle were translated as far back as the ninth century of our era. It is a curious treatise by the Arabic sage, Ibn Jasher, who was the teacher of Ibn Zohr, who was the teacher of Averroes. It was carried from Spain to Rome about the year 1000 by the learned Pope Sylvester the Second, who spoke Arabic and of whose library it formed part."

"Indeed!" Blondel responded, staring at it, "it must be of great value. How came it into your possession, Messer Basterga?"

Basterga opened his mouth and shut it again. "I do not think I can tell you that," he said drily.

"It contains, I suppose, some curious things?"

"Curious?" Basterga replied impulsively, "I should say so! Why, it was in that I found——" And there in apparent confusion he broke off. He laughed awkwardly, and then—"Well, you know," he resumed, "we students find many things interest us which would fail to touch the man of affairs." And, as if he wished to change the subject, he took the manuscript from the Syndic's hand and threw it carelessly on the table.

Messer Blondel thought the carelessness overdone, and, his interest aroused, he followed the manuscript, he scarcely knew why, with his eyes. "I think I have heard the name of Averroes?" he said. "Was he not a physician?"

"He was many things," Basterga answered negligently. "As a physician he was, I believe, rather visionary than practical. I have his Colliget, his most famous work in that line, but for my part in the case of an ordinary disease, I would rather trust myself," with a shrug of contempt, "to the Grand Duke's physician."

"But in the case—of an extraordinary disease?" the Syndic asked shrewdly.

Basterga frowned. "I meant in any disease," he said. "Did I say extraordinary?"

"Yes," Messer Blondel answered stoutly. The frown had not escaped him. "But I take it, you are something of a physician yourself?"

"I have studied in the school of Fallopius, the chirur-geon of Padua," the scholar answered coldly. "But I am a scholar, Messer Blondel, not a physician, much less a practitioner of the ancillary art, which I take to be but a base and mechanical handicraft."

"Yet, chemistry—you pursue that?" the other rejoined with a glance at the farther table and its load of strange-looking phials and retorts.

"As an amusement," Basterga replied with a gesture of haughty deprecation. "A parergon, if you please. I take it, a man may dip into the mystical writings of Paracelsus without prejudice to his Latinity; and into the cabalistic lore of the school of Cordova without losing his taste for the pure oratory of the immortal Cicero. Virgil himself, if we may believe Helinandus, gave the weight of his great name to such sports. And Cornelius Agrippa, my learned fore-runner in Geneva——"

"Went something farther than that!" the Syndic struck in with a meaning nod, twice repeated. "It was whispered and more than whispered—I had it from my father—that he raised the devil here, Messer Blondel; the very same that at Louvain strangled one of Agrippa's scholars who broke in on him before he could sink through the floor."

Basterga's face took on an expression of supreme scorn. "Idle tales!" he said. "Fit only for women! Surely you do not believe them, Messer Blondel?"

"I?"

"Yes, you, Messer Syndic."

"But this, at any rate, you'll not deny," Blondel retorted eagerly. "That he discovered the Philosopher's Stone?"

"And lived poor, and died no richer?" Basterga rejoined in a tone of increasing scorn.

"Well, for the matter of that," the Syndic answered more slowly, "that may be explained."

"How?"

"They say, and you must have heard it, that the gold he made that way turned in three days to egg-shells and parings of horn."

"Yet having it three days," Basterga asked with a sneer, "might he not buy all he wanted?"

"Well, I can only say that my father, who saw him more than once in the street, always told me—and I do not know anyone who should have known better——"

"Pshaw, Messer Blondel, you amaze me!" the scholar struck in, rising from his seat and adopting a tone at once contemptuous and dictatorial. "Do you not know," he continued, "that the Philosopher's Stone was and is but a figure of speech, which stands as some say for the perfect element in nature, or as others say for the vital principle—that vivifying power which evades and ever must evade the search of men? Do you not know that the sages whose speculations took that direction were endangered by accusations of witchcraft; and to evade these and to give their researches such an aspect as would command the confidence of the vulgar, gave out that they were seeking either the Philosopher's Stone, which would make all men rich, or the Elixir Vitæ which would confer immortality. Believe me, they were themselves no slaves to these expressions; nor were the initiated among their followers. But as time went on, tyros, tempted by sounds, and caught by theories of transmutation, began to interpret them literally, and, straying aside, spent their lives in the vain pursuit of wealth or youth."

Messer Blondel stared. Had Basterga, assailing him

from a different side, broached the precise story, to which, in the case of Agrippa or Albertus Magnus, the Syndic was prepared to give credence, he had received the overture with suspicion if not with contempt. He had certainly been very far from staking good florins upon it. But when the experimenter in the midst of the apparatus of science, and surrounded by things, which imposed on the vulgar, denied their value, and laughed at the legends of wealth and strength obtained by their means—this fact alone went very far toward convincing him that Basterga had made a discovery and was keeping it back.

The vital principle, the essential element, the final good, these were fine phrases, though they had a pagan ring. But men, the Syndic argued, did not spend money, and read much and live laborious days, merely to coin phrases. Men did not surround themselves with costly apparatus only to prove a theory that had no practical value. "He has discovered something," Blondel concluded in his mind, "if it be not the Philosopher's Stone or the Elixir of Life. I am sure he has discovered something." And with eyes grown sharp and greedy, the magistrate raked the room.

The scholar stood thoughtful where he had paused, and did not seem to notice him.

"Then do you mean," Blondel resumed after a while, "that all your work there"—he indicated by a nod the chemical half of the room—"has been thrown away?"

"Well——"

"Not quite, I think?" the Syndic said, his small eyes twinkling. "Eh, Messer Basterga, not quite? Now be candid."

"Well, I would not say," Basterga answered coldly, and as it seemed unwillingly, "that I have not derived something from the researches with which I have amused my leisure. But nothing of value to the general."

"Yet something of value to yourself," Blondel said, his head on one side.

Basterga frowned, then shrugged his shoulders. "Well, yes," he said at length. "As it happens, I have. But a thing of no use to anyone else, for the simple reason that——"

"You have only enough for yourself!"

The scholar looked astonished and a little offended.

"I do not know how you learned that," he said curtly, "but you are right. I had no intention of telling you as much. But, as you have guessed rightly so far, I do not mind adding that it is a remedy for a disease which the most learned physicians do not pretend to cure."

"A remedy?"

"Yes, vital and certain."

"And you discovered it?"

"No, I did not discover it," Basterga replied modestly. "But the story is so long that I will ask you to excuse me. I will tell it another time."

"I shall not excuse you, if you do not favour me with it now," the Syndic answered eagerly. As he leaned forward, there was a light in his eyes that had not been in them a few minutes before. His hand, too, shook as he moved it from the arm of his chair to his knee. "Nay, but, I pray you indulge me," he continued, in a tone anxious and almost submissive. "I shall not betray your secrets. I am no philosopher, and no physician, and, had I the will, I could make no use of your confidence."

"That is true," Basterga replied. "And, after all, the matter is simple. I do not know why I should refuse to oblige you. I have said that I did not discover this remedy. That is so. But it happened that in trying, by way of amusement, certain precipitations, I obtained not that which I sought—nor had I expected," he continued, smiling, "to obtain that, for it was the Elixir of Life, which, as I have told you, does not exist—but a substance new in my experience, and which seemed to me to possess some peculiar properties. I tested it in all the ways known to me, but without benefit or enlightenment; and in the end, was about to cast it aside, when I chanced on a passage in the manuscript of Ibn Jasher—the same, in fact, that I showed you a few minutes ago."

"And you found?" The Syndic's attitude as he leaned forward, with parted lips and a hand on each knee betrayed an interest so abnormal, it was odd that Basterga did not notice it.

Instead, "I found that he had made," the scholar replied quietly, "as far back as the tenth century the same experiment which I had just completed. And with the same result."

"He obtained the substance?"

Basterga nodded.

"And discovered? What?" Blondel asked eagerly. "Its use?"

"A certain use," the other replied cautiously. "Or, rather, it was not he, but an associate, called by him the Physician of Aleppo, who discovered it. This man was the pupil of the learned Rhazes, and the tutor of the equally learned Avicenna, the link in fact, between them; but his name, for some reason, perhaps because he mixed with his practice a greater degree of mysticism than was approved by the Arabian schools of the next generation, has not come

down to us. This man identified the product which had
defied Ibn Jasher's tests with a substance even then considered by most to be fabulous, or to be extracted only from
the horn of the unicorn if that animal existed. That it had
some of the properties of the fabled substance, he proceeded to prove to the satisfaction of Ibn Jasher by curing
of a certain incurable disease, five persons."

"No more than five?"

"No."

"Why?"

"The substance was exhausted."

Blondel gasped. "Why did he not make more?" he
cried. His voice was almost savage.

"The experiment," Basterga answered, "of which it was
the product was costly."

Blondel's face turned purple. "Costly?" he cried.
"Costly? When the lives of men hang in the balance."

"True," Basterga replied with a smile, "but I was about
to say that, costly as it was, it was not its price which hin-
dered the production of a farther supply. The reason was
more simple. He could not extract it."

"Could not? But he had made it once?"

"Precisely."

"Then why could he not make it again?" the Syndic
asked. He was red with indignation. It was strange how
seriously he took the matter.

"He could not," Basterga made answer. "He repeated
the process again and again, but the peculiar product, which
at the first trial had resulted from the precipitation, was
not obtained."

"There was something lacking!"

"Precisely, there was something lacking," Basterga answered. "But what that was which was lacking, or how it had entered into the alembic in the first instance could not be discovered. The sage tried the experiment under all known conditions, and particularly when the moon was in the same quarter and when the sun was in the same house. He tried it, indeed, thrice on the corresponding day of the year, but—the product did not issue."

"How do you account for that?"

"Probably, in the first instance, an impurity in one of the drugs introduced a foreign substance into the alembic. That chance never occurred again, as far as I can learn, until, amusing myself with the same precipitation, I—I, Cæsar Basterga of Padua—" the scholar continued, not boastfully but in a tone thoughtful and almost absent, "in the last year of the last century, hit at length upon the same result."

The Syndic leaned forward; his hands gripped his knees more tightly. "And you," he said, "can repeat it?"

Basterga shook his head sorrowfully. "No," he said, "I cannot. Not that I have myself essayed the experiment more than thrice. I could not afford it. But a correspondent, M. de Laurens, of Paris, physician to the King, has, at the expense of a wealthy patient, spent more than fifteen thousand florins in essays. And without result."

The big man spoke with his eyes on the floor. Had he turned them on the Syndic he must have seen that he was greatly agitated. Beads of moisture stood on his brow, his face was red, he swallowed often and with difficulty. At length, with an effort at composure, "Possibly your product—is not after all the same as Ibn Jasher's?" he said.

"I tested it in the same way," Basterga answered quietly.

"What? By curing persons of that disease?"

"Yes," Basterga rejoined. "And I would to Heaven," he continued, with the first spirit of feeling which he had allowed to escape him, "that I had held my hand after the first proof. Instead, I must needs try it again and again, and again——"

"For nothing?"

Basterga shrugged his shoulders. "No," he said, "not for nothing." And by a gesture he indicated the objects about him. "I am not a poor man now, Messer Blondel. Not for nothing, but too cheaply. And so often that I have now left but one portion of that substance which all the science of Padua cannot renew. One portion, only, alas!" he repeated with regret.

"Enough to cure one person?" the Syndic exclaimed.

"Yes."

"And the disease?" Blondel rose as he spoke. "The disease?" he repeated. He extended his trembling arms to the other. No longer, even if he wished it, could Basterga feign himself blind to the agitation, which shook, which almost convulsed the Syndic's meagre frame. "The disease? Is it not that which men call the Scholar's? Is it not that? But I know it is."

Basterga with something of astonishment in his face inclined his head.

"And I have that disease! I!" the Syndic cried, standing before him a piteous figure; and he raised his hands above his head in a gesture, which challenged the compassion of gods and men. "I! In two years——" his voice failed, he could not go on.

"Believe me, Messer Blondel," Basterga answered after a long and sorrowful pause, "I am grieved. Deeply grieved," he continued in a tone of feeling, "to hear this. Do the physicians give no hope?"

"Sons of the Horse-Leech!" the Syndic cried, a new passion shaking him in its turn. "They give me two years! Two years! And it may be less. Less!" he cried, raising his voice. "I, who go to and fro here and there, like other men with no mark upon me. I, who walk the streets in sunshine and rain like other men. Yet, for them the sky is bright, and they have years to live. For me, one more summer, and—night! Two more years at the most—and night! And I, but fifty-eight!"

The big man looked at him with eyes of compassion. "It may be," he said, after a pause, "that the physicians are wrong, Messer Blondel. I have known such a case."

"They are, they shall be wrong!" Blondel replied. "For you will give me your remedy! It was God led me here to-day, it was God put it in your heart to tell me this. You will give me your remedy and I shall live! You will, will you not? Man, you can pity and you will?" And with his outstretched hands he tried to seize and embrace the other's hand—to carry it to his lips.

"Alas, alas," Basterga replied, much and strongly moved. "I cannot."

"Cannot?"

"Cannot!"

The Syndic glared at him. "Why?" he cried. "Why not? If I give you——"

"If you were to give me the half of your fortune," Basterga answered solemnly, "it were useless! I myself have the first symptoms of the disease."

"You?"

"Yes, I."

The Syndic fell back in his chair. A groan broke from him that bore witness at once to the bitterness of his soul and the finality of the argument. He seemed in a moment shrunk to half his size. In a moment disease and the shadow of death clouded his features; his cheeks were leaden; his eyes, without light or understanding, conveyed no meaning to his brain. "You, too!" he muttered mechanically. "You, too!"

"Yes," Basterga replied in a sorrowful voice. "I, too. No wonder I feel for you. I have not known it long, nor has it proceeded far in my case. I have even hopes, at least there are times when I have hopes, that the physicians may be mistaken."

Blondel's small eyes bulged suddenly larger. "In that event?" he cried hoarsely. "In that event surely——"

"Even in that event I am helpless to aid you," the big man answered, spreading out his hands. "I am pledged by the most solemn oath to retain the one portion I have for the use of the Grand Duke, my patron. And apart from that oath, the benefits I have received at his hand are such as to give him a claim second only to my necessity. A claim, Messer Blondel, which—I say it sorrowfully—I dare not set aside for any private feeling or private gain."

Blondel rose violently, his hands clawing the air. "And I must die?" he cried, his voice thick with rage. "I must die because he *may* be ill? Because—because——" He stopped, struggling with himself, unable, it seemed, to articulate. By and by it became apparent that the pause had another origin, for when he spoke he had conquered his passion. "Pardon me," he said, still hoarsely, but in a different tone—the tone of one who saw that violence could not help him. "I was forgetting myself. Life—life is sweet to all, Messer Basterga, and we cannot lightly see it pass from us. To have life within sight, to know it within this room, perhaps within reach——"

"Not quite that," Basterga murmured, his eyes wandering to the steel casket, chained to the wall beside the hearth. "Still, I understand; and, believe me," he added in a tone of sympathy, "I feel for you, Messer Blondel. I feel deeply for you."

"Feel?" the Syndic muttered. And for an instant his eyes gleamed savagely, the veins of his temples swelled. "Feel!"

"But what can I do?"

Blondel could have answered, but to what advantage? What could words profit him, seeing that it was a life for a life, and that, as all that a man hath he will give for his life, so there is nothing another hath that he will take for it. Argument was useless; prayer, in view of the other's confession, beside the mark. The magistrate saw this, and made an effort to resume his dignity. "We will talk another day," he murmured, pressing his hand to his brow, "another day!" And he turned to the door. "You will not mention what I have said to you, Messer Basterga?"

"Not a syllable," his host answered as he followed him out. The abruptness of the departure did not surprise him. "Believe me, I feel for you, Messer Blondel."

The Syndic acknowledged the phrase by a gesture not without pathos, and, passing out, stumbled blindly down the narrow stairs. Basterga attended him with respect to the outer door, and there they parted in silence. The magistrate, his shoulders bowed, walked slowly to the left, where, turning into the town through the inner gate, the

Porte Tertasse, he disappeared. The big man waited awhile, sunning himself on the steps, his face toward the ramparts.

"He will come back, oh, yes, he will come back," he purred, smiling all over his large face. "For I, Cæsar Basterga, have a brain. And 'tis better, a brain than thews and sinews, gold or lands, seeing that it has all these at command when I need them. The fish is hooked. It will be strange if I do not land him before the year is out. But the bribe to his physician—it was a happy thought:—a happy thought of this brain of Cæsar Basterga, graduate of Padua, 'viri valde periti, doctissimique!' "

CHAPTER VI

THE house in the Corraterie, near the Porte Tertasse, differed in no outward respect from its neighbours. The same row of chestnut trees darkened
its lower windows, the same breezy view of the Rhone
meadows, the sloping vineyards and the far-off Jura light-
ened·its upper rooms. A kindred life, a life apparently as
quiet and demure, moved within its walls. Yet was the
house a house apart. Silently and secretly it had absorbed
and sucked and drawn into itself the hearts and souls and
minds of two men. It held for the one that which the old
prize above all things in this world—life; and for the
other, that which the young set above life—love.

Life? The Syndic did not doubt; the bait had been
dangled before his eyes with too much cunning, too much
skill. In a casket, in a room in that house in the Corraterie,
his life lay hidden; his life, and he could not come at it!
His life? Was it a marvel that waking or sleeping he
saw only that house, and that room, and that casket chained
to the wall; that he saw at one time the four steps rising
to the door, and the placid front with its three tiers of windows; at another time, the room itself with its litter of
scripts and dark-bound books, and rich furnishings, and

phials and jars and strangely shaped alembics. Was it a marvel that in the dreams of the night the sick man toiled up and up and up the narrow staircase, of which every point remained fixed in his mind; or that waking, whatever his task, or wherever he might be, alone or in company, in his parlour or in the Town House, he still fell a-dreaming of the room and the box—the room and the box that held his life?

Had this been the worst! But it was not. There were times, bitter times, dark hours, when the pains were upon him, and he saw his fate clear before him; for he had known men die of the disease which held him in its clutches, and he knew how they had died. And then he must needs lock himself into his room that other eyes might not witness the passionate fits of revolt, of rage and horror, and weak weeping, into which the knowledge cast him. And out of which he presently came back to—*the house*. His life lay there, in that room, in that house, and he could not come at it! He could not come at it! But he would! He would!

It issued in that always; in some plan or scheme for gaining possession of the philtre. Some of the plans that occurred to him were wild and desperate; dangerous and hopeless on the face of them. Others were merely violent; others again, of which craft was the mainspring, held out a prospect of success. For a whole day the notion of arresting Basterga on a charge of treason, and seizing the steel casket together with his papers, was uppermost. It seemed feasible, and was feasible; nay, it was more than feasible, it was easy; for already there were rumours of the man abroad, and his name had been mentioned at the Council table. The Syndic had only to give the word, and the arrest would be made, the search instituted, the papers and casket seized. Nay, if he did not give the word, it was possible that others might.

But when he thought of that step, that irrevocable step, he knew that he would not have the courage to take it. For if Basterga had so much as two minutes' notice, if his ear so much as caught the tread of those who came to take him, he might, in pure malignity, pour the medicine on the floor, or he might so hide it as to defy search. And at the thought —at the thought of the destruction of that wherein lay his only chance of life, his only hope of seeing the sun and feeling again the balmy breath of spring, the Syndic trembled and shook and sweated with rage and fear. No, he would not have the courage. He would not dare. For a week and more after the thought occurred to him, he dared not approach the scholar's lodging, or be seen in the neighbourhood, so great was his fear of arousing Basterga's suspicions and setting him on his guard.

At the end of eight days the choice of ways was presented to him in a concrete form; and with an abruptness which placed him on the edge of perplexity. It was at a morning meeting of the smaller council. The day was dull, the chamber warm, the business to be transacted monotonous; and Blondel, far from well and interested in one thing only—beside which the most important affairs of Geneva seemed small as the doings of an ant-hill viewed through a glass—had fallen asleep, or nearly asleep. Naturally a restless and wakeful man, of thin habit and nervous temperament, he had never done such a thing before: and it was unfortunate that he succumbed on this occasion, for while he drowsed the current of business changed; the debate grew serious, even vital. Finally he awoke to the knowledge of place and time with a name ringing in his ears; a name so fixed in his waking thoughts that, before he knew where he was or what he was doing, he repeated it in a tone that drew all eyes upon him.

"Basterga!"

Some knew he had slept and smiled; more had not noticed it, and turned, struck by the strange tone in which he echoed the name. Fabri, the First Syndic, who sat two places from him, and had just taken a letter from the Secretary, leaned forward so as to view him. "Ay, Basterga," he said. "An Italian, I take it. Do you know him, Messer Blondel?"

He was awake now, but, confused and startled, inclined to believe that he was on his trial; and that the faint parleyings with treason, small things hard to define, to which he had stooped, were known. Mechanically, to gain time, he repeated the name. "Basterga?"

"Yes," Fabri repeated. "Do you know him?"

"Cæsar Basterga, is it?"

"That is his name."

He was himself now, though his nerves still shook; himself so far as he could be, while ignorant of what had passed, and how he came to be challenged. "Yes, I know him," he said slowly, "if you mean a Paduan, a scholar of some note, I believe, who applied to me—I dare say it would be six weeks back—for a licence to stay awhile in the town."

"Which you granted?"

"In the usual course. He had letters from"—Blondel shrugged his shoulders—"I forget from whom. What of him?" with a steady look at Baudichon the Councillor, his life-long rival, and the quarter, whence if trouble were brewing, it was to be expected. "What of him?" he repeated, throwing himself back in his chair, and tapping the table with his fingers.

"This," Fabri answered, waving the letter which he had in his hands.

"But I do not know what that is," Blondel replied coolly. "I am afraid—" and he looked at his neighbour on either side—"was I asleep?"

"I fear so," said one, while the other smiled. They were his very good friends and allies.

"Well, it is not like me. I can say that I am not often," with a keen look at Baudichon, "caught napping! And now, M. Fabri," with his usual practical air, "I have delayed the business long enough. What is it? And what is that?" He pointed to the letter in the First Syndic's hands.

"Well, it is really your affair in the main," Fabri answered, "since as Fourth Syndic you are responsible for the Guard and the city's safety; and ours afterward. It is a warning," he continued, his eyes reverting to the page before him, "from our secret agent in Turin, whose name I need not mention"—Blondel nodded—"informing us of a fresh attempt to be made on the city before Christmas; by means of rafts formed of hurdles and capable of transporting whole companies of soldiers. These he has himself seen tried in the River Po, and they performed the work. Having reached the walls by their means the assailants are to mount by ladders which are being made to fit into one another. They are covered with black cloth, and can be laid against the wall without noise. It sounds —circumstantial?" Fabri commented, breaking off and looking at Blondel.

The Syndic nodded thoughtfully. "Yes," he said, "I think so. I think also," he continued, "that with the aid of my friend, Captain Blandano, I shall be able to give a good account of the rafts and the ladders."

Baudichon interposed. "But that is not all," he drawled, rolling ponderously in his chair as he spoke. He was a stout man with a double chin and a weighty manner; honest, but slow, and the spokesman of the more wealthy burghers. His neighbour Petitot, a man of singular appearance, lean, with a long thin drooping nose, commonly supported him. Petitot, who bore the nickname of "the Inquisitor," represented the Venerable Company of Pastors, and was viewed with especial distaste by the turbulent spirits whom the war had left in the city, as well as by the lower ranks, who upheld Blondel. In sense and vigour the Fourth Syndic was more than a match for the two precisians: but honesty of purpose has a weight of its own that slowly makes itself felt. "That is not all," Baudichon repeated after a glance at his neighbour and ally, Petitot, "I want to know——"

"One moment, Messer Baudichon, if you please," Fabri said cutting him short, amid a partial titter; the phrase "I want to know" was so often on the Councillor's lips that it had become ridiculous. "One moment; as you say, that is not all. The writer proceeds to warn us that the Grand Duke's Lieutenant, M. d'Albigny, has taken a house on the Italian side of the frontier, and is there constructing a huge petard on wheels which is to be dragged up to the gate——"

"With the ladders and rafts?"

"They seem to belong to another scheme," Fabri said, as he turned back and conned the letter afresh.

"THIS!" SAID FABRI, WAVING THE LETTER WHICH
HE HELD IN HIS HANDS

"With M. d'Albigny at the bottom of both?"

"Yes."

"Well, if he be not more successful with this," Blondel answered contemptuously, "than he was with the attempt to mine the Arsenal—which ended in supplying us with two or three casks of powder—I think Captain Blandano and I may deal with him."

A murmur of assent approved the boast; but it did not proceed from all. There were men at the table, who had children, who had wives, who had daughters, whose faces were grave. Just thirty years had passed over the world since the horrors of the massacre of St. Bartholomew, to be speedily followed by the sack of Antwerp, had paled the cheek of Europe. Just thirty years were to elapse and the sack of Magdeburg was to prove a match and more than a match for both, in horror and cruelty. That the papists, if they entered, would deal more gently with Geneva, the head and front of offence, or extend to the Mother of Heretics mercy which they had refused to her children, these men did not believe. The presence of an enemy ever lurking within a league of their gates, ever threatening them by night and by day, had shaken their nerves. They feared everything, they feared always. In fitful sleep, in the small hours, they heard their doors smashed in; their dreams were disturbed by cries and shrieks, by the din of bells, and the clash of weapons.

To these men Blondel seemed over-confident. But no one took on himself to gainsay him in his particular province, the superintendence of the Guard; and though Baudichon sighed and Petitot shook his head, the word was left with him. "Is that all, Messer Fabri?" he asked.

"Yes, if we lay it to heart."

"But I want to know," Baudichon struck in, puffing pompously, "what is to be done about—Basterga."

"Basterga? To be sure I was forgetting him," Fabri answered. "What is to be done? What do you say, Messer Blondel? What are we to do about him?"

"I will tell you if you will tell me what the point is that touches him. You forget, Messer Syndic"—with a somewhat sickly smile—"that I was asleep."

"The letter," Fabri replied, returning to it, "touches him seriously. It asserts that a person of that name is here in the Grand Duke's interest, that he is in the secret of these plots, and that we should do well to expel him, if we do not seize and imprison him."

"And you want to know——"

"I want to know," Baudichon answered, rolling in his chair as was his habit when delivering himself, "what you know of him, Messer Blondel."

Blondel turned rudely on him, perhaps to hide the sudden ebb of colour from his cheeks. "What I know?" he said.

"Ay, ay."

"No more than you know!"

"But," Petitot retorted in his dry, thin voice, "it was you, Messer Blondel, not Messer Baudichon, who gave him permission to reside in the town."

"And I want to know," Baudichon chimed in remorselessly, "what credentials he had. That is what I want to know!"

"Credentials? Oh, something formal! I don't know what," Blondel replied rudely. He looked to the Secretary who sat at the foot of the table. "Do you know?" he asked.

"No, Messer Syndic," the man replied. "I remember that a licence was granted to him in the name of Cæsar Basterga, graduate of Padua; and doubtless—for licences to reside are not granted without such—he had letters, but I do not recall from whom. They would be returned to him with the licence."

"And that is all," Petitot said, his long nose drooping, his inquisitive eyes looking over his glasses, "that you know about him, Messer Blondel?"

Did they know anything, and, if so, what did they know? Blondel hesitated. This persistence, this continual harping on one point began to alarm him. But he carried it bravely. "Do you mean as to his convictions?" he asked with a sneer.

"No, I mean at all!"

"I want to know," Baudichon added—the parrot phrase began to carry to Blondel's ears the note of fate—"what you know about him."

This time a pause betrayed Blondel's hesitation. Should he admit that he had been to Basterga's lodging; or dared he deny a fact that might imply an intimacy greater than he had acknowledged? A faint perspiration rose on his brow, as he decided that he dare not. "I know that he lives in a house in the Corraterie," he answered, "a house beside the Porte Tertasse, and that he is a scholar—I believe of some repute. I know so much," he continued boldly, "because he wrote to thank me for the licence, and, by way of acknowledgment, invited me to visit his lodging to view a rare manuscript of the Scriptures. I did so, and remained a few minutes with him. That is all I know of him. I suppose," with a grim look at Baudichon and the Inquisitor, who had exchanged meaning glances, "it is not alleged that I am in the plot with him? Or that he has confided to me the Grand Duke's plans?"

Fabri laughed heartily at the notion, and the laugh, which was echoed by four-fifths of those at the table, cleared the air. Petitot, it is true, limited himself to a smile, and Baudichon shrugged his shoulders. But for the moment the challenge silenced them. The game passed to Blondel's hands, and his spirits rose. "If M. Baudichon wants to know more about him," he said contemptuously, "I dare say that the information can be obtained."

"The point is," Fabri answered, "what are we to do?"

"As to——"

"As to expelling him or seizing him."

"Oh!" The exclamation fell from Blondel's lips before he could stay it. He saw what was coming, and the dilemma in which he was to be placed. He grew red.

"We have the letter before us," the First Syndic continued, "and apart from it, we know nothing for this person or against him." He looked round the table and met assenting glances. "I think, therefore, that it will be well to leave it to Messer Blondel. He is responsible for the safety of the city, and it should be for him to say what is to be done."

"Yes, yes," several voices agreed. "Leave it to Messer Blondel."

"You assent to that, Messer Baudichon?"

"I suppose so," the Councillor muttered reluctantly.

"Very good," said Fabri. "Then, Messer Blondel, it remains with you to say what is to be done."

The Fourth Syndic hesitated, and with reason: had Baudichon, had the Inquisitor known the whole, they could hardly have placed him in a more awkward dilemma. If

he took the course that prudence and his own interests dictated, and shielded Basterga, his action might expose him
to future criticism. If, on the other hand, he gave the
word to expel or seize him, he broke at once and for ever
with the man who held his last chance of life, in the hollow
of his hand.

And yet, if he dared adopt the latter course, if he dared
give the word to seize, there was a chance, and a good
chance, that he would find the Remedium in the casket;
for with a little arrangement Basterga might be arrested
out of doors, or be allured to a particular place and there
be set upon. But that way lay risk; a risk that chilled the
current of his blood. There was the chance that the attempt might fail; the chance that Basterga might escape;
the chance that he might have the Remedium about him
—and destroy it; the chance that he might have hidden it.
There were so many chances in a word that the Syndic's
heart stood still as he enumerated them, and pictured the
crash of his last hope of life.

He could not face the risk. He could not. Though
duty, though courage dictated the venture, craven fear—
fear for the loss of the new-born hope that for a week had
buoyed him up—carried it. Hurriedly at last, as if he
feared that he might change his mind, he pronounced his
decision.

"I doubt the wisdom of touching him," he said. "To
seize him if he be guilty proclaims our knowledge of the
plot; it will be laid aside and another, of which we may
not be informed, will be hatched. But let him be watched,
and it will be hard if with the knowledge we have we cannot do something more than frustrate his scheme."

After an interval of silence, "Well," Fabri said, drawing a deep breath and looking round, "I believe you are right. What do you say, Messer Baudichon?"

"Messer Blondel knows the man," Baudichon answered drily. "He is, therefore, the best judge."

Blondel reddened. "I see you are determined to lay the responsibility on me," he cried.

"The responsibility is on you already!" Petitot retorted. "You have decided. I trust it may turn out as you expect."

"And as you do not expect!"

"No; but you see"—and again the Inquisitor looked over his glasses—"you know the man, have been to his lodging, have conversed with him, and are the best judge what he is! I have had naught to do with him. By the way," he turned to Fabri, "he is at Mère Royaume's, is he not? Is there not a Spaniard of the name of Grio, lodging there?"

Blondel did not answer and the Secretary looked up from his register. "An old soldier, Messer Petitot?" he said. "Yes, there is."

"Perhaps you know him also, Messer Blondel?"

"Yes, I know him. He served the State," Blondel answered quietly. He had winked at more than one irregularity on the part of Grio, and at the sound of the name anger gave place to caution. "I have also," he continued, "my eye upon him, as I shall have it upon Basterga. Will that satisfy you, Messer Petitot?"

The Councillor leaned forward. "Fac salvam Genevam!" he replied in a voice low and not quite steady. "Do that, keep Geneva safe, guard well our faith, our wives and daughters—and I care not what you do!" And he rose from his seat.

The Fourth Syndic did not answer. Those words that

in a moment raised the discussion from the low level of detail on which the Inquisitor commonly wasted himself, and set it on the true plane of patriotism—for with all his faults Petitot was a patriot—silenced Blondel while they irritated and puzzled him. Why did the man assume such airs? Why talk as if he and he alone cared for Geneva? Why bear himself, as if he and he alone had shed and was prepared to shed his blood for the State? Why, indeed? Blondel snarled his indignation, but made no other answer.

A few minutes later, as he descended the stairs, he laughed at the momentary annoyance which he had felt. What did it matter to him, a dying man, who had the better or who the worse, who posed, or who believed in the pose? It was of moment indeed that his enemies had contrived to fix him with the responsibility of arresting Basterga, or of leaving him at large: that they had contrived to connect him with the Paduan, and made him accountable to an extent which did not please him for the man's future behaviour. But yet again what did that matter—after all? Of what moment was it—after all? He was a dying man. Was anything of moment to him except the one thing which Basterga had it in his power to grant or to withhold, to give or to deny?

Nothing! Nothing!

He pondered on what had passed, and wondered if he had not done foolishly. Certainly he had let slip a grand, a unique opportunity of seizing the man and of snatching the Remedium. He had put the chance from him at the risk of future blame. Now he was of two minds about it. Of two minds: but of one mind only about another thing. As he veered this way and that in his mind, now cursing his cowardice, and now thanking God that he had not taken the irrevocable step,

> " *Opportunity*
> *That work'st our thoughts into desires, desires*
> *To resolutions,*"

kindled in him a burning impatience to act. If he did not act, if he were not going to act, if he were not going to take some surer and safer step, he had been foolish and trebly foolish to let slip the opportunity that had been his.

But he would act. For a week he had abstained from visiting Basterga; he had even absented himself from the neighbourhood of the house lest the scholar's suspicions should be awakened. But to what purpose if he were not going to act? If he were not going to build on the ground so carefully prepared, to what end this wariness and this abstention?

Within an hour the Syndic, long so prudent, had worked himself into a fever and, rather than remain inactive, was ripe for any step, however venturesome, provided it led to the Remedium. He had still the wisdom to postpone action until night; but when darkness had fairly set in and the bell of St. Peter, inviting the townsfolk to the evening preaching, had ceased to sound—an indication that he would meet few in the streets—he cloaked himself, and, issuing forth, bent his steps across the Bourg du Four in the direction of the Corraterie.

Even now he had no plan in his mind. But amid the medley of schemes that for a week had been hatching in his brain, he hoped to be guided by circumstances to that one which gave surest promise of success. Nor was his courage as deeply rooted as he fancied: the day had told on his nerves; he shivered in the breeze and started at a sound. Yet as often as he paused or hesitated, the words "A dying man! A dying man!" rang in his ears and urged him on.

CHAPTER VII

A SECOND TISSOT

MESSER BLONDEL'S sagacity in forbearing completely and for so long a period the neighbourhood of Basterga proved an unpleasant surprise to one man; and that was the man most nearly concerned. For a day or two the scholar lived in a fool's paradise, and hugging himself on certain success, anticipated with confidence the entertainment which he would derive from the antics of the fish as it played about the bait, now advancing and now retreating. He had formed a low opinion of the magistrate's astuteness, and forgetting that there is a cunning which is rudimentary and of the primitives, he entertained for some time no misgiving. But when day after day passed by and still, though nearly a week had elapsed, Blondel did not appear, nor make any overture—when, watch he never so carefully in the dusk of the evening or at the quiet hours of the day, he caught no glimpse of the Syndic's lurking figure, he began to doubt. He began to fear. He began to wait about the door himself in the hope of detecting the other: and a dozen times between dawn and dark he was on his feet at the upper window, looking warily down, on the chance of seeing him in the Corraterie.

At last, slowly and against his will, the fear that the fish would not bite began to take hold of him. Either the Syndic was honest, or he was patient as well as cunning. In no other way could Basterga explain his dupe's inaction. And presently, when he had almost brought himself to accept the former conclusion, on an evening something more than a week later, a thing happened that added sharpness to his anxiety. He was crossing the bridge from the Quarter of St. Gervais; suddenly a man cloaked to the eyes slipped from the shadow of the mills, a little before him, and with a slight but unmistakable gesture of invitation proceeded in front of him without turning his head.

There was mist on the face of the river that rushed in a cataract below; a steady rain was falling, and darkness itself was not far off. There were few abroad, and those were going their ways without looking behind them. A better time for a secret rendezvous could not be, and Messer Basterga's heart leapt up and his spirits rose as he followed the cloaked figure. At the end of the bridge the man turned leftwards on to a deserted wharf between two mills; Basterga followed. Near the water's edge the projecting upper floor of a granary promised shelter from the rain; under this the stranger halted, and turning, lowered, with a brusque gesture, his cloak from his face. The eager, "Why, Messer Blondel——" that was on Basterga's lips died on them. He stood speechless with disappointment, choking with chagrin. The stranger noted this and laughed.

"Well," he said in French, his tone dry and sarcastic, "you do not seem overpleased to see me, Monsieur Basterga! Nor am I surprised. Large promises have ever small fulfilments!"

"His Highness has discovered that?" Basterga replied, in a tone no less sarcastic.

The stranger's eyes flickered, as if the other's words touched a sore. "His Highness is growing impatient!" he returned, his tone somewhat warmer. "That is what he has sent me to say. He has waited long, and he bids me convey to you that if he is to wait longer he must have some security that you are likely to succeed in your design."

"Or he will employ other means?"

"Precisely. Had he followed my advice," the stranger continued with an air of cool contempt, "he would have done so long ago."

"M. d'Albigny," Basterga answered, spreading out his hands with an ironical gesture, "would prefer to dig mines under the Tour du Pin near the College, and under the Porte Neuve! To smuggle fireworks into the Arsenal and the Town House; and then, on the eve of execution, to fail as utterly as he failed last time! More utterly than my plan can fail, for I shall not put Geneva on its guard —as he did! Nor set every enemy of the Grand Duke talking—as he did!"

M. d'Albigny—for he it was—let drop an oath. "Are you doing anything at all?" he asked, savagely, dropping the thin veil of irony that shrouded his temper. "That is the question. Are you moving?"

"That will appear."

"When? When, man? That is what His Highness wants to know. At present there is no appearance of anything."

"No," Basterga replied with fine irony. "There is not. I know it. It is only when the fireworks are discovered and

the mines opened and the engineers are flying for their lives
—that there is an appearance of something."

"And that is the answer I am to carry to the Grand
Duke?" d'Albigny retorted in a tone which betrayed how
deeply he resented such taunts at the lips of his inferior.
"That is all you have to tell him?"

Basterga was silent awhile. When he spoke again, it
was in a lower and more cautious tone. "No; you may
tell His Highness this," he said, after glancing warily behind him. "You may tell him this. The longest night in
the year is approaching. Not many weeks divide us from
it. Let him give me until that night. Then let him bring
his troops and ladders and the rest of it—the care whereof
is your lordship's, not mine—to a part of the walls which
I will indicate, and he shall find the guards withdrawn, and
Geneva at his feet."

"The longest night? But that is some weeks distant,"
d'Albigny answered in a grumbling tone. Still it was evident that he was impressed by the precision of the other's
promise.

"Was Rome built in a day? Or can Geneva be destroyed in a day?" Basterga retorted.

"If I had my hand on it!" d'Albigny answered trucu-
lently, "the task would not take more than a day!" He
was a Southern Frenchman and an ardent Catholic; an
officer of high rank in the employ of Savoy; for the rest,
proud, brave, and difficult.

"Ay, but you have not your hand on it, M. d'Albigny!"
Basterga retorted coolly. "Nor will you ever have it, without help from me."

"And that is all you have to say?"

"At present."

"Very good," d'Albigny replied, nodding contemptuously. "If His Highness be wise——"

"He is wise. At least," Basterga continued drily, "he
is wiser than M. d'Albigny. He knows that it is better to
wait and win, than leap and lose."

"But what of the discontented you were to bring to a
head?" d'Albigny retorted, remembering with relief another head of complaint, on which he had been charged to
deliver himself. "The old soldiers and rufflers whom the
peace has left unemployed, and with whom the man Grio
was to aid you? Surely waiting will not help you with
them! There should be some in Geneva who like not the
rule of the pastors and the drone of psalms and hymns!
Men who, if I know them, must be on fire for a change?
Come, Monsieur Basterga, is no use to be made of them?"

"Ay," Basterga answered, after stepping back a pace to
assure himself by a careful look that no one was remark-
ing a colloquy, which the time and the weather rendered
suspicious. "Use them if you please. Let them drink and
swear and raise petty riots, and keep the Syndics on their
guard! It is all they are good for, M. d'Albigny; and I
cannot say that aught keeps back the cause so much as
Grio's friends and their line of conduct!"

"So! that is your opinion, is it, Monsieur Basterga?"
d'Albigny answered. "And with it I must go as I came!
I am of no use here, it seems?"

"Of great use presently, of none now," Basterga replied
with greater respect than he had hitherto exhibited.
"Frankly, M. d'Albigny, they fear you and suspect you.
But if President Rochette of Chambéry, who has the confidence of the Pastors, were to visit us on some pretext or
other, say to settle such small matters as the Peace has left

in doubt, it might soothe their spirits and allay their suspicions. He, rather than M. d'Albigny, is the helper I need at present."

D'Albigny grunted, but it was evident that the other's boldness impressed him. "You think, then, that they suspect us?" he said.

"How should they not? Tell me that. How should they not? Rochette's task should be to lull those suspicions to sleep. In the meantime I——"

"Yes?"

"Will be at work," Basterga replied. And he laughed drily as if it pleased him to baulk the other's curiosity. Softly he added, under his breath,

> " *Captique dolis, lacrimisque coactis,*
> *Quos neque Tydides, nec Larrissæus Achilles*
> *Non anni domuere decem, non mille carinæ!* "

D'Albigny nodded. "Well, I trust you have a solid plan," he answered. "For you are taking a great deal upon yourself, Monsieur Basterga," he continued with a searching look. "I hope you understand that."

"I take all on myself," the big man answered.

The Frenchman was far from content, but he argued no more. He reflected a moment, considering whether he had forgotten anything: then, muttering that he would convey Basterga's views to the Grand Duke, he pulled his cloak more closely about his face and, with a curt nod of farewell, he turned on his heel, and was gone. A moment and he was lost to sight between the wooden mills and warehouses which flanked the bridgeway on either side, and rendered it at once as narrow and as picturesque as were most of the bridges of the day.

Basterga left solitary, waited awhile before he left his shelter. Satisfied at length that the coast was clear, he continued his way into the town, and thinking deeply as he went, came presently to the Corraterie. It cannot be said that his meditations were of the most pleasant, and perhaps for this reason he walked slowly. When he entered, shaking the moisture from his coat and cap, he found the others seated at table and well advanced in their meal. He was the only person late.

He was a clever man. But at times, in moments of irritation, the sense of his cleverness and of his superiority to the mass of men, led him to do the thing which he had better have left undone. It was so this evening. Face to face with d'Albigny, he had put a bold face on the difficulties which surrounded him: he had let no sign of doubt or uncertainty, no word of fear respecting the outcome escape him. But the moment he found himself at liberty, the critical situation of his affairs, if the Syndic refused to take the bait, recurred to his mind, and harassed him. He had no confidante, no one to whom he could breathe his fears, no one to whom he could explain the situation, or with whom he could take credit for his coolness: and the curb of silence, while it exasperated his temper, augmented, a hundredfold, the contempt in which he held the unconscious companions among whom chance and his mission had thrown him. A spiteful desire to show that contempt sparkled in his eyes as he took his seat at the table this evening; but for a minute or two after he had begun his meal, he kept silence.

On a mind such as his, outward things have small effect; otherwise the cheerful homeliness of the scene which met his eyes must have soothed him. The lamp, telling of

present autumn and approaching winter, had been lit: a
wood-fire crackled pleasantly in the great fireplace and
was reflected in rows of pewter plates on either dresser:
a fragrant stew scented the air; all that a philosopher of
the true type could have asked was at his service. But
Basterga belonged rather to the fifteenth century, the century of the south, which was expiring, than to the century
of the north which was opening. Splendour rather than
comfort, the gorgeousness of Venice, of red-haired dames,
stiff-clad in Titian velvets, of tables gleaming with silk
and gold and ruby glass, rather than the plain homeliness
which Geneva shared with the Dutch cities, held his mind.
To-night in particular his lip curled as he looked round.
To-night in particular, ill-pleased and ill-content, he found
the company well matched, the one and the other mean and
contemptible!

One there—Gentilis—marked the great man's mood,
and, cringing, after his kind, kept his eyes low on his platter. Grio, too, knew enough to seek refuge in sullen silence. Claude alone, impatient of the constraint which had
fallen on the party at the great man's coming, continued to
talk in a raised voice. "Good soup to-night, Anne," he
said. For some days past he had been using himself to
speak to her easily and lightly, as if she were no more to
him than to the others.

She did not answer—she seldom did. But "Good?"
Basterga sneered in his most cutting tone. "Ay, for schoolboys! And such as have no palate save for pap!"

Claude minded the thrust little, yet he returned it with
a boy's impertinence. "We none of us grow thin on it,"
he said.

Basterga's eyes gleamed. "Grease and dish-washings,"

he exclaimed. And then, as if he knew where he could most easily wound his antagonist, he turned to the girl.

"If Hebe had brought such liquor to Jupiter," he sneered, "do you think he had given her Hercules for a husband, as I shall presently give you Grio? Ha! You flush at the prospect, do you? You colour and tremble," he continued mockingly, "as if it were the wedding-day. You'll sleep little to-night, I see, for thinking of your Hercules!" With grim irony he pointed to his loutish companion, whose gross purple face seemed the coarser for the small peaked beard, that, after the fashion of the day, adorned his lower lip. "Hercules, do I call him? Adonis rather."

"Why not Bacchus?" Claude muttered, his eyes on his plate. In spite of the strongest resolutions, he could not keep silence.

"Bacchus? And why, boy?" frowning darkly.

"He were better bestowed on a tun of wine," the youth retorted, without looking up.

"That you might take his place, I suppose?" Basterga retorted swiftly. "What say you, girl? Will you have him?" And when she did not answer, "Bread, do you hear?" he cried harshly and imperiously. "Bread, I say!" And having forced her to come within reach to serve him, "What do you say to it?" he continued, his hand on the trencher, his eyes on her face. "Answer me, girl, will you have him?"

She did not answer, but that which he had quite falsely attributed to her before, a blush, slowly and painfully darkened her cheeks and neck. He seized her brutally by the chin, and forced her to raise her face. "Blushing, I see?" he continued. "Blushing, blushing, eh? So it is for him you thrill, and lie awake, and dream of kisses, is it? For this new youth and not for Grio? Nay, struggle not! Wrest not yourself away! Let Grio, too, see you!"

Claude, his back to the scene, drove his nails into the palms of his hands. He would not turn. He would not, he dared not see what was passing, or how they were handling her, lest the fury in his breast sweep all away, and he rise up and disobey her! When a movement told him that Basterga had released her—with a last ugly taunt aimed as much at him as at her—he still sat bearing it, curbing, drilling, compelling himself to be silent. Ay, and still to be silent, though the voice that so cruelly wounded her was scarcely mute before it began again.

"Tissot, indeed!" Basterga cried in the same tone of bitter jeering. "A fig for Tissot! No more shall we

> *Upon his viler metal test our purest pure,*
> *And see him transmutations three endure!*

And why? Because a mightier than Tissot is here! Because," with a coarse laugh,

> *Our stone angelical whereby*
> *All secret potencies to light are brought*

has itself suffered a transmutation! A transmutation do I say! Rather an eclipse, a darkening! He, whom matrons for their maidens fear, has come, has seen, has conquered! And we poor mortals bow before him."

Still Claude, his face burning, his ears tingling, put force upon himself, and sat mute, his eyes on the board. He would not look round, he would not acknowledge what was passing. Basterga's tone conveyed a meaning coarser and more offensive than the words he spoke; and Claude knew it, and knew that the girl, at whom he dared not look, knew it, as she stood helpless, a butt, a target for their gloating eyes. He would not look, for he remembered. He saw the scalding liquid blister the skin, saw the rounded arm quiver with pain; and remembering and seeing, he was resolved that the lesson should not be lost on him. If it was only by suffering he could serve her, he would serve her.

He dared not look even at Gentilis, who sat opposite him, and was staring in unmanly rapture at the girl's confusion, and the burning blushes, so long banished from her pale features. For to look at that mean mask of a man was the same thing as to strike! Unfortunately, as it happened, his silence and lack of spirit had a result which he had not foreseen. It encouraged the others to carry their brutality to greater and even greater lengths. Grio flung a gross jest in the girl's face: Basterga asked her mockingly how long she had loved. They got no answer; on which the big man asked his question again, his voice grown menacing; and still she would not answer. She had taken refuge from Grio's coarseness in the farthest corner of the hearth: where stooping over a pot, she hid her burning face. Had they gone too far at last? So far, that in despair she had made up her mind to resist? Claude wondered. He hoped that they had.

Basterga, too, thought it possible; but he smiled wickedly, in the pride of his resources. He struck the table sharply with his knife-haft. "What?" he cried. "You don't answer me, girl? You withstand me, do you? To heel! To heel! Stand out in front of me, you jade, and answer me at once. There! Stand there! Do you hear?" And with a mocking eye he indicated with his knife the spot that took his fancy.

She hesitated a moment, scarlet revolt in her face; she hesitated for a long moment; and the lad thought that surely the time had come. But then she obeyed. She obeyed! And at that Claude at last looked up; he could look up safely now for something, even as she obeyed, had put a bridle on his rage and given him control over it. That something was doubt. Why did she comply? Why obey, endure, suffer at this man's hands that which it was a shame a woman should suffer at any man's hands? What was his hold over her? What was his power? Was it possible that she had done anything to give him power? Was it possible—

"Stand there!" Basterga repeated, licking his lips. He was in a cruel temper: harassed himself, he would make someone suffer. "Remember who you are, wench, and where you are! And answer me! How long have you loved him?"

The face no longer burned: her blushes had sunk behind the mask of apathy, the pallid mask, hiding terror and the shame of her sex, which her face had worn before, which had become habitual to her. "I have not loved him," she answered in a low voice.

"Louder!"

"I have not loved him."

"You do not love him?"

"No." She did not look at Claude, but dully, mechanically, she stared straight before her.

Grio laughed boisterously. "A dose for young Hopeful!" he cried. "Ho! Ho! How do you feel now, Master Jackanapes?"

The big man smiled:

> *" Galle, quid insanis ? inquit, Tua cura Lycoris*
> *Perque nives alium perque horrida castra secuta est !"*

he murmured. He bowed ironically in Claude's direction. "The gentleman passes beyond the jurisdiction of the court," he said. "She will have none of him, it seems; nor we either! He is dismissed."

Claude, his eyes burning, shrugged his shoulders, and did not budge. If they thought to rid themselves of him by this fooling they would learn their mistake. They wished him to go: the greater reason he should stay. A little thing—the sight of a small brown hand twitching painfully, while her face and all the rest of her was still and impassive, had expelled his doubts for the time—had driven all but love and pity and burning indignation from his breast. All but these, and the memory of her lesson and her will. He had promised and he must suffer.

Whether Basterga was deceived by his inaction, or of set purpose was minded to try how far they could go with him, the big man turned again to his victim. "With you, my girl," he said, "it is otherwise. The soup was bad, and you are mutinous. Two faults that must be paid for. There was something of this, I remember, when Tissot—our good Tissot, who amused us so much—first came. And we tamed you then. You paid forfeit, I think. You kissed Tissot, I think; or Tissot kissed you."

"No, it was I kissed her," Gentilis said with a smirk. "She chose me."

"Under compulsion," Basterga retorted drily. "Will you ransom her again?"

"Willingly! But it should be two this time," Gentilis said grinning. "Being for the second offence, a double——"

"Pain," quoth Basterga. "Very good. Do you hear, my girl? Go to Gentilis, and see you let him kiss you twice! And see we see and hear it! And have a care! Have a care! Or next time your modesty may not escape so easily! To him at once, and——"

"No!" The cry came from Claude. He was on his feet, his face on fire. "No!" he repeated passionately.

"No?"

"Not while I am here! Not under compulsion," the young man cried. "Shame on you!" and he turned to the others, generous wrath in his face. "Shame on you to torture a woman so, a woman alone! And you three to one!"

Basterga's face grew dark. "You are right! We are three," he muttered, his hand slowly seeking a weapon in the corner behind him. "You speak truth there, we are three—to one! And——"

"You may be twenty, I will not suffer it!" the lad cried gallantly. "You may be a hundred——"

On that word in the full tide of speech he stopped. His voice sank as suddenly as it had been raised, he stammered, his bearing changed. He had met her eyes: he had read in them reproach, warning, rebuke. And too late he remembered his promise.

The big man leaned forward. "What may we be?" he asked. "You were going, I think, to say that we might be —that we might be——"

But Claude did not answer. He was passing through a

moment of such misery as he had never experienced. To
give way to them now, to lower his flag before them after
he had challenged them! To abandon her to them, to see
her—oh, it was more than he could do, more than he could
suffer! It was——

"Pray go on," Basterga sneered, "if you have not said
your say."

Oh bitter! But he remembered how the scalding liquor
had fallen on the tender skin. "I have said it," he muttered hoarsely. "I have said it," and by a movement of
his hand, pathetic enough had any understood it, he seemed
to withdraw himself and his opposition.

But when, obedient to Basterga's eye, the girl moved to
Gentilis' side and bent her cheek—which flamed, not by
reason of Gentilis or the coming kisses, but of Claude's
presence and his cry for her—he could not bear it. He
could not stay and see it, though to go was to abandon her
perhaps to worse treatment. He rose with a cry, and
snatched his cap, and tore open the door. With rage in his
heart and their laughter, their mocking, triumphant laughter, in his ears, he sprang down the steps.

A coward! That was what he must seem to them. A
coward's part, that was the part they had seen him play.
Into the darkness, into the night, what mattered whither,
when such fierce anger boiled within him? Such self-con-
tempt? What matter whither, when he knew how he had
failed! Ay, failed and played the Tissot! The Tissot
and the weakling!

CHAPTER VIII

ON THE THRESHOLD

HE hurried along the ramparts in a rage with those whom he had left, in a still greater rage with himself. He had played the Tissot with a vengeance. He had flown at them in weak passion, he had recoiled as weakly, he had left them to call him coward. Now, even now, he was fleeing from them, and they were jeering at him. Ay, jeering at him; their laughter followed him, and burned his ears.

The rain that beat on his fevered face, the moist wind from the Rhone Valley below, could not wipe out *that*—the defeat and the shame. The darkness through which he hurried could not hide it from his eyes. Thus had Tissot begun, flying out at them, fleeing from them, a thing of mingled fury and weakness. He knew how they had regarded Tissot. So they now regarded him.

And the girl? Surely shame lay on his manhood who had abandoned her! Who had left her to be their sport! His rage boiled over as he thought of her, and with the rain-laden wind buffeting his brow he halted and made as if he would return. But to what end if she would not have his aid, to what end if she would not suffer him? With a furious gesture, he hurried on afresh, only to be arrested, by and by, at the corner of the ramparts near the

Bourg du Four, by a dreadful thought. What if he had deceived himself? What if he had given back before them, not because she had willed it, not because she had looked at him, not in compliance with her wishes; but in face of the odds against him, and by virtue of some streak of cowardice latent in his nature? The more he thought of it, the more he doubted if she had looked at him; the more likely it seemed that the look had been a straw, at which his craven soul had grasped!

The thought maddened him. But it was too late to return, too late to undo his act. He must have left them a full half-hour. The town was growing quiet, the sound of the evening psalms was ceasing. The rustle of the wind among the branches covered the tread of the sentries as they walked the wall between the Porte Neuve and the Mint tower; only their harsh voices as they met midway and challenged came at intervals to his ears. It must be hard on ten o'clock. Or, no, there was the bell of St. Peter's proclaiming the half-hour after nine.

He was ashamed to return to the house, yet he must return; and by and by, reluctantly and doggedly, he set his face that way. The wind and rain had cooled his brow, but not his brain, and he was still in a fever of resentment and shame when his lagging feet brought him to the house. He passed it irresolutely once, unable to make up his mind to enter and face them. Then, cursing himself for a poltroon, he turned again and made for the door.

He was within half a dozen strides of it when a dark figure detached itself from the doorway, and stumbled down the steps. Its aim seemed to be to escape, and leaping to the conclusion that it was Gentilis, and that some trick was being prepared for him, Claude sprang forward.

His hand shot out, he grasped the other's neck. His wrath blazed up.

"You rogue!" he said. "I'll teach you to lie in wait for me!" And shifting his grasp from the man's neck to his shoulder, he turned him round regardless of his struggles. As he did so the man's hat fell off. With amazement Claude recognised the features of the Syndic Blondel.

The young man's arm fell, and he stared, open-mouthed and aghast, the passion with which he had seized the stranger whelmed in astonishment.

The Syndic, on the other hand, behaved with a strange composure. Breathing rather quickly, but vouchsafing no word of explanation, he straightened the crumpled linen about his neck, and set right his coat. He was proceeding, still in silence, to pick up his hat, when Claude, anticipating the action, secured the hat and restored it to him.

"Thank you," he said. And then, stiffly, "Come with me," he continued,

He turned as he spoke and led the way to a spot at some distance from the house, yet within sight of the door; and there he wheeled about. "I was coming to see you," he said, steadfastly confronting Claude. "Why have you not called upon me, young man, in accordance with the invitation I gave you?"

Claude stared. The Syndic's matter-of-factness and the ease with which he ignored what had just passed staggered him. Perhaps after all Blondel had come for this, and had been startled while waiting at the door by the quickness of his approach. "I—I had overlooked it," he murmured, trying to accept the situation.

"Then," the Syndic answered shrewdly, "I can see that you have not wanted anything."

"No."

"You lodge there?" Blondel continued, pointing to the house. "But I know you do. And keep late hours I fear. You lodge there," he continued, peering inquisitively into the young man's face. "And are not alone in the house I think."

"No," Claude replied; and as his mind went back to the house and those in it, there came on him the temptation to tell all to this man, a magistrate, and appeal to him in the girl's behalf. He could not speak to a more proper person if he sought the city through, and here was the opportunity, brought unsought, to his door. But then he had not the girl's leave to speak; could he speak without her leave? He shifted his feet, and to gain time, "No," he said slowly, "there are two or three—who lodge in the house."

"Is not the person with whom you quarrelled at the Inn one of them?" the Syndic asked, his eyes on the door of the house. "Eh? Is not he one?"

"Yes," Claude answered; and the recollection of the scene and of the support which the Syndic had given to Grio checked the impulse to speak. Perhaps after all the girl knew best.

"And a person of the name of Basterga, I think?"

Claude nodded. He dared not trust himself to speak now. Could it be that a whisper of what was passing in the house had reached the magistrates?

The Syndic coughed. He glanced from the distant door, now a dark blur in the obscurity, to his companion's face and back again to the door—of which he seemed reluctant to lose sight. For a moment he seemed at a loss how to proceed. When he did speak, after a long pause, it was in a dry, curt tone. "It is about him I wish to hear something," he said. "I look to you as a good citizen to afford such information as the State requires. The matter is more important than you think. I ask you what you know of that man."

"Messer Basterga!"

"Yes."

Claude stared. "I know no good," he answered, more and more surprised. "I do not like him, Messer Syndic."

"But he is a learned man, I believe. He passes for such, does he not?"

"Yes."

"Yet you do not like him. Why?"

Claude's face burned. "He puts his learning to no good use," he said. "He uses it to—to torture women. If I could tell you all—all, Messer Blondel," the young man continued, in growing excitement, "you would understand! He gains power over people, a strange power, and abuses it. He——"

"A strange power? What do you mean? What power?"

"God knows."

The Syndic stared a moment, his face expressive of something like contempt. This was not the line he had meant his questions to take. What did it matter to him how the man treated women? Pshaw! Then suddenly a light—as of satisfaction, or discovery—gleamed in his eyes. "Do you mean," he muttered, lowering his voice, "by sorcery?"

"God knows."

"By evil arts?"

The young man shook his head. "I do not know," he answered, almost pettishly. "How should I? But he has a power. A strange power! I do not understand him or it!"

The Syndic looked at him darkly thoughtful. "You did not know that that was said of him?" he asked.

"That he——"

"Has magical arts?"

Claude shook his head.

"Nor that he has a laboratory upstairs?" Blondel continued, fixing the young man gravely with his eyes. "A laboratory in which he reads much in unknown tongues? And speaks much when no one is present? And tries experiments with strange substances?"

Claude shook his head. "No!" he said. "Never! I never heard it." He never had, but in his eyes dawned none the less a look of horror. No man in those days doubted the existence of the devilish arts at which Blondel hinted—arts by the use of which one being could make himself master of the will and person of another. No man doubted their existence; and that such practices were rare, were difficult, were seldom brought within a man's experience made them only the more hateful without making them seem to the men of that day the less probable. That they were often exercised at the cost of the innocent and pure, who in this way were added to the accursed brood—few doubted this also; but the full horror of it could be known only to the man who loved, and who reverenced where he loved. Fortunately, men who never doubted the reality of witchcraft, seldom conceived of it as touching those they loved; and it was only slowly that Claude took in the meaning of the Syndic's suggestion, or discerned how perfectly it accounted for a thing otherwise unaccountable—the mysterious sway which the Scholar held over the young girl.

But he reached, he came to that point at last; and his silence and his agitation were more eloquent than words. The Syndic, who had not shot his bolt at a venture—for to accuse Basterga of the black art had passed through his mind before—saw that he had hit the mark; and he pushed his advantage. "Have you noted aught," he asked, "to bear out the idea that he is given to such practices?"

Claude was silent in sheer horror: horror of the thing suggested to him, horror of the punishment in which he might involve the innocent.

"I don't know!" he stammered at last, and almost incoherently. "I know nothing! Don't ask me! God grant it be not so!" And he covered his face.

"Amen! Amen, indeed," Blondel answered gravely. "But now for the woman, over whom you said he had power?"

"I said?"

"Ay, you, a minute ago! Who is she? Is she one of the household? Come, young man, you must answer me," the Syndic continued with severity proportioned to the other's hesitation. "I know much, and a little more light may enable us to act and to bring the guilty to punishment. Does she live in the house?"

Only the darkness hid Claude's pallor. "There is a woman," he muttered reluctantly, "who lives in the house. But I know nothing! I have no proof! Nothing, nothing!"

"But you suspect! You suspect, young man," the Syndic continued, eyeing him sternly, "and suspecting you would leave her in the clutches of the devil whose she must become, body and soul! For shame!"

"But I do not believe it!" Claude cried fiercely. "I do not believe it!"

"Of her?"

"Of her? No! *Mon dieu!* No! She is a child! She is innocent! Innocent as——"

"The day! you would say?" the Syndic struck in, almost solemnly. "The likelier prey? The choicest are ever the devil's morsels."

"And you think that she——"

"God help her, if she be in his power! This man," the Syndic continued, laying his hand on the other's arm, "has ruined hundreds by his secret arts, by his foul practices, by his sorceries. He has made Venice too hot for him. In Padua they will have him no more. Genoa has driven him forth. If you doubt this character of him there is an easy proof; for it is whispered, nay, it is almost certain, in what his power lies. Do you know his room?"

"No."

"No?" in a tone of dismay. "But is it not on a level with yours?"

"No," Claude answered, shivering. "It is over mine."

"No matter, there is an easy mode of proving him," the Syndic replied, and despite himself his tone grew eager. "If he be the man they say he is, there is in his room a box of steel chained to the wall. It contains the spell he uses. By means of it he can enter where he pleases, he can enslave women to his will, he——"

"And you do not seize it?" Claude cried in a tone of horror.

"He has the Grand Duke's protection," the Syndic answered smoothly, "and to touch him without clear proof might cause much trouble to the State."

"And for that you suffer him," Claude exclaimed, his voice trembling. "You suffer him to work his will?"

"I must follow the law," Blondel answered, shaking his head. He looked warily round; the dark ramparts were quiet. Basterga he knew was absent; he might not have such another chance. "I act but as a magistrate," he continued. "Were I a mere man and knew him, as I know him now, for what he is—a foul magician weaving his spells about the young, ensnaring, with his sorceries, the souls of innocent women, corrupting—but what is it, young man?"

"He is within?"

"No; he left the house a minute or so before you arrived. But what is it?" Seizing the young man's arm he restrained him. "Where are you going?"

"To his room!" Claude answered between his teeth. "Be he man or devil—to his room!"

"You dare?"

"I dare and I will!" And, resisting the Syndic's feigned efforts to hold him back, he strode toward the door. "That spell shall not be his another hour."

But Blondel, terrified by his sudden success, and, hesitating to put all on a cast, now the time was come, kept his hand on him. "Stay! Stay!" he babbled, dragging him back. "Do not be rash!"

"Stay, and leave him to ruin her!"

"Then listen! Whatever you do, listen!" the Syndic answered; and insisted, clinging to him. His agitation indeed was such that had Claude retained his powers of observation, he must have noticed something strange in this anxiety. "Listen! If you find the casket, on your life touch nothing in it! On your life!" Blondel repeated, his hands clinging more tightly to the other's arm. "Bring it entire, touch nothing! If you do not promise me I will raise the alarm here and now! To open it, I warn you, is to risk all."

"I will bring it!" Claude answered, his foot on the steps, his hand on the latch. "I will bring it!"

"Ay, but you do not know what hangs on it! You will bring it as you find it?"

His persistence was so strange, he clung to the young man's arm with so complete an abandonment of his ordinary manner that, with the latch half raised, Claude looked at him in wonder. "Very well, I will bring it as I find it!" he muttered. And then, notwithstanding a movement which the Syndic made to restrain him, he pushed the door.

It was not locked, and, in a moment, he stood in the living room which he had left little more than an hour before. It was untenanted, but not in darkness; a rushlight, set in an earthen vessel on the hearth, flung long shadows on the walls and ceiling, and gave to the room, so homely in its every-day aspect, a sinister look. The door of Gentilis' room was shut; probably he was asleep. That at the foot of the staircase was also shut. Claude stood a moment, frowning darkly; then he crossed the floor toward the staircase door. His heart beat fast, but his mind was fixed. Yet the spell of the other's excitement told on him; the · flicker of the rushlight made him start; half way across the room a sound, at his elbow, brought him up as if he had been stabbed. He turned his head slowly, expecting to find the big man's eyes bent on him from some corner. He found instead the Syndic, who had entered after him, and with a dark, anxious face was standing like a shadow of guilt between him and the door.

The young man resented the alarm which the other had caused him. "If you are going, go," he muttered. "And if you will do it yourself, Messer Blondel, so much the better." He pointed to the door of the staircase.

The Syndic recoiled, his beard wagging senilely. "No, no," he babbled. "No, I will go back."

It was no longer the formal magistrate, but a shivering man who stood at Claude's elbow. And this was so clear that superstition, which is of all things the most infectious, began to shake the young man's resolution. Desperately he threw it off, and went to open the door. Then he reflected that it would be dark upstairs, he must have a light; and re-crossing the floor on tiptoe, he brought the rushlight from the hearth. Holding it aloft he opened the creaking door and began to ascend the stairs.

With every step the awe of the other world fell on him more strongly; while the shadow, which he had found at his elbow below, followed him upwards. When he paused at the head of the flight the Syndic's face was on a level with his knee, the Syndic's eyes were fixed on his.

Claude did not understand this; but the man's company was welcome now, and the sight of Basterga's door, not three paces from the place where he stood, diverted his thoughts. He had not been above stairs since the day of his arrival, but he knew that Basterga's room was the nearer to the stairs. That was the door then; behind that door the Italian wrought his devilish spells!

The light, smoky and wavering, cast black shadows on the walls of the passage as he moved. The air seemed heavy and sulphurous, laden with some strange drug; the house was still, with the stillness which precedes horror. Not many men of his time, suspecting what he suspected, would have opened that door, or at that hour of the night would have entered that room. But Claude, though he feared, though he shuddered, though unearthly terrors pressed upon him, possessed a charm that bore up his courage: the memory of the scene in the room below, of the scalding drops falling on the white skin, of the girl looking at him with that drawn face of pain. The devil was strong, but there was a stronger; and in the strength of love the young man approached the door and tried it. It was locked.

Somehow the fact augmented his courage. "Where the devil is, is no need of locks," he muttered, and he felt above the door, then, stooping, groped under it. In the latter place he found the key, thrust out of sight between door and floor, where doubtless it was Basterga's custom to hide it. He drew it out, and with a grim face set it in the lock.

"Quick!" muttered a voice in his ear, and turning he saw that the Syndic was trembling with eagerness. "Quick, quick! Or he may return!"

Claude smiled sourly. If he did not fear the devil he certainly did not fear Basterga. And he was about to turn the key in the lock when a sound stayed his hand and rooted him to the spot. Yet it was only a laugh—but a laugh such as his ears had never caught before, a laugh full of a ghastly, strained unearthly mirth. It rang through the passage, through the house, through the night; but whence it proceeded, whether from some being at their elbows or from above stairs or below, it was impossible to say; and the blood gone from his face Claude stood, peering over his shoulder into the dark corners of the passage. Again that laugh rose, shrill, mocking, unearthly; and this time his hand fell from the lock.

The Syndic, utterly unmanned, leant sweating against the wall. He called upon the name of his Maker. "My God!" he muttered. "My God!"

"There is no God!"

The words, each syllable of them clear, though spoken in a voice shrill and cracked and strange, and such as neither had ever heard before, were beyond doubt. Close on them followed a shriek of weird laughter, and then the blasphemy repeated in the same tone of mockery. The hair crept on Claude's head, the blood withdrew to his heart. The key which he had drawn out of the lock fell from the hand it seemed to freeze.

With distended eyes he glared down the passage. The words were still in the air, the laughter echoed in his brain, the shadows cast by the shaking rushlight danced and took weird shapes. A rustling as of black wings gathered about him, unseen shapes hovered closer—was it his fancy or did he hear them?

He tried to disbelieve, he strove to withstand his terror; and a moment his fortitude held. Then, as the Syndic, shaking as with the palsy, tottered, with a hand on either wall down the stairs, and moaning aloud in his terror, felt his way across the room below, Claude's courage too, gave way; not in face of that he saw, but of that which he fancied. He turned too, and with a greater show of composure, and still carrying the light, he stumbled down the stairs and into the room below.

There, for an instant sense and nerve returned, and he stood. He turned even, and made as if he would re-ascend the staircase. But he had no sooner thrust his head into it, and paused to listen ere he ventured, than a faint echo of the same mirthless laughter reached him, and he turned shuddering, and fled—fled out of the room, out of the house, out of the light, to the same spot under the trees, whence he had started with so bold a heart a few minutes earlier.

The Syndic was there before him—or no, not the Syndic, but a stricken man, clinging to a tree; seized now and again with a fresh fit of trembling. "Take me home," he babbled. "There is no hope! There is no hope! Take me home!"

Claude, when he had a little recovered himself, assented, gave the tottering man his arm and supported him—he needed support—until they reached the dwelling in the Bourg du Four. Still a wreck, Blondel was by this time a little more coherent. But his nerves were utterly shattered, he foresaw solitude and dreaded it; he would have had the other enter and pass the night there. But the young man, already ashamed of his weakness, already doubting and questioning, refused, promising only to return on the morrow. With an aspect apparently composed, he insisted on taking his leave, turned abruptly from the door and retraced his steps to the Corraterie. But when he came to the house, he lacked, brave as he was, the heart to enter; and passing it, he spent the time until daybreak, in walking up and down the rampart within hearing of the sentries.

His mind grown somewhat calmer, he set himself to recall precisely and exactly the thing that had happened. But recall it as he might, he could not account for it. The words of blasphemy that had scorched his ears as the key

WITH DISTENDED EYES HE GLARED DOWN THE
PASSAGE

entered the lock, had been uttered, he was sure, in no voice known to him; nay more, in no voice of human intonation. How could he explain them? How account for them save in one way? How defend his cowardice save on one ground? He shuddered, gazing at the house, and murmuring now a prayer, and now a word of exorcism. But the day had come, the sky was red, and the sun was near its rising before he took courage and dared to cross the threshold.

CHAPTER IX

MELUSINA

EVEN then, with the daylight about him, he crept into the house under a weight of awe and dread. He left the door ajar that the daylight might enter with him and dispel the shadows: and when he had crossed the threshold, it was with a pale and frowning face that he advanced to the middle of the floor, and stood peering round the deserted living-room. No one was stirring above or below, the house and all within it slept: the rushlight stand, its wick long extinguished, remained where he had set it down in the panic of his flight.

With that exception—he eyed it darkly—no trace of the mysterious event of the night was visible. The room wore, or minute by minute assumed, its daylight aspect. Nor had he stood long gazing upon it before he breathed more freely and felt his heart lightened. What was to be thought, what could be thought in the circumstances, he was not prepared to say. But the panic of the night was gone with the darkness; and with it all idea—if in the depths he had really sunk so low—of relinquishing the woman he loved to the powers of evil.

To the powers of Evil! To a fate as much worse than death as the soul and the mind are higher than the body! Was he really face to face with that? Was this house, so quiet, so peaceful, so commonplace, in reality the theatre of one of those manifestations of Satan's power which were the horror of the age? His senses affirmed it, and yet he doubted. Such things were, he did not deny it. Few men of the time denied it. But presented to him, brought within his experience, they shocked him to the point of disbelief. He found that from the thing which he was prepared to admit in the general, he dissented fiercely and instinctively in the particular.

What, the woman he loved! Was he to believe her delivered, soul and body, to the power of Satan? Never! Never! All that was sane and wholesome and courageous in the man rebelled against the thought. He would not believe it. The pots and pans on the hearth, the simple implements of work and life, on which his eyes alighted wherever he turned them, and to none of which her hand was stranger, his memory of the love that was between her and her mother, his picture of the sacred life led by those two above stairs, all, all gave the lie to it! Her subjection to Basterga, her submission to contumely and to insult—there must be a reason for these, a natural and innocent reason could he hit on it. The strange occurrences of the night, the blasphemous words, the mocking laughter, at the worst they might not import a mastery over her. He shuddered as he recalled them, they rang in his ears and brain, the vividness of his memory of them was remarkable. But they might not have relation to her.

He stood long in moody thought, but his ears never for an instant relaxed their vigil, their hearkening for he knew not what. At length he passed into his bedcloset, and cooled his hot face with water and repaired his dress. Coming out again, he found the house still quiet, the door as he had left it, the daylight pouring in through the aperture. No one was moving, he was still safe from interruption; and a curiosity to visit the passage above and learn if aught abnormal was to be seen, took possession of him. It was just possible that Basterga had not returned; that the key still lay where he had dropped it!

He opened the door of the staircase and listened. He heard nothing, and he stole half way up the flight and again stood. Still all was silent. He mounted more boldly then, and he was within four steps of the top—whence, turning his head a little, he could command the passage—when a sound arrested him. It was a sound easily explicable though it startled him; for a moment later Anne Royaume appeared at the foot of the upper flight of stairs, and moved along the passage toward him.

She did not see him, and he could have escaped with ease had he retired at once. But he stood fixed to the spot by something in her appearance; a something that, as she moved slowly toward him, fancying herself alone, filled him with dread, and with something worse than dread—suspicion.

For if ever woman looked as if she had come from a witch's Sabbath; if ever girl, scarce more than child, walked as if she had plucked the fruit of the Tree and savoured it bitter, it was the girl before him. Despair—it seemed to him—rode her like a hag. Dejection, fear, misery, were in her whole bearing. Her eyes looked out from black hollows, her cheeks were pallid, her mouth was nerveless. Three sleepless nights, he thought, could not have changed a woman thus—no, nor thrice three; and he who had seen her last night, and saw her now, gazed fascinated and bewildered, asking himself what had happened, what it meant.

Alas, for answer there rose the spectre which he had been striving to lay; the spectre that had for the men of that day so appalling, so shocking a reality. Witchcraft! The word rang in his brain. The thing would account for this, ay, and for all; for her long submission to vile behests and viler men; for that which he had heard in this house at midnight; for that which the Syndic had whispered of Basterga; for that which he noted in her now! Would account for it; but by fixing her with a guilt, not of this world, terrible, abnormal: by fixing her with a love of things vile, unspeakable, monstrous, a love that must deprive her life of all joy, all sweetness, all truth, all purity! A guilt and a love that showed her thus!

But thus, for a moment only. The next she espied his face above the landing-edge, perceived that he watched her, detected, perhaps, something of his feeling. With startling abruptness her features and form underwent a change. Her cheeks flamed high, her eyes sparkled with resentment. "You!" she cried—and her causeless anger, her impatience of his presence confirmed the dreadful idea he had conceived. "You!" she repeated. "How dare you come here? How dare you? What are you doing here? Your room is below. Go down, sir!"

He did not move, but he met her eyes; he tried to read her soul, his own quaking. And his look, sombre and stern —for he saw a gulf opening at his feet—should have given her pause. Instead, her anger faced him down and mastered him. "Do you hear me?" she flung at him. "Do you hear me? If you have aught to say, if you are not as those others, go down! Go down, and I will hear you there!"

He went down then, giving way to her, and she followed

him. She closed the staircase door with care; and that done, in the living-room with her he would have spoken. But with a glance at Gentilis' door, she silenced him, and led the way through the outer door to the open air. The hour was still early, the sun was barely risen. Save for a sentry sleeping at his post on the ramparts, there was no one within sight, and she crossed the open space to the low wall that looked down upon the Rhone. There, in a spot where the partly stripped branches which shaded the rampart hid them from the windows, she turned to him. "Now," she said, breathing quickly—there was a smouldering fire in her eyes—"if you have aught to say to me, say it. Say it now!"

He hesitated. He had had time to think, and he found the burden laid upon him heavy. "I do not know," he answered dully, "that I have any right to speak to you."

"Right!" she cried; and let her bitterness have way in that word. "Right! Does any stay for that where I am concerned? Or ask my leave, or crave my will, sir? Right? You have the same right to flout and jeer and scorn me, the same right to watch and play the spy on me, to hearken at my door, and follow me, that they have! Ay, and the same right to bid me come and go, answer at your will, that others have! Do you scruple a little at beginning?" she continued mockingly. "It will wear off. It will come easy by and by! For you are like the others!"

"No!"

"You are as the others! You begin as they began!" she repeated, giving the reins to her indignation. "The day you came, last night even, I thought you different. I deemed you"—she pressed her hand to her bosom as if she stilled a pain—"other than you are! I confess it. But you are their fellow. You begin as they began, by listening on stairs and at doors, by dogging me and playing eaves-dropper, by hearkening to what I say and do. Right?" she repeated the word bitterly, mockingly, with fierce unhappiness. "You have the right that they have! The same right!"

"Have I?" he asked slowly. His face was sombre and strangely old.

"Yes!"

"Then how did I gain it?" he retorted with a dark look. "How—" his tone was as gloomy as his face—"did they gain it? Or—he?"

"He?" The flame was gone from her face. She trembled a little.

"Yes, he, Basterga," he replied, his eyes losing no whit of the change in her. "How did he gain the right which he has handed on to others, the right to shame you, to lay hand on you, to treat you as he does? This is a Free City. Women are no slaves here. What then is the secret between you and him?" Claude continued grimly. "What is your secret?"

"My secret!" She spoke faintly; her passion dwindled under his eyes, under his words.

"Ay," Claude answered, "and his! His secret and yours. What is the thing between you and him?" he continued, his eyes fixed sternly on her, "so dark, so weighty, so dangerous, you must needs for it suffer his touch, bear his look, be smooth to him though you loathe him? What is it?"

"Perhaps—love," she muttered, with a forced smile. But it did not deceive him for a moment.

"You loathe him!" he said.

"I may have loved him—once," she faltered.

"You never loved him," he retorted sternly. All the shyness of youth, all the bashfulness of man with maiden were gone. Under the weight of that thought, that dreadful thought, he had grown old in a few minutes. His tone was hard, his manner pitiless. "You never loved him!" he repeated, the very immodesty of her excuse confirming his fears. "And I ask you, what is it? What is it that is between you and him? What is it that gives him this power over you?"

"Nothing," she stammered, pale to the lips.

"Nothing! And was it for nothing that you were startled when you found me upstairs? When you found me watching you five minutes ago, was it for nothing you flamed with rage——"

"You had no right to be there."

"No. Yet it was an innocent thing enough—to be there," he answered. "To be there, this morning." And then he added, giving the words all the meaning of which his voice was capable, "To have been there last night—that were a different thing perhaps."

"Were you there?" Her voice was barely audible.

"I was."

It was dreadful to see how she sank under that, how she slid into herself and cringed before him, her anger gone, her colour gone, the light fled from her eyes—eyes grown suddenly secretive. It was a minute, it seemed a minute at least, before she could frame a word, a single word. Then, "What do you know?" she whispered. But for the wall against which she leant, she must have fallen.

"What do I know?"

She nodded, unable to repeat the words.

"WHAT DO YOU KNOW?" SHE WHISPERED. BUT
FOR THE WALL SHE WOULD HAVE FALLEN

"I was at the door of Basterga's room last night."

"Last night!"

"Yes. I had the key of his room in my hand. I was putting it into the lock when I heard——"

"Hush!" She stepped forward, she would have put her hand over his mouth. "Hush! Hush!"

The terror of her eyes, the glance she cast behind her, echoed the word—nay, spoke it—more clearly than her lips. "Hush! Hush!"

He could not bear to look at her. Her voice, her terror, the very defence she had striven to make confirmed him in his worst suspicions. The thing was too certain, too apparent; in mercy to himself as well as to her, he averted his eyes.

They fell instead on the hills on which he had gazed that morning barely three weeks earlier, when the autumn haze had mirrored her face; and all his thoughts, his heart, his fancy had been hers, her prize, her easy capture. And now he dared not look on her face. He could not bear to see it distorted by the terrors of an evil conscience. Even her words when she spoke next jarred on him.

"You knew the voice?" she whispered.

"I did not know it," he answered, brokenly. "I knew —whose it was."

"Mine?"

"Yes." He scarcely breathed the word.

She did not cry "Hush!" this time, but she caught her breath; and after a moment's pause, "Still—you did not recognise it?" she murmured. "You did not know that it was my voice?" Could it be that after all she hoped to blind him?

"I did not."

"Thank God!"

"Thank God!" He stood erect, staring at her, echoing the words in his astonishment. How dared she name the sacred name?

She read his thoughts. "Yes," she said hardily, "why not?"

He turned on her. "Why not?" he cried. "Why not? You dare to thank Him, who last night denied him? You dare to name His name in the light, who in the darkness—— You! And you are not afraid?"

"Afraid?" she repeated. There was a strange light, almost a smile he would have deemed it had he thought that possible—in her face, "Nay, perhaps; perhaps. For even the devils, we are told, believe and tremble."

His jaw fell; for a moment he gazed at her in sheer bewilderment. Then, as the full import of her words and her look overwhelmed him, he turned to the wall and bowed his face on his arms. His whole being shook, his soul was sick. What was he to say to her? What was he to do? Flee from her presence as from the presence of Antichrist? Avoid her henceforth as he valued his soul? Pluck even the memory of her from his mind? Or wrestle with her, argue with her, snatch her from the foul spells and enchantments that now held her—the tool and chosen instrument of the evil one—in their fiendish grip?

He felt a Churchman's horror—Protestant as he was—at the thought of a woman possessed. But for that reason, and because he was in the way of becoming a minister, was it not his duty to measure his strength with the Adversary. Alas! he could conceive of no words, no thoughts, no arguments adequate to that strife. Had he been a Papist he might have turned with hope, even with pious confidence, to the Holy Stoup, the Bell and Book and Candle, to the Relics and hundred Exorcisms of his Church. But the colder and more abstract faith of Calvin, while it admitted the possibility of such Possessions, supplied no weapons of a material kind.

He groaned in his impotence, stifled by the unwholesome atmosphere of his thoughts. He dared not even ponder too long on what she was who stood beside him; nor peer too closely through the murky veil that hid her being. To do so might be to risk his soul, to become a partner in her guilt. He might conjecture what dark thoughts and dreadful aptitudes lurked behind the girl's gentle mask, he might strive to learn by what black arts she had been seduced, what power over visible things had been the price of her apostasy, what Sabbath-mark, seal and pledge of that apostasy she bore—but at what peril! At what risk of soul and body! His brain reeled, his blood raced at the thought.

Such things had lately been, he knew. Had there not been a dreadful outbreak in Alsace—Alsace, the neighbour almost of Geneva—within the last few years. In Thann and Turckheim, places within a couple of days' journey of Geneva, scores had suffered for such practices; and some of these not old and ugly, but young and handsome, girls and pages of the Court and young wives! Had not the most unlikely persons confessed to practices the most dreadful? The most innocent in appearance to things unspeakable!

But—with a sudden revulsion of feeling—that was in Alsace, he told himself. That was in Alsace! Such things did not happen here at men's elbows! He must have been mad to think it or dream it. And, lifting his head, he looked about him. The sun had risen higher, the rich vale of the Rhone, extended at his feet, lay bathed in air and light and brightness. The burnished hills, the brown, tilled slopes, the gleaming river, the fairness of that rare landscape clad in morning freshness, gave the lie to the suspicions he had been indulging, gave the lie, there and then, to possibilities he dared not have denied in school or pulpit. Nature spoke to his heart, and with smiling face denied the unnatural. In Bamberg and Wurzburg and Alsace, but not here! In Magdeburg, but not here! In Edinburgh, but not here! The world of beauty and light and growth on which he looked would have none of the dark devil's world of which he had been dreaming: the dark devil's world which the sophists and churchmen and the weak-witted of two score generations had built up!

He turned and looked at her, the scales fallen from his eyes. She was still pale, but she had recovered her composure and she met his gaze without blenching. Now, however, behind the passive defiance, grave rather than sullen, which she presented to his attack, the weakness, the helplessness, the heart pain of the woman were visible.

He saw them and while he hungered for a more explicit denial, for a cry of indignant protest, for a passionate repudiation, he found some comfort in that look. And his heart spoke. "I do not believe it!" he cried impetuously, in perfect forgetfulness of the fact that he had not put his charge into words. "I do not: I will not! Only say that it is false! And I will say no more."

Her answer was as cold water thrown upon him. "I will tell you nothing," she said firmly.

"Why not? Why not?" he cried.

"You ask why not," she answered slowly. "Are you

so short of memory? Is it so long since, against my will
and prayers, you came into yonder house—that you forget what I said and what I did? And what you promised?"

"My God!" he cried. "You do not know where you
stand! You do not know what peril threatens you. This
is no time," he continued, holding out his hands to her in
growing agitation, "for sticking on scruples or raising
trifles. Tell me all!"

"I will tell you nothing!" she replied firmly. "I have
suffered. I suffer. Can you not suffer a little?"

"Not blasphemy!" he said. "Not that! Tell me"—
his voice, his eyes grew suppliant—"tell me that it was not
your voice. Tell me that it was not you who spoke! Tell
me—only that. I ask no more."

"I will tell you nothing!" she answered with the same
strange stolidity.

"You do not know——"

"I know what it is you have in your mind!" she replied.
"What it is you are thinking of me. That they will burn
me in the Bourg du Four presently, as they burned the girl
in Aix last year! As they burned the woman in Besançon
not many months since—I have seen those who saw it. As
they did to two women in Zurich—my mother was there!
As they did to five hundred people in Geneva in my grandfather's time. It is that," she continued, a strange wild
light in her eyes, "that you think they will do to me?"

"God forbid!" he cried.

"Nay, you may do it, too, if you choose," she answered,
gravely regarding him. "But I do not think you will, for
you are young, almost as young as I am, and, having done
it, you would have many years to live and think. You

would remember in those years that it was my mother that nursed your father, that it was you who came to us, not we to you, that it was you who promised to aid us, not I who sought your aid! You would remember all these things of a morning when you awoke early: and this—that in the end you gave me up to the law and burned me."

"God forbid!" he cried, and hid his face with his hands. The very quietness of her speech set an edge on horror. "God forbid!"

"Ay, but men allow!" she answered drearily. "What if I was mad last night, and in my madness denied my Maker? I am sane to-day, but I must burn, if it be known! I must burn!"

"Not by my mouth!" he cried, his brow damp with sweat. "Never, I swear it! If there be guilt, on my head be the guilt!"

"You mean it? You mean that?" she said.

"I do."

"You will be silent?"

"I will."

Her lips parted, in her eyes shone hope—hope which showed how deep her despair had been. "And you will ask no questions?" she whispered.

"I will ask no questions," he answered. He stifled a sigh.

She drew a deep breath of relief, but she did not thank him. It was a thing for which no thanks could be given. She stood a while, sad and thoughtful, reflecting, it seemed, on what had passed; then she turned slowly and left him, crossed the open space, and entered the house, walking as one under a heavy burden.

And he? He remained; troubled at one time by the

yearning to follow and comfort and cherish her; cast at another into a cold sweat by the recollection of that voice in the night, and the strange ties which bound her to Basterga. Innocent, it seemed to him, that connection could not be. Based on aught but evil it could hardly be. Yet he must endure, witness, cloak it. He must wait, helpless and inactive, the issue of it. He must lie on the rack, drawn one way by love of her, drawn the other by daily and hourly suspicions, suspicions so strong and so terrible that even love could hardly cast them out.

For the voice he had heard at midnight, and the horrid laughter, which greeted the words of sacrilege—were facts. And her subjection to Basterga, the man of evil past and evil name, was a fact. And her terror and her avowal were facts. He could not doubt, he could not deny them. Only—he loved her. He loved her even while he doubted her, even while he admitted that women as young and as innocent had been guilty of the blackest practices and the most evil arts. He loved her and he suffered: doubting, though he could not abandon her. The air was fresh about him, the world lay sunlit under his eyes. But the beauty of the world had not saved young and tender women, who on such mornings had walked barefoot, none comforting them, to the fiery expiation of their crimes. Perhaps—perhaps among the thousands who had witnessed their last agony, one man hidden in the crowd, had vainly closed ears and eyes, one man had died a hundred deaths in one.

CHAPTER X

AUCTIO FIT; VENIT VITA

IN his spacious chestnut-panelled parlour, in a high-backed oaken chair that had throned for centuries the Abbots of Bellerive, Messer Blondel sat brooding, with his chin upon his breast. The chestnut-panelled parlour was new. The shields of the Cantons which formed a frieze above the panels shone brightly, the or and azure, gules and argent of their quarterings, undimmed by time or woodsmoke. The innumerable panes of the long heavily leaded windows which looked out on the Bourg du Four were still rain-proof; the light they admitted still found something garish in the portrait of the Syndic—by Schouten—that formed the central panel of the mantelpiece. New and stately, the room had not its pair in Geneva; and dear to its owner's heart had it been a short, a very short time before. He had anticipated no more lasting pleasure, looked forward to no safer gratification for his declining years, than to sit, as he now sat, surrounded by its grandeur. In due time—not at once, lest the people take alarm or his enemies occasion—he had determined to rebuild the whole house after the same fashion. The plans of the oaken gallery, the staircase and dining-chamber, prepared by a trusty craftsman of Basle, lay at this moment in the drawer of the bureau beside his chair.

Now all was changed. A fiat had gone forth, which placed him alike beyond the envy of his friends, and the hatred of his foes. He must die. He must die, and leave these pleasant things, this goodly room, that future of which he had dreamed. Another man would lie warm in the chamber he had prepared; another would be Syndic and bear his wand. The years of stately plenty which he had foreseen, were already as last year's harvest. No wonder that the sheen of portrait and panel, the pride of echoing oak, were fled; or that the eyes with which he gazed on the things about him were dull and lifeless.

Dull and lifeless at one moment, and clouded by the apathy of despair; at another bright with the fierce fever of revolt. In the one phase or the other he had passed many hours of late, some of them amid the dead-sea grandeur of this room. And he had had his hours of hope also. Three weeks back a ray of hope, bright as the goblin light which shines the more brilliantly the darker be the night, had shone on him and amused and enchanted him. And then, in one moment, God and man—or if not God, the devil—had joined to quench the hope; and this morning he sat sunk in deepest despair, all in and around him dark. Hitherto he had regarded appearances. He had hidden alike his malady and his fears, his apathy and his mad revolt; he had lived as usual. But this morning he was beyond that. He could not rouse himself, he could not be doing. His servants, wondering why he did not go abroad or betake himself to some task, came and peeped at him, and went away whispering and pointing and nudging one another. And he knew it. But he paid no heed to them or to anything, until it happened that his eyes, resting dully on the street, marked a man who paused before the door and looked at the house, in doubt, it seemed, whether he should seek to enter or should pass on.

For an appreciable time the Syndic watched the loiterer without seeing him. What did it matter to a dying man —a man whom heaven, impassive, abandoned to the evil powers—who came or went? But by-and-by his eyes conveyed the identity of the man to his brain; he rose to his feet, and laid his hand on a bell which stood on the table beside him. In the act of ringing, however, he changed his mind, and laying the bell down, he strode himself to the outer door, the house door, and opened it. The man was still in the street. Scarcely showing himself, Blondel caught his eye, signed to him to enter, and held the door while he did so.

Claude Mercier—for he it was—entered awkwardly. He followed the Syndic into the parlour, and standing with his cap in his hand, began shamefacedly to explain that he had come to learn how the Syndic was, after—— after that which had happened——. He did not finish the sentence.

For that matter, Blondel did not allow him to finish. He had passed at sight of him, into the other of the two conditions between which his days were divided. His eyes glittered, his hands trembled. "Have you seen him?" he asked eagerly; and the voice in which he spoke surprised the young man. "Have you seen him?"

"Basterga, do you mean, Messer Syndic?"

"Who else? Who else?"

"No, Messer Blondel, I have not."

"Nor learned anything?"

"No, nothing."

"But you don't mean to leave it there?" Blondel cried,

his voice rising almost to a scream. And he sat down and
rose up again. "You have done nothing, but you are going to do something? What will it be? What?" And
then as he discerned the other's surprise, and read suspicion in his eyes, he curbed himself, lowered his tone, and
with an effort was himself. "Young man," he said, wiping
his brow, "I am oppressed, I am ridden—by what happened last night. I have lain, since we parted, under an
overwhelming sense of the presence of evil. Of evil," he
repeated, still speaking a little wildly, "such as this God-
fearing town should not know even by repute! You think
me over-anxious? But I have felt the hot blast of the
furnace on my cheek, my head bears even now the smell of
the burning. Hell gapes near us!" He was beginning
to tremble afresh, partly with impatience of this parleying, partly with anxiety to pluck from the other his answer. The glitter was returning to his eyes. "Hell gapes
near us," he repeated. "And I ask you, young man, what
are you going to do?"

"I?"

"Yes, you!"

Claude stared. "What would you have me do?" he
asked.

"What would you have done last night?" the Syndic
retorted. "Did you ask me then? Did you wait for my
permission? Did you wait even—for my presence?"

"No, but——"

"But what?"

"Things are changed."

"Changed? How?" Blondel's tone sank to one of unnatural calm; but his frame shook and his face was purple with the pressure he put upon himself. "What is

changed? Who has changed it?" he continued; to see his chance of life hang on the will of this imbecile was almost more than he could bear. "Speak out! Let me know what has happened."

"You know what happened as well as I do," Claude answered slowly. He had given his word to the girl that he would not interfere, but he began to see difficulties of which he had not thought. "It was enough for me! He may be all you said he was, Messer Syndic, but——"

"But you no longer burn to break the spell?" Blondel cried. "You no longer desire to snatch from him the woman you love? You will stand by and see her perish body and soul in this web of iniquity? You are frightened, and will leave her to the law!" He thrust out his thin flushed face, his pointed beard wagging malignantly. "For that is what will come of it! To the law, you understand! I warn you, the magistrates in Geneva bear not the sword in vain."

The young man's brow grew damp. The crisis was nearer than he had feared. "But—she has done nothing!" he faltered.

"The tool with the hand that uses it! The idol and him who made it!" the Syndic cried, swaying himself to and fro.

Claude stared. "But you know nothing!" he made shift to say after a pause. "You have nothing against her, Messer Blondel. He may be all you say, but she——"

"I have ears!"

The tone said more than the words, and Claude trembled. He knew the width of the net where witchcraft was in question. He knew that, were Basterga seized, all in the house would be taken with him, and though men otten escaped for the fright, women seldom went free so cheaply. The knowledge of this tied his tongue; and urgent as he felt the need to be, he could only glare helplessly at the magistrate.

Blondel, on his part, saw the effect of his words, and determined to force the young man to his will, he followed up the blow. "If you would see her burn, well and good!" he cried. "It is for you to choose. Break the spell, bring me the box, and set her free; or see the law take its course! Last night——"

"Last night," Claude replied, hurt to the quick, "you were not so bold, Messer Blondel!"

The Syndic winced, but merged his wrath in an anxiety a thousand times deeper. "Last night is not to-day," he answered. "Midnight is not daylight! I have told you where the spell is, where, at least, it is reputed to be, what it does, and under what sway it lays her; you who love her, and I see you do—you who have access to the house at all hours, who can watch him out——"

"We watched him out last night!" Claude muttered mutinously.

"Ay, but day is day! In the daylight——"

"But it is not laid on me to do this! I am not the only one whom it concerns."

"You love her!"

"Nor the only one who has access to the house."

"Are you a coward?"

Claude breathed hard. He was driven to the wall. Between his promise to her, and the Syndic's demand, he found himself helpless. And the demand was not so unreasonable. For it was true that he loved her, and true that he had access to the house; and if the plan suggested seemed unusual, if it was not the course most obvious or most natural, it was hardly for him to cavil at a scheme which promised to save her, not only from the evil influence which mysteriously swayed her, but from the law, and the danger of an accusation of witchcraft. Apart from his promise he would have chosen this course; even as it had been his first impulse to pursue it the evening before. But now he had given his word to her that he would not interfere, and he was conscious that he understood but in part how she stood. That being so——

"A coward!" the Syndic repeated, savagely and coarsely. He had waited in intolerable suspense for the other's answer. "That is what you are, with all your boasting!—A coward! Afraid of—why, man, of what are you afraid? Basterga?"

"It may be," Claude answered sullenly.

"Basterga? Why——" And there Blondel stopped; and over his face came a startling change. The rage died out of it and the flush; and fear, and a cringing embarrassment, took place of them. In the same instant the change was made, and Claude saw that which caused it. Basterga stood in the half-open doorway, looking toward them.

For a few seconds no one spoke. The magistrate's tongue clave to the roof of his mouth. Then the scholar advanced, cap in hand, and bowed to one and the other, the florid politeness of his bearing thinly veiling the sarcasm of his address.

"O mire conjunctio!" he said. "Happy is Geneva where age thinks no shame of consorting with youth! And youth, thrice happy, imbibes wisdom at the feet of age! Messer Blondel," he turned to him, and dropped in a degree the irony of his tone. "I have not seen you for so long, I feared that something was amiss and I come to inquire. It is not so, I hope?"

The Syndic, unable to mask his confusion, forced a sickly phrase of denial. He had dreaded nothing so much as to be surprised by Basterga in the young man's company: for his conscience warned him that to find him with Mercier and to read his plan, would be one and the same thing to the scholar's astuteness. And here was the discovery made, and made so abruptly and at so unfortunate a moment that to carry it off was out of his power, though he knew that every halting word and guilty look bore witness against him.

"No? That is well," Basterga answered, smiling broadly as he glanced from one face to the other. "That is well!" He had the air of a good-natured pedagogue who espies his boys in a venial offence, and will not notice it save by a sly word. "Very well! And you, my friend," he continued, addressing Claude, "is it not true what I said,

' Terque Quaterque redit !'

You fled in haste last night but we meet again! Your method in affairs is the reverse, I fear, of that which your friend here would advise: namely, that to carry out a plan one should begin slowly, and end quickly; thereby putting on the true helmet of Plato, as it has been called by a learned Englishman of our time."

Claude glowered at him, almost as much at a loss as the Syndic, but for another reason. To exchange commonplaces with the man who held the woman he loved by an evil hold, who owned a power so baneful, so mischievous

—to bandy words with such an one was beyond him. He could only glare at him in speechless indignation.

"You bear malice, I fear," the big man said. There was no doubt that he was master of the situation. "Do you not know that in the words of the same learned person whom I have already cited—a marvellous exemplar amid that fog-headed people—vindictive persons live the life of witches, who as they are mischievous so end they unfortunate."

The blood left Claude's face. "What do you mean?" he muttered, finding his voice at last.

"Who hates burns. Who loves burns also. But that is by the way."

"Burns?"

"Ay," with a grin, "burns! It seems to come home to you. Burns! Fie, young man; you hate, I fear, beyond measure, or love beyond measure, if you so fear the fire. What, you must leave us? It is not very mannerly," with sarcasm, "to go while I speak!"

But Claude could bear no more. He snatched his cap from the table, and with an incoherent word, aimed at the Syndic and meant for leave-taking, he made for the door, plucked it open and disappeared.

The scholar smiled as he looked after him. "A foolish young man," he said lightly, "who will assuredly, if he be not stayed, end unfortunate. It is the way of Frenchmen, Messer Blondel. They act without method and strike without intention, bear into age the follies of youth, and wear the gravity neither of the north nor of the south. But that reminds me," he continued, speaking low, and bending toward the other with a look of sympathy. "You are better, I hope?"

The words were harmless, but they conveyed more than their surface meaning, and they touched the Syndic to the quick. He had begun to compose himself; now he could have gnashed his teeth in the scholar's face. "Better?" he ejaculated bitterly. "What chance have I of being better? Better? Are you?" He began to tremble, his hands on the arms of his chair. "Otherwise, if you are not, you will soon have cause to know what I feel."

"I am better," Basterga answered with fervour. "I thank Heaven for it."

Blondel rose to his feet, his hands still clutching the chair. "What!" he cried. "You—you have not tried the——"

"The remedium?" The scholar shook his head. "No, on the contrary, I am relieved from my fears. The alarm was baseless. I have it not, I thank Heaven. I have not the disease. Nor, if there be any certainty in medicine, shall have it."

The Syndic, alas for human nature, could have struck him in the face!

"You have it not?" he snarled. "You have it not?" And then regaining control of himself, "I suppose I ought," with a forced and ghastly smile, "to felicitate you on your escape."

"Rather to felicitate yourself," Basterga answered. "Or so I had hoped two days ago."

"Myself?"

"Yes," Basterga answered lightly. "For as soon as I found that I had no need of the remedium, I thought of you. That was natural. And it occurred to me—nay, calm yourself!"

"Quick! Quick!"

"Nay, calm yourself, my dear Messer Blondel," Basterga repeated with outward solicitude and inward amusement. "Be calm, or you will do yourself an injury; you will indeed! In your state you should be prudent—you should govern yourself—one never knows. And besides, the thought, to which I refer—I see you recognise what it was——"

"Yes! yes! Go on! Go on!"

"Proved futile."

"Futile?"

"Yes, I am sorry to say it. Futile."

"Futile!" The wretched man's voice rose almost to a scream as he repeated the word. He rose and sat down again. "Then how did you—why did you——" he stopped, fighting for words, and unable to frame them, clutched the air with his hands. A moment he mouthed dumbly, then "Tell me!" he gasped. "Speak, man, speak! How was it? Cannot you see—that you are killing me?"

Basterga saw indeed that he had gone nearer to it than he had intended: for a moment the starting eyes and purple face alarmed him. In all haste, he gave up playing with the other's fears. "It occurred to me," he said. "That as I no longer needed the medicine myself, there was only the Grand Duke to be considered. I thought that he might be willing to waive his claim, since he is as yet free from the disease. And four days ago I despatched a messenger whom I could trust to him at Turin. I had hopes of a favourable reply, and in that event, I should not have lost a minute in waiting upon you. For I am bound to say, Messer Blondel," the big man rubbed his chin and eyed the other benevolently—"your case appealed to me in an especial manner. I felt myself moved,

I scarcely know why, to do all I could in your behalf. Alas, the answer dashed my hopes."

"What was it?" Blondel's voice sounded hollow and unnatural. Sunk in the high-backed chair, his chin fallen on his breast, it was in his eyes alone, peering from below bent brows, that he seemed to live.

"He would not waive his claim," Basterga answered gently, "save on a—but in substance that was all."

Blondel raised himself slowly and stiffly in the chair. His lips parted. "In substance?" he muttered hoarsely. "There was more then?"

Basterga shrugged his shoulders. "There was. Save, the Grand Duke added, on the condition—but the condition which followed was inadmissible."

Blondel gave vent to a cackling laugh. "Inadmissible?" he muttered. "Inadmissible." And then, "You are not a dying man, Messer Basterga, or you would think—few things inadmissible."

"Impossible, then."

"What was it? What was it?"—with a gesture eloquent of the impatience that was choking him.

"He asked," Basterga replied reluctantly, "a price."

"A price?"

The big man nodded.

The Syndic rose up and sat down again. "Why did you not say so? Why did you not say so at once?" he cried fiercely. "Is it about that you have been fencing all this time? Is that what you were seeking? And I fancied— A price, eh? I suppose—" in a lower tone, and with a gleam of cunning in his eyes, "he does not really want— the impossible? I am not a very rich man, Messer Basterga, you know that; and I am sure you would tell him.

You would tell him that men do not count wealth here, as they do in Genoa or Venice, or even in Florence. I am sure you would put him right on that," with a faint whine in his tone. "He would not strip a man to the last rag. He would not ask—thousands for it."

"No," Basterga answered, with something of asperity and even contempt in his tone. "He does not ask thousands for it, Messer Blondel. But he asks, none the less, something you cannot give."

"Money?"

"No."

"Then—what is it?" Blondel leant forward in growing fury. "What is it, man?"

Basterga did not answer for a moment. At length, shrugging his shoulders, and speaking between jest and earnest, "The town of Geneva," he said. "No more, no less."

The Syndic started violently, then was still. But the hand which in the first instant of surprise he had raised to shield his eyes, trembled; and behind it drops of sweat rose on his brow, and bore witness to the conflict in his breast.

"You are jesting," he said at last, without removing his hand.

"It is no jest," Basterga answered soberly. "You know the Grand Duke's keen desire. We have talked of it before. And were it only a matter," he shrugged his shoulders, "of the how—of ways and means in fact—there need be no impossibility, your position being what it is. But I know the feeling you entertain on the subject, Messer Blondel; and though I do not agree with you, for we look at the thing from different sides, I had no hope that you would come to it."

"Never!"

"No. So much so, that I had it in my mind to keep the condition to myself. But——"

"Why did you not, then?"

"Hope against hope," the big man answered, with a shrug and a laugh. "After all, a live dog is better than a dead lion—only you will not see it. We are ruled, the most of us, by our feelings, and die for our side without asking ourselves whether a single person would be a ducat the worse if the other side won. It is not philosophical," with another shrug. "That is all."

Apparently Blondel was not listening, for "The Duke must be mad," he ejaculated, as the other uttered his last word.

"Oh, no."

"Mad!" The Syndic repeated, his eyes still shaded by his hand. "Does he think," with bitterness, "that I am the man to run through the streets crying 'Viva Savoia!' To raise a hopeless *émeute* at the head of the drunken ruffians who, since the war, have been the curse of the place! And be thrown into the common gaol, and hurried thence to the scaffold! If he looks for that——"

"He does not."

"He is mad."

"He does not," Basterga repeated, unmoved. "The Grand Duke is as sane as I am."

"Then what does he expect?"

But the big man laughed. "No, no, Messer Blondel," he said. "You push me too far. You mean nothing, and meaning nothing, all's said and done. I wish," he continued, rising to his feet, and reverting to the tone of sympathy which he had for the moment laid aside, "I wish I might endeavour to show you the thing as I see it, in a word, as a philosopher sees it, and as men of culture in all ages, rising above the prejudices of the vulgar, have seen it. For after all, as Persius says,

' Live while thou liv'st ! for death will make us all,
A name, a nothing, but an old wife's tale.'

But I must not," reluctantly. "I know that."

The Syndic had lowered his hand; but he still sat with his eyes averted, gazing sullenly at the corner of the floor.

"I knew it when I came," Basterga resumed after a pause, "and therefore I was loth to speak to you."

"Yes."

"You understand, I am sure?"

The Syndic moved in his chair, but did not speak, and Basterga took up his cap with a sigh. "I would I had brought you better news, Messer Blondel," he said, as he rose and turned to go. "But 'Cor ne edito!' I am the happier for speaking, though I have done no good!" And with a gesture of farewell, not without its dignity, he bowed, opened the door, and went out, leaving the Syndic to his reflections.

HE WENT OUT, LEAVING THE SYNDIC TO HIS
REFLECTIONS

CHAPTER XI

BY THIS OR THAT

LONG after Basterga, with an exultant smile and the words, "I have limed him!" on his lips, had passed into the Bourg du Four and gone to his lodging, the Syndic sat frowning in his chair. From time to time a sigh deep and heart-rending, a sigh that must have melted even Petitot, even Baudichon, swelled his breast; and more than once he raised his eyes to his painted effigies over the mantel, and cast on it a look that claimed the pity of men and heaven.

Nevertheless with each sigh and glance and, though sigh and glance lost no whit of their fervour, it might have been observed that his face grew brighter; and that little by little, as he reflected on what had passed, he sat more firmly and strongly in his chair.

Not that he purposed buying his life at the price which Basterga had put on it. Never! But when a ship is on the lee shore it is pleasant to know that if one anchor fails to hold there is a second, albeit a borrowed one. The knowledge steadies the nerves and enables the mind to deal more firmly with the crisis. Or—to put the image in a shape nearer to the fact—though the power to escape by a shameful surrender may sap the courage of the garrison, it may also enable it to array its defences without

155

panic. The Syndic, for the present at least, entertained no thought of saving himself by a shameful compliance; it was indeed because the compliance was so shameful, and the impossibility of stooping to it so complete, that he sighed thus deeply, and raised his eyes so piteous to his own portrait. He who stood almost in the position of Pater Patriæ to Geneva, to betray Geneva! He the father of his country to betray his country! Perish the thought! But, alas, he too must perish, unless he could hit on some other way of winning the Remedium.

Still, it is not to be gainsaid that the Syndic went about the search for this other way in a more cheerful spirit; and revolved this plan and that plan in a mind more at ease. The ominous shadow of the night, the sequent gloom of the morning were gone; in their place rode an almost giddy hopefulness to which no scheme seemed too fanciful, no plan without its promise. Betray his country! Never, never! Though after all there was small scope for such a man as himself in the Republic, and he had received and could receive but a tithe of the honour he deserved! While other men, Baudichon and Petitot for instance, to say nothing of Fabri and Du Pin, reaped where they had not sown.

That, by the way; for it had naught to do with the matter in hand—the discovery of a scheme which would place the Remedium within his grasp. He thought awhile of the young student. He might make a second attempt to use him. But Claude's flat refusal to go farther with the matter, a refusal on which, up to the time of Basterga's abrupt entrance, the Syndic had made no impression, was a factor; and reluctantly, after some thought, Blondel put him out of his mind.

To do the thing himself was the natural course. But the scare of the night before had given him a distaste for the house; and he shrank from the attempt with a timidity he did not understand. He held the room in abhorrence, the house in dread; and though he told himself that in the last resort—perhaps he meant the last but one—he should venture, while there was any other way he put that aside.

And there was another way: there were others through whom the thing could be done. Grio, indeed, who had access to the room and the box, was Basterga's creature; and the Syndic dared not tamper with him. But there was a third lodger, a young fellow, of whom the inquiries he had made respecting the house had apprised him. Blondel had met Gentilis more than once, and marked him; and the lad's weak chin and shifty eyes, no less than the servility with which he saluted the magistrate had not been lost on the observer. The youth, granted he was not under Basterga's thumb, was unlikely to refuse a request backed by authority.

As he reflected the very person who was in his thoughts passed the window, moving with the shuffling gait and sidelong look which betrayed his character. The Syndic took his presence for an omen: he rose, seized his head-gear and cane, and hurried into the street. He glanced up and down, and, espying Louis in the distance moving in the direction of the College, he followed him. Three or four youths, bearing books, were hastening in the same direction through the narrow street of the Coppersmiths, and the Syndic fell in behind them. He dared not hasten over much, for a dozen curious eyes watched him from the noisy beetle-browed stalls on either side; and presently finding he did not gain, he was making up his mind to await a better occasion, when Louis, abandoning a companion who had just joined him, dived into one of the brass founders' shops.

The Syndic walked on slowly, returning here and there a reverential salute. He was nearly at the gate of the College, when Louis, late and in haste, overtook him, and hurried by him. Blondel doubted an instant what he should do; doubted, now the moment was come, the wisdom of the step he had in his mind. But a feverish desire to act had seized upon him, and after a moment's hesitation he raised his voice. "Young man," he said, "a moment! Here!"

Louis, not quite out of earshot, turned, found the magistrate's eye upon him, wavered, and at last came to him. He cringed low, wondering what he had done amiss.

"I know your face," Blondel said, fixing him with a penetrating look. "Do you not lodge, my lad, in a house in the Corraterie? Near the Porte Tertasse?"

"Yes, Messer Syndic," Louis answered, overpowered by the honour of the great man's address, and still wondering what evil was in store for him.

"The Mère Royaume's?"

"Yes, Messer Syndic."

"Then you can do me—or rather"—with an expression of growing severity—"you can do the State a service. Step this way, and listen to me, young man!" And his asperity increased by the fear that he was taking an unwise step, he told the youth, in curt stiff sentences, such facts as he thought necessary.

The young student listened, thunder-struck, his mouth open, and an expression of fatuous alarm on his face.

HE CRINGED
LOW,
WONDERING
WHAT HE HAD
DONE AMISS

"Letters?" he muttered, when the Syndic had come to a certain point in the story he had decided to tell.

"Yes, papers of importance to the State," the Syndic replied weightily, "of which it is necessary that possession should be taken as quietly as possible."

"And they are——"

"They are in the steel box chained to the wall of his apartment. Be it your task, young man, to bring the box and the letters unread and untouched to me. Opportunities of securing them in Messer Basterga's absence cannot but occur," he continued more benignly. "Choose one wisely, use it boldly, and the care of your fortunes will be in better hands than yours! A word to Basterga, on the other hand," Blondel continued slowly, and with a deadly look—he had not failed to notice that Louis winced at the name of Basterga—"and you will find yourself in the prison of the Two Hundred, destined to share the fate of the conspirators."

The young man began to shake. "Conspirators?" he cried. The word brought vividly before him the horrors of the scaffold and the wheel. "Oh, Lord! Oh, Lord! Why did I go to that house to lodge?"

"Do your duty," the Syndic said, "and you need fear nothing."

"But if I cannot—do it?" the youth stammered, his teeth chattering. He to penetrate to Basterga's room unbidden! He to rob the formidable man and perhaps be caught in the act! He to deceive him and meet his eye at meals! Impossible! "But if I cannot—do it?" he repeated, cowering.

"The State knows no such word!" the Syndic returned grimly. "Cannot," he continued slowly, "means will not.

Do your duty and fear nothing. Do it not, pause, hesitate, breathe but a syllable of that which I have told you and you will have all to fear. All!"

He saw too late that it was he himself who had all to fear; that in taking the lad before him into his confidence, he had placed himself in the hands of a craven. But he had done it. He had gone too far, moved by the foolish impulse of the moment, to retreat. His sole chance lay in showing the lad on which side danger pressed him most closely; on frightening him completely. And when Louis did not reply,

"You do not answer me?" Blondel said in his sternest tones. "You do not reply? Am I to understand that you decline? That you refuse to perform the task which the State assigns to you? In that case be sure you will perish with those whom the Two Hundred know to be the enemies of Geneva, and for whom the rack and the wheel are at this moment prepared."

"No!" Louis cried passionately; he almost fell on his knees in the open street. "No, no! I will go anywhere, do anything, Messer Syndic! I swear I will; I am no enemy! No conspirator!"

"You may be no enemy. But you must show yourself a friend!"

"I will! I will! I will indeed."

"And no syllable of this will pass your lips?"

"As I live, Messer Syndic! Nothing! Nothing!"

When he had repeated this several times with the earnestness of extreme terror, and appeared to have laid to heart such particulars as Blondel thought he should know, the Syndic dismissed him, letting him go with a last injunction to be silent—and a last threat.

By mere force of habit the lad would have gone on and entered the College; but on the threshold he felt how unfit he was to meet his fellows' eyes, and he turned and hastened as fast as his trembling limbs would carry him, toward his home. The streets, to his excited imagination, were full of spies; he fancied his every movement watched, his footsteps counted. If he lingered they might suppose him lukewarm, if he paused they might think him ill-affected. His speed must show his zeal. His poor little heart beat in his breast as if it would spring from it, but he did not stay nor look aside until the door of the house in the Corraterie closed behind him.

Then within the house there fell upon him—alas! what a thing it is to be a coward—a new fear. The fear was not the fear of Basterga, the bully and cynic, whom he had known and fawned on and flattered; but of Basterga the dark and dangerous conspirator, of whom he now heard, ready to repay with the dagger the least attempt to penetrate his secrets! On his entrance the lad had flung himself face downward on his pallet in the little closet where he slept; but at this thought he sprang up, suffocated by it; already he fancied himself in the hands of the desperadoes whom he had betrayed, already he pictured slow and lingering deaths. But again, at thought of the task laid upon him he flung himself prostrate, writhing, and cursing his fate, and shedding tears of panic. He to beard Basterga! He to betray him! Impossible! Yet if he failed, the rack and the wheel awaited him. Either way lay danger, on either side yawned torture and death. And he was a coward. He wept and shuddered, abandoning himself to a very paroxysm of terror.

When his door was pushed open a minute or two later,

he did not hear the movement; his head buried in the pillow he did not see the face of wonder, not unmingled with alarm, which viewed him from the doorway. He had forgotten that it was Anne Royaume's custom to attend to the young men's rooms during their absence at the afternoon lecture; and when her voice, asking in startled accents what was amiss and if he was ill, reached his ears, he only sought, with a smothered shriek, to cover his head with the bed-clothes. He fancied Basterga was upon him!

"What is the matter?" she repeated, advancing slowly to the side of the bed. Then, getting no answer, she dragged the coverlet off him. "What is it? Don't you know me?"

He sat up then, unwillingly, saw who it was, and came gradually to himself, but with many sighs and tears. She stood, looking down on him with contempt. "Has some-one been beating you?" she asked, and searched with hard eyes—he had been no friend to her—for signs of ill-treatment.

He shook his head. "Worse," he sobbed. "Oh, what will become of me? What will become of me? Lord, have mercy upon me! Lord, have mercy upon me!"

Her lip curled. Perhaps she was comparing him with another youth who had spoken to her that morning in a different strain.

"I don't think it matters much," she said scornfully, "what becomes of you."

"Matters?" he exclaimed.

"If you are such a coward as this! Tell me what it is. What has happened? If it is not that someone has beaten you, I don't know what it is—unless you have been doing

something, and they have put you out of the University?
Is it that?"

"No!" he cried, fretfully. "Worse, worse! And do
you leave me! You can do nothing! No one can do anything!"

She had her own troubles, and to-day was almost sinking under them. But this was not her way of bearing them.
She shrugged her shoulders contemptuously. "Very well,"
she said, "I will go if I can do nothing."

"Do?" he cried, vehemently. "What can you do?" And
then, in the act of turning from him, she stood; so startling
was the change, so marvellous the transformation which
she saw come over his face. "Do," he repeated, trembling,
and speaking in a tone as much altered as his expression.
He rose to his feet. "Do? Perhaps you—you can do
something—still. Wait. Please wait a minute! I—I
was not quite myself." He passed his hand across his
brow. She did not know that behind his face of frightened stupor his mind was working cunningly, following up
the idea that had occurred to him.

She began to think him mad. But though she held him
in distaste, she had no fear of him; and even when he
closed the door with a cringing air, and a look that im-
plored indulgence, she held her ground. Only, "You
need not close the door," she said coldly. "There is no one
in the house except my mother."

"Messer Basterga?"

"He has gone out. Is it of him," in sudden enlightenment, "that you are afraid?"

He nodded sullenly. "Yes," he said; and then he
paused, eyeing her in doubt if he could trust her. At last,
"It is, but, if you dared do it, I know how I could draw his

teeth! How I could"—with the cruel grin of the coward
—"squeeze him! squeeze him!" and he went through the
act with his nervous, shaking fingers. "I could hold him
like that! I could hold him powerless as the dog that
would bite and dare not!"

She stared at him. "You?" she said; it was hard to say
whether incredulity or scorn were written more plainly on
her face. "You?"

"I! I!" he replied, with the same gesture of holding
something. "And I know how to put him in your power
also."

"In my power!"

"Ay."

Her face grew hard as if she too held her enemy passive in her grip. Then her lip curled, and she laughed in
scorn. "Ay! And what must I do? Something, I suppose, you dare not, Louis?"

"Something you can do more easily than I," he answered doggedly. "A small thing, too," he continued,
clasping his hands in his eagerness and looking at her with
imploring eyes. "A nothing, a mere nothing!"

"And yet it will do so much?"

"I swear it will."

"Then," she retorted, eyeing him shrewdly, "if it is so
easy to do why were you undone a minute ago? And pul-
ing like a child in arms?"

"Because," he said, flushing under her eyes, "it—it is
not easy for me to do. And I did not see my way."

"It looked like it."

"But I see it now if you will help me. You have only
to take a packet of letters from his room—and you go
there when you please—and he is yours! While you have

the letters he dare not stir hand or foot—lest you bring
him to the scaffold!"

"Bring him to the scaffold?"

"Get the letters, give them to me, and I will answer for
the rest." Louis' voice was low, but he shook with excitement. "See!" he continued, his eyes at all times promi-
nent, almost starting from his head, "it might be done this
minute. This minute!"

"It might," the girl replied, watching him coldly. "But
it will not be done either this minute or at all unless you
tell me what is in the letters, and how you come to know
about them."

Should he tell her? He fancied that he had no choice.
"Messer Blondel the Syndic wants the letters," he answered sullenly. And, urged further by her expression of
disbelief, he told the astonished girl the story which Blondel had told him. The fact that he believed it went far
with her; why, for the rest, doubt a story so extraordinary
that it seemed to bear the stamp of truth?

"And that is all?" she said when he came to the end.

"Is it not enough?"

"It may be enough," she replied, her resolute manner
in strange contrast with his cowardly haste. "Only there
is a thing not clear. If the Syndic knows what is in the letters, why does he not seize them and Basterga with them
—the traitor with the proof of his treason?"

"Because he is afraid of the Grand Duke," Louis cried.
"If he seize Basterga and miss the proof of his treason,
what then?"

"Then he is not sure that the letters are there?" Anne
replied keenly.

"He is not sure that they would be there when he came

to seize them," Louis answered. "Basterga might have a dozen confederates in the house ready at a sign to destroy the letters."

She nodded.

"And that is what they will make us out to be," he continued, his voice sinking as his fears returned upon him. "The Syndic threatened as much; and such things have happened a hundred times. I tell you, if we do not do something, we shall suffer with him. But do it, and he is in your power! And if he has any hold on you, it is gone!"

The blood surged to her face. Hold upon her? Ah! Rage—or was it hope?—lightened in her eyes and transformed her face. She was thinking, he guessed, of the hundred insults she had undergone at Basterga's hands, of the shame-compelling taunts to which she had been forced to listen, of the loathed touch she had been forced to bear. If there was aught in her mind beyond this, any motive deeper or more divine, he did not perceive it; enough, that he saw that she wavered, and he pressed her.

"You will be free," he cried passionately. "Freed from him! Freed from fear of him! Say you will do it! Say that you will do it," he continued fervently, and he made as if he would kneel before her. "Do it, and I swear that never shall a word to displease you pass my lips."

With a glance of scorn that pierced even his selfishness, "Swear only," she said, "that you have told me the truth! I ask no more."

"I swear it on my salvation!"

She drew a deep breath.

"I will do it," she said. "The steel box which is chained to the wall?"

"Yes, yes," he panted, "you cannot mistake it. The key——"

"I know where he keeps it."

She said no more, but turned, and regarding his thanks as little as if they had been the wind passing by her, she opened the door, crossed the living room, and vanished up the staircase. He followed her as far as the foot of the stairs, and there stood listening and shifting his feet and biting his nails in an agony of suspense. She had not deigned to bid him watch for Basterga's coming, but he did so; his eyes on the outer door, through which the scholar must enter, and his tongue and feet in readiness to warn her or save himself, according as the pressure of danger directed the one or the other step.

Meanwhile his ears were on the stretch to catch what she did. He heard her try the door of the room. It was locked. He heard her shake it. Then he guessed that she fetched a key, for after an interval, which seemed an age, he caught the grating of the wards in the lock. After that she was quiet so long, that but for the apprehensions of Basterga's coming, which weighed on his coward soul, he must have gone up in sheer jealousy to see what she was doing.

Not that he distrusted her. Even while he waited, and while the thing hung in the balance, he smiled to think how cleverly he had contrived it. On the side of the authorities he would gain favour by delivering the letters; on the other side, if Basterga retained power to harm, it was not he who had taken the letters, nor he who would be exposed to the first blast of vengeance—but the girl. The blame for her, the credit for him! From the nettle danger his wits had plucked the flower, safety. But for his fears he could have chuckled; and then he heard her come out and relock the door. With a gasp of relief, he retired a pace or two, and waited, his eyes fixed on the doorway through which she must enter.

She was long in coming, and when she came, his hand extended to receive the letters fell by his side, the whispered question died on his lips. For her face told him that she had failed. It might have told him also that she had built far more on the attempt than she had let him perceive. But what was that to him? It was enough for him that she had not the letters. He could have torn her with his hands. "Where are they? Where are they?" he cried, advancing upon her. "You have not got them?"

"Got them?" And she straightened herself, with a passionate glance at the door. "No! And he has not come in time to take me in the act, it seems. As I have no doubt you planned, you villain! That I might be more and deeper in his power!"

"No! No!" he cried, recoiling. "I never thought of it!"

"Yes, yes!" she retorted.

He wrung his hands. How was he to make her understand? "I swear," he cried, and he fell on his knees with uplifted hands. "I swear on my knees I thought of no such thing. The tale I told you was true! True, every word of it! And the letters——"

"There are no letters!" she said.

"In the box?"

"None."

He sprang to his feet. He shook his fist at her in low ignoble rage. "You lie!" he cried. "You have not looked. You have played with me. You have gone into the room and come out again, but you have not looked, you have not dared to look."

"I have looked," she answered quietly. "In the box that is chained to the wall. There are no papers in it. There is nothing in it except a small phial."

"A phial?"

"Of some golden liquid."

"That is all?"

"All!"

Louis Gentilis stared at her, open-mouthed. Had the Syndic deceived him? Or had someone deceived the Syndic?

CHAPTER XII

THE CUP AND THE LIP

BLONDEL could not hide the agitation he felt as he listened to his unexpected visitors and saw whither their errand tended. Fabri, who was leader of the deputation of three, who had come upon him without warning, discerned this; much more Baudichon and Petitot, whose eyes were on the watch for the least sign of weakness. And Blondel was conscious that they saw it, and for that strove the more to mask his feelings under a show of decision. "I have little doubt that I shall have news within the hour," he said. "Before night, I must have news." And nodding with the air of a man who knew much which he could not impart, he leant back in the old Abbot's chair.

But Fabri had not come for that, nor was he to be satisfied with that; and, after a pause, "Yes," he replied, "I know. That may be so. But you see, Messer Blondel, this affair is not quite where it was yesterday, or we should not have come to you to-day. The King of France—I am sure we are much indebted to him—does not write on light occasions, and his warning is explicit. From Paris, then, we get the same story as from Turin. And this being so, and the King's tale agreeing with our agent's——"

"He does not mention Basterga!" Blondel objected. He repented the moment he had said it.

"By name, no. But he says——"

"Enough for anyone with eyes!" Petitot exclaimed.

"He says," Fabri repeated, requesting the other by a gesture to be silent, "that the Grand Duke's emissary is a Paduan expelled from Venice or from Genoa. That is near enough. And I confess, were I in your place, Messer Blondel——"

"With your responsibilities," Petitot muttered through closed teeth.

"I should want to know—more about him." This from Baudichon.

Fabri nodded. "I think so," he said. "I really think so. In fact, I may go farther and say that were I in your place, Messer Blondel, I should seize him to-day."

"Ay, within the hour!"

"This minute!" said Baudichon, last of the trio. And all three, their ultimatum delivered, looked at Blondel, a challenge in their eyes. If he stood out longer, if he still declined to take the step which prudence demanded, the step on which they were all agreed, they would know that there was something behind, something of which he had not told them.

Blondel read the look, and it perturbed him. But not to the point of sapping the resolution which he had formed at the Council Table, and to which, once formed, he clung with the obstinacy of an obstinate man. The Remedium first; afterwards what they would, but the Remedium first. He was not going to risk life, warm life, the vista of sunny unending to-morrows, of springs and summers and the melting of snows, for a craze, a scare, an imaginary danger! Why at that very minute the lad he had commissioned to seize the thing, might be on the way with it. At any minute a step might sound on the threshold, and herald the promise of life. And then—then they might deal with Basterga as they pleased. Then, they might hang the Paduan high as Haman, if they pleased. But until then—his mind was made up.

"I do not agree with you," he said, his underlip thrust out, his head trembling a little.

"You will not arrest him?"

"No, I shall not arrest him," he replied, hardening himself to meet their protestant and indignant eyes. "Nor would you," he continued with bravado, "in my place. If you knew as much as I do."

"But if you know," Baudichon said, "I would like to know also."

"The responsibility is mine." Blondel swayed himself from side to side in his chair as he said it. "The responsibility is mine, and I am willing to bear it. It is the old difference of policy between us," he continued, addressing Petitot. "You are willing to grasp at every petty advantage, I am willing——"

"To risk much to gain much," Petitot exclaimed.

"To take some risk to gain a real advantage," Blondel retorted, correcting him with an eye to Fabri; whom alone, as the one impartial hearer, he feared. "For to what does the course which you are so eager to take amount? You seize Basterga: later, you will release him at the Grand Duke's request. What are we the better? What is gained?"

"Safety."

"No, on the other hand, danger. Danger! For, warned that we have detected their plot, they will hatch another plot, and instead of working as at present under our eyes, they will work below the surface with augmented care and secrecy: and will, perhaps, deceive us. No, my friends"—throwing himself back in his chair with an air of patronage, almost of contempt—for by dint of repeating his argument he had come to believe it, and to plume himself upon it—"I look farther ahead than you do, and for the sake of future gain am willing to take—present responsibility."

They were silent awhile: his old mastery was beginning to assert itself. Then Petitot spoke. "It is a heavy responsibility," he said, "a heavy charge, Messer Blondel. And what if harm come of it?"

Blondel shrugged his shoulders.

"You have no wife, Messer Blondel."

Blondel stared, taken by surprise.

"You have no daughters," Petitot continued, a slight quaver in his tone. "You have no little children, you sleep well of nights, the fall of wood-ash does not rouse you, you do not listen when you awake. You do not——" he paused, the last barrier of reserve broken down, the tears standing openly in his eyes—"it is foolish perhaps—you do not yearn, Messer Blondel, to take all you love in your arms, and shelter them and cover them from the horrors that threaten us, the horrors that may fall on us—any night! You do not"—he looked at Baudichon and the stout man's face grew pale, he averted his eyes—"you do not dream of these things, Messer Blondel, nor awake to fancy them, but we do. We do!" he repeated in accents which went to the hearts of all, "day and night, rising and lying down, waking and sleeping. And we—dare run no risks."

In the silence which followed Blondel's fingers tapped restlessly on the table. He cleared his throat and voice.

"But there, I tell you there are no risks," he said. He was moved nevertheless.

Petitot bowed, humbly for him. "Very good," he said. "I do not say that you are not right. But——"

"And moment by moment I expect news. It might come at this minute, it might come at any minute," the Syndic continued. With a glance at the window he moved his chair, as if to shake off the spell that Petitot had cast over him. "Besides, you do not expect the town to be taken in an hour from now?"

"No."

"In broad daylight?"

Petitot shook his head. "God knows what I expect!" he murmured despondently.

"When the information we have points to a night attack?"

Fabri nodded. "That is true," he said.

"And the walls are well guarded at night."

Fabri nodded again. "Yes," he said, "it is true. I think, Messer Petitot," he went on, turning to him, "we are a little over fearful."

The two others were silent and Blondel eyed them harshly, aware that he had mastered them—yet hating them. Petitot's appeal to his feelings—which had touched and moved the Syndic even while he resented it as something cruel and unfair—had lacked but a little of success. But missing, failing by ever so little, it left the three ill-equipped to continue the struggle on lower grounds. They sat silent, Fabri almost convinced, the others dejected: and Blondel sat silent also, hardened by his victory, and hating them for the manner of it. Was not his life as dear to him as their wives and children were to them? And was

it not at stake? Yet he did not whine and pule to them.
God! They whine, they complain, who had long years to
live and rose of mornings without counting the days, and,
at the worst and were Geneva taken, had but the common
risks to run and many a chance of escape! While he—
yet he did not pule to them! He did not stab them un-
fairly, cruelly, striving to reach their tender spots, to take
advantage of their kindness of heart. He had no thought,
no notion of betraying them; but, had he such, it would
serve them right! It would repay them selfishness for
selfishness, greed for greed! In his place they would not
hesitate. He could see at what a price they set their petty
lives, and how little they would scruple to buy them in
the dearest market. Well was it for Geneva that it was
he and not they whom God saw fit to try. And he glowered
at them. Wives and daughters! What were wives and
daughters beside life, warm life, life stretching forward
pleasantly, indefinitely, morning after morning, day after
day—life and a continuance of good things?

Immersed as he was in this train of thought, it was none
the less he who first caught the sound of a foot on the
threshold, and a summons at the door. He rose to his
feet in sudden hope. Already in his mind's eye he saw
Basterga cast to the lions: and why not? The sooner the
better if the Remedium were really at the door. "There
may be news even now," he said, striving to master his
emotion, and to speak with the superiority of a few minutes before. "One moment, by your leave! I will see
and let you know if it be so, Messer Fabri."

"Do, by all means," Fabri answered earnestly. "You
will greatly relieve me."

"Ay, indeed, I hope it is so," Petitot murmured.

"I will see, and—and return," Blondel repeated, beginning to stammer. "I—I shall not be a minute." The struggle for composure was vain; his head was on fire, his limbs twitched. Had it come?

Yet when he reached the door he paused, afraid to open. What if it were not the Remedium, what if it were some trifle? What if—but as he hesitated, his hand, half eager, half reluctant, rested on the latch, the door slid ajar, and his eyes met the complacent smirking face of his messenger. He fancied that he read success in Gentilis' looks, and his heart leapt up. "I shall be back in a moment," he babbled, speaking over his shoulder to those whom he left. "In a moment, gentlemen, one moment!" And going out he closed the door behind him—closed it jealously, that they might not hear.

"I hope he has news will decide him," Petitot muttered lowering his voice involuntarily. "Messer Blondel is over courageous for me!" He shook his head dismally.

"He is very courageous," Fabri assented in the same undertone. "Perhaps even—a little rash."

Baudichon grunted. "Rash!" he repeated. "I would like to know what he expects? I would like to know——"

A cry as of a wild beast cut short the word: a blow, a shriek of pain followed, the door flew open; as they rose to their feet in wonder, into the room fell a lad—it was Louis Gentilis—a red weal across his face, his arm raised to protect his head. Close on him, his eyes flaming, his cane quivering in the air, pressed Messer Blondel. In their presence he aimed another blow at the youth: but the blow fell short, and before he could raise his stick a third time the astonished looks of the three in the room reminded him where he was, and in a measure sobered him. But he

ON HIS HEELS,

HIS EYES

FLAMING, HIS

CANE

QUIVERING IN

THE AIR,

PRESSED

MESSER BLONDEL

was still unable to articulate: and the poor smarting wretch cowering behind the magistrates was not more deeply or more visibly moved.

"Steady, steady, Messer Blondel!" Fabri said. "I fear something untoward has happened. What is it?" And he put himself more decidedly between them.

"He has ruined us!"

"Not that, I hope?"

"Ruined us! Ruined us!" Blondel panted, his rage almost choking him. "He had it in his hands and let it go. He let it go!"

"That which you——"

"That which I"—a pause—"commissioned him to get."

"But you did not—oh, worshipful gentlemen," Gentilis wailed, turning to them; "indeed, he did not tell me to bring aught but papers! I swear he did not."

"Whatever was there, I said. Whatever was there!" the Syndic screamed.

"No, worshipful sir!" amid a storm of sobs. "No, no! Indeed no! And how was I to know? There was naught but that in the box, and who would think treason lay in a——"

"Mischief lay in it!"

"In a bottle!"

"And treason," Blondel thundered, drowning his last word, "for aught you knew! Who are you to judge where treason lies, or may lie? Oh, pig, dog, fool!" he continued, carried away by a fresh paroxysm of rage, at the thought that he had had it in his grasp and let it go! "If I could score your back!" And he brandished his cane.

"You have scored his face pretty fairly," Baudichon muttered. "To score his back too——"

"Were nothing for the offence! Nothing! As you would say if you knew it," Blondel panted.

"Indeed?"

"Ay."

"Then I would like to know it. What is it he has done?"

"He has left undone that which he was ordered to do," Blondel answered more soberly than he had yet spoken. He had recovered something of his power to reason. "That is what he has done. But for his default we should at this moment be in a position to seize Basterga."

"Ay?"

"Ay, and to seize him with proof of his guilt! Proof and to spare."

"But I could not know," Louis whimpered. "Worshipful gentlemen, I could not know. I could not know what it was you wanted."

"I told you to bring the contents of the box."

"Letters, ay! Letters, worthy sir, but not——"

"Silence, and go into that room!" Blondel pointed with a shaking finger to a small inner serving-room at the end of the parlour. "Go!" he repeated peremptorily, "and stay there until I come to you."

Then, but not until the lad had taken his tear-bedabbled face into the closet and had closed the door behind him, the Syndic turned to the three. "I ask your pardon," he said, making no attempt to disguise the agitation which still moved him. "But it was enough, it was more than enough to try me." He paused and wiped his brow, on which the sweat stood in beads. "He had under his hand the papers," looking at them a little askance as if he doubted whether the explanation would pass, "that we need! The papers that would convict Basterga. And be-

cause they did not wear the appearance he expected—
because they were disguised, you understand—they were
in a bottle in fact—and were not precisely what he expected——"

"He left them?"

"He left them."   There was something like a tear, a
leaden drop, in the corner of the Fourth Syndic's eye.

"Still if he had access to them once," Petitot suggested
briskly, "what has been done once may be done twice.   He
may gain access to them again.   Why not?"

"He may, but he may not.   Still, I should have thought
of that and—and made allowance," Blondel answered with
a fair show of candour.   "But too often an occasion let
slip does not return, as you well know.   The least disorder
in the box he searched may put Basterga on the alert, and
wreck my plans."

They did not answer.   They felt one and all, Petitot
and Baudichon no less than Fabri, that they had done this
man an injustice.   His passion, his chagrin, his singleness
of aim, the depth of his disappointment, disarmed even
those who were in the daily habit of differing from him.
Was this—this the man whom they had secretly accused of
lukewarmness?   And to whom they had hesitated to en-
trust the safety of the city?   They had done him wrong.
They had not credited him with a tithe of the feeling, the
single-mindedness, the patriotism which it was plain he possessed.

They stood silent, while Blondel, aware of the preci-
pice, to the verge of which his improvident passion had
drawn him, watched them out of the corner of his eye, uncertain how far their comprehension of the scene had gone.
He trembled to think how nearly he had betrayed his se-

cret; and took the more shame to himself, inasmuch as in cooler blood, he saw the lad's error to be far from irremediable. As Petitot said, that which could be done so easily and quickly, could be done a second time. If only he had not struck the lad! If only he had commanded himself, and spoken him fairly and sent him back! Almost by this time the Remedium might be here. Ay, here, in the palm of his hand! The reflection stabbed Blondel so poignantly, the sense of his folly went so deep, he groaned aloud.

That groan, fairly won over Baudichon, who was by nature of a kind heart. "Tut, tut," he said. "You must not take it to heart, Messer Blondel. Try again."

"Unless, indeed," Petitot murmured—but with respect, "Messer Blondel knows the mistake to be fraught with consequences more grave than we suppose."

The Fourth Syndic smiled awry: that was precisely what he did know. But "No," he said, "the thing can be cured. I am sorry I lost my temper. Not a moment must be wasted, however. I will see this young man: if he raises any difficulty, I have still another agent whom I can employ. And by to-morrow at latest——"

"You may still have the thing in your hands."

"I think so. I certainly think so."

"Good. Then till to-morrow," Fabri answered, as he took his cap from the table and with the others turned toward the door. "Good luck, Messer Blondel. We are reassured. We feel that our interests are in good hands."

"Yes," said Petitot, almost warmly. "Still, caution,. caution! Messer Blondel. One bad man within the gates——"

"May be hung!" Blondel cried gaily.

"Ay, may be! But unhung is a graver foe than five

hundred men without! It is that which I would have you bear in mind."

"I will bear it in mind," the Fourth Syndic answered. "And when I can hang him," with a vindictive look, "be sure I will—and high as Haman!"

He attended them with solicitude to the door, being set by what had happened a little more upon his behaviour. This done and the outer door closed upon them, he returned to the parlour, but did not at once seek the young man, upon whom he had taken the precaution of turning the key.

Instead he stood awhile, pondering with a pale face; a haggard, paler replica he seemed, of the stiff, hard portrait on the panel over the mantel. He was wondering why he had let himself go so foolishly; he was recognising with a sinking heart that it was to his illness he owed it that he had so frequently of late lost control of himself.

For a man to discover that the power of self-mastery is passing from him is only a degree less appalling than the consciousness of insanity itself; and Blondel cowered, trembling under the thought. If aught could strengthen his purpose it was the suspicion that the insidious disease from which he suffered was already sapping the outworks of that mind, on whose clever combinations he depended for his one chance of cure.

Yet while the thought strengthened, it terrified him. "I must make no second mistake—no second mistake!" he muttered, his eyes on the door of the serving-room. "No second mistake!" And he waited awhile considering the matter in all its aspects. Should he tell Louis more than he had told him already? It seemed needless. To send the lad with curt, stern words to fetch that which he had omitted to bring—this seemed the more straightforward way: and the more certain, too, since the lad had now seen the other magistrates, and could have no doubt of their concurrence or of the importance of the task entrusted to him. Blondel decided on that course, and advancing to the door he opened it and called to his prisoner to come out.

To his credit be it said the sight of the lad's wealed face gave the Syndic something of a shock. He was soon to be more gravely shaken. Instigated partly by curiosity, partly by the desire to fix Louis' scared faculties, he began by asking what was the aspect of the phial which the lad had omitted to bring. "What was its colour and size, and how full was it?" he proceeded, striving to speak gently and to make allowance for the cowering weakness of the youth before him. "Do you hear?" he urged. "Of what shape was it? You can tell that at least. You handled it, I suppose? You took it out of the metal box?"

Louis burst into tears.

Blondel had much ado—for it was true, he had small command of himself—not to strike the lad again. Instead, "Fool," he said, "what do your tears help you or advance me? Speak, I tell you, and answer my question! What was the appearance of this flask or bottle, or what it was—that you left there?"

The lad sank to his knees. Fear and pain had robbed him of the petty cunning he possessed. He no longer knew what to tell nor what to withhold. And in a breath the truth was out. "Don't strike me!" he wailed, guarding his smarting face with his arm. "And I'll tell you all! I will indeed!"

The Syndic knew then that there was more to learn.

"All?" he repeated, aghast.

"Ay, the truth. All the truth," Louis moaned. "I

did not see it. I didn't go to it! I dared not! I swear I dared not!"

"You didn't see it?" the Syndic said slowly. "The phial? You did not see the phial?"

"No."

This time Messer Blondel did not strike. He leant heavily upon the table; his face which a moment before had been swollen with impatience turned a sickly white. "You—you didn't see it?" he muttered—his tone had sunk to a whisper. "You didn't see it? Then—all you told me was a lie? There was nothing—no bottle in the box? But how then did you know anything of a bottle? Did he—" with a sharp spasm of pain—"send you here —to tell me this?"

"No, no! She told me. She looked—for me—in the box."

"Who?"

"Anne. Anne Royaume! I was afraid," the lad continued, speaking with a little more confidence, as he saw that the Syndic made no movement to strike him, "and she said that she would look for me. She could go to his room, and run little risk. But if he had caught me there he would have killed me! He would have killed me!" he repeated desperately, as he read the storm-signs that began to darken the Syndic's face.

"You told her then?"

"I could not do it myself! I could not."

He cowered lower; but he fared better than he expected. The Syndic drew a long fluttering breath, a breath of returning life, of returning hope. The colour, too, began to come back to his cheeks. After all it might have been worse. He had thought it worse. He had thought himself discovered, tricked, discomfited by the man against whom he had pitted his wits, with his life for stake. Whereas—it seemed a small thing in comparison —this· meant only the inclusion of one more in the secret, the running of one more risk, the hazarding another tongue. And the lad had not been so unwise. She had easier access to the room than he, and ran less risk of suspicion or detection. Why not employ her—in place of the lad?

The youth grovelling before him wondered to see him calm, and plucking up spirit stood upright. "You must go back to her, and ask her to get it for you," Blondel said firmly. "You can be back within the half-hour, bringing it."

Louis began to shrink. His eyes sank. "She will not give it me," he muttered.

"No?" Blondel, as he repeated the word, wondered at his own moderation. But the shock had been heavy; he felt the effect of it. He was languid, almost half-hearted. Moreover, a new idea had taken root in his mind. "You can try her," he said.

"I can try her, but she will not give it me," Louis repeated with a new obstinacy. As the Syndic grew mild he grew sullen. The change was in the other, not in himself. Subtly he knew that the Syndic was no longer in the mood to strike.

Blondel ruminated. It might be better, it might even be safer, if he saw the girl himself. The story—of treason and a bottle—which had imposed on his colleagues might not move her much. It might be wiser to attack her on other grounds, grounds on which women lay more open. And self-pity whispered with a tear that the truth, than which he could conceive nothing more moving, nothing more sublimely sad, might go farther with a woman than bribes or threats or the most skilful inventions. He made up his mind. He would tell the truth, or something like it, something as like it as he dared tell her.

"Very well," he said, "you can go! But be silent! A word to him—and I shall learn it sooner or later—and you perish on the wheel! You can go now. I shall put the matter in other hands."

CHAPTER XIII

A MYSTERY SOLVED

WHETHER Basterga, seeing that Claude was less pliant than he had looked to find him, shunned occasion of collision with him, or the Paduan being in better spirits was less prone to fall foul of his companions, certain it is that life for a time after the outbreak at supper ran more quietly in the house in the Corraterie. Claude's gloomy face—he had not forgiven —bade beware of him; and little save on the subject of Louis' disfigured cheek—of which the most pointed questions could extract no explanation—passed among them at table. But outward peace was preserved and a show of ease. Grio's brutal nature broke out, once or twice when he had had wine; but discouraged by Basterga, he subsided quickly. And Louis, starting at a voice and trembling at a knock, with the fear of the Syndic always upon him, showed a nervousness which more than once drew the Italian's eye to him. But on the whole a calm prevailed; a stranger entering at noon or during the evening meal, might have deemed the party ill-assorted and silent, but lacking neither in amity nor ease.

Meantime, under cover of this calm, destined to be short-lived and holding in suspense the makings of a storm of no mean violence, two persons were drawing nearer to one another. A confidence, even a confidence not perfect, is a tie above most. Nor does love play at any time a higher part than when it repeats "I do not understand, I trust." By the common light of day, which showed Anne moving to and fro about her household tasks, at once the minister and the providence of the home, the dark suspicion that had for a moment—a moment only!—mastered Claude's judgment, lost shape and reality. It was impossible to see her bending over the hearth, or arranging her mother's simple meal, impossible to witness her patience, her industry, her deftness, to behold her, ever gentle yet supporting with a man's fortitude the trials of her position, trials of the bitterness of which she had given him proof—it was impossible, in a word, to watch her in her daily life, without perceiving the wickedness as well as the folly of the thought, which had possessed him.

True, the more he saw of her, the graver seemed the mystery; and the more deeply he wondered. But he no longer dreaded the answer to the riddle; nor did he fear to meet at some turn or corner a Megæra head that should freeze his soul. Wickedness there might be, cruelty there might be, and shame; but the blood ran too briskly in his veins and he had looked too often into the girl's candid eyes—reading something there which had not been there formerly—to fear to find them at her door.

He had taken to coming to the living-room a little before nightfall; there he would seat himself beside the hearth while she prepared the evening meal. The glow of the wood-fire, reflected in rows of burnished pewters, or returned by the night-backed casements, the savour of the coming meal, the bubbling of the black pot between which and the table her nimble feet carried her a dozen times in as many minutes, the pleasant, homely room with its touches of refinement and its winter comfort, these were excuses enough had he not brought the book which lay unheeded on his knee.

But in truth he offered her no excuses. With scarce a word an understanding had grown up between them that not a million words could have made more clear. Each played the appropriated part. He looked and she bore the look, and if she blushed the fire was warrant, and if he stared it was the blind man's hour between day and night, and why should he not sit idle as well as another? Soon there was not a turn of her head or a line of her figure that he did not know; not a trick of her walk, nor a pose of her hand as she waited for a pot to boil that he could not see in the dark; not a gleam from her hair as she stooped to the blaze, nor a turn of her wrist as she shielded her face that was not as familiar to him as if he had known her from childhood.

In these hours she let the mask fall. The apathy, which had been the least natural as it had been the most common garb of her young face, and which had grown to be the cover and veil of her feelings, dropped from her. Seated in the shadow, while she moved, now in the glow of the burning embers, now obscured, he read her mind without disguise—save in one dark nook—watched unrebuked the eye fall and the lip tremble, or in rarer moments saw the shy smile dimple the corner of her cheek. Not seldom she stood before him sad: sad without disguise, her bowed head and drooping shoulders the proof of gloomy thoughts, that strayed, he fancied, far from her work or her companion. And sometimes a tear fell and she wiped it away, making no attempt to hide it; and sometimes she would shiver and sigh as if in pain or fear.

At these times he longed for Basterga's throat; and the blood of old Engerrande de Beauvais, his ancestor, dust these four hundred years at "Damietta of the South," raced in him, and he choked with rage and grief, and for the time could scarcely see. Yet with this pulse of wrath were mingled delicious thrills. The tear which she did not hide from him was his gage of love. The brooding eye, the infrequent smile, the start, the reverie were for him only, and for no other. They were the gift to him of her secret life, her secret heart.

It was an odd love-making, and bizarre. To Grio, even to men more delicate and more finely wrought, it might have seemed no love-making at all. But the wood-smoke that perfumed the air, sweetened it, the firelight wrapped it about, the pots and pans and simple things of life, amid which it passed, hallowed it. His eyes attending her hither and thither without reserve, without concealment, unabashed, laid his heart at her feet, not once, but a hundred times in the evening; and as often, her endurance of the look, more rarely her sudden blush or smile, accepted the offering.

And scarce a word said: for though they had the room to themselves, they knew that they were never alone or unheeded. Basterga, indeed, sat above stairs and only descended to his meals; and Grio also was above when he was not at the tavern. But Louis sulked in his closet beside them, divided from them only by a door, whence he might emerge at any minute. As a fact he would have emerged many times, but for two things. The first was his marked face, which he was chary of showing: the second the notion he had got that the balance of things in the house was changing, and the reign of petty bullying in

which he had so much delighted, approaching its end.
With Basterga exposed to arrest, and the girl's help of
value to the authorities, it needed little acumen to discern
this. He still feared Basterga; nay, he lived in such terror, lest the part he had played should come to the scholar's
ears, that he prayed for his arrest night and morning, and
whenever during the day an especial fit of dread seized
him. But he feared Anne also, for she might betray him
to Basterga; and of young Mercier's quality—that he was
no Tissot to be brow-beaten, or thrust aside—he had had
proof on the night of the fracas at supper. Essentially a
coward, Louis' aim was to be on the stronger side; and
once persuaded that this was the side on which they stood,
he let them be.

On several consecutive evenings the two passed an hour
or more in this silent communion. On the last the door
of Louis' room stood open, the young man had not come
in, and for the first time they were really alone. But the
fact did not at once loosen Claude's tongue; and if the girl
noticed it, or expected aught to come of it, more than had
come of their companionship on other evenings, she hid
her feelings with a woman's ease. He remarked, however,
that she was more thoughtful and downcast than usual,
and several times he saw her break off in the middle of a
task and listen nervously, as for something she expected.
Presently,

"Are you listening for Louis?" he asked.

She turned on him, her eyes less kind than usual. "No,"
she said, almost defiantly. "Was I listening?"

"I thought so," he said.

She turned from him and went on with her work. But
by-and-by as she stooped over the fire a tear fell and pat-

tered audibly in the wood-ash on the hearth; and another. With an impatient gesture she wiped away a third. He saw all—she made no attempt to hide them—and he bit his lip and drove his finger-ends into his palms in the effort to be silent. Presently he had his reward.

"I am sorry," she said in a low tone. "I was listening, and I knew I was. I do not know why I deceived you."

"If you would tell me all!" he cried.

"I cannot!" she answered, her breast heaving passionately. "I cannot!" And for the first time she broke down before him, and sinking on a bench with her back to the table she sobbed bitterly, her face in her hands. For some minutes she rocked herself to and fro in a paroxysm of trouble.

He had risen and stood watching her awkwardly, longing to comfort her, but ignorant how to go about it, and feeling acutely his helplessness and his *gaucherie*. Sad she had always been, and at her best despondent, with gleams of cheerfulness as fitful as brief. But this evening her abandonment to her grief convinced him that something more than ordinary was amiss, that some danger more serious than ordinary threatened. He felt no surprise, therefore when a little later she arrested her sobbing, raised her head, and with suspended breath and tear-stained face listened with that scared intentness which had impressed him before.

She feared! He could not be mistaken. Fear looked out of her expectant eyes, fear hung breathless on her parted lips. He was sure of it. And "Is it Basterga?" he cried. "Is it of him that you are afraid? If you are——"

"Hush!" she said, raising her hand in warning.

"Hush!" And then, "You did not —hear anything?"
For an instant her eyes met his.

"No." He met her look, puzzled; obeying her gesture,
he listened afresh. "No, I heard nothing. But——"

He heard nothing now; but, whatever it was, that
sharpened her hearing to an abnormal pitch, it was clear
that she did. She was up, on the instant; with a startled
cry she was on the farther side of the table and half way
across the room, while he stared, the word suspended on
his lips. A second, and her hand was on the latch of the
staircase door. Then as she opened it, he sprang forward
to accompany her, to help her, to protect her if necessary.
"Let me come!" he said. "Let me help you. Whatever
it is, I can do something."

She turned on him fiercely. "Go back!" she said. All
the confidence, the gentleness, the docility of the last three
days were gone; and in their place suspicion glared at him
from eyes grown spiteful as a cat's. "Go back!" she repeated. "I do not want you! I do not want any one, or
any help! Or any protection! Go, do you hear, and let
me be!"

As she ceased to speak, an odd sound from above stairs
—a sound which this time, the door being open, did reach
his ears, froze the words on his lips. It was a voice, yet no
common voice, heaven be thanked! A moment she continued to confront him, her face one mute, despairing
denial! Then she slammed the door in his teeth, and he
heard her panting breath and fleeing footsteps speed up the
stairs and along the passage, and—more faintly now—he
heard her ascend the upper flight. Then—silence.

Silence! But he had heard enough. He paused a moment irresolute, uncertain, his hand raised to the latch.

Then the hand fell to his side, he turned, and went softly —very softly back to the hearth. The firelight playing on his face showed it much moved; moved and softened almost to the semblance of a woman's. For there were tears in his eyes — eyes singularly bright; and his features worked, as if he had some ado to repress a sob. In truth he had. In a breath, in the time it takes to utter a single sound, he had hit on the secret, he had come to the bottom of the mystery, he had learnt that which Basterga, favoured by the position of his room on the upper floor, had learned two months before, that which Grio might have learned, had he been anything but the dull gross toper he was! He had learned, or in a moment of intuition guessed —all. The power of Basterga, that power over the girl which had so much puzzled and perplexed him, was his also now, to use or misuse, hold or resign.

Yet his first feeling was not one of joy; nor for that matter his second. The impression went deeper, went to the heart of the man. An infinite tenderness, a tenderness which swelled his breast to bursting, a yearning that, man as he was, stopped little short of tears, these were his, these it was that thrilled his soul to the point of pain. The room in which he stood, homely as it showed, plain as it was, seemed glorified, the hearth transfigured. He could have knelt and kissed the floor which the girl had trodden, coming and going, serving and making ready—under that burden; the burden that dignified and hallowed the bearer. What had it not cost her—that burden? What had it not meant to her, what suspense by day, what terror of nights, what haggard awakenings—such as that of which he had been the ignorant witness—what watches above, what slights and insults below! Was it a marvel that the cheeks

had lost their colour, the eyes their light, the whole face
its life and meaning? Nay, the wonder was that she had
borne the weight so long, always expecting, always dread-
ing, stabbed in the tenderest affection, with for confidante
an enemy and for stay an ignorant! Viewed through the
medium of the man's love, which can so easily idealise
where it rests, the love of the daughter for the mother, that
must have touched and softened the hardest—or so, but
for the case of Basterga, one would have judged—seemed
so holy, so beautiful, so pure a thing that the young man
felt that, having known it, he must be the better for it all
his life.

And then his mind turned to another point in the story,
and he recalled what had passed above stairs on the day
when he had entered a stranger, and gone up. With what
a smiling face of love had she leant over her mother's Bed.
With what cheerfulness had she lied of that which passed
below, what a countenance had she put on all—no house
more prosperous, no life more gay—how bravely had she
carried it! The peace and neatness and comfort of the
room with its windows looking over the Rhone valley,
and its spinning-wheel and linen chest and blooming bow-
pot, all came back to him; and he understood many things
which had passed before him then, and then had roused
but a passing and a trifling wonder.

Her anxiety lest he should take lodging there and add
one more to the chances of espial, one more to the wit-
nesses of her misery; her secret nods and looks, and that
gently checked outburst of excitement on Madame Royaume's part, which even at the time had seemed odd—all
were plain now. Ay, plain; but suffused with a light so
beautiful, set in an atmosphere so pure and high, that no

view of God's earth, even from the eyrie of those lofty
windows, and though dawn or sunset flung its fairest
glamour over the scene, could so fill the heart of man with
gratitude and admiration!

Up and down in the days gone by, his thoughts followed
her through the house. Now he saw her ascend and enter, and finding all well, mask—but at what a cost—her
aching heart under smiles and cheerful looks and soft
laughter. He heard the voice that was so seldom heard
downstairs murmur loving words, and little jests, and dear
foolish trifles; heard it for the hundredth time reiterate
the false assurances that affection hallowed. He was witness to the patient tendance, the pious offices, the tireless
service of hand and eye, that went on in that room under
the tiles; witness to the long communion hand in hand,
with the world shut out; to the anxious scrutiny, to the
daily departure. A sad departure, though daily and more
than daily taken; for she who descended carried a weight
of fear and anxiety. As she descended the weary stairs,
he saw the brightness die from eye and lip, and pale fear
or dull despair seize on its place. He saw—and his heart
was full—the slender figure, the pallid face enter the room
in which he stood—it might be at the dawning when the
cold shadow of the night still lay on all, from the dead
ashes on the hearth to the fallen pot and displaced bench;
or it might be at mid-day, to meet sneers and taunts and
ignoble looks; and his heart was full. His face burned,
his eyes filled, he could have kissed the floor she had walked
over, the wooden spoon her hand had touched, the trencher-
edge—done any foolish thing to prove his love.

Love? It was a deeper thing than love, a holier, purer
thing—that which he felt. Such a feeling as the rough

spearsmen of the Orléannais had for Joan the maid; ur the great Florentine for the girl whom he saw for the first time at the banquet at the house of the Portinari; or as that man, who carried to his grave the Queen's glove, yet had never touched it with his bare hand.

Alas, that such feelings cannot last, nor such moments endure; that in the footsteps of the priest, be he never so holy, treads ever the grinning acolyte with his mind on sweet things. They pass, these feelings, and too quickly. But once to have had them, once to have lived such moments, once to have known a woman and loved her in such wise leaves no man as he was before; leaves him at least with a memory, of a higher life.

That the acolyte in Claude's case took the form of Louis Gentilis made him no more welcome. Claude was still dreaming on his feet, still viewing in a kind of happy amaze the simple things about him, things that for him wore

" The light that never was on land or sea,"

and that this world puts on but once for each of us, when Gentilis opened the door and entered, bringing with him a rush of rain, and a gust of night air. The lad breathed quickly as if he had been running, yet having closed the door, he paused before he advanced into the room; and he seemed surprised, and at a nonplus. After a moment, "Supper is not ready?" he said.

"It is not time," Claude answered curtly. The vision of an angel does not necessarily purify at all points, and he had small stomach for Master Louis at any time.

The youth winced under the tone, but stood his ground. "Where is Anne?" he asked, something sullenly.

"Upstairs. Why do you ask?"

"Messer Basterga is not coming to supper. Nor Grio. They bade me tell her. And that they would be late."

"Very well, I will tell her."

But it was evident that that was not all Louis had in his mind. He remained fidgeting by the door, his cap in his hand; and his face—but Claude had already turned a contemptuous shoulder on him—was a picture of doubt and indecision. At length, "I've a message for you," he muttered nervously. "From Messer Blondel the Syndic. He wants to see you—now."

Claude turned, and if he had not looked at the other before, he made up for it now. "Oh!" he said, after a stare that bespoke both surprise and suspicion. "He does, does he? And who made you his messenger?"

"He met me in the street—just now."

"He knows you then?"

"He knows I live here," Louis muttered.

"He pays us a vast amount of attention," Claude replied with polite irony. "Nevertheless"—he turned again to the fire—"I cannot pleasure him," he continued curtly, "this time."

"But he wants to see you," Gentilis persisted desperately. It was plain that he was on pins and needles. "At his house. Cannot you believe me?" in a querulous tone. "It is all fair and above board. I swear it is."

"Is it?"

"It is, I swear it is. He sent me. Do you doubt me?" he added with undisguised eagerness.

Claude was about to say, with no politeness at all, that he did, and to repeat his refusal in stronger terms, when his ear caught the same sound which had revealed so much

to him a few minutes earlier at the foot of the stairs. It
came more faintly this time, deadened by the closed door
of the staircase, but to his enlightened senses it proclaimed
so clearly what it was—the echo of a cracked, shrill voice,
of a laugh insane, uncanny, elfish—that he trembled lest
Louis should hear it also and gain the clue. That was a
thing to be avoided; and even as this occurred to him he
saw the way to avoid it. Basterga and Grio were absent:
if this fool could be removed also, even for an hour or
two, Anne would have the house to herself, and by midnight the crisis might be overpast.

"I will come with you," he said.

Louis uttered a sigh of relief. He had expected—and
he had very nearly received—another answer. "Good,"
he said. "But he does not want me."

"Both or neither," Claude replied coolly. "For all I
know 'tis an ambush."

"No, no!"

"In which event I shall see that you share it. Or it may
be a scheme to draw me from here, and then if harm be
done while I am away——"

"Harm? What harm?" Louis muttered.

"Any harm! If harm be done, I say, I shall then have
you at hand to pay me for it. So—both or neither!"

For a moment Louis' hang-dog face—none the hand-
somer for the mark of the Syndic's cane—spelt refusal.
Then he changed his mind. He nodded sulkily. "Very
well," he said. "But it is raining, and I have no great wish
to—hush! What is that?" He raised his hand in the
attitude of one listening and his eyes sought his companion's. "What is that? Did you not hear something—like
a scream upstairs?"

"I hear something like a fool downstairs!" Claude retorted gruffly.

"But it was—I certainly heard something!" Louis persisted, raising his hand again. "It sounded———"

"If we are to go, let us go!" Claude cried with temper.
"Come, if you want me to go! It is not my expedition,"
he continued, moving noisily hither and thither in search
of his staff and cloak. "It is your affair, and—where is
my cap?"

"I should think it is in your room," Louis answered
meekly. "It was only that I thought it might be Anne.
That there might be———"

"Two fools in the house instead of one!" Claude broke
in, emerging noisily, and slamming the door of his closet
behind him. "There, come, and we may hope to be back
to supper some time to-night! Do you hear?" And
jealously shepherding the other out of the house, he withdrew the key, when both had passed the threshold. Lock-
ing the door on the outside, he thrust the key under it.
"There!" he said, smiling at his cleverness, "now, who
enters—knocks!"

CHAPTER XIV

"AND ONLY ONE DOSE IN ALL THE WORLD!"

IN his picture of the life led by the two women on the upper floor of the house in the Corraterie, that picture which by a singular intuition he had conceived on the day of his arrival, Claude had not gone far astray. In all respects but one the picture was truly drawn. Than the love between the mother and daughter, no tie could be imagined at once more simple and more holy; no union more real and pure than that which bound together these two women, left lonely in days of war and trouble in the midst of a city permanently besieged and menaced by an enduring peril. Almost forgotten by the world below, which had its own cares, its alarums and excursions, its strivings and aims, they lived for one another. The weak health of the one and the brave spirit of the other had gradually inverted their positions; and the younger was mother, the elder, daughter. Yet each retained, in addition, the pious instincts of the original relation. To each the welfare of the other was the prime thought. To give the other the better portion, be it of food or wine, of freedom from care or ease of mind, and to take the worse, was to each the ground plan of life, as it was its chiefest joy.

In their eyrie above the anxious city they led an existence all their own. Between them were a hundred jests,

Greek to others; and whimsical ways, and fond sayings and old smiles a thousand times repeated. And things that must be done after one fashion or the sky would fall; and others that must be done after another fashion or the world would end. When the house was empty of boarders, or nearly empty—though at such times the cupboard also was apt to be bare—there were long hours spent upstairs and surveys of household gear, carried up with difficulty, and reviews of linen and much talk of it, and small meals, taken at the open windows that looked over the Rhone valley and commanded the sunset view. Such times were times of gaiety though not of prosperity, and far from the worst hours of life—could they but have persisted.

But in the March of 1601 a great calamity fell on these two. A fire, which consumed several houses near the Corraterie and flung wide through the streets the rumour that the enemy had entered, struck the bedridden woman—aroused at midnight by shouts and the glare of flames—with so dire a terror, not on her own account but on her daughter's, that she was never the same again. For weeks at a time she appeared to be as of old, save for some increase of weakness and tremulousness. But below the surface the brain was out of poise, and under the least pressure of excitement she betrayed the change in a manner so appalling—by the loud negation of those beliefs which in saner moments were most dear to her, and especially by a denial of the Providence and goodness of God —that even her child, even the being who knew her and loved her best, shuddered lest Satan, visible and triumphant, should rise to confront her.

Fortunately the fits of this mysterious malady were short as they were appalling, and to the minds of that day, suspicious. And in the beginning Anne had the support of an old physician, well-nigh their only intimate. True, even he was scared by a form of disease, new and beyond his science; but he prescribed a sedative and he kept counsel. He went further: for sufficiently enlightened himself to believe these attacks innocent, he none the less explained to the daughter the peril to which her mother's aberrations must expose her were they known to the vulgar; and he bade her hide them with all the care imaginable.

Anne, on this, would fain have adopted the safest course and kept the house empty; to the end that to the horror of her mother's fits of delirium might not be added the chance and the danger of eavesdropping. But to do this was to starve, as well as to reveal to Madame Royaume the fact of those seizures of which no one in the world was more ignorant than the good woman who suffered under them. It followed that to Anne's burden of dread by reason of the outer world, whom she must at all costs deceive, was added the weight of concealment from one, from whom she had never kept anything in her life. A thing which augmented immeasurably the loneliness of her position and the weight of her load.

Presently the drama, always pitiful, increased in intensity. The old leech who had been her stay and helper died, and left her alone to face the danger. A month later Basterga discovered the secret and began to hold it over her. From this time she led a life of which Claude, in his dreams upon the hearth, had exaggerated neither the tragedy nor the beauty. The load had been heavy before. Now to fear was added contumely, and to vague apprehensions, the immediate prospect of discovery and peril. The grip of the big scholar, subtle, cruel, tightening day by day and hour by hour, was on her youth; slowly it paralysed in her all the buoyancy of spirit, all the nerves of life and hope, that were part of her age.

That through all she showed an indomitable spirit, we know. We have seen how she bore herself when confronted by an unexpected danger on the morning when Claude Mercier, after overhearing her mother's ravings, had his doubts confirmed by the sight of her depression on the stairs. How boldly she met his attack, unforeseen as it was, how bravely she shielded her other and dearer self, how deftly she made use of the chance the young man's soberer sense afforded her, will be remembered. But not even in that pinch, no, nor in that worse hour when Basterga, having discovered his knowledge, gave her—as a cat plays with a mouse which it is presently to tear to pieces—a little law and a little space, did she come so near to despair as on this evening when the echo of her mother's insane laughter drew her from the living-room, at an hour without precedent.

For hitherto Madame Royaume's attacks had come on in the night only. With a regularity not unknown in the morbid world they had occurred about midnight, an hour when her daughter could attend to her and when the house below lay wrapped in sleep. A change in this respect doubled the danger, therefore. It did more: the prospect of being summoned at any hour shook, if it did not break, the last remains of Anne's strength. To be liable at all times to such interruptions, to tremble while serving a meal or making a bed lest the dreadful sound arise and reveal all, to listen below and above and never to feel safe for a minute, never, never!—who could face, who could endure, who could lie down and rise up under this burden?

It could not be. As Anne ascended the stairs she felt that the end was coming, was come. Strive as she might, war as she might, with all the instinct, all the ferocity, of a mother defending her young—the end was come. The secret could not be kept longer. Even while she administered the medicine with shaking hands, while with tears in her voice she strove to still the patient and silence her wild words, even while she restrained by force the feeble strength that would and could not, while in a word she omitted no precaution, relaxed no effort, her heart told her with every pulsation that the end was come.

And presently, when Madame was quiet and slept, the girl bowed her head over the unconscious object of her love and wept, bitterly, passionately, wetting with her tears the long grey hair that strewed the pillow, as she recalled with pitiful clearness all the stages of concealment, all the things which she had done to avert this end. Vainly, futilely, for it was come. The dark mornings of winter recurred to her mind, those mornings when she had risen and dressed herself by rushlight, with this fear redoubling the chill gloom of the cold house; the nights, too, when all had been well, and in the last hour before sleep, finding her mother sane and cheerful, she had nursed the hope that the latest attack might be the last. The evenings brightened by that hope, the mornings darkened by its extinction, the rare hours of brooding, the days and weeks of brave struggle, of tendance never failing, of smiles veiling a sick heart—she lived all these again, looking pitifully back, straining tenderly in her arms the dear being she loved.

And then, stabbing her back to life in the midst of her exhaustion, the thought pierced her that even now she was hastening the end by her absence. They would be asking for her below; they must be asking for her already. The supper-time was come, was past, perhaps; and she was not there! She tried to picture what would happen, what already must be happening; and rising and dashing the tears from her face she stood listening. Perhaps Claude would make some excuse to the others; or, perhaps—how much had he guessed?

Her mother was passive now, sunk in the torpor which followed the attack and from which the poor woman would awake in happy unconsciousness of the whole. Anne saw that her charge might be left, and hastily smoothing the tangle of luxuriant hair which had fallen about her face, she opened the door. Another might have stayed to allay the fever of her cheeks, to remove the traces of her tears, to stay the quivering of her hands; but such small cares were not for her, nor for the occasion. She could form no idea of the length of time she had spent upstairs, a half-hour, or an hour and a half; and without more ado she raised the latch, slipped out, and turning the key on her patient ran down the upper flight of stairs.

She anticipated many things, but not that which she encountered—silence on the upper landing, and below when she had descended and opened the staircase door—an empty room. The place was vacant; the tables were as she had left them, half laid; the pot was gently simmering over the fire.

What had happened? The supper-hour was past, yet none of the four who should have sat down to the meal were here. Had they overheard her mother's terrible cry —those words which voiced the woman's despair on finding, as she fancied, the city betrayed? And were they gone to denounce her? The thought was discarded as soon as formed; and before she could hit on a second explanation a hasty knocking on the door turned her eyes that way.

The four who lodged in the house were not in the habit of knocking, for the door was only locked at night when the last retired. She approached it then, wondering, hesitated an instant, and at last, collecting her courage, raised the latch. The door resisted her impulse. It was locked.

She tried it twice, and only as she drew back the second time did she see the key lying at the foot of the door. That deepened the mystery. Why had they locked her in? Why, when they had done so, had they thrust the key under the door and so placed it in her power? Had Claude Mercier done it that the others might not enter to hear what he heard and discover what he had discovered? Possibly. In which case the knocker—who at that instant made a second earnest attack upon the door—must be one of the others, and the sooner she opened the door the less would be the suspicion created.

With an apology trembling on her lips she hastened to open. Then she stood bewildered; she saw before her not one of the lodgers, but Messer Blondel. "I wish to speak to you," the magistrate said. Before she knew what was happening he had motioned to her to go before him into the house, and following had locked the door behind them.

She knew him by sight, as did all Geneva; and the blood, which surprise at the appearance of a stranger had brought to her cheeks, fled as she recognised the Syndic. Had they betrayed her, then, while she lingered upstairs? Had they locked her in while they summoned the magistrate? And was he here to make inquiries about—something he had heard?

His voice cut short her thoughts without allaying her

fears. "I wish to speak to you alone," he said. "Are you alone, girl?" His manner masked excitement. His eyes scrutinised her and searched the room by turns.

She nodded, unable to speak.

"There is no one in the house with you?"

"My mother," she murmured.

"She is bedridden, is she not? She cannot hear us?" he added imperiously.

"No, but I am expecting the others—to return," she muttered.

"Messer Basterga?"

"Yes."

"He will not return before morning," the Syndic replied with decision, "nor his companion. The two young men are safe also. If you are alone therefore, I wish to speak to you."

She bowed her head nervously.

"The young man who lodges here—of the name of Gentilis—he came to you some time ago and told you that the State needed certain letters which the man Basterga kept in a steel box upstairs? That is so, is it not?"

"Yes, Messer Syndic."

"And you looked for them?"

"Yes, I—I was told that you desired them."

"You found a phial? You found a phial, I say?" the Syndic repeated, passing his tongue over his lips. His face was flushed; his eyes shone with a peculiar brightness.

"I found a small bottle," she answered slowly. "There was nothing else."

He raised his hand. If she had known how the delay of a second tortured him! "Describe it to me!" he said. "What was it like?"

Wondering, the girl tried to describe it. "It was small and of a strange shape, of thin glass, Messer Syndic," she said. "Shot with gold, or there was gold afloat in the liquid inside. I do not know which."

"It was not empty?"

"No, it was three parts full."

His hand went to his mouth, to hide the working of his lips. "And there was with it—a paper, I think?"

"No."

"A scrap of parchment then? Some words, some figures?" His voice rose as he read a negative in her face. "There was something surely?"

"There was nothing," she said. "Had there been a scrap even of writing——"

"Yes, yes?" He could not control his impatience.

"I should have sent it to you. I should have thought," she continued earnestly, "that it was that you needed, Messer Syndic; that it was that the State needed. But there was nothing."

"Well, be there papers with it or be there not, I must have that phial!"

Anne stared. "But I do not think—" she began with hesitation—and then as she gained courage, she went on more firmly—"that I can take it! I dare not, Messer Syndic."

"Why not?"

"Papers—for the State—were one thing," she stammered, in confusion. "But to take this—a bottle—would be stealing!"

The Syndic's eyes sparkled. His passion overcame him. "Girl, don't play with me!" he cried. "Don't dare to play with me!" And then as she shrank back alarmed by his tone, and shocked by this sudden peeping forth of the tragic and the real, lo, in a twinkling he was another man, trembling, holding out shaking hands to her. "Get it for me!" he said. "Get it for me, girl! I will tell you what it is! If I had told you before, I had had it now, and I should be whole and well! whole and well. You have a heart and can pity! Women can pity. Then pity me! I am rich, but I am dying! I am a dying man, rising up and lying down, counting the days as I walk the streets, and seeing the shroud rise higher and higher upon my breast!"

He paused for breath, endeavouring to gain some command of himself; while she, carried off her feet by this rush of words, stared at him in stupefaction. Before he came he had made up his mind to tell her the truth—or something like the truth. But he had not intended to tell her the truth in this way until, face to face with her and met by her scruples, he let the impulse to tell the whole story carry him away.

He steadied his lips with a shaking hand. "You know now why I want it," he resumed, speaking huskily and with restrained emotion. "'Tis life! Life, girl! In that——" he fought with himself before he could bring out the word —"in that phial is my life! Is life for whoever takes it! It is the Remedium, it is strength, life, youth, and but one —but one dose in all the world! Do you wonder—I am dying!—that I want it? Do you wonder—I am dying!— that I will have it? But"—with a strange grimace intended to reassure her—"I frighten you, I frighten you."

"No, no!" she said, though in truth she had unconsciously retreated almost to the door of the staircase before his extended hands. "But I—I scarcely understand, Messer Blondel. If you will please to tell me——"

"Yes, yes!"

"What Messer Basterga—how he comes to have this?" She must parley with him until she could collect her thoughts; until she could make up her mind whether he was sane or mad and what it behoved her to do.

"Comes to have it!" he cried vehemently. "God knows! And what matter? 'Tis the Remedium I tell you, whoever has it! It is life, strength, youth!" he repeated, his eyes glittering, his face working, and the impulse to tell her not the truth only, but more than the truth, if he might thereby dazzle her, carrying him away. "It is health of body, though you be dying, as I am! And health of mind though you be possessed of devils! It is a cure for all ills, for all weaknesses, all diseases, even," with a queer grimace, "for the Scholar's evil! Think you, if it were not rare, if it were not something above the common, if it were not what leeches seek in vain, I should be here! I should have more than enough to buy it, I, Messer Blondel of Geneva!" He ceased, lacking breath.

"But," she said timidly, "will not Messer Basterga give it to you? Or sell it to you?"

"Give it to me? Sell it to me? He?" Blondel's hands flew out and clawed the air as if he had the Paduan before him, and would tear it from him. "He give it me? No, he will not. Nor sell it! He is keeping it for the Grand Duke! The Grand Duke, curse him! Why should he escape more than another?"

Anne stared. Was she dreaming or had her brain given way? Or was this really Messer Blondel the austere Syndic, this man standing before her, shaking in his limbs as he poured forth this strange farrago of Remedia and scholars and princes and the rest? Or if she were not mad was

ne mad? Or could there be truth, any truth, any fact in
the medley? His clammy face, his trembling hands answered for his belief in it. But could there be such a thing
in nature as this of which he spoke? She had heard of
panaceas, things which cured all ills alike; but hitherto they
had found no place in her simple creed. Yet that he believed she could not doubt; and how much more he knew
than she did! Such things might be; in the cabinets of
princes, perhaps, purchasable by a huge fortune and by
the labour, the engrossment, the devotion of a life. She
did not know; and for him his acts spoke.

"It was this that Louis Gentilis was seeking?" she murmured.

"What else?" he retorted, opening and shutting his
hands. "Had I told him the truth, as I tell it you, the
thing had been in my grasp now!"

"But are you sure," she ventured to ask with respect,
"that it will do these things, Messer Blondel?"

He flung up his hands in a gesture of impatience. "And
more! And more!" he cried. "It is life and strength, I
tell you! Health and youth! For body or mind, for the
old or the young! But enough! Enough, girl!" he resumed in an altered tone, a tone grown suddenly peremptory, urgent, dangerous. "Get it me! Do you hear?
Stand no longer talking! At any moment they may return, and—and it may be too late."

Too late! It was too late already. Even as he spoke,
the door shook under an angry summons. As he stiffened
where he stood, his eyes fixed upon it, his hand still pointing her to his bidding, a face showed white at the window
and vanished again. An instant he imagined it Basterga's;
and hand, voice, eyes, all hung frozen. Then he saw his

mistake—to whomsoever the face belonged it was not Basterga's; and finding voice and breath again, "Quick," he muttered, "do you hear, girl? Get it! Get it before they enter!"

Her hand was on the latch of the inner door. Another second and swayed by his will she would have gone up and got the thing he needed, and the stout door would have shielded them, and within the staircase he might have taken it from her and no one been the wiser. But as she turned, there came a second attack on the door, so loud, so persistent, so furious, that she faltered, remembering that the duplicate key of Basterga's chamber was in her mother's room, and that she must mount to the top of the house for it.

He saw her hesitation, and shaken by the face which had looked in out of the night, and which still might be watching his movements, his resolution gave way. The habits of a life of formalism prevailed. The thing was as good as his, she would get it presently. Why, then, cause talk and scandal by excluding these persons, whoever they were, when the thing might be had without talk?

"To-night!" he cried rapidly. "Get it to-night, then! Do you hear, girl? You will be sure to get it?" His eyes flitted from her to the door and back again. "Basterga will not return until to-morrow. You will get it to-night?"

She murmured some form of assent.

"Then open the door! open the door!" he urged impatiently. And with a stifled oath, "A little more and they will rouse the town!"

She ran to obey, the door flew open, and into the room bundled first Louis without his cap; and then on his heels and gripping him by the nape, Claude Mercier. Nor did the latter seem in the least degree abashed by the presence in which he found himself. On the contrary, he looked at the Syndic, his head high; as if he, and not the magistrate, had the right to an explanation.

But Blondel had recovered himself. "Come, come!" he said, sternly. "What is this, young man? Are you drunk?"

"Why was the door locked?"

"That you might not interrupt me," Blondel replied severely, "while I asked some questions. I have it in my mind to ask you some also. You took him to my house?" he continued, addressing Louis.

Louis whined that he had.

"You were late then?" His cold eye returned to Claude. "Attend me to-morrow at nine, young man. Do you hear? Do you understand?"

"Yes."

"Then have a care you are there, or the officers will fetcn you. And you," he continued, turning more graciously to Anne, "see, young woman, you keep counsel. A still tongue buys friends, and is a service to the State. With that—good-night."

He looked from one to the other with a sour smile, nodded, and passed out.

He left Claude staring in the middle of the room. The love, the pity, the admiration of which the lad's heart had been full an hour before, still hungered for expression; but it was not easy to vent them before Louis nor at a moment when the Syndic's cold eye and the puzzle of his presence had chilled for the time the atmosphere of the room.

Claude, indeed, was perplexed, nay, more than that, he was alarmed by what he had seen; and before he could decide what he would do, Anne, ignoring the need of explanation, had taken the matter into her hands. She had begun to put on the meal, and Louis, smiling maliciously, had seated himself in his place. To speak with effect then, or to find words adequate to the feelings that had moved him a while before was impossible. A moment later, the opportunity was gone.

"You must please to wait on yourselves," the girl said wearily. "My mother is not well, and I may not come down again this evening." As she spoke, she lifted from the table the little tray which she had prepared.

He was in time to open the door for her; and even then, had she glanced at him, his eyes must have told her much, perhaps enough. But she did not look at him. She was preoccupied with something else; she passed him as if he had been a stranger, her eyes on the tray. Worshipping, he stood, and saw her turn the corner at the head of the flight; then with a full heart he went back to his place. His time would come.

And she? At the door of Basterga's room she paused and stood long in thought, gazing at the rushlight she carried on the tray—yet seeing nothing. A sentence, one sentence of all those which Blondel had poured forth—not Blondel the austere Syndic, who had set the lads aside as if they had been schoolboys, but Blondel the man, trembling, holding out suppliant hands—rang again and again in her ears.

"It is health of body, though you be dying as I am, and health of mind, though you be possessed of devils!" Health of body! Health of mind! Health of body!

Health of mind! The words wrote themselves before her eyes in letters of fire. Health of Body! Health of Mind!

And only one dose in all the world. Only one dose in all the world! She recalled that too.

CHAPTER XV

ON THE BRIDGE

TO say that the Syndic, as soon as he had withdrawn, repented of his weakness and wished with all his heart that he had not opened until the Remedium was in his hand—is only to say that he was human. He did more than this, indeed. When he had advanced some paces in the direction of the Porte Tertasse he returned, and for a full minute he stood before the Royaumes' door irresolute; half-minded to knock and say that he must have at once that for which he had come. He would get it, if he did, he was certain of that. For the rest, what the young men said or thought, or what others who heard their story might say or think, mattered not a straw now that he came to consider it; since he could have Basterga seized on the morrow, and all would pass for a part of his affair.

Yet he did not knock. A downward step on the slope of indecision is hard to retrace. He reflected that he would get the Remedium in the morning. He would certainly get it. The girl was won over, Basterga was away. Practically, he had no one to fear. And to make a stir when the matter could be arranged without a stir, was not the part of a wise man in a magistrate's position. Slowly he turned and walked away.

But, as if his good angel touched him on the shoulder, under the Porte Tertasse he had qualms; and again he stood. And when, after a shorter interval and with less indecision, he resumed his course, it was by no means with the air of a victor. He would receive what he needed in the morning: he dared not admit a doubt of that. And yet—was it a vague presentiment weighed on him as he walked, or only the wintry night wind that caused the blood to run more slowly and more tamely in his veins? He had not fared ill in his venture, he had made success certain. And yet he was unreasonably, he was unaccountably, he was undefinably depressed.

He grew more cheerful when he had had his supper and, seated before a half-flagon of wine, gave the reins to his imagination. For the space of a golden hour he held the Remedium in his grasp, he felt its life-giving influence course through his frame, he tasted again of health and strength and manhood, he saw before him years of success and power and triumph! In comparison of it the bath of Pelias, though endowed with the virtues which lying Medea attributed to it, had not seemed more desirable, nor the Elixir of life, nor the herb of Anticyra. Nor was it until he had taken the magic draught once and twice and thrice in fancy, and as often hugged himself on health renewed and life restored that a thought, which had visited him at an earlier period of the evening, recurred and little by little sobered him.

This was the reflection that he knew nothing of the quantity of the potion which he must take, nothing of the time or of the manner of taking it. Was it to be taken all at once, or in doses? Pure, or diluted with wine, or with water, or with aqua vitæ? At any hour, or at midnight, or at a particular epoch of the moon's age, or when this or that star was in the ascendant?

The question bulked larger, as he considered it; for in life no trouble is surmounted but another appears to confront us; nor is the most perfect success of an imperfect world without its drawback. Now that he held the elixir his, now that in fancy he had it in his grasp, the problem of the mode and the quantity which had seemed trivial and negligeable a few days or hours before, grew to formidable dimensions; nor could he of himself discover any solution of it. He had counted on finding with the potion some scrap of writing, some memorandum, some hieroglyphics at least, that, interpreted by such skill as he could command, would give him the clew he sought. But if there was nothing, as the girl asserted, not a line nor a sign, the matter could be resolved in one way only. He must resort to pressure. With the potion and the man in his possession, he must force the secret from Basterga; force it by threats or promises or aught that would weigh with a man who lay helpless and in a dungeon. It would not be difficult to get the truth in that way; not at all difficult. It seemed, indeed, as if Providence—and Fabri and Petitot and Baudichon—had arranged to put the man in his power *ad hoc.*

He hugged this thought to him, and grew so enamoured of it that he wondered that he had not had the courage to seize Basterga in the beginning. He had allowed himself to be disturbed by phantoms; there lay the truth. He should have seen that the scholar dared not for his own sake destroy a thing so precious, a thing by which he might, at the worst, ransom his life. The Syndic wondered that he had not seen that point before: and still in sanguine humour he retired to bed, and slept better than he had slept for weeks, ay, for months. The elixir was his, as good as his; if he did not presently have Messer Basterga by the nape he was much mistaken.

He had had the scholar watched and knew whither he was gone, and that he would not return before noon. At nine o'clock, therefore, the hour at which he had directed Claude to come to him at his house, he approached the Royaumes' door. Pluming himself on the stratagem by which twice in the twenty-four hours he had rid himself of an inconvenient witness, he opened the door boldly and entered.

On the hearth, cap in hand, stood not Claude, but Louis Gentilis. The lad wore the sneaking air, as of one surprised in a shameful action which such characters wear even when innocently employed. But his actions proved that he was not surprised. With finger on lip, and eyes enjoining caution, he signed to the Syndic to be silent, and himself set the example of listening.

The Syndic was not the man to suffer fools gladly, and he opened his mouth. He closed it—all but too late. All but too late, if—the thought sent cold shivers down his back—if Basterga had really returned. With an air almost as furtive and mean as that of the lad before him, he signed to him to approach.

Louis crossed the room on tiptoe; with a show of caution the more strange as the early December sun was shining and all without was cheerful. "Has he come back?" Blondel whispered.

"Claude?"

"Fool!" Low as the Syndic pitched his tone it expressed a world of contempt. "No, Basterga?"

The youth shook his head, and again laying his finger to his lips listened.

What! It was not that? Blondel's colour returned, his eyes bulged out with passion. What did the imbecile mean? Because he knew certain things did he think himself privileged to play the fool? The Syndic's fingers tingled. Another second and he had broken the silence with a vengeance, when,

"You are—too late!" Louis muttered. "Too late!" he repeated with protruded lips.

Blondel glared at him as if he would annihilate him. Too late? What did this creature know? Or how could it be too late—if Basterga had not returned? Yet the Syndic was shaken. His fingers no longer tingled for the other's cheek; he no longer panted to break the silence in a way that should startle him. On the contrary, he listened, while his eyes passed swiftly round the room, to gather what was amiss. But all seemed in order. The lads' bowls and spoons stood on the table, the great roll of brown bread lay beside them, and a book, probably Claude's, lay face downward on the board. The door of one of the bedrooms stood open. The Syndic's suspicious gaze halted at the closed door. He pointed to it.

Louis shook his head; then, seeing that this was not enough, "There is no one there," he whispered. "But I cannot tell you here. I will follow you, honoured sir, to——"

"The Porte Tertasse."

"Mercier would meet us by your leave," Louis rejoined with a faint grin.

The magistrate glared at this tool who on a sudden had

turned adviser. Still for the time he must humour him.
"The mills, then, on the bridge," he muttered. And he
opened the door with care and went out. With a dreadful
sense of coming evil he went along the Corraterie and took
his way down the steep slope to the bridge which, far below, curbed the blue rushing waters of the Rhone. The
roar of the icy torrent and of the busy mills, stupendous as
it was, did not prove loud enough to deaden the two words
that clung to his ears, "Too late! Too late!" Nor did the
frosty sunshine, gloriously reflected from the line of snowy
peaks to eastward, avail to pierce the gloom in which he
walked. For Louis Gentilis, if it should turn out that he
had inflicted this penance for naught—there was preparing
an evil hour.

The magistrate turned aside on a part of the bridge between two mills. With his back to the wind-swept lake,
and its wide expanse of ruffled waves, he stood a little apart
from the current of crossers, on a space kept clear of
loiterers by the keen breeze. He seemed, if any curious
eye fell on him, to be engaged in watching the swirling torrent pour from the narrow channel beneath him, as in
warmer weather many a one stood to watch it. Here two
minutes later Louis found him; and if Blondel still cherished hope, if he still fought against fear or maintained
courage, the lad's smirking face was enough to end all.

For a moment, such was the effect on him, Blondel could
not speak. Then with an effort, "What is it?" he said.
"What has happened?"

"Much," Louis replied glibly. "Last night, after you
had gone, honoured sir, I judged by this and that, that
there was something afoot. And being devoted to your interests, and seeking only to serve you——"

"The point! The point!" the Syndic ejaculated. "What has happened?"

"Treachery," the young man answered, mouthing his words with enjoyment—it was for him a happy moment. "Black, wicked treachery!" with a glance behind him. "The worst, sir, the worst, if I rightly apprehend."

"Curse you," Blondel cried—contrary to his custom, for he was no swearer, "you will kill me, if you do not speak."

"But——"

"What has happened? What has happened, man?"

"I was going to tell you, honoured sir, that I watched her——"

"Anne? The girl?"

"Yes, and an hour before midnight she took that which you wished me to get, you know—the bottle. She went to Basterga's room, and——"

"Took it! Well? Well?" The Syndic's face, grey a moment before, was dangerously suffused with blood. The cane that had inflicted the bruise Louis still wore across his visage, quivered ominously. Public as the bridge was, open to obloquy and remark, as an assault must lay him, Blondel was within an inch of striking the lad again. "Well? Well?" he repeated. "Is that all—you have to tell me?"

"Would it were!" Louis replied, raising his open hands with sanctimonious fervour. "Alas, sir!"

"You watched her?"

"I watched her back to her room."

"Upstairs?"

"Yes, the room which she occupies with her mother. And kneeling and listening, and seeing what I could for your sake," the knave continued, not a feature evincing the shame he should have felt, "I saw her handle the phial at a little table opposite the door, but hidden by a curtain from the bed."

The Syndic's eyes conveyed the question his lips refused to frame. No man, submitted to the torture, has ever suffered more than he was suffering.

But Louis had as much mind to avenge himself as the bravest—if he could do so safely; and he would not be hurried. "She held it to the light," he said, dwelling on every syllable, "and turned it this way and that, and I could see bubbles as of gold——"

"Ah!"

"Whirling and leaping up and down in it as if they lived —God guard us from the evil one! Then she knelt——"

The Syndic uttered an involuntary cry.

"And prayed," Louis continued, confirming his astonishing statement by a nod. "But whether to it—'twas on the table before her—or to the devil, or otherwise, I know not. Only"—with damnatory candour—"it had a strange aspect. Certainly she knelt, and it was on the table in front of her, and her forehead rested on her hands, and——"

"What then? What then? By Heaven, the point!" gasped Blondel, writhing in torture. "What then? Blind worm that you are, can you not see that you are killing me? What did she do with it? Tell me!"

"She poured it into a glass, and——"

"She drank it?"

"No, she carried it to her mother," Louis explained as slowly as he dared. Fawning on the hand that had struck him, he would fain bite it if he could do so safely. "I did not see what followed," he went on, "they were behind the screen. But I heard her say that it was Madame's medicine. And I made out enough——"

"Ah!"

"To be sure that her mother drank it."

Blondel stared at him a moment, wide-eyed; then, with a cry of despair, bitter, final, indescribable, the Syndic turned and hurried away. He did not hear the timid remonstrances which Louis, who followed a few paces behind, ventured to utter. He did not heed the wondering looks of those whom he jostled as he moved into the current of passers and thrust his way across the bridge in the direction whence he had come. The one impulse in his blind brain was to get home, to get home that he might think and moan and bewail himself unwatched; even as the first instinct of the wounded beast is to seek its lair and lie hidden, there to await with piteous eyes and the divine patience of animals the coming of death.

But this man had the instinct only, not the patience. In his case would come with thought wild rages, gnawings of regret, tears of blood. That he might have, and had not, that he had failed by so little, that he had been worsted by his own tools—these things and the bitter irony of life's chances would madden and torment him. In an hour he would live a lifetime of remorse; yet find in his worst moments no thought more poignant than the reflection that had he played the game with courage, had he grasped the nettle boldly, had he seized Basterga while it was yet time, he might have lived! He might have lived! Ah, God!

Meanwhile Louis, though consumed with desire to see what would happen next, remained on the bridge. He had tasted a fearful joy, and would fain savour more of it if

"SHE HELD IT TO THE LIGHT AND TURNED IT
THIS WAY AND THAT"

he could do so with a whole skin. But to follow seemed too perilous; he held the Syndic's mood in too great awe for that. He did, therefore, the next best thing. He hastened to a projecting part of the bridge a few paces from the spot where they had conferred; there he raised himself on the parapet that he might see which way Blondel turned at the end of the bridge. If he entered the town no more could be made of it: but if he turned right-handed and went by the rampart to the Corraterie, Louis' mind was made up to risk something. He would follow to the Royaumes' house. The magistrate could hardly blame him for going to his own lodging!

It was a busy hour, and, cold as it was, a fair number of people were passing between the island and the upper town. For a moment, look as he might he could not discern the spare figure of his late companion. He was beginning to think that he had missed him, when he saw something that in a twinkling turned his thoughts. On the bank a little beside the end of the bridge stood Claude Mercier. He carried a heavy stick in his hand, and he was waiting: waiting, with his eyes fixed on our friend, and a look in those eyes that even at that distance raised a gentle sweat on Louis' brow.

It required little imagination to follow Claude's past movements. He had gone to the Syndic's house at nine, and finding himself tricked a second time had returned hot-foot to the Corraterie. Thence he had somehow tracked the two to this place. But how long had he been waiting, Louis wondered; and how much had he seen? Something, for certain. His face announced that; and Louis hot all over, despite the keen wind and frosty air, recognised this and augured the worst. Cowards however

have always one course open. The way was clear behind
him. He could cross the island to the St. Gervais bank,
and if he were nimble he might give his pursuer the slip in
the maze of small streets beside the water. It was odd if
the lapse of a few hours did not cool young Mercier's
wrath, and restore him to a frame of mind in which he
might be brought to hear reason.

No sooner planned than done. Or rather it would have
been done if turning to see that the way was clear behind,
he had not discovered a second watcher, who from a spot
on the edge of the island was marking his movements with
grim attention. This watcher was Basterga. Moreover
the glance which apprised Louis of this showed him that
the scholar's face was black as thunder.

Then, if the gods looked down that day upon any mortal with pity, they must have looked down on this young
man; who was a coward. At the one end of the bridge,
Claude, with an ugly weapon and a face to match! At the
other, Basterga, with a black brow and Heaven alone could
say how much knowledge of his treachery! The scholar
could hardly know of his loss indeed, of the loss of the
phial; for apparently he had only just returned to the city
by the St. Gervais gate. But that he soon would know of
it, that he knew something already, that he had been a witness to the colloquy with the Syndic, this was certain.

At any rate Louis thought so, and his knees trembled
under him. He had no longer a way of retreat, and out of
the corner of his eye he saw Claude beginning to advance
upon him. What was he to do? The perspiration burst
out on him. He turned this way and that, now casting wild
eyes at the whirling current below, now piteous eyes—the
eyes of a calf on its way to the shambles and as little re-

garded—on the thin stream of passers. How could they go on their way and leave him to the mercies of this madman?

He smothered a shriek as Claude, now less than twenty paces away, sped a fierce look at him. Claude, indeed, was thinking of Anne and her wrongs; and of a certain kiss. His face told this so plainly, and that passion was his master, that Louis' cheek grew white. What if the ruffian threw him into the river? What if—then like every coward, he chose the remoter danger. With Claude at hand, he turned and fled, dashed blindly through the passers on the bridge, flung himself on Basterga, and, seizing him by the arm, strove to shelter himself behind him.

"He is mad!" he gasped. "Mad! He is going to throw me over!"

"Steady!" Basterga answered; and he opposed his huge form to Claude's rush. "Young man, what is this? Coming to blows in the street? For shame! For shame!" He moved again so as still to confront him.

"Give him up!" Claude panted, scarcely preventing himself from attacking both. "Give him up, I say, and——"

"Not till I have heard what he has done! Steady, young man, keep your distance!"

"I will tell you everything! Everything!" Louis whined, clinging to his arm.

"Do you hear what he says?" Basterga replied. "In the meantime, I tell you to keep your distance, young man. I am not used to be jostled!"

Claude hesitated a moment, scowling. Then "Very well!" he said, drawing off with a gesture of menace. "It is but put off: I shall pay him another time. It is waiting for you, sneak, bear that in mind!" And shrugging his shoulders he turned with as much dignity as he could and moved off.

Basterga wheeled from him to the other. "So!" he said. "You have something to tell me, it seems?" And taking the trembling Louis by the arm, he drew him aside, a few paces from the approach to the bridge. In doing so he hung a moment searching the bridge and the farther bank with a keen gaze. He knew, and for some hours had known, on what a narrow edge of peril he rested, and that only Blondel's influence protected him from arrest. Yet he had returned: he had not hesitated to put his head again into the lion's mouth. Still if Louis' words meant that arrest awaited him, he was not too proud to save himself.

He could discern no officers on the bridge, however, and satisfied on the point of immediate danger, he turned to his shivering ally. "Well, what is it?" he said. "Speak!"

"I'll tell you the truth," Louis gabbled.

"You had better!" Basterga replied, in a tone that meant much more than he said. "Or you will find me worse to deal with than yonder hot-head! I will answer for that."

"Messer Blondel has been at the house," Louis murmured glibly, his mind centred on the question how much he should tell. "Last night and again this morning. He has been closeted with Anne and Mercier. And there has been some talk—of a box or a bottle."

"Were they in my room?" Basterga asked, his brow contracting.

"No, downstairs."

"Did they get—the box or the bottle?" There was a dangerous note in Basterga's voice; and a look in his eyes that scared the lad. Louis, as his instinct was, lied again, fleeing the more pressing peril. "Not to my knowledge," he said.

"And you?" The scholar eyed him with bland suavity. "You had nothing to do—with all this, I suppose?"

"I listened. I was in my room, but they thought I was out. When I went," the liar continued, "they discovered me; and Messer Blondel followed me and overtook me on the bridge and threatened—that he would have me arrested if I were not silent."

"You refused to be silent, of course?"

But Louis was too acute to be caught in a trap so patent. He knew that Basterga would not believe in his courage if he swore to it. "No, I said I would be silent," he answered. "And I should have been," he continued with candour, "if I had not run into your arms."

"But if you assented to his wish," Basterga retorted, eyeing him keenly, "why did he depart after that fashion?"

"Something happened to him," Louis said. "I do not know what. He seemed to be in distress, or to be ill."

"I could see that," the scholar answered drily. "But, Master Claude? What of him? And why was he so enamoured of you that he could not be parted from you?"

"It was to punish me for listening. They followed me different ways."

"Ah, I see. And that is the truth, is it?"

"I swear it is!"

The scholar saw no reason why it should not be the truth. Louis, a facile tool, had always been of his, the stronger, party. If Blondel tampered with anyone, he would naturally, if he knew aught of the house, suborn Claude or Anne. And Louis, spying and fleeing, and when overtaken, promising silence, was quite in the picture. The only thing, indeed, which stood out awkwardly, and refused to fall into place, was the fashion in which the Syndic had turned and gone off the bridge. And for that there might be reasons. He might have been seized with a sudden attack of his illness, or he might have perceived Basterga watching him from the farther bank.

On the whole the scholar, forgetting that cowards are ever liars, saw no reason to doubt Louis' story. It did but add one more to the motives he had for action: immediate, decisive, striking action, if he would save his neck, if he would succeed in his plans. That the Syndic alone stood between him and arrest, that by the Syndic alone he lived, he had learned at a meeting at which he had been present the previous night at the Grand Duke's country house four leagues distant. D'Albigny had been there, and Brunaulieu, Captain of the Grand Duke's Guards, and Father Alexander, who dreamed of the Episcopate of Geneva, and others—the chiefs of the plot, his patrons. To his mortification they had been able to tell him things he had not learned, though he was within the city, and they without. Among others, that the Council had knowledge of him and his plans, and but for the urgency of Blondel would have arrested him a fortnight before.

His companions at the midnight supper had detected his dismay, and had derided him, thinking that with that there was an end of the mysterious scheme which he had refused to impart. They fancied that he would not return to the city, or venture his head a second time within the lion's jaws. But they reckoned without their man. Basterga, if he was a villain, was brave; he had failed in too many schemes to resign this one lightly.

" ' *Si fractus illabatur orbis*
Impavidum ferient ruinæ,' "

he murmured; and he had ventured, he had passed the
Gates, he was here. Here, with his eyes open to the peril,
and open to the necessity of immediate action if the slender
thread by which all hung were not to snap untimely.

Blondel! He lived by Blondel. And Blondel—why
had he left the bridge in that strange fashion? Abruptly,
desperately, as if something had befallen him. Why? He
must learn, and that quickly.

CHAPTER XVI

A GLOVE AND WHAT CAME OF IT

MEANWHILE, Claude, robbed of his prey, had gone into the town, in great disgust. As he passed from the bridge, and paused before he entered the huddle of narrow streets that climbed the hill, he had on his left the glittering heights of snow, rising ridge above ridge to the blue; and most distant among them Mont Blanc itself, etherealised by the frosty sunshine and clear air of a December morning. But Mont Blanc might have been a marsh, the Rhone pouring its icy volume from the lake, might have been a brook, for him. Aware at length of the peril in which Anne stood, and not doubting that these colloquies of Messer Blondel and Louis, these manœuvrings to be rid of his presence, were part of a conspiracy against her, he burned with the desire to thwart it. They had made a puppet of him; they had sent him to and fro at their will and pleasure; and they had done this no doubt, in order that in his absence they might work—Heaven knew what vile and miserable work! But he would know, too! He was going to know! He would not be so tricked thrice.

His indignation went beyond the Syndic. The smug-faced towns-folk whom he met and jostled in the narrow ways, and whose grave starched looks he countered with

hot defiant glances—he included them in his anathema. He
extended to them the contempt in which he held Blondel
and Louis and the rest. They were all of a breed, a big-
oted breed; all dull, blind worms, insensible to the beauty
of self-sacrifice, or the purity of affection. All, self-suffi-
cient dolts, as far removed, as immeasurably divided from
her whom he loved, as the gloomy lanes of this close city
lay below the clear loveliness of the snow-peaks! For
after all, he had lifted his eyes to the mountains.

One thing only perplexed him. He understood the attitude of Basterga and Grio and Louis toward the girl.
He discerned the sword of Damocles that they held over
her, the fear of a charge of witchcraft, or of some vile
heresy, in which they kept her. But how came Blondel in
the plot? What was his part, what his object? If he had
been sincere in that attempt on Basterga's secrets, which
Madame's delirious words had frustrated, was he sincere
now? Was his object now as then—the suppression of the
devilish practices of which he had warned Claude, and in
the punishment of which he had threatened to include the
girl with her tempter? Presumably it was, and he was still
trying to reach the goal by other ways, using Louis as he
had used Claude, or tried to use him.

And yet Claude doubted. He began to suspect that
Blondel had behind this a more secret, a more personal, a
more selfish aim. Had the young girl, still in her teens,
caught the fancy of the man of sixty? There was nothing unnatural in the idea; such things were, even in Geneva; and Louis was a go-between, not above the task. In
that case she who had showed a brave front to Basterga
all these months, who had not blenched before the daily
and hourly persecution, to which she had been exposed in

her home, was not likely to succumb to the senile advances of a man, who might be her grandfather!

If he did not hold her secret. But if he did hold it? If he did hold it, and the cruel power it gave? If he did hold it, he who had only to lift his hand to consign her to duress on a charge so dark and dangerous that innocence itself was no protection against it? So plausible that even her lover had for a short time held it true? What then?

Claude, who had by this time reached the Tertasse gate, and passed through it from the town-side, paused on the ramparts and bared his head. What then?

He had his answer. Framed in the immensity of sky and earth that lay before him, he saw his loneliness and hers, his insignificance and hers, his helplessness and hers; he, a foreigner, young, without name or reputation, or aught but a strong right hand; she, almost a child, alone or worse than alone, in this great city—one of the weak things which the world's car daily and hourly crushes into the mud, their very cries unheard and unheeded. Of no more account than the straw which the turbid Rhone bore one moment on its swirling tide, and the next swallowed from sight beneath its current!

They were two—and a madwoman! And against them were Blondel and Basterga and Grio and Louis, and presently all the town of Geneva! All these gloomy, narrow, righteous men, and shrieking, frightened women—frightened lest any drop of the pitch fall on them and destroy them! Love is a marvellous educator. Almost as clearly as we of a later day, he saw how outbreaks of superstition, such as that which he dreaded, began, and came to a head, and ended. A chance word at a door, a spiteful rumour or a sick child, the charge, the torture, the widening net of accusation, the fire in the market-place. So it had been in Bamberg and Wurzburg, in Geneva two generations back, in Alsace scarce as many years back: at Edinburgh in Scotland where thirty persons had suffered in one day—ten years ago that; in the district of Como, where a round thousand had suffered!

Nobility had not availed to save some, nor court-favour others; nor wealth, nor youth, nor beauty. And what had he or she to urge, what had they to put forward that would in the smallest degree avail them? That could even for a moment stem or avert the current of popular madness which power itself had striven in vain to dam. Nothing!

And yet he did not blench, nor would he; being half French and of good blood, at a time when good French blood ran the more generously for a half century of war. He would not have blenched, even if he had not, from the sunlit view of God's earth and heaven which lay before his eyes, drawn other thoughts than that one of his own littleness and insignificance. As this view of vale and mountain had once before lifted his judgment above the miasma of a cruel superstition, so it raised him now above creeping fears and filled him with confidence in something more stable than magistrates or mobs. Love, like the sunlight, shone aslant the dark places of the prospect and filled them with warmth. Sacrifice for her he loved took on the beauty of the peaks, cold but lovely; and hope and courage, like the clear blue of the vault above, looked smiling down on the brief dangers and the brief troubles of man's making.

The clock of St. Gervais was striking eleven as, still in exalted mood, he turned his back on the view and entered the house in the Corraterie. He had entered on his return from his fruitless visit to Blondel, and had satisfied himself that Anne was safe. Doubtless she was still safe, for the house was quiet.

In his new mood he was almost inclined to quarrel with this. In the ardour of his passion he would fain have seen the danger immediate, the peril present, that he might prove to her how much he loved her, how deeply he felt for her, what he would dare for her. To die on the hearth of the living-room, at her feet and saving her, seemed for a moment the thing most desirable—the purest happiness!

That was denied him. The house was quiet, as in a morning it commonly was. So quiet that he recalled without effort the dreams which he had dreamed on that spot and the thoughts which had filled his heart to bursting a few hours before. The great pot was there, simmering on its hook; and on the small table beside it, the table that Basterga and Grio occupied, stood a platter with a few dried herbs and a knife fresh from her hand. Claude made sure that he was unobserved, and raising the knife to his lips, kissed the haft gently and reverently, thinking what she had suffered many a day while using it. What fear, and grief and humiliation, and—

He stood erect, his face red: he listened intently. Upstairs, breaking the long silence of the house, opening as it were a window to admit the sun, a voice had uplifted itself in song. The voice had some of the tones of Anne's voice, and something that reminded him of her voice. But when had he heard her sing? When had aught so clear, so mirthful, or so young, fallen from her as this—this melody, laden with life and youth and abundance, that rose and fell, and floated to his ears through the half-open door of the staircase?

He crept to the staircase door and listened; yes, it was her voice, but not such as he had ever heard it. It was her voice as he could fancy it in another life, a life in which she was as other girls, darkened by no fear, pinched by no anxiety, crushed by no contumely; such as her voice might have been uplifted in the garden of his old home on the French border, amid bees and flowers and fresh-scented herbs. Her voice, doubtless, it was; but it sorted so ill with the thoughts he had been thinking, that with his aston- ishment was mingled something of shock and of loss. He had dreamed of dying for her or with her, and she sang! He was prepared for peril, and her voice vied with the lark's in joyous trills.

Leaning forward to hear more clearly, he touched the door. It was open but an inch or two; before he could hin- der it, it closed with a sharp sound. The singing ceased, with an abruptness that told, or he was much mistaken, of self-remembrance. And presently, after an interval of no more than a few seconds, during which he pictured the singer listening, he heard her begin to descend.

Two men may do the same thing from motives as far apart as the poles. Claude did what Louis would have done. As the foot drew near the staircase door, treading, less willingly, less lightly, more like that of Anne with every step, he slid into his closet, and stood. Through the crack between the hinges of the open door, he would be able to view her face when she appeared.

A second later she came, and he saw. The light of the song was still in her eyes, but mingled, as she looked round the room to learn who was there, with something of ex- altation, and defiance. Christian maidens might have worn some such aspect, he thought—but he was in love—as they passed to the lions. Or Esther, when she went unbidden into the inner court of the King's House, and before the golden sceptre moved. Something had happened to her. But what?

She did not see him, and after standing a moment to assure herself that she was alone, she passed to the hearth. She lifted the lid of the pot, bent over it, and slowly stirred the broth; then, having covered it again, she began to chop the dried herbs on the platter. Even in her manner of doing this, he fancied a change; a something unlike the Anne he had known, the Anne he had come to love. The face was more animated, the action quicker, the step lighter, the carriage more free. She began to sing, and stopped; fell into a reverie, with the knife in her hand, and the herb half cut; again roused herself to finish her task; finally having slid the herbs from the platter to the pot, she stood in a second reverie, with her eyes fixed on the window.

He began to feel the falseness of his position. It was too late to show himself, and if she discovered him what would she think of him? Would she believe that in spying upon her, he had some evil purpose, some low motive, such as Louis might have had? His cheek grew hot. And then —in a trice he forgot himself.

Her eyes had left the window and fallen to the window-seat. It was the thing she did then which drew him out of himself. Moving to the window—he had to stoop forward to keep her within the range of his sight—she took from it a glove, held it a moment, regarding it; then with a tender yet whimsical laugh, a laugh half happiness, half ridicule of herself, she kissed it.

It was Claude's glove. And if, with that before his eyes he could have restrained himself, the alternative was not his. She turned in the act, and saw him; and with a startled cry she put—none too soon—the table between them.

They faced one another across it, he flushed, eager, with love in his eyes, and on his lips; she blushing but not ashamed, her new-found joy in her eyes, and in the pose of her head.

"Anne!" he cried. "I know now! I know! I have seen and you cannot deceive me!"

"In what?" she said, a smile trembling on her lips. "And of what, Messer Claude, are you so certain, if you please?"

"That you love me!" he replied. "But not a hundredth part—" he stretched his arms across the table toward her —"as much as I love you, and have loved you for weeks! As I loved you even before I learned last night——"

"What?" Into her face—that had not found one hard look to rebuke his boldness—came something of her old silent, watchful self. "What did you learn last night?"

"Your secret!"

"I have none!" Quick as thought the words came from her lips. "I have none! God is merciful"—with a gesture of her open arms, as if she put something from her, "and it is gone! If you know, if you guess aught of what it was," her eyes questioned his and read in them if not that which he knew, that which he thought of her—"I ask you to be silent."

"I will, after I have——"

"Now! Always!"

"Not till I have spoken once!" he cried. "Not till I have told you once what I think of you! Last night—I heard. And I understood. I saw what you had gone through, what you had feared, what had been your life all these weeks, rising and lying down! I saw what you meant when you bade me go anywhere but here, and why you suffered what you did at their hands, and why they dared to treat you—so! And had they been here I would have killed them!" he added, his eyes sparkling. "And had you been here——"

"Yes?" She did not seek to check him now. Her bearing was changed, her eyes, soft and tender, met his as no eyes had ever met them.

"I should have worshipped you! I should have knelt as I kneel now!" he cried. And sinking on his knees he extended his arms across the table and took her unresisting hands. "If you no longer have a secret, you had one, and I bless God for it! For without it I might not have known you, Anne! I might not have——"

"Perhaps you do not know me now," she said; but she did not withdraw her hands or her eyes. Only into the latter grew a shade of trouble. "I have done—I am a thief."

"Pah!"

"It is true. I am a thief."

"What is it to me?" He laughed a laugh as tender as her eyes. "You are a thief, for you have stolen my heart. For the rest, do you think that I do not know you now? That I can be twice deceived? Twice take gold for dross, and my own for another thing? I know you!"

"But you do not know," she said tremulously, "what I have done, what I did last night, or what may happen."

"I know that it will happen, not to one but to two," he replied bravely. "And that is all I ask to know. That, and that you are content it shall be so?"

"Content?"

"Yes."

SINKING ON HIS KNEES, HE EXTENDED HIS ARMS
ACROSS THE TABLE

"Content!"

There are things, other than wine, that bring truth to the surface. That which had happened to the girl in the last few hours, that which had melted her into unwonted song, was of these things; and the tone of her voice as she repeated the word "Content!" the surrender of her eyes that placed her heart in his keeping, as frankly as she left her hands in his, proclaimed it. The reserves of her sex, the tricks of coyness and reticence men look for in maids, were shaken from her; and as man to man her eyes told him the truth, told him that if she had ever doubted she no longer doubted that she loved him. In the heart which a single passion, the purest of which men and women are capable, had engrossed, Nature, who, expel her as you will, will still return, had won her right and carved her kingdom.

And she knew it was well with her; whatever the upshot of last night. To be lonely no more; to be no longer the protector always, but the protected; to know the comfort of the strong arm as well as of the following eye, the joy of receiving as well as of giving; to know that, however dark the future might lower, she had no longer to face it alone, no longer to plan and hope and fear and suffer alone, but with *him*—the sense of these things so mingled with her gratitude on her mother's account that the new affection, instead of weakening the old, became as it were part of it; while the old stretched onward its pious hand to bless the new.

If Claude did not read all this in her eyes, and in that one word "Content?" he read so much that never devotee before relic rose more gently or more reverently to his feet. Because all was his he would take nothing. "As I stand by you, may God stand by me," he said still holding her hands in his, and with the table between them.

"I have no fear," she replied in a low voice. "Yet— if you fail, may He forgive you as fully as I must forgive you. What shall I say to you—on my part, Messer Claude?"

"That you love me."

"I love you," she murmured with an intonation which ravished the young man's heart and brought the blood to his cheeks. "I love you. What more?"

"There is no more," he cried. "There can be no more. If that be true nothing matters."

"No!" she said beginning to tremble under a weight of emotion too heavy for her, following as it did the excitement of the night. "No!" she continued, raising her eyes which had fallen before the ardour of his gaze. "But there must be something you wish to ask me. You must wish to know——"

"I have heard what I wished to know."

"But——"

"Tell me what you please."

She stood in thought an instant: then, with a sigh, "He came to me last evening," she said, "when you were at his house."

"Messer Blondel?"

"Yes. He wished me to procure for him a certain drug that Messer Basterga kept in his room."

Claude stared. "In a steel casket chained to the wall?" he asked.

"Yes," with some surprise. "You knew of it, then? He had tried to procure it before through Louis, and on the pretence that the box contained papers needed by the State.

Failing in that he came last evening and told me the truth."

"The truth?" Claude asked, wondering. "But was it the truth?"

"It was." Her eyes, like stars on a rainy night, shone softly. "I have proved it." And, again, with a ring of exultation in her voice, "I have proved it!" she cried.

"How?"

"There was in the box a drug, he told me, possessed of an almost miraculous power over disease of body and mind; so rare and so wonderful that none could buy it, and he knew of but this one dose, of which Messer Basterga had possessed himself. He begged me to take it and to give it to him. He had on him, he said, a fatal illness, and if he did not get this—he must die." Her voice shook. "He must die! Now God help him!"

"You took it."

"I took it." Her face, as her eyes dropped before his, began to betray trouble and doubt. "I took it," she continued, trembling. "If I have done wrong, God forgive me. For I stole it."

His face betrayed his amazement, but he did not release her hands. "Why?" he said.

"To give to her," she answered. "To my mother. I thought then that it was right—it was a chance. I thought —Now I don't know, I don't know!" she repeated. The shade on her face grew deeper. "I thought I was right then. Now—I am frightened." She looked at him with eyes in which her doubts were mirrored. She shivered, she who had been so joyous a moment before; and her hands, which hitherto had lain passive in his, returned his pressure feverishly. "I fear now!" she exclaimed. "I fear! What is it? What has happened—in the last minute?"

He would have drawn her to him, seeing that her nerves were shaken; but the table was between them, and before he could pass to her, a sound caught his ear, a shadow fell between them, and looking up he discovered Basterga's face peering through the nearer casement. It was pressed against the small leaded panes, and possibly it was this which by flattening the huge features imparted to them a look of malignity. Or the look—which startled Claude, albeit he was no coward—might have been only the natural expression of one, who suspected what was afoot between them and came to mar it. Whatever it meant, the girl's cry of dismay found an echo on Claude's lips. Involuntarily he dropped her hands; but—and the action was symbolical of the change in her life—he stepped at the same moment between her and the door. Whatever she had done, right or wrong, was his concern now.

CHAPTER XVII

THE REMEDIUM

WE have seen that for Claude, as he hurried from the bridge, the faces he met in the narrow streets were altered by the medium through which he viewed them; and appeared gloomy, sordid, fanatical. In the eyes of Blondel, who had passed that way before him, the same faces wore a look of selfishness, stupendously and heartlessly cruel. And not the faces only; the very houses and ways, the blue sky overhead, and the snow peaks—when for an instant he caught sight of them—bore the same aspect. All wore their every day air, and mocked the despair in his heart. All flung in his teeth the fact, the incredible fact, that whether he died or lived, stayed or went, the world would proceed; that the eternal hills, ay, and the insensate bricks and mortar would be standing when he was gone into the darkness.

There are few things that to the mind of man in his despondent moods are more strange, more shocking, than the permanence of trifles. The small things to which his brain and his hand have given shape, which he can, if he will, crush out of form, and resolve into their primitive atoms, outlive him! They lie on the table when he is gone, are unchanged by his removal, serve another master as they have served him, preach to another generation the same lesson. The face is dust, but the canvas smiles from the wall. The hand is withered, but the pencil is still in the tray and is used by another. There are times when the irony of this thought bites deep into the mind, and goads the mortal to revolt. Had Blondel, as he climbed the hill, possessed the power of Orimanes to blast at will, few of those whom he met, few on whom he turned the gloomy fire of his eyes, would have reached their houses or seen another sun.

He was within a hundred paces of his house, when a big man, passing along the Bourg du Four, but on the other side of the way, saw him, and came across the road to intercept him. It was Baudichon, his double chin more pendulent, his massive face more dully wistful than ordinary; for the times had got upon the Councillor's nerves, and day by day he grew more anxious, slept worse of nights, and listened much before he went to bed.

"Messer Blondel," he called out, in a voice more peremptory than was often addressed to the Fourth Syndic's ear. "Messer Syndic! One moment, if you please!"

Blondel stopped and turned to him. Outwardly the Syndic was cool, inwardly he was at a white heat that at any moment might impel him to the wildest action. "Well," he said. "What is it, M. Baudichon?"

"I want to know——"

"Of course!" The sneer was savage and undisguised. "What, this time, if I may be so bold?"

Baudichon breathed quickly, partly with the haste he had made across the road, partly in irritation at the gibe. "This only," he said. "How far you purpose to try our patience? A week ago you were for delaying the arrest you know of—for a day. It was a matter of hours then."

"It was."

"But days have passed, and are passing! and we have no explanation; nothing is done. And every night we run a fresh risk, and every morning—so far—we thank God that our throats are still whole; and every day we strive to see you, and you are out, or engaged, or about to do it, or awaiting news! But this cannot go on for ever! Nor," puffing out his cheeks, "shall we always bear it!"

"Messer Baudichon!" Blondel exclaimed, the passion he had so far restrained gleaming in his eyes, and imparting a tremor to his voice, "are you Fourth Syndic or am I?"

"You! You, certainly. Who denies it?" the stout man said. "But——"

"But what? But what?"

"We would know what you think we are, that we can bear——"

"I will tell you what I think you are!"

"By your leave?"

"*A fat hog!*" the Syndic shrieked. "And as brainless as a hog fit for the butcher! That for you! and your like!"

And before the astounded Baudichon, whose brain was slow to take in new facts, had grasped the full enormity of the insult flung at him, the Syndic was a dozen paces distant. He had eased his mind, and that for the moment was much; though he still ground his teeth, and, had Baudichon followed him, would have struck the Councillor without thought or hesitation. The pigs! The hogs! To press him with their wretched affairs: to press him at this moment when the grave yawned at his feet, and the coffin opened for him!

To be sure he might now do with Basterga as he pleased without thought or drawback; but for their benefit— never! He paused at his door, and cast a haggard glance up and down; at the irregular line of gables he had known from childhood, the steep, red roofs, the cobble pavement, the bakers' sign that hung here and there and with the wide eaves darkened the way; and he cursed all he saw in the frenzy of his rage. Let Basterga, Savoy, d'Albigny do their worst! What was it to him? Why should he move? He went into his house despairing.

Unto this last hour a little hope had shone through the darkness. At times the odds had seemed to be against him, at one time heaven itself had seemed to declare itself his foe. But the Remedium had existed, the thing was still possible, the light burned, though distant, feeble, flicker- ing. He had told himself that he despaired; but he had not known what real despair was until this moment, until he sat, as he sat now, among the Dead Sea splendours of his parlour, the fingers of his right hand drumming on the arm of the Abbot's chair, his shaggy eyelids drooping over his brooding eyes.

Ah, God! If he had stayed to take the stuff when it lay in his power! If he had refused to open until he held it in his hand! If, even after that act of folly, he had re- fused to go until she gave it him! How inconceivable his madness seemed now, his fear of scandal, his thought of others! Others? There was one of whom he dared not think, for when he did his head began to tremble on his shoulders; and he had to clutch the arms of the chair to stay the palsy that shook him. If *she,* the girl who had de- stroyed him, thought it was all one to him whom the drug advantaged, or who lived or who died, he would teach her—before he died! He would teach her! There was no extremity of pain or shame she should not taste, accursed witch, accursed thief, as she was! But he must not think of that, or of her, now; or he would die before his time. He had a little time yet, if he were careful, if he were cool, if he were left a brief space to recover himself. A little, a very little time!

Whose were that foot and that voice? Basterga's? The Syndic's eyes gleamed, he raised his head. There was another score he had still to pay! His own score, not Baudichon's. Fool, to have left his treasure unguarded for every thieving wench to take! Fool, thrice and again, for putting his neck back into the lion's mouth. Stealthily Blondel pulled the handbell nearer to him and covered it with his cloak. He would have added a weapon, but there was no arm within reach, and while he hesitated between his chair and the door of the small inner room the outer door opened, and Basterga appeared and advanced to greet him.

"Your servant, Messer Syndic," he said lightly. "I heard that you had been inquiring for me in my absence, and I am here to place myself at your disposition. You are not looking——" he stopped short, in well-feigned surprise. "There is nothing wrong, I hope?"

Had the scholar been such a man as Baudichon, Blondel's answer would have been one frenzied shriek of insults and reproaches. But face to face with the massive quietude of this man, with his giant bulk, with that air, at once masterful and cynical, which proclaimed to those with whom he talked that he gave them but half his mind while reading theirs, the wrath of the smaller man cooled. A moment his lips writhed, without sound; then "Wrong?" he cried, his voice harsh and broken. "Wrong? All is wrong!"

"You are not well?" Basterga said, eyeing him with concern.

"Well? I shall never be better! Never!" Blondel shrieked. And after a pause, "Curse you!" he added. "It is your doing!"

Basterga stared. He was in the dark as to what had happened, though the Syndic's manner on leaving the bridge had prepared him for something. "My doing, Messer Blondel?" he said. "Why? What have I done?"

"Done?"

"Ay, done! It was not my fault," the scholar continued, with a touch of sternness, "that I could not offer you the Remedium on easy terms. Nor mine, that hard as the terms were, you did not accept them. Besides," he continued, slowly and with meaning,

> " ' *Terque quaterque redit !* '

You remember the Sibylline books? How often they were offered, and the terms? It is not too late, Messer Blondel —even now. While there is life there is hope, there is more than hope. There is certainty."

"Is there?" Blondel cried; he extended a lean hand, shaking with vindictive passion. "Is there? Go and look in your casket, fool! Go and look in your steel box!" he hissed. "Go! And see if it be not too late!"

For a moment Basterga peered at him, his brow contracted, his eyes screwed up. The blow was unexpected. Then, "Have you taken the stuff?" he muttered.

"I? No! But she has!" And then, seeing the change

in the other's face—for, for once the scholar's mask slipped and suffered his consternation to appear — he laughed triumphantly: in torture himself, he revelled in a disaster that touched another. "She has! She has!"

"She? Who?"

"The girl of the house! Ay, Anne you call her! Curse her! child of perdition! Anne Royaume! She! Curse her!" And he clawed the air.

"She has taken it?" Basterga spoke incredulously, but his brow was damp, his cheeks were a shade more sallow than usual; he did not deceive the other's penetration. "Impossible!" he continued, striving to rally his forces. "Why should she take it? She has no illness, no disease! Try—" he swallowed something—"to be clear, man. Try to be clear. Who has told you this cock-and-bull story?"

"It is the truth."

"She has taken it?"

"To give to her mother—yes."

"And she?"

"Has taken it? Yes."

The scholar, ordinarily so cool and self-contained, could not withhold an execration. His small eyes glittered, his face swelled with rage; for a moment he was within a little of a fit. Of what mad, what insensate folly, unworthy of a schoolboy, worthy only of a sot, an imbecile, a Grio, had he been guilty! To leave the potion, that if it had not the virtues which he ascribed to it, had virtue—or it had not served his purpose of deceiving the Syndic during some days or hours—to leave the potion unprotected, at the mercy of a chance hand, of a treacherous girl! Safeguarded, in appearance only, and to blind his dupe! It seemed incredible that he could have been so careless!

True, he might replace the stuff at some expense; but not in a day or an hour. And how—with one dose in all the world!—keep up the farce? The dose consumed, the play was at an end. An end—or, no, was he losing his wits, his courage? On the instant, in the twinkling of an eye, he shaped a fresh course.

He cursed the girl anew, and apparently with the same fervour. "A month's work it cost me!" he cried. "A month's work! And ten gold pieces!"

The Syndic, pale, and almost in a state of collapse—for the bitter satisfaction of imparting the news no longer supported him, stared. "A month's work?" he muttered. "A month? Years you told me! And a fortune!"

"I told you? Never!" Basterga replied slowly, and opened his eyes in seeming amazement. "Never, good sir, in all my life!" he repeated emphatically. "But—" returning grimly to his former point—"ten gold pieces, or a fortune—no matter which, she shall pay dearly for it, the thieving jade!"

The Syndic sat heavily in his seat, and, with a hand on either arm of the Abbot's chair, stared dully at the other. "A fortune, you told me," he said, in a voice little above a whisper. "And years. Was it a fiction, all a fiction? About Ibn Jasher, and the Physician of Aleppo and Monsieur Laurens of Paris, and—and the rest?"

Basterga deliberately took a turn to the window, came back, and stood looking down at him. "Mon Dieu!" he muttered. "Is it possible?"

"Eh?"

"I can scarcely believe it!" The scholar spoke with a calmness half cynical, half compassionate. "But I suppose you really think that of me, though it is almost in-

credible! You are under the impression, that the drug
this jade stole was the Remedium of Ibn Jasher, the one
incomparable and sovereign result of long years of study
and research? You believe that I kept this in a mere
locked box, the key accessible by all who knew my habits,
and the treasure at the mercy of the first thief! Mon
Dieu! Mon Dieu! If I said it a thousand times I could
not express my astonishment. I might be the vine grower
of the proverb,

' Cui saepe viator
Cessisset magna compellans voce cucullum!' "

The Syndic heard him without changing the attitude of
weakness and exhaustion into which he had fallen on sitting down. But midway in the other's harangue, his lips
parted, he held his breath, and in his eyes grew a faint
light of dawning hope. "But if it be not so?" he muttered
feebly. "If this be not so, why——"

"Mon Dieu! Mon Dieu!"

"Why did you look so startled a moment ago?"

"Why, man? Because ten pieces of gold are ten pieces!
To me at least! And the potion, which was made after a
recipe of that same Messer Laurens of Paris, cost no less.
It is a love-philtre, beneficent to the young, but if taken by
the old so noxious, that had you swallowed it," with a grin,
"you had not been long Syndic, Messer Blondel!"

Blondel shook his head. "You do not deceive me," he
muttered. For though he was anxious to believe, as yet
he could not. He could not; he had seen the other's face.
"It is the Remedium she has taken! I feel it."

"And given to her mother?"

Blondel inclined his head.

The scholar laughed contemptuously. "Then is the test easy," he said. "If it be the Remedium you will find her mother, who has not left her bed for three years, grown strong and well and vigorous, and like to him who lifted up his bed and walked. But if it be the philtre you have but to come with me, and you will find her——" He did not finish the sentence, but a shrug of his shoulders, and a mysterious smile filled the gap.

Imperceptibly Blondel had raised himself in his chair. The gleam of hope, once lighted in his eyes, was growing bright. "How?" he asked. "How shall we find her? If it be the philtre only that she has taken—as you say?"

"If it be the love-philtre? The mother, you mean?"

"Yes."

"Mad! Mad!" Basterga repeated with decision, "and beside herself. As you had been," he continued grimly, "had you by any chance taken the Aqua Medeæ."

"That you kept in the steel box?"

"Ay."

"You are sure it was not the Remedium?" Blondel leaned forward: if only he could believe it, if only it were the truth how great the difference! No wonder that the muscles of his lean throat swelled, and his hands closed convulsively on the arms of his great chair, as he strove to read the other's mind.

He had as soon read a printed page without light. The scholar saw that it needed but a little to convince him, and took his line with confidence; and not without some pride in the wits that had saved him. "The Remedium?" he repeated with impatient wonder. "Do you not know that the Remedium is unique? That it is a man's life? That in the world's history it scarce appears once in five hundred

years? That all the wealth of kings cannot produce it,
nor the Spanish Indies furnish it? Do you remember these
things, Messer Blondel, and do you ask if I kept it like a
common philtre in a box in my lodgings?" He snorted in
contempt, and going disdainfully to the hearth spat in the
fire as if he could not brook the idea. Then returning to
the Syndic's side, he took up his story in a different tone.
"The Remedium," he said, "my good friend, is in the
Grand Duke's Treasury at Turin. It is in a steel box it is
true, but in one with three locks and three keys, sealed with
the Grand Duke's private signet and with mine; and laid
where the Treasurer himself cannot meddle with it."

The Syndic sat up straight, and with his eyes fixed sullenly on the floor fingered his beard. He was almost persuaded but not quite. Could it be, could it really be that
the thing still existed, that it was still to be obtained, that
life by its means was still possible?

"Well?" Basterga said, when the silence had lasted
some time.

"The proof!" Blondel retorted, excitement once more
overmastering him. "Let me have the proof! Let me
see, man, if the woman be mad."

But the scholar, leaning Atlas-like, against the wall beside the long low window, with his arms crossed, and his
great head sunk on his breast, did not move. He saw that
this was his hour and he must use it. "To what purpose?"
he answered slowly: and he shrugged his shoulders. "Why
go to the trouble of that? The Remedium is in Turin.
And if it be not, it is the Grand Duke's affair only and
mine, since you will not come to his terms. I would, I confess," he continued, in a more kindly tone, "that it were
your affair also, Messer Blondel. I would I could have

made you see things as they are and as I see them. As, believe me, Messer Petitot would see them were he in your place; as Messer Fabri and Messer Baudichon—I warrant it—do see them; as—pardon me—all who rank themselves among the wise and the illuminate, see them. For all such, believe me, these are times of enlightening, when the words which men have woven into shackles for their minds fall from them, and are seen to be but the straw they are; when men move, like children awaking from foolish dreams, and life——"

The Syndic's eyes glowed dully.

"Life," Basterga continued sonorously, "is seen to be that which it is, the one thing needful which makes all other things of use, and without which all other things are superfluities! Bethink you a minute, Messer Blondel! Would Petitot give his life to save yours?"

The Syndic smiled after a sickly fashion. Petitot? The stickling pedant! The thin, niggling whipster!

"Or Messer Fabri?"

Blondel shook his head.

"Or Messer Baudichon?"

"I called him but now—a fat hog!"

It was Basterga's turn to shake his head. "He is not one to forget," he said gravely. "I fear you will hear of that again, Messer Blondel. I fear it will make trouble for you. But if these will not, is there any man in Geneva, any man you can name, who would give his life for you?"

"Do men give life—so easily?" Blondel answered, moving painfully in his chair.

"Yet you will give yours for them! You will give yours! And who will be a ducat the better?"

"I shall at least die for freedom," the Syndic muttered, gnawing his moustache.

"A word!"

"For the religion, then."

"It is that which men make it!" the scholar retorted. "There have been good men of all religions, though we dare not say as much in public, or in Geneva. 'Tis not the religion. 'Tis the way men live it! Was John Bernardino of Assisi, whom some call St. Francis, a worse man than Arnold of Brescia, the Reformer? Or is your Beza a better man than Messer Francis of Sales? Or would the heavens fall if Geneva embraced the faith of the good Archbishop of Milan? Words, Messer Blondel, believe me, words!"

"Yet men die for them!"

"Not wise men. And when you have died for them, who will thank you?" The Syndic groaned. "Who will know, or style you martyr? Baudichon, whom you have called a fat hog? He will sit in your seat. Petitot—he said but a little while ago that he would buy this house if he lived long enough."

"He did?" The Syndic came to his feet as if a spring had raised him.

"Certainly. And he is a rich man, you know."

"May the Bise search his bones!" Blondel cried, trembling with fury. For this was the realisation of his worst fears. Petitot to live in his house, lie warm in his bed, sneer at his memory across the table that had been his, rule in the Council where he had been first! Petitot, that miserable crawler who had clogged his efforts for years, who had shared, without deserving, his honours, who had spied on him and carped at him day by day and hour by hour!

Petitot to succeed him! To be all and own all, and sun himself in the popular eye, and say, "Geneva, it is I!" While he, Blondel, lay rotting and forgotten, stark, beneath snow and rain, winter wind and summer drought!

Perish Geneva first! Perish friend and foe alike!

The Syndic wavered. His hand shook, his thin, dry cheek burned with fever, his lips moved unceasingly. Why should he die? They would not die for him. Nay, they would not thank him, they would not praise him. A traitor? To live he must turn traitor? Ay, but try Petitot, and see if he would not do the same! Or Baudichon, who could not sleep of nights for fear—how would he act with death staring him in the face? The bravest soldiers when disarmed, or called upon to surrender or die, capitulated without blame. And that was his position.

Life, too; dear, warm life! Life that might hold much for him still. Hitherto these men and their fellows had hampered and thwarted him, marred his plans and balked his efforts. Freed from them and supported by an enlightened and ambitious prince, he might rise to heights hitherto invisible. He might lift up and cast down at will, might rule the Council as his creatures, might live to see Berne and the Cantons at his feet, might leave Geneva the capital of a great and wealthy country.

All this at his will; or he might die! Die and rot and be forgotten like a dog that is cast out.

He did not believe in his heart that faith and honour were words; fetters woven by wise men to hamper fools. He did not believe that all religions were alike, and good or bad as men made them. But on the one side was life and on the other death. And he longed to live.

"I would that I could make you see things as I

see them," Basterga resumed, in a gentle tone. Patiently waiting the other's pleasure he had not missed an expression of his countenance, and, thinking the moment ripe, he used his last argument. "Believe me, I have the will, all the will, to help you. And the terms are not mine. Only I would have you remember this, Messer Blondel: that others may do what you will not, so that you may after all find that you have cast life away, and no one the better. Baudichon, for instance, plays the Brutus in public. But he is a fearful man, and a timid, and to save himself and his family—he thinks much of his family—he would do that you will not."

"He would do it!" the Syndic cried passionately. And he struck the table. "He would, curse him!"

"And he would not forget," Basterga continued, with a meaning nod, "that you had miscalled him!"

"No! But I will be before him!" The Syndic was on his feet again, shaking like a leaf.

"Ay?" Basterga blew his nose to hide the flash of triumph that shone in his eyes. "You will be wise? Well, I am not surprised. I thought that you would not be so mad —that no man could be so mad as to throw away life for a shadow!"

"But mind you," Blondel snarled, "the proof. I must have the proof," he repeated. He would fain persuade himself that his surrender depended on a condition; fain hide his shame under a show of bargaining. "The proof, man, or I will not take a step."

"You shall have it."

"To-day?"

"Within the hour."

"And if she be not mad—I believe you are deceiving

me, and it was the Remedium the girl took—if she be not mad——" the Syndic, stammering and repeating himself, broke off. He could not meet the other's eyes, and between a shame new to him, and the overpowering sense of what he had done, he was in a pitiable state. "Curse you," with violence, "I believe you have laid a trap for me!" he cried. "I say if she be not mad, I have done."

"Let it stand so," Basterga answered placidly. "Trust me, if she has taken the philtre she will be mad enough. Which reminds me that I also have a crow to pick with Mistress Anne."

"Curse her!"

"We will do more than that," Basterga murmured. "If she be not very good we will burn her, my friend.

> ' *Uritur infelix Dido, totaque videtur*
> *Urbe furens!* ' "

His eyes were cruel, and he licked his lips as he uttered the quotation.

CHAPTER XVIII

THE BARGAIN STRUCK

CLAUDE, at the first sign of peril, had put himself between Anne and the door; and, had not the fear which seized the girl at the sight of Basterga robbed her of the power to think, she must have thrilled with a new and delicious sensation. She, who had not for years known what it was to be sheltered behind another, was now to know the bliss of being protected. Nor did her lover remain on the defensive. He challenged the intruders.

"What is it?" he asked, as the Syndic crossed the threshold; which was darkened a moment later by the scholar's huge form. "What is your business here, Messer Syndic?"

"With you, none!" Blondel answered curtly, and pausing a little within the door, he cast a look, cold and searching, round the apartment. His outward composure hid a tumult of warring passions; shame and rage were at odds within him, and rising above both was a venomous desire to exact retribution from someone. "Nothing, with you!" he repeated. "You may stand aside, young man, or, better, go to your classes. What do you here at this hour, and idle, were the fitting question; and not, what is my business! Do you hear, sirrah?" with a rap of his staff of office on the floor. "Begone to your work!"

But Claude, who had been thirsting this hour past for realms to conquer and dragons to subdue, and who, with his mistress beside him, felt himself a match for any ten, was not to be put aside. His manhood rebelled against the notion of leaving Anne with men whose looks boded the worst. "I am at home," he replied, breathing a little more quickly, and aware that in defying the Syndic he was casting away the scabbard. "I am at home in this house. I have done no wrong. I am in no inn now, and I know of no right which you have to expel me without cause from my own lodging."

Blondel's lean face grew darker. "You beard me?" he cried.

"I beard no one," Claude answered hardily. "I am at home here, that is all. If you have lawful business here, do it. I am no hindrance to you. If you have no lawful business—and as to that," he continued, recalling with indignation the tricks which had been employed to remove him, "I have my opinion—I have as much right to be here as you! The more, as it is not very long," he went on, with a glance of defiance, directed at Basterga, "since you gave the man who now accompanies you the foulest of characters! Since you would have me rob him! Since you called him reprobate of the reprobate! Is he reprobate now?"

"Silence!"

"A corrupter of women, as you called him?"

"Liar!" the Syndic cried trembling with passion. "Be silent!" The thrust had found him unprepared. "He lies!" he stuttered, turning to his ally.

Basterga laughed softly. He had guessed as much; none the less he thought it time to interfere, lest his tool be put too much out of countenance. "Gently, young man," he said, "or perhaps you may go too far. I know you."

"He is a liar!" Blondel repeated.

"Probably," Basterga said, "but it matters not. It is enough that our business here lies not with him, but with this young woman. You seem to have taken her under your protection," he continued, addressing Claude, "and may choose, if you please, whether you will see her haled through the streets by force, or will suffer her to answer our questions here. As you please."

"Your questions?" Claude cried, recalling with rage the occasions on which he had heard this man insult her. "Hear me one moment, and I will very quickly prove——"

He was silent with the word on his lips. It was her hand on his arm that recalled the necessity of prudence. He bit his lip and stood glowering at them, longing to leap upon them. Meanwhile it was she who spoke.

"What do you wish?" she asked in a low voice.

Naturally courageous as she was, she could not have uttered a word but for the support of her lover. For the unexpected, the unimagined conjunction of these two, and their entrance together, had stricken her with a great fear. "What is your desire?" she repeated faintly.

"To see your mother," Basterga answered. "We have no business with you—at present," he added after a perceptible pause, and with a slight emphasis.

She caught her breath. "You want to see — my mother?" she faltered.

"I spoke plainly," Basterga replied with sternness. "That was what I said."

"What do you want with her?"

"That is our affair."

Pale to the lips, she hesitated. Yet, after all, why should they not go up and see her mother? Things were not to-day as they had been yesterday: or she had done in vain that which she had done, had sinned in vain if she had sinned. And that was a thing not to be considered. If they found her mother as she had left her, if they found the promise of the morning fulfilled, even their unexpected entrance would do no harm. Her mother was sane to-day: sane and well, as other people, thank God! It was on that account she had let her heart rise like a bird's to her lips.

Yet, when she opened her mouth to assent, she found the words with difficulty. "I do not know what you want," she said faintly, "but if you wish to see her, you can go up."

"Good!" Basterga replied, and advancing, he opened the staircase door, then made way for the Syndic to ascend first. "Good! The uppermost floor, Messer Blondel," he continued, holding the door wide. "The stairs are narrow, but I think I can promise you that at the top you will find all you want."

He could not divest his tone of the triumph he felt. Slight as the warning was, it sufficed; while the last word was still on his lips, she snatched the door from his grasp, closed it and stood panting before it. What inward monitors had spoken to her, what she had seen, what she had heard, besides that note of triumph in Basterga's voice matters not. Her mind was changed.

"No!" she cried. "You do not go up! No!"

"You will not let us see her?" Basterga exclaimed.

"No!" Her breast heaving, she confronted them without fear.

In his surprise at her action the scholar had recoiled a step: he was fiercely angry. "Come, girl, no nonsense," he said, roughly and brutally. "Make way! Or we shall have a little to say to you of what you did in my room last night! Do you mark me?" he continued. "I might have you punished for it, wench! I might have you whipped and branded for it! Do you mind me? You robbed me, and that which you took——"

"I took at his instigation!" she retorted, pointing an accusing finger at Blondel, who stood gnawing his beard, hating the part he was playing, and hating still more this white-faced girl who had come so near to ruining, if she had not ruined, his last chance of life. Hate her? The Syndic hated her for the hour of anguish through which he had just passed, hated her for the price—he shuddered to think of it—which he must now pay for his life. He hated her for his present humiliation, he hated her for his future shame. She seemed to blame for all.

"You took it," Basterga answered, acknowledging her words only by a disdainful shrug, "and gave it to your mother. Why, I care not. Now that you see we know so much, will you let us go up?"

"No!" She faced him bravely and steadfastly; love cast out fear. "No. If you know so much, you know also why I took it, and why I gave it to her." And then, the radiance of unselfish love illuminating her pallid face, "I would do it again were it to do," she said. "And again, and yet again! For you, I have done you wrong, I have robbed you, and you may punish me. I must bear it. But as to him," pointing to Messer Blondel, "I am innocent! Innocent," she repeated firmly. "For he would have done it himself and for himself; it was he would have had me do it. And if I have done it, I have done it for another. I have robbed you, if need be I must pay the price; but that man has naught against me in this! And for the rest, my mother is well."

"Ah?"

"Ay, well! well!" she repeated, the light of joy soften-ing her eyes as she repeated the word. "Well! and I fear nothing."

Basterga laughed unpleasantly. "Well?" he said. "Well is she? Then let us go up and see her. If she be well, why not?"

"No!"

"Why not?"

She did not answer, but she did not make way.

"Why not? I will tell you if you please," he said. "And it will make you pipe to another tune. You have given her, young woman, that which will make her worse, and not better!"

"She is better!"

"For an hour, or for twelve hours!" he retorted. "That certainly. Then worse."

"No!"

"No? But I see what it is," he continued—and alas his voice strengthened the fear that like a dead hand was clos-ing on her heart and staying it; deepened the terror that like a veil was falling before her eyes and darkening the room; so that she had much ado, gripping finger-nails into palms, to keep her feet and let herself from fainting. "I see what it is. You would fain play Providence," he con-tinued, "that is it, is it? You would play Providence? Then come! Come then, and see what kind of Providence it is you have played. We will see if you are right or I am right! And if she be well, or if she be ill!" And again he moved toward the staircase door.

But she stood obstinately between him and the door. "No," she said. "You do not go up!" She was resolute. The fear that as she listened to his gibing tones had driven the colour from her face, had hardened it too. For—if he were right? If for that fear there were foundation? If that which the Syndic had led her to give and that which she had given, proved—though for a few hours it had seemed to impart marvellous vigour—useless or worse than useless? Then the need to keep these men from her mother was the greater, the more desperate. How they could be kept from her, or for how long it was possible to keep them, she did not pause to consider, any more than the she-wolf that crouches, snarling, between her whelps and the hunt, counts odds. It was enough for her that if they were right the worst had come, and naught lay between her mother's weakness and their cruel eyes and judgments but her own feeble strength.

Or no! she was wrong in that; she had forgotten! As she spoke, and as Basterga with a scowl repeated the order to stand aside, Claude put her gently but irresistibly by, and took her place. The young man's eyes were bright, his colour high. "You will not go up!" he said, a mocking note of challenge, replying to Basterga's tone, in his voice. "You will not go up."

"Fool! Will you prevent us?"

"You will not go up! No!"

In the very act of falling on the lad, Basterga recoiled. Claude had not been idle while the others disputed. He had gone to the corner for his sword, and it was the glittering point, suddenly whipped out and flickered before his eyes that gave the scholar pause, and made him leap back. "Pollux!" he cried. "Are you mad? Put down! Put down! Do you see the Syndic? Do you know," stamping his foot, "that it is penal to draw in Geneva?"

"I know that you are not going upstairs!" Claude answered gently. He was radiant. He would not have exchanged his position for a crown. She was looking, and he was going to fight.

"You fool," Basterga retorted, "we have but to call the watch from the Tertasse and you will be haled to the lock-up, and gaoled and whipped, if not worse! And that jade with you; *Stultus es?* Do you hear? Messer Syndic, will you be thwarted in this fashion? Call these lawbreakers to order and bid them have done!"

"Put up!" the Syndic cried, hoarse with rage. He was beside himself, when he thought of the position in which he had placed himself. He looked at the two as if he would fain have slain them where they stood. "Or I call the watch, and it will be the worse for you," he continued. "Do you hear me? Put up?"

"He shall not go upstairs!" Claude answered, breathing quickly. He was pale, but utterly and fixedly resolved. If Basterga made a movement to attack him, he would run him through whatever the consequences.

"Then, fool, I will call the watch!" Blondel babbled, fairly beside himself.

Claude had no answer to that; only they should not go up. It was the girl's readier wit furnished the answer.

"Call them!" she cried, in her clear voice. "Call the watch, Messer Syndic, and I will tell them the whole story. What Messer Blondel would have me do, and get, and give."

"It was for the State!" the Syndic hissed.

"And is it for the State that you come to-day with that man?" she retorted, and with her outstretched finger accused Basterga of unspoken things. "That man! Last night you would have had me rob him. The day before he was a traitor. To-day he and you are one. Are one! What are you plotting together?"

Strange how the Syndic shrank from the other's side under the prick of her words—words that, uttered at random, flew, straight as the arrow that slew Ahab, to the joint of his armour! "To-day you and that man are one," she repeated. "One! What are you plotting together?"

She knew as much as that, did she? She knew that they were one, that they were plotting together; while in the Council men were clamouring for the Paduan's arrest, and were growing suspicious because he was not arrested —Baudichon, whom he had called a fat hog, and Petitot, that slow, plodding sleuth-hound of a patriot. What if light fell on the true state of things—and less than the girl had said might cast that light? Then the warrant might go, not for the Paduan only, but for himself. Ay, for him! For with an enemy lying ever within a league of the gates warrants flew quickly in Geneva. Men who sleep ill of nights, and take the cock-crow for war's alarum, are suspicious, and, once roused, without ruth or mercy.

There was the joint in his harness. Once let his name be published with Basterga's—as must happen if the watch were summoned and the girl spoke out—and no one could say where the matter might end, or what suspicions might not be awakened. Nay, the matter was worse, more perilous and more lightly balanced; for, setting himself aside, none the less was a brawl that brought up Basterga's name, a thing to be shunned. The least thing might precipitate the scholar's arrest; his arrest must lead to the loss of the Remedium, if it existed; and the loss of the Remedium to the loss of that, which Messer Blondel had come to value the more dearly the more he sacrificed to keep it—the Syndic's life.

He dared not call the watch, and he dared not use or permit violence. As he awoke to those two facts, he stood blinking in dismayed silence, swallowing his rage, and hating the girl and hating the man with a dumb hatred. Though the reasons which weighed with him were unknown to the two, they could not be blind to his fear, to his baffled mien; and had he been alone they might have taken victory for certain. But Basterga was not one to be so lightly thwarted. He had impressed on them a vivid sense of his personality. His intellect, his wit, his very mass intimidated. And therefore it was with as much relief as surprise that Anne read in his face the reflection of the other's doubts, and saw that he, too, gave back.

"You are two fools!" he said. "Two great, big fools!" There was resignation, there was something that was almost approval in his tones. "You do not know what you are doing! Is there no way of making you hear reason?"

"You cannot go up," Anne said. She had won, it seemed, without knowing how she had won.

Basterga grunted; and then "Ah, well," he said, addressing Claude, "if I had you in the fields, my lad, it would not be that bit of metal would save you!" And he spouted with appropriate gesture—

    " ' —*Illum fidi aequales, genua aegra trahentem*
       Jactantemque utroque caput, crassumque cruorem

Ore ejectantem mixtosque in sanguine dentes
Ducunt ad navis! '

Half an hour in my company, and you would not be so
bold."

Claude smiled with pardonable contempt, but made no
reply, nor did he change his attitude.

"Come!" Blondel muttered, addressing his ally with his
eyes averted. "I have reasons at present for letting them
be!" They were strange reasons, to judge by the hang-
dog look of the proud magistrate. "But I shall know how
to deal with them by and by. Come, man, come!" he repeated impatiently. And he turned toward the door and
unlocked it.

Basterga moved reluctantly after him. "Ay, we go
now," he said, with a look full of menace. "But wait
awhile! Cæsar Basterga does not forget, and his turn will
come! Where is my cap?"

He had let it fall on the floor, and he turned to pick it
up, stooping slowly and with difficulty as stout men do.
As he raised himself, his head still low, he butted it suddenly and with an activity for which no one would have
given him credit full into Claude's chest. The unlucky
young man, who had lowered his weapon the instant before, fell back with a "sough" against the wall, and leant
there, pale and breathless. Anne uttered one scream, then
the scholar's huge arm enfolded her neck and drew her
backward against his breast.

"Up! up! Messer Blondel!" he cried sharply. "Now
is your chance! Up and surprise her!" And with his dis-
engaged hand he gripped Claude, for further safety, by
the collar. "Up! I will keep them quiet!"

The Syndic wasted a moment in astonishment, then he took in the situation and the other's cleverness. Before Basterga had ceased to speak, he was at the door of the staircase, and had dragged it open. But as he set his foot on the lowest stair, Anne, held as she was against Basterga's breast, and almost stifled by the arm which covered her mouth, managed to clutch the Syndic by his skirts, and, once having taken hold, held him with the strength of despair. In vain he struggled and strove and wrestled to jerk himself free; in vain Basterga, hampered by Claude, tried to drag the girl away—Blondel came away with her! She clung to him, and even, freeing her mouth for a moment, succeeded in uttering a scream.

"Curse her!" Basterga foamed: and had he had a hand to spare would have struck her down. "Pull, man, have you no strength! Let go, you vixen! Let go, or——"

He tried to press her throat, but in changing his hold, allowed her to utter a second scream, louder, more shrill, more full of desperate passion than the other. At the same instant a chair, knocked down by Blondel in his efforts, fell with a crash, throwing down a pewter platter; and Claude, white and breathless as he was, began to struggle seeing his mistress so handled. The four swayed to and fro. Another moment, and either the Syndic must have jerked himself free, or the contest must have attained to dimensions that could not escape the notice of the neighbours, when a sound—a sound from within, from upstairs, stayed the tumult, as by magic.

Blondel ceased to struggle, and stood aghast. Basterga relaxed his hold upon his prisoners and listened. Claude leant back against the wall. The girl alone—she alone moved. Without speaking, without looking, as a bird flies to its young, she sprang to the stairs and fled up them.

The maniacal laugh, the crazy words—a moment only, they heard them; and then the door above, which the poor woman, so long bedridden, had managed in her frenzy of fear to open, closed on the sounds and stifled them. But enough had been heard: enough to convince Blondel, enough to justify Basterga, enough to change the fortunes of more than one in the room. The scholar's eyes met the Syndic's.

"Are you satisfied?" he asked, in a low tone.

Blondel, breathing hard, nodded.

"You heard?"

He nodded a second time. He looked scared.

"Then you have enough to burn the old witch and the young one with her!" Basterga replied. He turned his small eyes, sparkling with malignity, on the young man, who stood against the wall, pale, and but half recovered from the blow he had sustained. "You thought to thwart me, did you, Messer Claude? You thought yourself clever enough to play with Cæsar Basterga, did you? To hold at bay—oh, clever fellow—a magistrate and a scholar! And defy us both! Now I will tell you what will come of it!" He shook his great finger in front of the young man. "Your pretty bit of pink and white will burn! Burn, see you! A show for the little boys, a holiday for the young men and the young women, a treat for the old men, who will see her white limbs writhe in the smoke! Ha!" as Claude, with a face of horror, would have waved him away, "that touches you, does it? You had not thought of that? Nay, you had not thought of other things. I tell you, before the sun sets this evening, this house shall

be anathema! Before night what we have heard will be
known abroad, and there will be much added to it. There
was a child died in the fourth house from this on Sunday!
It will be odd if she did not overlook it. And the young
wife of the Lieutenant at the Porte Tertasse, who has
ailed since her marriage—a pale thing; who knows but
he looked this way once and Mistress Anne thought ill of
his defection? Ha! Ha! You would cross Cæsar Basterga, would you? No, Messer Claude," he set his huge
foot on the fallen sword which Claude had made a movement to recover. "I fight with other weapons than that!
And if you lay a finger on me"—he extended his arms to
their widest extent—"I will crush the life out of you. That
is better," as Claude stood glaring helplessly at him, "I
teach you prudence, at any rate. And as," with a sneer,
"you are so apt at learning, I will do you, if you choose,
a greater kindness than man ever did you, or woman
either!"

The young man, breathing quickly, did not speak. Perhaps his eyes were watching for an opening; for at the
least appearance of one he would have flung himself upon
his enemy.

"You do not choose. And yet I will do it. In one
word—Go!

> *' Teque bis, puer, eripe flammis! ' "*

He pointed to the door with a gesture tragic enough.
"Go! Go and live, for if you stay you die! Wait not until the chain is drawn before the door, until boards darken
the windows, and men cross the street when they would
pass! Until women hide their heads as they go by, and

the market will not sell, nor the water run for you! For then, as surely as she will perish miserably, you will perish with her!"

"So be it!" Claude cried. And in his turn he pointed, not without dignity, to the door. "Go you, and our blood be upon your head!"

Basterga shrugged his shoulders, and in a moment put the thing and his grand manner away from him. "Enough! we will go," he said. "You are satisfied, Messer Syndic? Yes. Farewell, young sir, you have my last word." And while the young man stood glowering at him, he opened the street door, and the two passed out.

"You will not go on with this?" Blondel muttered with a backward gesture, as the two paused.

"Nothing," Basterga answered in a low voice, "will suit our purpose better. It will amuse Geneva, and fill men's mouths, till the time comes. For you, too, Messer Blondel," he continued with a piercing look, "will live and not die, I take it?"

The other knew, then, that the hour had come to set his seal to the bargain: and equally, that if at this eleventh hour he would return, the path was open. But *facilis*— too well known is the rest, and the grip which a strong nature gains on a weaker, and how hardly fear, once admitted, is cast out. Within the Syndic's sight rose one of the gates, almost within touch rose the rampart of the city, long his own, which he was asked to betray. The mountains of his native land, pure, cold and sunlit, stood up against the blue depth of winter sky, eloquent of the permanence of things, and the insignificance of men. The contemplation of the one and the other turned his cheek a shade paler and struck terror to his heart, but did not stay him. His eyes avoiding the other's gaze, his face shrinking and pitiable, shame already his portion, he nodded.

"Precisely," Basterga said. "Then nothing can better serve our purpose than this. Let your officers know what you have heard, and know that you would hear more— of this house. That, and a hint of evil practices and witch's spells, dropped here and there, will give your townsfolk something to talk of and stare at and swallow, until our time comes."

"But if I bid them watch this house," Blondel muttered weakly—how fast, how fast the thing was passing out of his hands!—"attention will be called to you, and then, Messer Basterga——"

"My work is done here," Basterga replied calmly. "I have crossed that threshold for the last time. When I leave you—and it is time we parted—I go out of the gates, not again to return until—until things have been brought to the point at which we would have them, Messer Blondel."

"And that," the Syndic said with a shudder, and a scared look round, "will be—when?"

"Toward the longest night. Say, in a week or so from now. The precise moment—that and other things, I will let you know by a safe mouth."

"But the Remedium? That first!" the Syndic muttered, a scowl, for a second, darkening his face.

Basterga smiled. "Have no fear," he replied. "That first, by all means. And afterward, Geneva."

CHAPTER XIX

THE DEPARTURE OF THE RATS

THE wood-ash on the hearth had sunk lower and grown whiter. The last flame that had licked the black sides of the great pot in the chimney-place had died down among the expiring embers. Only under the largest log glowed a tiny cavern, carbuncle-hued; and still Claude walked restlessly from the window to the door, or listened with a frowning face at the foot of the stairs. One hour, two hours had passed since the Syndic's departure with Basterga; and still Anne remained with her mother and made no sign. Once, spurred by anxiety and the thought that he might be of use, Claude had determined to mount and seek her; but half way up the stairs his courage had failed, he had recoiled from a scene so tender, and so sacred. He had descended and fallen again to moving to and fro, and listening, and staring remorsefully at the weapon—it lay where he had dropped it, on the floor—that had failed him in his need.

He had their threats in his ears, and by and by the horror of inaction, the horror of sitting still and awaiting the worst with folded hands, overcame him; and in a panic planning flight for them all, flight, however hopeless, however desperate, he hurried into his bed-closet, and began to pack his possessions. He packed impulsively until even the fat text-books bulked in his bundle, and the folly of flying for life with a Cæsar and Melancthon on his back struck him. Then he turned all out on the floor in a fury of haste, lest she should surprise him, and think that he had had it in his mind to desert her.

Back he went on that to the living-room with its dying fire and lengthening shadows; and there he resumed his solitary pacing. The room lay silent, the house lay silent; even the rampart without, which the biting wind kept clear of passers. He tried to reason on the position, to settle what would happen, what steps Basterga and Blondel would take, how the blow they threatened would fall. Would the officers of the Syndic enter and seize the two helpless women and drag them to the guard-house? In that case, what should he do, what could he do, since it was most unlikely that he would be allowed to go with them or see them? For a time the desperate notion of bolting and barring the house and holding it against the law possessed his mind; but only to be quickly dismissed. He was not yet mad enough for that. In the meantime was there anyone to whom he could appeal? Any course he could adopt?

The sound of the latch rising in its socket drew his eyes to the outer door. It opened and he saw Louis Gentilis on the threshold. Holding the door ajar, the young man peered in. He met Claude's eyes, and looked round, as if to seek the protection of Anne's presence; failing to find her, he made as if he would shut the door again, and go. But apparently he saw that Claude, thoroughly dispirited, was making no motion to carry out his threats of vengeance, and he thought better of it. Coming slowly in, he closed the door after him. Turning his cap in his hand he crossed the floor, and with his eyes slyly fixed on Claude, he made without a word for his bed-closet, and closed the door behind him.

His silence was strange, and his furtive manner impressed Claude unpleasantly. They seemed to imply a knowledge that boded ill; nor was the impression they had made weakened when, two minutes later, the closet door opened again, and he came out.

"What is it?" Claude asked, speaking sharply. He was not going to put up with mystery of this sort.

For answer Louis' eyes met his a moment; then the young man, without speaking, slid across the room to a chair on which lay a book. He took up the volume; it was his. He took further stock of the room, and discovered another possession—or so it seemed—approached it and took seisin of it in the same dumb way; and so with another and another. Then blinking and looking askance, he passed his eyes from side to side to learn if he had overlooked anything.

But Claude's patience, though prolonged by curiosity, was at an end. He took a step forward, and had the satisfaction of seeing Louis drop his air of mystery, and recoil two paces. "If you don't speak," Claude cried, "I will break every bone in your body! Do you hear, you sneaking rogue? Do you forget that you are in my debt already? Tell me in two words what this dumb show means, or I will have payment for all!"

Master Louis cringed, divided between the desire to flee and the fear of losing his property. "You will be foolish if you make any fuss here," he muttered, his arm raised to ward off a blow. "Besides, I'm going," he continued, swallowing nervously as he spoke. "Let me go."

"Going?"

"Yes."

"Do you mean," Claude exclaimed in astonishment, "that you are going for good?"

"Yes, and"—with a look of sinister meaning in his blinking eyes—"if you will take my advice you will go too. That is all."

"Why? Why?" Claude repeated.

Louis' only answer was a shudder, which told Claude that if the other did not know all, he knew much. Dismayed and confounded, Mercier stepped back, and, with a secret grin of satisfaction, Louis turned again to his task of searching the room. He found at last that for which he had been looking—his cloak. He disentangled it, with a peculiar look, from a woman's hood, contact with which he avoided with care. That done he cast it over his arm, and got back into his closet. Claude heard him moving there, and presently he emerged a second time.

Precisely as he did so Claude caught the sound of a light footstep on the stairs, the stair door opened, and Anne, her face weary, but composed, came in. Her first glance fell on Louis, who, with his sack and cloak on his arm, was in the act of closing the closet door. Habit carried her second look to the hearth.

"You have let the fire go out," she said. Then, turning to Louis, in a voice cold and even, "You are going?" she continued.

He muttered that he was, his face a medley of fear and spite and shame.

She nodded, but to Claude's astonishment expressed no surprise. Meanwhile, Louis, after dropping first his cloak and then his sack, in his haste to be gone, shuffled his way to the door. The two looked on, without moving or speaking, while he opened it, carried out his bag, and, turning about, closed the door upon himself. They heard his footsteps move away.

At length Claude spoke. "The rats, I see, are leaving," he muttered.

"Yes, the rats!" she echoed, and carried for a moment her eyes to his. Then she knelt on the hearth, and uncovering the under side of the log, where a little fire still smouldered, she fed it with two or three fir-cones, and, stooping low, blew steadily on them until they caught fire and blazed. He stood looking down at her and marvelled at the strength of mind that allowed her to stoop to trifles, or to think of fires at such a time as this. He forgot that habit is of all stays the strongest, and that to women a thousand trifles make up—God reward them for it—the work of life: a work which instinct moves them to pursue, though the heavens fall.

Several hours had elapsed since he had entered hot-foot to see her; and the day was beginning to wane. The flame of the blazing fir-cones, a hundred times reflected in the rows of pewter plates and the surface of the old oaken dressers, left the corners of the room in shadow. Immediately within the windows the daylight held its own; but when she rose and turned to him her back was toward the casement, and the firelight which lit up her face flickered uncertainly, and left him in doubt whether she were moved or not.

"You have eaten nothing!" she said—while he stood pondering what she would say. "And it is four o'clock! I am sorry!" Her tone, which took shame to herself, gave him a new surprise.

He stopped her as she turned to the dresser. "Your mother is better, I hope?" he said gently.

"She is herself now," she replied, with a slight quaver, and without looking at him. And she went about her work.

Did she know? Did she understand? In his world was only one fact, in his mind only one tremendous thought: the fact of their position, the thought of their isolation, of their peril. In her treatment of Louis, she had seemed to show knowledge and a comprehension as wide as his own. But if she knew all, could she be thus calm? Could she go about her daily tasks? Could she cut and lay and fetch with busy fingers, and all in silence?

He thought not; and though he longed to consult her, to reassure her and comfort her, to tell her that the very isolation, the very peril in which they stood were a happiness and a joy to him, whatever the issue, because he shared them with her, he would not, by reason of that doubt. He did not yet know the courage that underlies the gentlest natures: nor did he guess that even as it was a joy to him to stand beside her in peril, so it was a joy to her, even in that hour, to come and go for him, to cut his bread and lay for him, to draw his wine from the great cask under the stairs, and pour for him in the tall horn mug.

And little said. By him, because he shrank from opening her eyes to the danger of their position; by her, because her mind was full and she could not trust herself to speak calmly. But he knew that she, too, had fasted since morning, and he made her eat with him: and it was in the thoughts of each that they had never eaten together before. For commonly Anne took her meal with the mother, or ate as the women of her time often ate, standing, alone, when others had finished. There are moments when the simplest things put on the beauty and significance of rites, and this first eating together at the small table on the fire-lit hearth, was one of such moments. He saw that she did eat; and this care for her, and the reverence of his manner, so moved her, that at last tears rose and choked her, and to give her time and to hide his own feelings, he stood up and affected to get something from the fireside.

Before he turned again, the latch rattled and the door flew open. The freezing draught that entered, arrested him between the table and the fire. The intruder was Grio. He stood an instant scowling on them, then he entered and closed the door. He eyed the two with a sneering laugh, and, turning, flung his cloak on a chair. It was ill-aimed and fell to the ground.

"Why the devil don't you light?" he cried violently. "Eh?" And he added something in which the words "Old hag's devilry!" were alone audible. "Do you hear?" he continued, more coherently. "Why don't you light? What black games are you playing, I'd like to know? I want my things!"

Claude's fingers tingled, but danger and responsibility are sure teachers, and he restrained himself. Neither of them answered, but Anne fetched the lamp, and kindling a splinter of wood lighted it, and placed it on the table. Then bringing the Spaniard's rushlight from the three or four that stood on the dresser, she lighted it and held it out to him.

"Set it down!" he said, with tipsy insolence. He was not quite sober. "Set it down! I am not going to—hic!

—risk my salvation! Avaunt Satan! It is possible to palm the evil one, like a card, I am told, and—hic!—soul out, devil in, all lost as easy as candle goes out!"

He had taken his candle with an unsteady hand, and had blown it out. She restrained Claude by a look, and patiently taking the rushlight from Grio, she re-lit it and set it on the table for him to take.

"As a candle goes out!" he repeated, eyeing it with drunken wisdom. "Candle out, devil in, soul lost, there you have it in three words, clever as any of your long-winded preachers! But I want my things. I'm going before it is too late. Advise you to go too, young man," he hiccoughed, "before you are overlooked. She is a witch! She's the devil's mark on her, I tell you! I'd like to have the finding it!" And with an ugly leer he advanced a step as if he would lay hands on her.

She shrank back then, and Claude's eyes blazed. Fortunately, the bully's mind passed to the first object of his coming; or, perhaps, he was sober enough to read a warning in the younger man's face.

"Oh! time enough," he said. "You are not so nice always, I'll be bound. And things come—hic—to those who wait! I don't belong to your Sabbaths I suppose, or you'd be freer! But I want my things, and I am going to have them! I defy thee, Satan! And all thy works!"

Still growling under his breath he burst open the staircase door, and stumbled noisily upward, the light wavering in his hand. Anne's eyes followed him; she had advanced to the foot of the stairs, and Claude understood the apprehension that held her. But the sounds did not penetrate to the room on the upper floor, or Madame Royaume did not take the alarm; perhaps she slept. After assuring herself that Grio had entered his room the girl returned to the table.

The Spaniard had spoken with brutal plainness; it was impossible to ignore what he had said, or to be under any illusion as to the girl's knowledge of her peril. Claude's eyes met hers: for a moment the anguished human soul peered through the mask of constancy, for a moment the woman in her, shrinking from the ordeal and the fire, from shame and death, thrust aside the veil, and held out quivering, piteous hands to him. But it was for a moment only. Before he could speak she was brave as before, quiet as he had ever seen her, patient, mistress of herself. "It is as you said," she muttered, smiling wanly, "the rats are leaving us."

"Vermin!" he whispered. He could not trust himself to say more. His voice shook and his eyes were full.

"They have not—lost time," she continued in a low tone. She did not cease to listen, nor did her eyes leave the staircase door. "Louis first, and now Grio. How has it reached them so quickly, do you think?"

"Louis is hand in glove with the Syndic," he murmured.

"And Grio?"

"With Basterga."

She nodded. "What do you think they will do—first?" she whispered. And again—it went to his heart—the woman's face, fear-drawn, showed as it were beneath the mask with which love and faith and a noble resignation had armed her. "Do you think they will denounce us at once?"

He shook his head in sheer inability to foresee; and then, seeing that she continued to look anxiously for his answer, that answer which he knew to be of no value, for minute by minute the sense of his helplessness was weighing upon him, "It may be," he muttered. "God knows. When Grio is gone we will talk about it."

She began, but always with a listening ear and an eye to the open door, to remove from the table the remains of their meal. Midway in her task, she glanced askance at the window, under the impression that someone had looked through it; and in any case now the lamp was lit it exposed them to the curiosity of the rampart. She was going to close the shutters when Claude interposed, raised the heavy shutters and bolted and barred them. He was turning from them when Grio's step was heard descending.

Strange to say the Spaniard's first glance was at the windows, and he looked genuinely taken aback, when he saw that they were closed. "Why the devil did you shut?" he exclaimed, in a rage; and passing Anne with a sidelong movement, he flung a heavy bundle on the floor by the door. As he turned to go up again he met her eyes, and backing from her he made with two of his fingers the ancient sign which southern peoples still use to ward off the evil eye. Then, half shamefacedly, half recklessly, he blundered upstairs again. A moment, and he came stumbling down; but this time he was careful to keep the great bundle he bore between himself and her eyes, until he had got the door open.

That precaution taken, as if he thought the free cold air which entered would protect him from spells, he showed himself at his ease, threw down his bundle and faced her with an air of bravado.

"I need not have feared," he said with a tipsy grin, "but I had forgotten what I carry. I have a hocus-pocus here" —he touched his breast—"written by a wise man in Ra-

HE MADE,

WITH TWO

FINGERS, THE

ANCIENT SIGN

USED TO WARD

OFF THE

EVIL EYE

venna, and sealed with a dead Goth's hand, that is proof against devil or dam! And I defy thee, mistress."

"Why?" she cried. "Why?" And the note of indignation in her voice, the passionate challenge of her eyes, enforced the question. In the human mind is a desire for justice that will not be denied; and even from this drunken ruffian a sudden impulse bade her demand it. "Why should you defy me or fear me? What have I done to you, what have I done to anyone," she continued, with noble resentment, "that you should spread this of me? You have eaten and drunk at my hand a hundred times; have I poisoned or injured you? I have looked at you a hundred times; have I overlooked you? You have lain down under this roof by night a hundred times; have I harmed you sleeping or waking, full moon or no moon?"

For answer he leered at her slyly. "Not a whit," he said. "No."

"No?" Her colour rose.

"No; but you see"—with a grin—"it never leaves me, my girl." He touched his breast. "While I wear that, I am safe."

She gasped. "Do you mean that I——"

"I do not know what you would have done—but for that!" he retorted. "Maimed me or wizened me, perhaps! Or, may be, made me waste away as you did the child that died three doors away last Sunday!"

Her face changed slowly. Prepared as she had been for the worst by many an hour of vigil beside her mother's bed, the horror of this precise accusation—and such an accusation—overcame her. "What?" she cried hoarsely. "You dare to say that I——that I——" she could not finish.

But her eyes lightened, her form dilated with passion; and tipsy, ignorant, brutish as he was, the Spaniard could not be blind to the indignation, the resentment, the very wonder which stopped her breath and choked her utterance. At the sight some touch of shame, some touch of pity, made itself felt in the dull recesses even of his brain. "I don't say it," he muttered awkwardly. "It is what they are saying in the street."

"In the street?"

"Ay, where else?" He knew who said it, for he knew whence his orders came: but he was not going to tell her. Yet the spark of kindliness which she had kindled still lived—how could it be otherwise in presence of her youth and gentleness? "If you'll take my advice," he continued roughly, "you'll not show yourself in the streets unless you wish to be mishandled, my girl. It will be time enough when the time comes. Even now, if you were to leave your old witch of a mother and get good protection, there is no knowing but you might be got clear! You are a fair bit of red and white," with a grin. "And it is not far to Savoy! Will you come if I risk it?"

A gesture, half refusal, half loathing, answered him.

"Oh, very well!" he said. The short-lived fit of pity passed from him; he scowled. "You'll think differently when they have the handling of you. I'm glad to be going, for where there's one fire there's apt to be more; and I am a Christian, no matter who's not! Let who will burn, I'll not!"

He picked up one bundle and, carrying it out, raised his voice. A man, who had shrunk, it seemed, from entering the house, showed his face in the light which streamed from the door. To this fellow he gave one bundle, and shouldering the other, he went heavily out, leaving the door wide open behind him.

Claude strode to it and closed it angrily; but not so quickly that he had not a glimpse of three or four pairs of eyes staring in out of the darkness; eyes so curious, so fearful, so quickly and noiselessly withdrawn—for even while he looked, they were gone—that he went back to the hearth with a shiver of apprehension.

Fortunately, she had not seen them. She stood where he had left her, in the same attitude of amazement into which Grio's accusation had cast her. As she met his gaze —then, at last, she melted. The lamplight showed her eyes brimming over with tears; her lips quivered, her breast heaved, under the storm of resentment.

"How dare they say it?" she cried. "How dare they? That I should harm a child? A helpless child?" And unable to go on, she held out protesting hands to him. "And my mother? My mother, who never injured anyone or harmed a hair of anyone's head! That she—that they should say that of her! That they should set that to her! But I will go this instant—with resolution—to the child's mother. She will hear me. She will know and believe me. A mother? Yes, I will go to her!"

"Not now," he said. "Not now, Anne!"

"Yes, now," she persisted, deaf to his voice. She snatched up her hood from the ground on which it had fallen, and began to put it on.

He seized her arm. "No, not now," he said firmly. "You shall not go now. Wait until daylight. She will listen to you more coolly then."

She resisted him. "Why?" she said.

"I am sure of it," he urged. "People fancy things at

night. I know it is so. If she saw you enter out of the darkness"—the girl with her burning eyes, her wet cheeks, her disordered hair looked wild enough—"she might refuse to believe you. Besides——"

"What?"

"I will not have you go now," he said firmly. That instant it had flashed upon him that one of the faces he had seen outside was the face of the dead child's mother. "I will not let you go," he repeated. "Go in the daylight. Go to-morrow morning. Go then if you will!" He did not choose to tell her that he feared for her instant safety, if she went now; that, if he had his will, the streets would see her no more for many a day.

She gave way. She took off her hood, and laid it on the table. But for several minutes she stood, brooding darkly and stormily, her hands fingering the strings. To foresee is not always to be forearmed. She had lived for months in daily and hourly expectation of the blow which had fallen; but not the more easily for that could she brook the concrete charge. Her heart burned, her soul was on fire. Justice, give us justice though the heavens fall, is an instinct planted deep in man's nature! Of the Mysterious Passion of our Lord our finite minds find no part worse than the anguish of innocence condemned. A child? She to hurt a child? And her mother? Her mother, so harmless, so ignorant, so tormented! She to hurt a child?

After a time, nevertheless, the storm began to subside. But with it died the hope which is inherent in revolt; and in proportion, as she grew more calm, the forlornness of her situation rose more clearly before her. At last that had happened which she had so long expected to happen. The thing was known. Soon the full consequences would be upon her, the consequences on which she dared not dwell. Shudderingly she tried to close her eyes to the things that might lie before her, to the things at which Grio had hinted, the things of which she had lain thinking—even while they were distant and uncertain—through many a night of bitter fear and fevered anticipation.

They were at hand now, and though she averted her thoughts, she knew it. But the wind is tempered to the shorn. Even as the prospect of future ill can dominate the present, embitter the sweetest cup, and render thorny the softest bed, so, sometimes, present good has the power to obscure the future evil. As Anne sank back on the settle, her trembling limbs almost declining to bear her, her eyes fell on her companion. Failing to rouse her, he had seated himself on the other side of the hearth, his elbows on his knees, his chin on his hands, in an attitude of deep thought. And little by little, as she looked at him, her cheeks grew, if not red, less pale, her eyes lost their tense and hopeless gaze. She heaved a quivering sigh, and slowly carried her look round the room.

Its homely comfort, augmented by the hour and the firelight, seemed to lap them round. The door was locked, the shutters were closed, the lamp burned cheerfully. And he sat opposite—sat as if they had been long married. The colour grew deeper in her face as she gazed; she breathed more quickly; her eyes shone. What evil cannot be softened, what misfortune cannot be lightened to a woman by the knowledge that she is loved by the man she loves? That where all have fled, he remains, and that neither fear of death nor word of man can keep him from her side?

He looked up in the end, and caught the look on her face, the look that a woman bestows on one man only in her life. In a moment he was on his knees beside her, holding her hands, covering them with kisses, vowing to save her, to save her—or to die with her!

CHAPTER XX

IN THE DARKENED ROOM

CLAUDE flung the cloak from his head and shoulders, and sat up. It was morning—morning, after that long, dear sitting together—and he stared confusedly about him. He had been dreaming, all night he had slept uneasily; but the cry that had roused him, the cry that had started that quick beating of the heart, the cry that still rang in his waking ears and frightened him, was no dream.

As he rose to his feet, his senses began to take in the scene; he remembered what had happened and where he was. The shutters were lowered and open. The cold grey light of the early morning at this deadest season of the year fell cheerlessly on the living-room; in which for the greater safety of the house he had insisted on passing the night. Anne, whose daily task it was to open the shutters, was up and had been down then; she had been down or whence the pile of fresh cones and splinters that crackled, and spirted flame about the turned log. Perhaps it was her mother's cry that had roused him; and she had re-ascended to her room.

He strode to the staircase-door, opened it softly and listened. No, all was silent above; and then a new notion struck him, and he glanced round. Her hood was gone. It was not on the table on which he had seen it last night.

It was so unlikely, however, that she had gone out without telling him that he dismissed the notion; and, somewhat recovered from the strange agitation into which the
cry had cast him, he yawned. He returned to the hearth
and knelt and re-arranged the sticks so that the air might
have freer access to the fire. Presently he would draw the
water for her, and fill the great kettle, and sweep the floor.
The future might be gloomy, the prospect might lower,
but the present was not without its pleasures.

All his life his slowness to guess the truth on this occasion was a puzzle to him. For the materials were his.
Slowly, gradually, as he crouched sleepily before the fire,
it grew upon him that there was a noise in the air; a confused sound, not of one cry, but of many, that came from
the street, from the rampart. A noise, now swelling a
little, now sinking a little, that seemed as he listened not
so distant as it had sounded a while ago. Not distant at
all, indeed; quite close—now! A sound of rushing water,
rather soothing; or, as it swelled, a sound of a crowd, a
gibing, mocking crowd. Yes, a crowd; and then in one
instant the change was wrought.

He was on his feet; he was at the door. He, who a moment before had nodded over the fire, watching the flames
grow, was transformed in five seconds into a furious man,
tugging at the door, wrestling madly with the unyielding
oak. Wrestling, and still the noise rose! And still he
strained in vain, back and sinew, strained until with a cry
of despair he found that he could not win. The door was
locked, the key was gone! He was a prisoner!

And still the noise that maddened him, rose. He sprang
to the right-hand window, the window nearest the commotion. He tore open a panel of the small leaded panes,

and thrust his head between the bars. He saw a crowd;
for an instant, in the heart of the crowd and raised above it,
he saw an uplifted arm and a white woman's face from
which blood was flowing. He drew in his head, and laid
his hands to one of the bars and flung his weight this way
and that, flung it desperately, heedless of injury. But in
vain. The lead that soldered the bar into the strong stone
mullion held, and would have held against the strength of
four. With heaving breast, and hands from which the
blood was starting, he stood back, glared round him, then
with a cry flung himself upon the other window, tore it open
and seized a bar—the middle one of the three. It was
loose he remembered. God! why had he not thought of it
before? Why had he wasted time?

He wasted no more, with those shouts of cruel glee in
his ears. The bar came out in his hands. He thrust himself feet first through the aperture. Slight as he was, it
was small for him, and he stuck fast at the hips, and had
to turn on his side. The rough edges of the bars scraped
the skin, but he was through, and had dropped to his feet,
the bar which he had plucked out still in his hands. For
a fraction of a second, as he alighted staggering, his eyes
took in the crowd, and the girl at bay against the wall. She
was raised a little above her tormentors by the steps on
which she had taken refuge.

On one side her hair hung loose, and the cheek beneath
it was cut and bleeding, giving her a piteous and tragic
aspect. Four out of five of her assailants were women;
one of these had torn her face with her nails. Streaks
of mud were mingled with the blood which ran down
her neck; and even as Claude recovered himself after the
drop from the window, a missile, eluding the bent arm

with which she strove to shield her face, struck and be-
spattered her throat where the collar of her frock had
been torn open—perhaps by the same rough clutch which
had dragged down her hair. The ring about her—like
all crowds in the beginning—were strangely silent; but a
yell of derision greeted this success, and a stone flew, nar-
rowly missing her, and another, and another. A woman,
holding a heavy Bible after the fashion of a shield, was
stooping and striking at her knees with a stick, striving to
bring her to the ground; and with the cruel laughter that
hailed the hag's ungainly efforts were mingled other and
more ugly sounds, low curses, execrations, and always one
fatal word, "Witch! Witch!"—fatal word spat at her by
writhing mouths, hissed at her by pale lips, tossed broad-
cast on the cold morning wind, to breed wherever it flew,
fear and hate and suspicion. For, even while they mocked
her they feared her, and shielded themselves against her
power with signs and crossings and the Holy Book.

To all, curse and blow and threat, she had only one
word. Striving patiently to shield her face, "Let me go!"
she wailed pitifully. "Let me go! Let me go!" Strange
to say, she cried even that but softly; as who should say,
"If you will not, kill me quietly, kill me without noise!"
Ay, even then with the blood running down her face, and
with those eyes more cruel than men's eyes hemming her
in, she was thinking of the mother whom she had sheltered
so long.

"Let me go! Let me go!" she cried.

"Witch, you shall go!" they answered, ruthlessly. "To
Hell!"

"Ay, with her dam! To the water with her! To the
water!"

"LET ME GO! LET ME GO!" SHE WAILED

"Look for the devil's mark! Search her! Again, Martha! Bring her down! Bring her down, and we'll soon see whether she bears it!"

Then he reached them. The man, one of the few present, who had bidden them search her fell headlong on his face in the gutter, struck behind as by a thunderbolt. The great Bible flew one way, the hag's stick flew another—and in its flight felled a second woman. In a twinkling Claude was on the steps, and in the heart of the crowd stood two people, not one; in a twinkling his arm was round the girl, his flaming, furious face confronted her tormentors, his blazing eyes beat down theirs! More than all, his iron bar, brandished recklessly this way and that, threatened the brains of the man or the woman who was bold enough to withstand him.

For he was beside himself with rage. He learned in that moment that he was of those who fight with joy and rejoicing, and laugh where others shake. The sight of that white, bleeding face, of that hanging hair, of that suppliant arm; above all, the sound of that patient "Let me go! Let me go!" that expected nothing and hoped nothing, had turned his blood to fire. The more numerous his opponents—if they were men—the better he would be pleased; and if they were women, such women, unsexed by hate and superstition, as he saw before him, women looking a millionfold more like witches than the girl they accused, the worse for them! His arm would not falter!

It seemed of steel indeed. The bar quivered like a reed in his grasp, his eyes darted hither and thither, he stood an inch taller than at other times. He was like the warhorse that sniffs the battle.

And yet he was cool, after a fashion. He must get her

home, and to do so he must not lose a moment. The
vantage of the steps on which they stood, raised a hand's
breadth above their assailants, was a thing to be weighed;
but it would not serve them, if these cursed women mus-
tered, and the cowardly crew before him throve to a mob.
He must home with her. But—the door was locked, and
she could only go in as he had come out. Still, she must go.

He thought all this between one stride and another—
and other thoughts thick as leaves falling in a wind. Then,
"Fools!" he thundered, and had her down the steps, and
was dragging her toward her own door before they
awoke from their surprise, or thought of attacking him.
The woman with the big Bible had had her fill—though
he had not struck her but her stick—and sat where she had
fallen in the mud. The other woman hugged herself in
pain. The man was in no hurry to be up, having once felt
Claude's knee in the small of his back. For a few seconds
no one moved; and when they recovered themselves he
was half way to the Royaumes' door.

They snatched up mud, then, and flung it after the pair
with shrill execrations. And the woman who had picked
up the stick hurled it in a frenzy after them, but wide of
the mark. A dozen stones fell round them, and the cry
of "The Witch! The Witch!"—cry so ominous, so cruel,
cry fraught with death for so many poor creatures—followed hard on them. But they were within five paces of
the door now, and if he could lift her to the window—

"The key!" she murmured in his ear. "The key is in
the lock!"

She had her wits, too, then, and her courage! He felt
a glow of pride, his arm pressed her more closely to him.
"Unlock it!" he answered, and leaving her to it, hav-

ing now no fear that she would faint or fall, he turned on the rabble with his bar.

But they were for words, not blows, a rabble of cowards and women. They turned tail with screams and fled to a distance, more than one falling in the sudden *volte face*. He made no attempt to pursue them along the rampart, but looked behind him, and found that she had opened the door. She had taken out the key, and was waiting for him to enter.

He went up the steps, entered, and she closed the door quickly. It shut out in a moment the hootings of the returning women. While she locked it on the inside, he raised the bars and slid them into their places. Then, not till then, he turned to her.

Her face averted, she was stanching the blood which trickled from her cheek. "It was the child's mother!" she faltered, a sob in her voice. "I went to her. I thought —that she would believe. Get me some water, please! I must go upstairs. She will be frightened."

He was astonished: on fire himself, with every pulse beating madly, he was prepared for her to faint, to fall, to fling herself into his arms in gratitude; prepared for everything but this self-forgetfulness. "Water?" he said doubtfully, "but had you not better—take some wine, Anne?"

"To wash! To wash!" she replied sharply, almost angrily. "How can I go to her in this state? And do you shut the shutters."

A stone had that moment passed through one of the panes. The rout of women were gathering before the house; the step she advised was plainly necessary. Fortunately the Royaumes' house, like all in the Corraterie—

which formed an inner line of defence pierced by the Tertasse Gate—had outside shutters of massive thickness, capable of being lowered from within. He closed these in
haste, and found, when he turned from the task and looked
for her—a small round hole in each shutter made things
dimly visible—that she was gone to soothe her mother.

He could not but love her the more for it. He could
not but respect her the more for her courage, for her
thoughtfulness, her self-denial. But when the heart is full
and would unburden itself, when the brain teems with
pent-up thoughts, when the excitement of action and of
peril wanes, and the mind would fain tell and hear and
compare and remember—then to be alone, to be solitary, is
to sink below one's self.

For a time, while his pulses still beat high, while the
heat of battle still wrought in him, and the noise without
continued, and there seemed a prospect of things to be
done, he stood up against this. Thump! Thump! They
were stoning the shutters. Let them! He placed the settle across the hearth, and in this way cut off the firelight
that might have betrayed those in the room to eyes peeping through the holes. By and by the shrill vixenish cries
rose louder, he caught the sound of voices in altercation,
and hoarse orders: then slowly and reluctantly the babel
seemed to pass away. An anxious moment followed: fear-
fully he listened for the knock of the law, the official summons which must make all his efforts useless. But it did
not come.

It was when the silence which ensued had lasted some
minutes that the strangeness and aloofness of his position
in this darkened room began to weigh on his spirits. His
eyes had adapted themselves to the gloom, and he could

make out the shapes of the furniture. But it was morning.
It was day.   Outside, the city was beginning to go about
its ordinary work, its ordinary life.   The streets were filling, the classes were mustering.   And he sat here in the
dark.   The longer he stared into the strange, depressing
gloom, the farther he seemed from life; the more solitary,
the more hopeless, the more ominous seemed the position.

Alone with two women whom the worst of fates threatened!   Whose pains and ultimate lot the brawl in which
he had lately taken part foreshadowed too clearly.   For
thus and with as little cause perished in those days thousands of the helpless and the friendless.   Alone with these
two, under the roof from which all others had fled, barred
with them behind the gloomy shutters until the hour came,
and their fellows, shuddering, cast them out—what chance
had he of escaping their lot?

Or what desire to escape it?   None, he told himself.
None!   But he who fights best when blows are to be struck
and things can be done finds it hard to sit still when it is
the inevitable that must be faced.   And while Claude told
himself that he had no desire to escape, since escape for her
was impossible, his mind sought desperately the means of
saving all.   The frontier lay but a league away.   Conceivably they might lower themselves from the wall by
night; conceivably his strength might avail to carry her
mother to the frontier.   But, alas! the crime of witchcraft
knew no frontier; the reputation of a witch once thrown
abroad, flew fast as the swiftest horse.   Before they had
been three days in Savoy, the women would be reported,
seized and examined; and their fate at Faucigny or Bonne-
ville would be no less tragic than in the Bourg du Four of
Geneva.

Yet, something must be done, something could surely be done. But what? The bravest caught in a net struggles the most desperately, and involves himself the most hopelessly. Claude felt himself caught in a net. He felt the deadly meshes cling about his limbs, the ropes fetter and benumb him. From the sunshine of youth, from freedom, from a life without care, he had passed in a few days into the grip of this anagke, this dire necessity, this dark ante-chamber of death. Was it wonderful that for a moment, recognising the sacrifice he was called upon to make and its inefficacy to save, he rebelled against the love that had drawn him to this fate, that had led him to this, that in others' eyes had ruined him? Ay, but for a moment only. Then with a heart bursting with pity for her, with love for her, he was himself. If it must be, it must be. The prospect was dark as the room in which he stood, confined and stifling, sordid, shameful; the end one which would make his name a marvel and an astonishment. But the prospect and the end were hers too; they would face them together. Haply he might spare her some one pang, haply he might give her some one moment of happiness, the support of one at least who knew her pure and spotless. And while he thought of it—surprise of surprises— he bowed his head on his folded arms and wept.

Not in pity for himself, but for her. It was the thought of her gentleness, her loving nature, her harmlessness— and the end this, the reward this—which overcame him; which swelled his breast until only tears could relieve it. He saw her as a dove struggling in cruel hands; and the pity which, had there been chance or hope, or any to smite, would have been rage, could find no other outlet. He wept like a woman, but it was for her.

And she who had descended unheard, and stood even now at the door, with a something almost divine in her face—a something that was neither love nor compassion, maid's fancy nor mother's care, but a mingling of all these, saw; and her heart bled for him. Her arms in fancy went round him, in fancy his head was on her breast, she comforted him. She, who a moment before had almost sunk down on the stairs, worn out by her sufferings and the strain of hiding them from her mother's eyes, forgot her weakness in thought for him.

She had no contempt for his tears. She had seen him stand between herself and her tormentors, she had seen the flash of his eye, she had heard his voice, and knew him brave. But the fate, for which long thought and hours on her knees had prepared her—so that it seemed but a black and bitter passage with peace beyond—appalled her for him; and might well appal him. The courage of men is active, of women passive; with a woman's instinct she knew this, allowed for it, and allowed, too, for another thing—that he was fasting.

When he looked up, startled by the tinkle of pewter and the rustle of her skirt, she was kneeling between the settle and the fire, preparing food. He flattered himself that in the dark she had not seen him, and when he had regained his self-control he stepped to the settle-back and looked over it.

"You did not see me?" he said.

She did not answer at once, but finished what she was doing. Then she stood up and handed him a bowl. "The bread is on the table," she said, indicating it. She was a woman, and, dark as it was, she kept the disfigured cheek averted from him.

He would have replied, but she made a sign to him to eat, and, seating herself on a stool in the corner with her plate on her lap, she set him an example. Apart from her weary attitude, and the droop of her head, he might have deemed the scene in which they had taken part a figment of his brain. But round them was the gloom of the closed room.

"You did not see me?" he repeated, presently.

She stood up. "I would I had never seen you!" she cried; and her anguished tone bore witness to the truth of her words. "It is the worst, it is the bitterest thing of all! of all!" she repeated. The settle was between them, and she rested her hands on the back of it. He stooped, and, in the darkness, covered them with kisses, while his breast heaved with the swell of the storm which her entrance had cut short. "For all but that I was prepared," she continued, "I was ready. I have seen for weeks the hopelessness of it, the certain end, the fate before us. I have counted the cost, and I have learned to look beyond for —for all we desire. It is a sharp passage, and peace. But you," she continued on the same tragic note of monotony, "are outside the sum, and spoil all. A little suffering will kill my mother, a little, a very little fear. I doubt if she will live to be taken hence. And I—I can suffer. I have known all, I have foreseen all—long! I have learned to think of it, and I can learn by God's help to bear it! And in a little while, a very little while, it will be over, and I shall be at rest. But you—you, my love——"

Her voice broke, her head sunk forward. His lips met hers in a first kiss; a kiss, salted by the tears that ran unchecked down his face. For a long minute there was silence in the room, a silence broken only by the low, inarticulate murmur of love—love whispered brokenly on her tear-wet lips, on her cold, closed eyelids. She made no attempt to withdraw her face, and presently the murmur grew to words of defiance, of love that mocked at peril, mocked at shame, mocked at death, having assurance of its own, having assurance of her.

They fell on her ears as warm thaw-rain on frozen sward; and slowly into the pallor of her face, the whiteness of her closed eyelids, crept a tender blush. Strange that for a few brief moments they were happy; strange, proof marvellous of the dominance of the inner life over the outer, of love over death.

"My love, my love!"

"Again!" he murmured.

"My love, my love!"

But at length she came to herself, she remembered. "You will go?" she said. She put him from her and held him fondly at arm's length, her hands on his shoulders. "You will go? It is all you can do for me. You will go and live?"

"Without you?"

"Yes. Better, a hundred times better so for me."

"And for me? Why may I not save you—and her?"

"It is impossible!"

"Nothing is impossible to love," he answered. "The nights are long, the wall is not too high! No wall is too high for love! It is but a league to the frontier, and I am strong."

"Who would receive us?" she asked sadly. "Who would shelter us? In Savoy, if we were not held for sorcery, we should be delivered to the Inquisition."

"We might gain friends?"

"With what? No," she continued, her hands cleaving more tightly to him, "you must go, dear love! Dear love! You must go! It is all you can do for me, and it is much! Oh, indeed, it is much! It is very much!"

He drew her to him as near as the settle would permit, until she was kneeling on it, and in spite of her faint resistance he could look into her eyes. "Were you in my place, would you leave me?" he asked.

"Yes," she lied bravely, "I would."

But the flash of resentment in her eyes gave her voice the lie, and he laughed joyfully. "You would not!" he said. "You would not leave me on this side of death!"

She tried to protest.

"Nor will I you," he continued, stopping her mouth with fresh kisses. "Nor will I you till death! Did you think me a coward?" He held her from him and looked into her reproachful eyes. "Or a Tissot? Tissot left you. Or Louis Gentilis?"

But she made him know that he was none of these in a way that satisfied him; and a moment later her mother's voice called her from the room. He thought, having no experience of a woman's will, that he had done with that; and in her absence he betook himself to examining the defences of the house. He replaced the bar which he had wrested from the window; wedging it into its socket with a morsel or two of molten lead. The windows of the bedrooms, his own and Louis', looked into a narrow lane, the Rue de la Cité, that ran at the back of the Corraterie in a line with the ramparts; but not only were they almost too small to permit the passage of a full-grown man, they were strongly barred. Against such a rabble, as had assaulted Anne, or even a more formidable mob, the house was secure. But if the law intervened neither bar nor bolt could save them.

He fell to thinking of this, and stood arrested in the middle of the darkened room that, as the hours went by, was beginning to take on a familiar look. The day was passing, all without remained quiet, nothing had happened. Was it possible that nothing would happen? Was it possible that the girl through long brooding exaggerated the peril? And that the worst to be feared was such an outbreak as had occurred that morning? Such an outbreak as might not take place again, since mobs were fickle things.

He dwelt awhile on this more hopeful view of things. Then he recalled Basterga's threats, the Syndic's face, the departure of Louis and Grio; and his heart sank as lead sinks. The rumour so quickly spread—by what hints, what innuendoes, what cunning inquiries, what references to the old, invisible, bedridden woman, he could but guess —that rumour bore witness to a malice and a thirst for revenge which were not likely to stop at words. And Louis' flight? And Grio's? And Basterga's?—for he did not return. To believe that all these, taken together, these and the outrage of the morning, portended anything but danger, anything but the worst, demanded a hopefulness that even his youth and his love could not compass.

Yet when she descended he met her with brave looks.

CHAPTER XXI

THE GOLDEN WATER

BLONDEL'S thin lips were warrant—to such of the world as had eyes to see—that in the ordinary things of life he would have been one of the last to put faith in a man of Basterga's stamp: and one of the first, had the case been other than his own, to laugh at the credulity he was displaying. He would have seen—no one more clearly—that, in making the bargain he had made, he was in the position of a drowning man who clutches at a straw; not because he believes that the straw will support him, but because he has no other hope, and is loath to sink.

He would have seen, too, another thing, which indeed he did see dimly. This was that, talk as he might, make terms as he might, repeat as firmly as he pleased "The Remedium first and then Geneva," he would be forced, when the time came, to take the word for the deed. If he dared not trust Basterga, neither dared the scholar trust him. Once safe, once snatched from the dark fate that scared him, he would laugh at the notion of betraying the city. He would snap his fingers in the Paduan's face; and Basterga knew it. The scholar, therefore, dared not trust him; and either there was an end of the matter or he must trust Basterga, must eat his own words, and, content with the possession of something, must wait for proof of its efficacy until the die was cast!

In his heart he knew this. He knew that on the brink of the fatal extremity to which circumstances and Basterga were slowly pushing him it might not be in his power to check himself: that he must trust, whether he would or no, and where instinct bade him place no trust. And this doubt, this suspicion that when all was done he might find himself tricked, and learn that for nothing he had given all, added immeasurably to the torment of his mind; to the misery of his reflections when he awoke in the small hours and saw things coldly and clearly, and to the fever and suspense in which he passed his days.

He clung to one thought and got what consolation he could from it; a bitter and saturnine comfort it was. The thought was this; if it turned out that, after all, he had been tricked, he could but die; and die he must if he made no bargain. And to a dead man what matter was it what price he had paid that he might live! What matter who won or who lost Geneva, who lived, who died, who were slaves, who free!

And again, the very easiness of the thing he was asked to do tempted him. It was a thing that to one in his position presented no difficulty and scarcely any danger. He had but to withdraw the guards, or the greater part of them, from a portion of the wall, and to stop on one pretext or another—the bitter cold of the wintry weather would avail—the rounds that at stated intervals visited the various posts. That was all; as a man of tried loyalty, intrusted with the safeguarding of the city, and to whom the officer of the watch was answerable, he might make the necessary arrangements without incurring, even after the catastrophe, more than a passing odium, a breath of suspicion.

And Baudichon and Petitot? He tasted, when he thought of them, the only moments of comfort, of pleasure, or of ease, that fell to his lot throughout these days. They would thwart him no more. Petty worms, whose vision went no farther than the walls of the city, he would have done with them when the flag of Savoy fluttered above St. Pierre; and when for the confines of a petty canton was substituted, for those who had eyes to see and courage to adapt themselves, the wide horizon of the Italian Kingdom. When he thought of them—and then only—he warmed to the task before him; then only he could think of it without a shiver and without distaste. And not the less because on that side, in their suspicion, in their grudging jealousy, in their unwinking integrity, lay the one difficulty.

A difficulty exasperated by the insult that, in a moment of bitter disappointment, he had flung in Baudichon's face. That hasty word had revealed to the speaker a lack of self-control that terrified him, even as it had revealed to Baudichon a glimpse of something underneath the Fourth Syndic's dry exterior that might well set a man thinking as well as talking. This matter Blondel saw plainly he must deal with at once, or it might do harm. To absent himself from the next day's Council, or to show himself backward, might rouse a storm beyond his power to weather; or, short of that, might give rise at a future day to a dangerous amount of gossip and conjecture.

He was early at the meeting, therefore, but to his surprise found it in session before the hour. This, and the fact that the hubbub of voices and discussion died down at his entrance—died down and was succeeded by a chilling silence—put him on his guard. He had not come unprepared for opposition; and to meet it he had wound himself to a pitch, telling himself that after this all would be easy; that he had this one peril to face, this one obstacle to surmount, and having succeeded might rest. Nevertheless, as he passed up the Great Council Chamber amid that silence, and met strange looks on faces that were wont to smile, his courage for one moment, even in that familiar scene—conscience makes cowards of all—wavered. His smile grew sickly, his nerves seemed suddenly unstrung, his knees shook under him. It was a dreadful instant of physical weakness, of mental terror under the eyes of all. To himself, he seemed to be self-betrayed, self-convicted!

Then—and so brief was the moment of weakness no eye detected it—he moved on to his place, and with his usual coolness took his seat. He looked round.

"You are early," he said, ignoring the glances, hostile or doubtful, that met his gaze. "The hour has barely struck, I believe?"

"We were of opinion," Fabri answered, with a dry cough, "that minutes were of value."

"Ah!"

"That not even one must be lost, Messer Blondel!"

"In doing?" Blondel asked in a negligent tone, well calculated to rouse those who were eager in the matter. "In doing what, if I may ask?"

"In doing, Messer Syndic," Petitot answered sharply, "that which should have been done a week ago; and better still a fortnight ago. In issuing a warrant for the arrest of the person whose name has been several times in question here."

"Messer Basterga?"

"The same."

"You may save yourselves the trouble," the Syndic replied, with a little contempt. "The warrant has been issued. It was issued yesterday, and would have been executed in the afternoon, if he had not got wind of it, and left the town. And let me say one more word on this," Blondel continued, leaning forward and speaking in sudden heat, before anyone could take up the question, "That word is this. If it had not been for the importunity of some who are here, the warrant had *not* been issued, the man had still been within the walls, and we had been able still to trace his plans! We had not been as we now are, and as I foretold we should be, in the dark, ignorant from which quarter the blow may fall, and not a whit the wiser for the hint given us."

"You have let him escape!" The words were Petitot's.

"I? No, I have not let him escape! But those who forced my hand!" Blondel retorted in passion, so real, or so well simulated, that it swept away the majority of his listeners. "They have let him escape! Those who had no patience nor craft! Those whose only notion of statesmanship, whose only method of making use of the document we had under our hand was to tear it up! Only yesterday morning I was with him——"

"Ay?" Baudichon cried, his eyes glowing with dull passion. "You were with him? And he went in the afternoon! Mark that!" He turned quickly to his fellows. "He went in the afternoon! Now, I would like to know——"

Blondel stood up. "Whether I am a traitor?" he said,

in a tone of fury; and he extended his arms in protest. "Whether I am in league with this Italian, I, Philibert Blondel of Geneva? That is what you ask, what you wish to know! Whether I sought him yesterday in the hope of worming his secrets from him, of doing what I could for the benefit of the State in a matter too delicate to be left to underlings? Or went there, one with him, to betray my country? To sell the Free City? That—that is what you ask?"

His passion was full, overpowering, convincing; so convincing—it almost stopped his speech—that he believed in it himself, so convincing that it swept away all but his steady and professed opponents. "No, no!" cried a dozen voices, in tones that reflected his indignation. "No, no! Shame!"

"No?" Blondel took up the word, his eyes sparkling, his adust complexion heated and full of fire. "But it is —yes, they answer! Yes, they say whom you have to thank if we have lost our clew, they who met me going to him but yesterday and threatened me! Threatened me!" he repeated, in a voice of astonishment. "Me, who desired only, sought only, was going only to do my duty! I used yesterday, I admit the fault, I do not strive to defend it," he allowed his voice to drop to a tone more like his own, "words that I now regret. But is blood water? Does no man besides Councillor Baudichon love his country? Is the suspicion, the open suspicion of such an one, no insult, that he must cavil if he be repaid in insult? I have given my proofs. If any man can be trusted to sound the enemy, it is I! But I have done! Had Messer Baudichon not pressed me to issue the warrant, not driven me beyond my patience, it had not been issued yesterday. It had been in the office, and the man within the walls! Ay, and not only within, but fresh from a conference with the Sieur d'Albigny, primed with all we need to know, and in doubt by which side he could most profit!"

"It was about that you saw him?" Petitot said slowly, his eyes fixed like gimlets to the other's face.

"It was about that I saw him," Blondel answered. "And I think in a few hours more I had won him. But in the street he had some secret word or warning; for when I handed the warrant—against my own will—to the officers, they, who had never lost sight of him between gate and gate, answered that he had crossed the bridge and left the town an hour before. Mon Dieu!"—he struck his two hands together and snapped his teeth—"when I think how foolish I was to be over-ridden, I could—I could say more, Messer Baudichon"—with a saturnine look—"than I said yesterday!"

"At any rate the bird is flown!" Baudichon replied, with sullen temper. "That is certain! And it was you who were set to catch him!"

"But it was not I who scared him," Blondel rejoined.

"I don't know what you would have had of him!"

"Oh, I see that plainly," said Fabri. He was an honest man, without prejudice, and long the peacemaker between the two parties.

"I thank you," Blondel said drily. "But, by your leave, I will make it clear to Messer Baudichon also, who will doubtless like to know more. I would have had of him the time and place and circumstance of the attack, if such be in preparation. And then, when I knew all, I would have made dispositions, not only to safeguard the city, but to give the enemy such a reception that Italy should ring with it! Ay, and such as should put an end for the rest of our lives, to these treacherous attacks."

The picture which he drew, of a millennium of safety, charmed not only his own adherents, but all who were neutral, all who wavered. They saw how easily the thing might have been done, how completely the treacherous blow might have been parried and returned. Veering about they eyed Baudichon, on whom the odium of the lost opportunity seemed to rest, with resentment—as an honest man, but a simpleton, a dullard, a block! And when Blondel added, after a pause, "But there, I have done! The office of Fourth Syndic I leave to you to fill," they barely allowed him to finish.

"No! No!" came from almost all mouths, and from every part of the Council table.

"No," Fabri said, when silence was made. "There is no provision for a change, unless a definite accusation be laid."

"But Messer Baudichon may have one to make," Blondel said, proudly. "In that case let him speak."

Baudichon breathed hard, and seemed to be on the point of pouring forth a torrent of words. But he said nothing. Instinct told him that his enemy was not to be trusted, but he had the wit to discern that Blondel had forestalled him, and had drawn the sting from his charges. He could have wept in dull, honest indignation; but for accusations, he saw that the other held the game, and he was silent. "Fat hog!" the man had called him. "Fat hog!" A tear gathered slowly in his eye as he recalled it.

Fabri gave him time to speak; and then with evident relief, "He has none to make, I am sure," he said.

"Let him understand, then," Blondel replied firmly,

"let all understand, that while I will do my duty I am no
longer in that position to guard against sudden strokes, in
which I should have been, had I been allowed to go my own
way. If a misfortune happen after this, it is not on me the
blame must rest." He spoke solemnly, laughing in his
sleeve at the cleverness with which he was turning his
enemy's petard against him. "All that man can do in
the dark shall be done," he continued. "And I do not—
I am free to confess that—anticipate anything while the
negotiations with the President Rochette are in progress."

"No, it is when they are broken off, the enemy will fall
back on the other plan," one of the councillors said with
an air of much wisdom.

"I think that is so. Nor do I think that anything will
be done during the present severe weather."

"They like it no better than we do!"

"But the roads are good in this frost," Fabri said. "If
it be a question of moving guns or wagons——"

"But it is not, by your leave, Messer Fabri, as I am
informed," the man who had spoken before objected;
supporting his opinion simply because he had voiced it, a
thing seen every day in such assemblies. Fabri replied on
him in the other sense; and presently Blondel had the satisfaction of listening to a discussion in which the one party
said a dozen things that he saw would be of use to him—
some day.

One only said not a word, and that was Petitot. He
listened to all with a puzzled look. He resented the insult which Blondel had flung at his friend Baudichon, but
he saw all going against them, and no chance of redress;
nay, capital was being made out of that which should have
been a disadvantage. Worst of all, he was uneasy, fancy-

ing—he was very shrewd—that he caught a glimpse, under the Fourth Syndic's manner, of another man: that he detected signs of emotion, a feverishness and imperiousness not quite explained by the circumstances.

He got the notion from this that the Fourth Syndic had learned more from Basterga than he had disclosed. His notion, even so, went no farther than the suspicion that Blondel was hiding knowledge out of a desire to reap all the glory. But he did not like it. "He was always for risking, for risking!" he thought. "This is another case of it. God grant it go well!" His wife, his children, his daughters, rose in a picture before him, and he hated Blondel, who had none of these. He would have put him to death for running the tithe of a risk.

When the Council broke up, Fabri drew Blondel aside. "The bird is flown, but what of the nest?" he asked. "Has he left nothing?"

"Between you and me," Blondel replied under his breath—and his eyes sought the other's—"I hope to make him speak yet. But not a word!"

"Ah!"

"Not a word! But there is just a chance. And it will be everything to us if I can induce him to speak."

"I see that. But the house? Could you not search it?"

"That would be to scare him finally."

"You have made no perquisition there?"

"None. I have heard," Blondel continued, hesitating as if he had not quite made up his mind to speak, "some things—strange things in respect to that house. But I will tell you more of that when I know more."

He was too clever to state that he held the house in suspicion for sorcery and kindred things. Charges such as that, he knew, spread upward from the lower classes, not downward to them. The poison, disseminated as he had known how to disseminate it, by hints and innuendoes dropped among his officers and ushers, was in the air, and would do its work. Fabri, a man of sense, might laugh to-day, and to-morrow; but the third day, when the report came to him from a dozen quarters, mainly by women's mouths, he would not laugh. And presently he would shrug his shoulders and stand aside, and leave the matter in more earnest hands.

Blondel dropped no more than that hint, therefore, and as he passed homeward applauded his discretion. He was proud of the turn things had taken at the Council, of the part he had played, of the proof he had given of his mastery. Now he felt able to carry anything through. His mind, leaping over the immediate future, pictured a wider theatre, in which his powers would have full scope, and a larger stage on which he might aspire to play the first part. He saw himself not only wealthy, but ennobled, the fount of honour, the favourite, and in time the master of princes. Such as he was to-day the Medicis had been, and many another whom the world held noble. He had but to live and to dare; only to live and to dare! Only in order to do the one he must—it was no choice of his—do the other!

Before he was five minutes older he was reminded of the necessity. At the door of his house the pains of the disease from which he suffered—aggravated, perhaps, by the excitement through which he had just passed, or by the cold of the weather—seized him with unusual violence. He leant, pale and almost fainting, against the door-jamb, unable at the moment to do so much as to raise the latch. The golden dreams in which he had lost him-

self by the way, the visions of power and fame, vanished
as he had so many times seen the after-glow vanish from
the snow peaks; leaving only cold images of death and
desolation.   Presently, with an effort, he staggered within
doors, poured out such medicine as he had, and, bent double and almost without breath, swallowed it; and so, by
and by, a wan and wild-eyed image of himself, came out
of the fit.

He told himself in after days that it was that decided
him; that but for that sharp fit of pain and the prospect
of others like it, he would not have yielded to the temptation, no, not to be the Grand Duke's favourite, not to
be Minister of Savoy!   He ignored, in his looking backward, the visions of glory and ambition in which he had
revelled.   He saw himself on the rack; with life and im-
munity from pain on the one side, the prospect of a miserable death on the other; and he pleaded that no man
would have decided otherwise.   After that experience the
straw did not float, so thin that he was not ready to grasp
it rather than die, rather than suffer again.   Nor did the
fact that the straw at that moment lay on the table beside
him go for much.

It did lie there.   When he felt a little stronger and
began to look about him, he found a note at his elbow.
It was a small, common-looking letter, sealed with a B,
that might signify Blondel, or Basterga, or for the matter of that, Baudichon.   He did not know the handwrit-
ing, and he opened it idly, in the scorn of small things
that pain induced.

He had not read a line of the contents, before his countenance changed.   The letter was from Basterga, and
cunningly contrived.   It gave him the directions he

needed, yet it was so worded that even after the event it might pass for a trifling communication from a physician. The place and the hour were specified—the latter so near that for a moment his cheek grew pale. On that ensued the part which interested him most; but as the whole was brief, the whole may be given.

"Sir" (here followed a cabalistic sign such as physicians were in the habit of using to impose on the vulgar). "After paying a visit in the Corraterie, where I have an appointment on Saturday evening next between late and early, I will be with you. But the mixture with the necessary directions shall be sent to you twelve hours in advance, so that before my visit you may experience its good effects. As surely as the wrong potion in the case you wot of deprived of reason, so surely (as I hope for salvation) will this potion have the desired effect.

"The Physician of Aleppo."

"Saturday next, between late and early!" Blondel muttered, gazing at the words with fascinated eyes. "It is for the day after to-morrow! The day after to-morrow!" And in his thoughts he passed again over the road he had travelled since his first visit to Basterga's room, since the hour when the scholar had unrolled before him the map of the town he called "Aurelia," and had told him the story of Ibn Jasher and the Physician of Aleppo.

.   .   .   .

"No, I am not well," he answered. He sat, warmly wrapped up, in the high chair in his parlour, his face so drawn with want of sleep that Captain Blandano of the city guard, who had come to take his orders, had no difficulty in believing him. "I am not well," he repeated, peevishly. "It is the weather." He had some soup before him, and beside it stood a tiny phial of medicine; a phial strangely-shaped and strange looking, containing something not unlike the green cordial of the Carthusians.

"It troubles me a good deal, too," Blandano said. "There are seven men absent in the fourth ward. And two men, whose wives are urgent with me that they should have leave."

"Leave?" the Syndic cried. "Do they think naught" —leaning forward in a passion—"of the safety of the city? If I were not ill, I would take service on the wall myself to set an example!"

"There is no need of that," the Captain answered, respectfully, "if I might have permission to withdraw a few men from the west side so as to fill the places on the east——"

"Ay, ay!"

"From the Rhone side of the town——"

"From the Corraterie, you mean? Well, that is least open to assault."

"Yes, from that part perhaps would be best," Blandano said, nodding. "Yes, I think so. Well, if I might do that, I think I could manage."

"Good, then, do it," Blondel answered. "And make a note that I assented to your suggestion to take them from the Corraterie and put them on the lower part of the wall. After all, the nights are very bitter now, and there are limits. Do the men grumble much?"

"It is as much as I can do to make them go the rounds," Blandano answered. "Some plead the weather; and some argue that, with President Rochette, whose word is as good as his bond, on the point of coming to an agreement with us, the rounds are a farce!"

The Syndic shrugged his shoulders. "Well!" he muttered, rubbing his chin and looking thoughtfully before him, "we must not wear the men out. There is no moon now, is there?"

"No."

"And the enemy can attempt nothing without light," Blondel continued, thinking aloud. "See here, Blandano, we must not put too heavy a burden on our people. I see that. As it is so cold, I think you may pass the word to pretermit the rounds to-night—save two. At what hours would you suggest?"

Blandano considered his own comfort—as the other expected he would—and answered, "Early and late, say an hour before midnight and an hour before dawn."

"Then, let it be as you suggest. But see"—with returning asperity—"that those rounds go, and at their hours. Let there be no remissness. I will make a note," he continued, "of the hours fixed. An hour before midnight and an hour before dawn."

He extended his arm and drew the ink-horn toward him. Midway in the act, whether it was that his hand shook by reason of his illness, or that he was in a hurry to close an interview which tried him more severely than appeared, his sleeve caught the little phial of green liquid that stood beside the soup on the table. It reeled an instant on its edge, toppled on its side, and rolling, in one-tenth of the time it takes to tell the tale, to the verge of the table —fell over.

Messer Blondel made a strange noise in his throat.

But the Captain had seen what was happening. He caught the bottle dexterously in his huge palm, and with an air of modest achievement was going to set it back on the table, when he saw that the Syndic had sank down in his chair, his face ghastly. Blandano was more used to death in the field than in the house; and in a panic he took two steps toward the door to call for help. Before he could take a third, Blondel gasped, and made an uncertain wavering movement with his hand, as if he would reassure him.

Blandano returned and leant over him. "You are ill, Messer Syndic," he said anxiously. "Let me call someone."

The Syndic could not speak, but he pointed to the table. And when Blandano, unable to make out what he wanted, and suspecting a stroke of a mortal disease, turned again to the door, persisting in his intention of getting aid, the Syndic found strength to seize his sleeve; and almost instantly regained his speech. "There!" he gasped, "there! The phial! Put it down!"

Captain Blandano in some wonder placed it on the table. "I was afraid you were ill, Messer Blondel," he said.

"I was ill," the Syndic answered; and he pushed his chair back so that no part of him was in contact with the table. He looked at the little bottle with fascinated eyes, and slowly, as he looked, the colour returned to his face. "I was ill," he repeated, with a sigh that seemed to relieve his breast. "I had a fright!"

"You thought it was broken?" Blandano said, wondering much, and looking in his turn at the phial.

"Yes, I thought that it was broken. I am much obliged to you. Much, very much obliged to you," the Syndic repeated, with a deep sigh, his hands still moving nervously about his dress. Then, after a moment's pause, "Will you ring the bell?" he said.

The Captain, marvelling much, rang the hand-bell which lay on a neighbouring table. He marvelled still more when he heard Messer Blondel order the servant to place six bottles of his best wine in a basket and take them to the Captain's lodging.

Blandano stared. He knew the wine to be choice and valuable; and he eyed the tiny phial respectfully. "It is something rare, I expect?" he said.

The Syndic nodded.

"And costly too, I doubt not?" with an admiring glance.

"Costly?" Messer Blondel repeated the word, and when he had done so turned on the other a look that led the Captain to think that he was going to be ill again. Then, "It cost me—it will cost me"—again a spasm contorted the Syndic's face—"I don't know what it will not have cost me before it is paid for, Captain Blandano!"

CHAPTER XXII

TWO NAILS IN THE WALL

THE long day during which the lovers had drained a cup at once so sweet and so bitter, and one of the two had felt alike the throb of pain and the thrill of kisses, came to an end at last; and without farther incident. Encouraged by the respite—for who that is mortal does not hope against hope—they ventured on the following morning to open the shutters and this to a great extent restored the house to its normal aspect. Anne would have gone so far as to attend the morning preaching at St. Pierre—it was Friday; but her mother awoke low and nervous, the girl dared not quit her side, and Claude had no field for the urgent dissuasions which he had prepared himself to use.

The greater part of the day she remained above-stairs, busied in the petty offices, and moving to and fro—he could hear her tread—upon the errands of love, to see her in the midst of which might well have confuted the slanders that crept abroad. But there were times in the day when Madame Royaume slept; and then, who can blame Anne if she stole down and sat hand in hand with Claude on the settle, whispering sometimes of those things of which lovers whisper, and will whisper to the world's end; but more often of the direr things before these two lovers, and so of faith and hope and the love that does not die. For the most part it was she who talked. She had so much to tell him of the long nightmare, the nightmare of months, that had oppressed her; of her prayers, and fears and fits of terror; of Basterga's discovery of the secret and the cruel use he had made of it; of the slow-growing resignation, the steadfast resolve, the onward look to something, beyond that which the world could do to her, that had come to be hers. With her face hidden on his breast she told him of her thoughts upon her knees, of the pain and obloquy through which, if the worst came, she knew she must pass, and of her trust that she would be able to bear them; speaking in such terms, so simply and so bravely, with so lofty a contemplation that he who listened, and had been but a week before a young man as other young men, grew as he listened to another stature, and thought for himself thoughts that no man can have and remain as he was, before the tongues of fire touched his heart.

And then again, once—but that was in the darkening of the Friday evening when the wound in her cheek burned and smarted and recalled the wretched moment of infliction —she showed him another side; as if she would have him know that she was not all heroic. Without warning she broke down, overcome by the prospect of death; she clung to him, weeping and shuddering, and begging him and imploring him to save her. To save her! Only to save her! At that sight and at those sounds, under the despairing grasp of her arms about his neck, the young man's heart was red-hot; his eyes burned. Vainly he held her closer and closer to him; vainly he tried to comfort her. Vainly he shed tears of blood. He felt her writhe and shudder in his arms.

And what could he do? He strove to argue with her. He strove to show her that accusation of her mother, condemnation of her mother, dreadful as they must be to her, so dreadful that he scarcely dared speak of them, need not involve her own condemnation. She was young, of blameless life, and without enemies. What could any cast up against her, what adduce in proof of a charge so dark, so improbable, so abnormal?

For answer she touched the pulsing wound in her cheek. "And this?" she said. "And the child—that I killed?" —with a bitter laugh unlike her own. "If they say so much already, if they say that to-day, what will they say to-morrow? What will they say when they have heard her ravings? Will it not be, the old and the young, the witch and her brood—to the fire? To the fire?"

The spasm that shook her as she spoke defied his efforts to soothe her. And how could he comfort her? He knew the thing to be too likely, the argument too reasonable, as men reasoned then; strange and foolish as their reasoning seems to us now. But what could he do? What? He who sat there alone with her, a prisoner with her, witness to her agony, scalded by her tears, tortured by her anguish, burning with pity, sorrow, indignation—what could he do to help her or save her?

He had wild thoughts, but none of them effectual; the old thoughts of defending the house, or of escaping by night over the town wall; and some new ones. He weighed the possibility of Madame Royaume's death before the arrest; surely, then, he could save the girl, and they two, young, active and of ordinary aspect, might escape somewhither? Again, he thought of appealing to Beza, the aged divine, whom Geneva revered and Cal-

vinism placed second only to Calvin. He was a Frenchman, a man of culture and of noble birth; he might stand
above the common superstition, he might listen, discern,
defend. But, alas, he was so old as to be bedridden and
almost childish. It was improbable, nay, it was most unlikely that he could be induced to interfere.

All these thoughts Anne drove out of his head by begging him, on a sudden and in moving terms of self-re-
proach, to forgive her her weakness. She had regained
her composure as abruptly, if not as completely, as she had
lost it; and would have had him believe that the passion
he had witnessed was less deep than it seemed, and rather
a womanish need of tears than a proof of suffering. A
minute later she was quietly preparing the evening meal,
while he, with a sick heart, raised the shutters and lighted
the lamp. As he looked up from the latter task, he found
her eyes fixed upon him, with a peculiar intentness: and
for a while afterward he remarked that she wore an
absent air. But she said nothing, and by and by, promising to return before bed-time, she went upstairs to her
mother.

The nights were at their longest, and the two had closed
and lighted before five. Outside the cold stillness of a
winter night and a freezing sky settled down on Geneva;
within, Claude sat with sad eyes fixed on the smouldering
fire. What could he do? What could he do? Wait and
see her innocence outraged, her tenderness racked, her
gentle body given up to unspeakable torments? The collapse which he had witnessed gave him as it were a fore-
taste, a bitter savour of the trials to come. It did not seem
to him that he could bear even the anticipation of them.
He rose, he sat down, he rose again, unable to endure the

intolerable thought. He flung out his arms; his eyes, cast upward, called God to witness that it was too much! It was too much!

Some way of escape there must be. Heaven could not look down on, could not suffer such deeds in a Christian land. But men and women, girls and young children had suffered these things; had appealed and called Heaven to witness, and gone to death, and Heaven had not moved, nor the angels descended! But it could not be in her case. Some way of escape there must be. There must be.

Why should she not leave her mother to her fate? A fate that could not be evaded? Why need she, whose capacity for suffering was so great, who had so much of life and love and all good things before her, remain to share the pains of one whose span in any case was nearing its end? Of one who had no longer power—or so it seemed—to meet the smallest shock, and must succumb before she knew more of suffering than the name. One whom a rude word might almost extinguish, and a rough push thrust out of life? Why remain, when to remain was to sacrifice two lives in lieu of one, to give and get nothing, to die for a prejudice? Why remain, when by remaining she could not save her mother, but, on the contrary, must inflict the sharpest pang of all, since she destroyed the being who was dearest to her mother, the being whom her mother would die to save?

He grew heated as he dwelt on it. Of what use to any, the feeble, flickering light upstairs, that must go out were it left for a moment untended? The light that would have gone out this long time back had she not fostered it and cherished it and sheltered it in her bosom? Of what avail that weak existence? Or, if it were of avail, why, for its sake, waste this other and more precious life that still could not redeem it?

Why?

He must speak to her. He must persuade her, press her, convince her; carry her off by force were it necessary. It was his duty, his clear call. He rose and walked the room in excitement as he thought of it. He had pity for the old, abandoned and left to suffer alone; and an enlightening glimpse of the weight that the girl must carry through life by reason of this desertion. But no doubt, no hesitation, he told himself, no scruple. To die that her mother might live was one thing. To die—and so to die—merely that her mother's last hours might be sheltered and comforted, was another, and a thing unreasonable.

He must speak to her. He would not hesitate to tell her what he thought.

But he did hesitate. When she descended half-an-hour later, and paused at the foot of the stairs to assure herself that her passage downstairs had not roused her mother from sleep, the light fell on her listening face and tender eyes; and he read that in them which checked the words on his lips, that which, whether it were folly or wisdom—a wisdom higher than the serpent's, more perfect than the most accurate calculation of values and chances—drove for ever from his mind the thought that she would desert her charge. He said no word then of what he had thought; the indignant reasoning, the hot, conclusive arguments fell from him and left him bare. With her hands in his, seeking no more to move her or convince her, he sat silent; and by mute looks and dumb love—more potent than eloquence or oratory—strove to support and console her.

She, too, was silent. Stillness had fallen on both of them. But her hands clung to his, and now and again pressed them convulsively; and now and again, too, she would lift her eyes to his, and gaze at him with a pathetic intentness, as if she would stamp his likeness on her brain. But when he returned the look, and tried to read her meaning in her eyes, she smiled. " You are afraid of me?" she whispered. "No, I shall not be weak again."

But even as she reassured him he detected a flicker of pain in her eyes, he felt that her hands were cold; and but that he feared to shake her composure he would not have rested content with her answer.

This sudden silence, this new way of looking at him, were the only things that perplexed him. In all else, silent as they sat, their communion was perfect. It was in the mind of each that the women might be arrested on the morrow; in the mind of each that this was their last evening together, the last of few, yet not so few that they did not seem to the man and the girl to bulk large in their lives. On that hearth they had met, there she had proved to him what she was, there he had spoken, there spent the clouded never to be forgotten days of their troubled courtship. No wonder that as they sat hand in hand, their hair almost mingling, their eyes on the red glow of the smouldering log, and not daring to look forward, looked back— no wonder that their love grew to be something other than the common love of man and maid, something higher and more beautiful, touched—as the hills are touched at sunset—by the evening glow of parting and self-sacrifice.

Silent amid the silence of the house; living moments never to be forgotten; welcoming together the twin companions, love and death.

But from the darkest outlook of the mind, as of the eye, morning dispels some shadows; into the most depressing atmosphere daylight brings hope, brings actuality, brings at least the need to be doing. Claude's heart, as he slipped from his couch on the settle next morning, and admitted the light and turned the log and stirred the embers, was sad and full of foreboding. But as the room, its disorder abated, took on a more pleasant aspect, as the fire crackled and blazed on the hearth, and the flush of sunrise spread over the east, he grew—he could not but grow, for he was young—more cheerful also. He swept the floor and filled the kettle and let in the air; and had done almost all he knew how to do, before he heard Anne's foot upon the stairs.

She had slept little and looked pale and haggard; almost more pale and wan than he had ever seen her look. And this must have sunk his heart to zero, if a certain particular in her aspect had not at the same time diverted his attention. "You are not going out?" he cried in astonishment. She wore her hood.

"I am not going to defend myself again," she answered, smiling sadly. "Have no fear. I shall not repeat—that mistake. I am only going——"

"You are not going anywhere!" he answered firmly.

She shook her head with the same wan smile. "We must live," she said.

"Well?"

"And to live must have water."

"I have filled the kettle."

"And emptied the waterpot," she retorted.

"True," he said. "But surely it will be time to refill it when we want it."

"I shall attract less attention now," she answered quietly, "than later in the day. There are few abroad. I will draw my hood about my face, and no one will heed me."

He laughed in tender derision. "You will not go!" he said. "Did you think that I would let you run a risk rather than fetch the water from the conduit?"

"You will go?"

"Where is the pot?"

He fetched the jar from its place under the stairs, snatched up his cap, and turning the key in the lock was in the act of passing out when she seized his arm. "Kiss me," she murmured. She lifted her face to his, her eyes half closed.

He drew her to him, but her lips were cold; and as he released her she sank passively from his arms, and was near falling. He hesitated. "You are not afraid to be left?" he said, looking down at her. "You are sure?"

"I am afraid of nothing if I know you safe," she answered faintly. "Go! go quickly, and God be with you!"

"Tut! I run no danger," he rejoined. "I have a strong arm and they will leave me alone." He thought that she was overwrought, that the strain was telling on her; his thoughts did not go beyond that. "I shall be back in five minutes," he continued, cheerfully. And he went, bidding her lock the door behind him and open only at his knock.

He made the more haste for her fears, passed into the town through the Porte Tertasse, and hastened to the conduit. The open space in front of the fountain, which a little later in the day would be the favourite resort of gossips and idlers, was a desert; the bitter morning wind saw to that. But about the fountain itself three or four women, closely muffled, were waiting their turns to draw. One looked up, and, as he fancied, recognised him, for she nudged her neighbour. And then first the one woman and then the other, looking askance, muttered something; it might have been a prayer, or a charm, or a mere word of gossip. But he liked neither the glance nor the action, nor the furtive, curious looks of the women; and as quickly as he could he filled his pot and carried it away.

He had splashed his fingers, and the cold wind quickly numbed them. At the Tertasse Gate, where the view commanding the river valley opened before him, he was glad to set down the vessel and change hands. On his left, the watch at the Porte Neuve, the gate in the ramparts which admitted from the country to the Corraterie—as the Tertasse admitted from the Corraterie to the town proper —was being changed, and he paused an instant, gazing on the scene. Then remembering himself, and the need of haste, he snatched up his jar and, turning to the right, hurried to the steps before the Royaume's door, swung up them and, with his eyes on the windows, set down his burden.

He knocked gently, sure that she would not keep him waiting. But she did not come at once; and by and by, seeing that a woman at an open door a little farther down the Corraterie was watching him with scowling eyes —and that strange look, half fear, half loathing, which he was growing to know—he knocked more loudly, and stamped to warm his feet.

Still, to his astonishment, she did not come; he waited, and waited, and she did not come. He would have begun to feel alarmed for her, but, what with the cold and the early hour, the place was deserted; no idle gazers such as a commotion leaves behind it were to be seen. The wind, however, began to pierce his clothes; he had not brought his cloak, and he shivered. He knocked more loudly.

Perhaps she had been called to her mother? That must be it. She had gone upstairs and could not on the instant leave her charge. He clothed himself in reproaches, then; but they did not warm him, and he was beginning to stamp his feet again when, happening to look down, he saw beside the water-can and partly hidden by its bulge, a packet about the size of a letter but a little thicker. If he had not mounted the steps with his eyes on the windows, searching for her face, he would have seen it at once, and spared himself these minutes of waiting. He took it up in a kind of maze, and turned it in his numbed hands; it was heavy, and from it, leaving only a piece of paper in his grasp, his purse fell to the ground. More and more astonished, he picked up the purse, and put it in his pocket. He looked at the window, but no one showed; then at the paper in his hand. Inside the latter were three lines of writing.

His face fell as he read them. *"I shall not admit you,"* they ran. *"If you try to enter, you will attract notice and destroy me. Go, and God bless and reward you. You cannot save me, and to see you perish were a worse pang than the worst."*

The words swam before his eyes. "I will beat down the door," he muttered, tears in his voice, tears welling up in his heart and choking him. And he raised his hand. "I will——"

But he did nothing. *"You will attract notice and destroy me."* Ah, she had thought it out too well. Too well, out of the wisdom of great love, she had known how to bridle him. He dared not do anything that would direct notice to the house.

But desert her? Never; and after a moment's thought he drew off, his plans formed. As he retired, when he had gone some yards from the door, he heard the window close sharply behind him. He looked back, and saw his cloak lying on the ground. Tears rose again to his eyes as he returned, took it up, donned it, and with a last lingering look at the window, turned away. She would think he had taken her at her word; but no matter!

He walked along the Corraterie, and passing the four square watch-towers with pointed roofs that stood at intervals along the wall, he came to the two projecting demilunes, or bastions, that marked the angle where the ramparts met the Rhone; a point from which the road descended to the bridge. In one of these bastions he ensconced himself; and selecting a place whence he could command without being seen, the length of the Corraterie, he set himself to watch the Royaumes' house. By and by he would go into the town and procure food, and, returning, keep guard until nightfall. After dark, if the day passed without event, he would find his way into the house by force or fraud. In a rapture of anticipation he pictured his entrance, her reluctant joy, her tears and smiles, and fond reproaches. As he loved her, as he must love her the more for the trick she had played him, she must love him the more for his return in her teeth. And the next day was Sunday, when it was unlikely that any steps would be taken. That whole day he would have with her, through it he would sit with her! A whole day without fear? It seemed an age. He did not, he would not look beyond it!

He had not broken his fast, and hunger presently drove

him into the town. But within half an hour he was at his post again. A glance at the Royaumes' house showed him that nothing had happened, and, resuming his seat in the deserted bastion, he began a watch that as long as he lived stood clear in his memory of the past. The day was cold and bright and frosty, with a nipping wind. Mont Blanc and the long ranges of snow-clad summits that flanked it rose dazzlingly bright against the blue sky. The most distant object seemed near; the wavelets on the unfrozen water of the lake gave to the surface, usually so blue, a rough, grey aspect. The breeze which produced this appearance kept the ramparts clear of loiterers; and even those who were abroad preferred the more sheltered streets, or went hurriedly about their business. The guards were content to shiver in the guard-rooms of the gate-towers, and if Claude blessed once the kind afterthought which had dropped his cloak from the window, he blessed it a dozen times. Even in its thick folds, it was all he could do to hold his ground against the cold. Without it he must have withdrawn or succumbed.

Through the morning he watched the house jealously, trembling at every movement which took place at the Tertasse Gate; lest it herald the approach of the officers to arrest the women. But nothing happened, and as the day wore on he grew more hopeful. He might, indeed, have begun to think Anne over-timid and his fears unwarranted, if he had not seen, a little before sunset, a thing which opened his eyes.

Two women and some children came out of a house not far from the bastion. They passed toward the Tertasse Gate, and he watched them. Before they came to the Royaumes' house, the children paused, flung their cloaks

over their heads, and, thus protected, ran past the house.
The women followed, more slowly, but gave the house a
wide berth, and each passed with a flap of her hood held
between her face and the windows; when they had gone
by they exchanged signals of abhorrence. The sight was
no more than of a piece with the outrage on Anne; but,
coming when it did, coming when he was beginning to
think he had been mistaken, when he was beginning to
hope, it depressed Claude dismally.

For comfort he looked forward to the hour when it
would be dark. "By hook or by crook," he muttered, "I
shall enter then."

He had barely finished the sentence, when he observed
moving along the ramparts toward him a figure he knew.
It was Grio. There was nothing strange in the man's presence in that place, for he was an idler and a sot; but Claude
did not wish to meet him, and debated in his mind whether
he should retreat before the other came up. Pride said one
thing, discretion another. He wanted no fracas, and was
still hanging doubtful, measuring the distance between
them, when—away went his thoughts. What was Grio
doing?

The Spaniard had come to a stand, and was leaning
on the wall, looking idly into the fosse. The posture
would have been the most natural in the world on a warm
day. On that day it caught Claude's attention; and—was
he mistaken, or were the hands that rested on the wall,
under cover of the cloak, busy about something?

In any case, he must make up his mind whether he
moved or stayed. For Grio was coming on again.
Claude hesitated a moment. Then he determined to stay.
The next instant he was glad he had so determined, for

when Grio had strolled on in seeming carelessness to a point not twenty yards from him, and well commanded from his seat, the Spaniard leant again on the wall, and seemed to be enjoying the view. This time Claude was sure, from the movement of his shoulders, that his hands were employed.

"In what?" The young man asked himself the question; and noted that beside Grio's left heel lay a piece of broken tile of a peculiar colour. The next moment he had an inspiration. He drew up his feet on the seat, drew his cloak over his head and affected to be asleep. What Grio, when he came upon him, thought of a man who chose to sleep in the open in such weather he did not learn, for after standing awhile—as Claude's ears told him—opposite the sleeper, the Spaniard turned and walked back the way he had come. This time, and though he now had the wind at his back, he walked briskly; as a man would walk in such weather, or as a man might walk who had done his business.

Claude waited until his coarse, heavy figure had disappeared through the Porte Tertasse; nay, he waited until the light began to fail. Then, while he could still pick out the red potsherd, he approached the wall, leant over it, and, failing to detect anything with his eyes, passed his fingers down the stones.

They alighted on a nail; a nail thrust lightly into the mortar below the coping stone. For what purpose? His blood beginning to move more quickly, Claude asked himself the question. To support a rope? And so to enable someone to leave the town? The nail, barely pushed into the mortar, would hardly support the weight of a dozen yards of twine.

Perhaps the nail was there by chance, and Grio had naught to do with it. He could settle that doubt; in a few moments he had settled it. Under cover of the growing darkness, he walked to the place at which he had seen Grio pause for the first time. A short search discovered a second nail as lightly secured as the other. Had he not been careful it must have fallen beneath his touch.

What did the nails there? Claude was not stupid, yet he was long in hitting on an explanation. It was a fanciful, extravagant notion, when he got it, but one that set his chilled blood running, and his hands tingling, one that might mean much to himself and to others. It was un-likely, it was improbable, it was out of the common—but it was an explanation. It was a mighty thing to hang upon two weak nails; but such as it was—and he turned it over and over in his mind before he dared entertain it—he could find no other. And presently, his eyes alight, his pulses riotous, his foot dancing, he walked down the Cor-raterie—with scarce a look at the house which had held his thoughts all day—and passed into the town. As he passed more slowly through the gateway he cast an inquisitive eye into the guard-room of the Tertasse. It was nearly empty. Two men sat drowsing before the fire, their boot-heels among the embers, a black jack between them.

The fact weighed something in the balance of probabil-ities: and in growing excitement, Claude hurried on, sought the cookshop at which he had broken his fast—a humble place, licensed for the scholars—and ate his sup-per, knowing not what he ate, nor with whom he ate it. It was only by chance that his ear caught, at a certain mo-ment, a new tone in the goodwife's voice; and that he looked up, and saw her greet her husband.

"Ay!" the man said, putting off his bandoleer and answering the exclamation of surprise which his entrance had evoked. "It's bed for me to-night. It's so cold they will send but half the rounds."

"Whose order is that?" asked a scholar at Claude's table.

"Messer Blondel's."

"Shows his sense!" the goodwife cried roundly. "A good man, and knows when to watch and when to ha' done!"

Claude said nothing, but he rose with burning cheeks, paid his share—it was seven o'clock—and, passing out, made his way back. It should be said that in addition to the Tertasse Gate, two lesser gates, the Treille on the one hand and the Monnaye on the other led from the town proper to the Corraterie; and this time he chose to go out by the Treille. Having ascertained that the guard-room there also was almost denuded of men, he passed along the Corraterie to his bastion, hugging the houses on his right, and giving the wall a wide berth. Although the cold wind blew in his face he paused several times to listen, nor did he enter his bastion until he had patiently made certain that it was untenanted.

The night was very dark: it was the night of December the 12th, old style, the longest and deadest of the year. Far below him in the black abyss on which the wall looked down a few feeble oil lamps marked the island and the town beyond the Rhone. Behind him, on his left, a glimmer escaping here and there from the upper windows marked the line of the Corraterie, of which the width is greatest at the end farthest from the river. Near the far extremity of the rampart, a bright light marked the Porte

Neuve, distant about two hundred yards from his post, and about seventy or eighty from the Porte Tertasse, the inner gate which corresponded with it. Straight from him to the Porte Neuve ran the rampart, a few feet high on the inner side, some thirty feet high on the outer, but shrouded for the present in a black gloom that defied his keenest vision.

He waited more than an hour, his ears on the alert. At the end of that time, he drew a deep breath of relief. A step that might have been the step of a sentry pacing the rampart, and now pausing, now moving on, began to approach him. It came on, paused, came on, paused—this time close at hand. Two or three dull sounds followed, then the sharper noise of a falling stone. Immediately the foot of the sentry, if sentry it was, began to retreat.

Claude drove his nails into the palms of his hands and waited, waited through an eternity, waited until the retreating foot had almost reached, as he judged, the Porte Tertasse. Then he stole out, groped his way to the wall, and passed his hand along the outer side until he came to the nail. He found it. It had been made secure, and from it depended a thin string.

He set to work at once to draw up the string. There was a small weight attached to it, which rose slowly until it reached his hand. It was a stone about as large as the fist, and of a whitish colour.

CHAPTER XXIII

IN TWO CHARACTERS

AFTER the wave, the trough of the wave; after action, passion. Not to sink a little after rising to the pitch of self-sacrifice, not to shed, when the deed is done, some bitter tears of regret and self-pity, were to be cast in a mould above the human.

When the cloak—dear garment!—had slipped from her hands, and the head bent that its owner might raise the cloak had passed from sight—when Anne had fled to the farther side of the room, to the farther side of the settle, and had heard his step die away, she would have given the world to see him again, to feel his arm about her, to hear the sound of his voice. The tears streamed down her face; in vain she tried to stay them with her hands, in vain she chid herself for her weakness. "It is for him! for him!" she moaned, and hid her face in her hands. But words stay no tears; and on the hearth which his coming had changed for her, standing where she had first seen him, where she had heard his first words of love, where she had tried him, she wept bitter tears for him.

The storm died away at last—for after every storm falls a calm—but it left the empty house, the empty heart, silence. Her mother? She had still her mother, and with lagging footsteps she went upstairs to her. But she found

her in a deep sleep, and she descended again, and going
to his room began to put together his few belongings, the
clothes he had worn, the books he had read; that if the
house were entered they might not be lost to him. She
buried her face in his garments and kissed them fondly,
tenderly, passionately, lingering over the task, and at last
putting the things from her with reluctance. A knot of
ribbon which she had seen him wear in the neck of his
shirt on holidays she took and hid in her bosom, and
fetching a length of her own ribbon she put it in place
of the other. This she thought she could do without fear
of bringing suspicion on him, for he alone would discern
the exchange. Would he notice it? Would he weep when
he found the ribbon as she wept now? And fondle it tenderly? At the thought her tears gushed forth.

The day wore on. Supported by the knowledge that
even a slight shock might cast her mother into one of her
fits, Anne hid her fears from her, though the effort was
as the lifting of a great weight. On the pretext that the
light hurt the invalid's sight, she shaded the window, and
so hid the hollows under her eyes and the wan looks that
must have betrayed the forced nature of her cheerfulness.
As a rule Madame Royaume's eyes, quickened by love,
were keen; but this day she slept much, and the night was
fairly advanced when Anne, in the act of preparing to lie
down, turned and saw her mother sitting erect in the bed.

The old woman's eyes were strangely bright. Her face
wore an intent expression which arrested her daughter
where she stood.

"Mother, what is it?" she cried.

"Listen!" Madame Royaume answered. "What is
that?"

"I hear nothing," Anne said, hoping to soothe her. And she approached the bed.

"I hear much," the mother retorted. "Go! Go and see, child, what it is!" She pointed to the door, but before Anne could reach it, she raised her hand for silence. "They are crossing the ditch," she muttered, her eyes dilated. "One, two, many, many of them! Many of them! They are throwing down hurdles and wattles, and crossing on them! And there is a priest with them——"

"Mother!"

"A priest!" Her voice dropped a little. "The ladders are black," she whispered. "Black ladders! Ay, swathed in black cloth; and now they set them against the wall. The priest absolves them, and they begin to mount. They are mounting! They are mounting now!"

"Mother!" There was sharp pain in Anne's voice. Who does not know the heartache with which it is seen that the mind of a loved one is wandering from us? And yet she was puzzled. She dreaded one of those scenes in which her young strength was barely sufficient to control and soothe the frail form before her. But they did not begin as a rule in this fashion; here, though the mind wandered, was an absence of the wildness to which she had become inured. Here—and yet as she listened, as she looked, now at her mother, now into the dimly-lighted corners of the room, where those dilated eyes seemed to see things unseen by her, black things, she found this phase no less disquieting than the other.

"Hush!" Madame Royaume continued, heeding her daughter's interruption no farther than by that word and an impatient movement of the hand. "A stone has fallen and struck one down. They raise him, he is lifeless! No, he moves, he rises. They set other ladders against the wall. They mount now by tens and twenties—and—it is growing dark—dark, child. Dark!" She seemed to try to put away a curtain with her hands.

"Mother!" Anne cried, bending over the bed and taking her mother's hand. "Don't, dear! Don't! You frighten me."

The old woman raised her hand for silence, and continued to gaze before her. Anne's arm was round her; the girl marked with astonishment, almost with awe, how strongly and stiffly she sat up. She marvelled still more when her mother sighed, murmured in the same tone, "I can see no more," and sank gently back. Anne bent over her. "I can—see no more," Madame Royaume repeated; "I can——" She was asleep!

Anne bent over her, and after listening awhile to her easy breathing, heaved a deep sigh of relief. Her mother had been talking in her sleep; and she, Anne, had alarmed herself for nothing. Nevertheless, as she turned from the bed she looked nervously over her shoulder. The other's wandering or dream, or what it was, had left a vague disquiet on her mind, and presently she took the lamp and, opening the door, passed out, and, with her hand still on the latch, listened.

Suddenly her heart bounded, her startled eyes leapt upward to the ceiling. Close to her, above her, she heard a sound.

It came from a trap door that led to the tiles; a trap that even as her eyes reached it, lifted itself with a rending sound. Save for the bedridden woman, Anne was alone in the house; and for one instant it was a question whether she held her ground or fled shrieking into the room she had left. For an instant; then the instinct to shield her mother won the day, and with fascinated eyes she watched the legs of a man drop through the aperture, watched a body follow, and—and at last a face!

Claude's face! But changed. Even while she sank gasping against the wall—for the relief was too much for her—even while he took the lamp from her shaking hand and supported her, and comfort and joy began to run like wine through her veins, she knew it. The forceful look, the tightened lips, the eyes gleaming with determination—all were new to her; they gave him an aspect so old, so strange, that when he had kissed her once she put him from her.

"What is it?" she said. "Oh Claude! What is it? What has happened?"

Letting a smile appear—but such a smile as did not reassure her—he signed to her to go before him downstairs. She complied; but at the foot of the first flight she stopped, she could bear the suspense no longer. She turned to him again. "What is it?" she cried. "Something has happened."

"Something is happening," he answered. His eyes shone, exultant. "But it is a matter for others! We may be easy!"

"What is it?"

"The Savoyards are in Geneva."

She stared incredulously. "In Geneva? Here?" she exclaimed. "The enemy?"

He nodded.

"Here? In Geneva?" she repeated. She could not have heard aright.

"Yes."

But she still looked at him; she could not reconcile his words with his manner. This, the greatest calamity that could happen, this which she had been brought up to fear as the worst and most awful of catastrophes—could he talk of it, could he announce it after this fashion, with a smile, in a tone of pleasantry? He must be playing with her. She passed her hand over her eyes, and tried to be calm. "But all is quiet?" she said.

"All is quiet now," he answered. "At twelve the trouble will begin."

Still she could not understand him. His face said one thing, his voice another. Besides, the town was quiet: no sound of riot or disturbance, no clash of steel, no tramp of feet penetrated the walls. And their house stood on the ramparts where the first alarm would be given. "Do you mean," she asked at last, her eyes fixed steadfastly on him, "that they are going to attack the town at twelve?"

"They are here now," he replied, shrugging his shoulders. "They scaled the walls after the guard had gone round at eleven, and they are now lying by tens and twenties along the outer side of the Corraterie, waiting for the hour and the signal."

She passed her hand across her closed eyes, and looked again, perplexedly. "And you," she said, "you? I do not understand. If this be so, what are you doing here?"

"Here?"

"Ay, here! Why have you not given the alarm in the town?"

"Why should I give the alarm?" he retorted coolly. "To save those who hounded you through the streets two days ago? To save those who to-morrow may put you to the torture and burn you like the vilest of creatures?

Save them?" with a grim smile. "No, let them save themselves!"

"But——"

"I would save you! not them! I would save your mother! not them! And it is done. Let the Grand Duke triumph to-night, let Savoy take Geneva, and our good townsfolk will have other matters to occupy their thoughts to-morrow! Ay, and through many and many a morrow to come! Save them?" with a grim cynical note in his voice, "No, I save you. Let them save themselves! It is God's mercy on us, and His judgment on them! Or why happens it to-night? To-night of all nights in the year?"

She was very pale, and for a moment remained silent: whether she felt the temptation to which he had succumbed, or was seeking what she should say to move him, is uncertain. At last, "It is impossible," she murmured, in a low voice. And she shivered. "You have not thought of the women and children, of the fathers and mothers who will suffer."

"And your mother!"

"Is one. God forbid that I should save her at the expense of all! God forbid! God forbid!" she wailed, as if she feared her own strength, as if the temptation almost overcame her. And then laying her hand on his arm and looking up to him—his face was set so hard. "You will not do this!" she said. "You will not do this! Could we be happy after? Could we be happy with blood on our heads, and on our hands, and on our hearts! Happy, oh no! Claude, dear heart, dear husband, we cannot buy happiness so, or life so, or love so! We cannot save ourselves—so! We cannot play God's part—so!"

"It is not we who do it," he answered stubbornly.

"It is we who may prevent it!" she answered, leaning more heavily on his arm, looking up to him more earnestly; with pleading eyes which it was hard to refuse. "Would you, to save us, have betrayed Geneva?"

He groaned—she had moved him. "God knows!" he answered. "To save you—I think I would!"

"You would not! You would not!" she repeated. "Neither must you do this! Honour, faith, duty, all forbid it!"

"And love!" he cried.

"And love!" she answered bravely. "For who would love dishonoured? Who would love in shame? No; go as you have come, and give the alarm! And do, and help! Go, as you have come! But how"—with a startled look as she thought of the trap door—"did you come?"

"By the Tertasse Gate," he explained. "There were but two men on guard, and they were asleep. I passed them unseen, climbed the stairs to the leads—I have been up twice before—and crossed the roofs. I knew I could come this way unseen, and if I had come by the door——"

She understood and she cut him short. "Then go as you came and rouse the watch in the gate!" she cried feverishly. "Rouse them all, and Heaven grant you be not too late! Go, Claude, for the love of me, for the love of God, go quickly!" Her hands on his arm shook with eagerness. "So that, if there be treachery here——"

"There is treachery!" he said darkly. "Grio——"

"We at least shall have no part in it! You will go? You will go?" she repeated, clinging to his arm, trembling against him, looking up to him with eyes which he could not resist. Love wrestled here, on the higher, the nobler,

the unselfish side, and came the stronger out of the contest.
There were tears in his eyes as he answered.

"I will go. You are right, Anne. But you will be
alone."

"I run no greater risk than others," she answered.

He held her to him, and their lips met once. And in
that instant, her heart beating against his, she comprehended to what she was sending him, into what peril of
life, into what a hell of force and darkness and fire
and blood; and her arms clung to him as if she could
not let him go. Then, "Go, and God keep you!" she
murmured in a choked voice. And she thrust him from
her.

A moment later he was on the roof, and she was kneeling where he had left her, bowed down, with her face on
the bare stairs in an agony of prayer for him. But not
for long; she had her part to do. She hurried down to the
living-room and made sure that the strong shutters were
secured; then up to Basterga's room and to Grio's, and
as far as her strength went she piled the furniture against
the iron-barred casements that looked on to the ramparts.
While she worked her ears listened for the alarm, but,
until she had finished and was ascending with the light to
her mother's room she heard nothing. Then a distant cry,
a faint challenge, the drum-drum of running feet, a second
cry—and silence. It might be his death-cry she had heard;
she stood with a white face, shivering, waiting, bearing
the woman's burden of suspense. To lie down by her
mother was impossible; rapine, murder, fire, all the horrors, all the perils of a city taken by surprise, crowded
into her mind. Yet they moved her not so much as the
dangers he ran, whom she had sent forth to confront them,

whom she had plucked from her own breast that he might face them!

Meanwhile, Claude, after gaining the tiles, paused a moment to consider his next step. Far below him, on the narrow, black triangle of the Corraterie, lay the Savoyards, some three hundred in number, who had scaled the wall. Out of the darkness of the plain, beyond and below them, rose the faint, distant quacking of alarmed ducks, proving that others of the enemy moved there. Even as he listened, the whirr of a wild goose, winging its flight over the city came to his ear. On his left, where a dim oil lamp or two marked the meeting of four ways, the town slept unsuspicious, recking nothing of the fate prepared for it.

It was a solemn moment, and Claude, on the roof under the night sky, felt it to be so. Restored to his higher self, he breathed a prayer for guidance and for her, and was as eager now as he had before been cold. But not the less for that did he ply the wits that, working freely in this hour of peril, proved him one of those whom battle owns for master. He had gathered enough, lying on his face in the bastion, to feel sure that the forlorn hope which had gained a footing on the wall, would not move until the arrival of the main body whom it was its plan to admit by the Porte Neuve. To carry the alarm to the Porte Neuve, therefore, and secure that gate, seemed to be the first and most important step; since to secure the Tertasse and the other inner gates would be of little avail, if the main body of the enemy were once in possession of the ramparts. The course that at first sight seemed the most obvious—to enter the town, give the alarm at the town hall, and set the tocsin ringing—he rejected; for while the town was arming, the three hundred who had entered might seize the Porte Neuve and so secure an entrance for the main body.

These calculations occupied no more than a few seconds; then, his mind made up to the course he must pursue, he crawled as quickly, but also as quietly, as he could along the dark parapets until he gained the leads of the Tertasse. Safe so far he proceeded with equal or greater caution to descend the narrow corkscrew staircase, that led to the guard-room on the ground floor.

He forgot that it is more easy to ascend without noise than to descend. With all his care he stumbled when he was within three steps of the bottom. He tried to save himself, but fell against the half-open door, flung it open, and, barely keeping his feet, found himself confronted by the two watchmen, who, startled by the noise, had sprung to their feet, thinking the devil was upon them. One, with an oath upon his lips, reached for his half-pike: his fellow, less sober, steadied himself by resting one hand on the table.

If they gave the alarm, his plan was gone. The enemy, finding themselves discovered, would seize the Porte Neuve. "One minute!" he cried breathlessly. "Let me explain!"

"You!" the more sober retorted, glaring fiercely at him. "Who the devil are you? And where have you been?"

"Quiet, man, quiet!"

"What is it?"

"Treason!" Claude answered, imploring silence by a gesture. "Treason! That is what it is! But for God's sake no noise! No noise, man, or our throats are as good as cut! Savoy has the wall!"

The man stared, and no wonder. "You are mad," he said, "or drunk! Savoy——"

"Fool, it is so!" Claude cried, beside himself with impatience.

"Savoy?"

"They are under the trees on the ramparts within a few yards of us now! Three hundred of them! A word and you will feel their pikes in your breast! Listen to me!"

But with a laugh of derision the drunken man cut him short.

"Savoy here—on the wall!" he hiccoughed. "And we on guard!"

"It is so!" Claude urged. "Believe me, it is so! And we must be wary!"

"You lie, young man! And I'll—hic—I'll prove it! See here! Savoy on the wall, indeed! Savoy? And we on guard?"

He lurched in two steps to the outer door, seized it, and supported himself by it. Claude leant forward to stop him, but could not reach, being on the other side of the table. He called to the other to do so. "Stop him!" he said. "Stop him!"

The man might have done so, but he did not stir; and "Stop him?" the sot answered, his hand on the door. "Not—two of you—will stop him! Now, then! Savoy, indeed! On the wall? I'll show you!"

He let the door go, and reeled three paces into the darkness outside, waving his hands as if he drove chickens. "Savoy! Savoy!" he cried; but whether in drunken bravado, in derision, or in pure disbelief, Heaven only knows! For the word had barely passed his lips the second time before a gurgling scream followed, freezing the hearts of the two listeners; and, before the second guard could close the door or move from his place on the hearth, four men sprang in out of the darkness, and bore him back. Before he had struck a blow they had pinned him against the wall.

Claude owed his escape to his position behind the door. They did not see him as they sprang in, intent on the one they did see. He knew resistance to be futile, and a bound carried him into the darkness of the corkscrew staircase. Once there, he dared not move. He saw or heard what followed.

The man pinned against the wall, with the point of a knife flickering before his eyes, begged piteously for his life.

"Then silence!" Basterga answered—for the foremost who had entered was he. "A word and you die!"

"Better let me finish him at once!" Grio growled. The prisoner's face was ashen, his eyes were starting from his head. "Dead men give no alarms."

"Mercy! Mercy!" the man gasped.

"Ay, ay, let him live," Basterga said good-naturedly. "But he must be gagged. Turn your face to the wall, my man!"

The poor wretch complied with gratitude. In a twinkling the Paduan's huge fingers closed round his neck, and over his windpipe. "Now strike," the big man hissed. "He will make no noise!"

With a sickening thud Grio's knife sank between the shoulders, a moment the body writhed in Basterga's herculean grip, then sank lifeless to the floor. "Had you struck him, fool," Basterga muttered wrathfully, wiping a little blood from his sleeve, "as you wanted to strike him—he had squealed like a pig! Now 'tis the same, and no noise. Ha! Seize him!"

He spoke too late. Claude had seen his opportunity, and as the treacherous blow was struck had crept forth. At the moment the other saw him and cried the alarm, he was in the act of bounding over the threshold. As his feet touched the ground outside, a man who stood there lunged at him with a pike but missed him—a chance, for Claude had not seen the striker. The next moment the young man had launched himself into the darkness and was running for his life across the Corraterie in the direction of the Porte Neuve.

He knew that his foes were lying on every side of him, and the cry of "Seize him! Seize him!" went with him, making every step a separate peril. He could not see a yard, but he was young and fleet, and active; and the darkness covered him, the men were confused. Over more than one black object he bounded like a deer. Once a man rising in front of him brought him heavily to the ground, but by good fortune it was his foot struck the man, and on the head, and the fellow lay still and let him rise. A moment later another gripped him, but Claude and he fell together, and the younger man, rolling nimbly sideways, got clear and to his feet again, made for the wall on his right, turned left again, and already thought himself over the threshold of the Porte Neuve. The cry "Aux Armes! Aux Armes!" was already on his lips, he thought he had succeeded; when, between his eyes and the faintly lighted gateway, a dozen forms rose as by magic and poured in before him—so near to him that, unable to check himself, he jostled the hindmost.

He might have entered with them—so near was he.

But he saw that he was too late; he guessed that the out-cry behind him had precipitated the attack, and arresting himself outside the ring of light, but within a few paces of the gateway, he threw himself on the ground and awaited the event. It was not long in declaring itself. For a few seconds a dull roar of shots and shouts and curses filled the gate. Then out again, helter-skelter, with a flash of exploding powder and a whirl of steel and blows, came defenders and assailants in a crowd, the former bent on escaping, the latter on cutting them off from the Porte Tertasse and the town. For an instant after they had poured out the gate seemed quiet. With his eyes upon it, Claude rose, first to his knees and then to his feet, paused a moment in doubt, then darted in and entered the guard-room.

The firelight—the other lights in the small, dingy chamber had been trampled under foot—showed him two wounded men groaning on the floor, and the body of a third who lay apparently dead. Claude bent over one, found what he wanted, a half-pike, and made for the door of the stairs that led to the roof. It was in the same position as in the Tertasse. He opened it, passed through it, mounted two steps, and in the darkness came against someone who seized him by the throat.

The man had no weapon—at any rate he did not strike; and Claude, taken by surprise, could not level his pike in the narrow stairway. For a moment they wrestled, Claude striving to bring his weapon to bear on his foe, the latter trying to strangle him. But the advantage of the stairs lay with the first-comer, who was uppermost, and grad-ually he bore Claude back. The young man, however, would not let go such hold as he had, and they were on the point of falling out together on the floor of the guard-room when the light disclosed Claude's face.

"You are of us!" his opponent panted. And abruptly he released his grip.

"Geneva!"

"I know you!" The man was one of the guard who, in the alarm, had escaped into the stairway. "I know you! You live in the Corraterie!"

Claude wasted not a second. "Up!" he cried. "We can hold the roof! Up, man, for your life! For your life! It is our only chance!"

With the fear of death upon him, the other needed no second telling. He turned, and groped upward; and Claude followed, treading on his heels; nor a moment too soon. While they were still within the narrow staircase, which their elbows rubbed on either side, they heard the enemy swarm into the room below. Cries of triumph, of "Savoy! Savoy!" of "Ville gagnée! gagnée!" hummed dully up to them, and proclaimed the narrowness of their escape. Then the night air met their faces, they bent their heads and passed out upon the leads; they had above them the stars, and below them all the world of night, with its tramp of hidden feet, its swaying lights so tiny and so distant, and here and there its cry of "Savoy! Savoy!" that showed that the enemy, relying on their capture of the Porte Neuve, were casting off disguise.

Claude heard and saw all, but lost not a moment. He had not made this haste for his life only: before he had risen to his knees or set foot in the gate, he had formed his plan. "The portcullis!" he cried. "The portcullis! Where are the chains? On this side?" Less than a week before he had stood and watched the guard as they released it, and raised it again for practice.

The soldier, familiar with the tower, should have been able to go to the chains at once. But though he had struggled for his life and was ready to struggle for it again, he had not recovered his nerve, and he shrank from leaving the stairs, in holding which their one chance of life consisted. He muttered, however, that the winch was on such and such a side, and, with his head in the stairway, indicated the direction with his hand. Claude groped his way thither, his breath coming fast; fortunately he laid his hand at once on the chains and felt for the spike, which he knew he must draw or knock out. That done, the winch would fly round, and the huge machine fall by its own weight.

On a sudden, "They are coming!" the soldier cried in a terrified whisper. "My God, they are coming! Come back! Come back!" For Claude had their only weapon, and the guard was defenceless. Defenceless by the side of the stairs up which the foe was climbing!

The hair rose on Claude's head, but he set his teeth; though the man died, though he died, the portcullis must fall! More than his own life, more than the lives of two, more than the lives of a hundred or a thousand hung on that bolt; the fate of millions yet unborn, the freedom and the future of a country hung on that spike—which would not give way, though now he had found it and was hammering it. Grinding his teeth, the sweat on his brow, he beat on it with the pike, struck the iron with the strength of despair, stooped to see what was amiss—still with the frenzied prayers of the other in his ears—saw it, and struck again and again—and again!

Whirr! The winch flew round, barely missing his head. With a harsh grinding sound that rose with incredible swiftness to a scream, piercing the night, the ponderous grating slid down, crashed home, and barred all entrance, closed the Porte Neuve. It did more, though Claude did not know it. It cut off the engineer from the outer gate, of which the keys were at the Town Hall, and against which in another minute, another sixty seconds, he had set his petard. That set and exploded, Geneva had lain open to its enemies. As it was so small was the margin, so fatally accurate the closing, that the day at its rising disclosed a portent. When the victors assembled to examine the spot they found beneath the portcullis the mangled body of one of the engineers, and beside him lay his petard.

CHAPTER XXIV

ARMES! ARMES!

CLAUDE did not know all that he had done, or the narrow margin of time by which he had succeeded. But he did know that he had saved the gate; that gate on the outer side of which four thousand of the picked troops of Savoy were waiting the word to enter. He knew that he had done it with death at his elbow and with the cries of his panic-stricken companion in his ears. And in the moment of success he rose above the common level. He felt himself master of fear, lord of death; in the exultation of his triumph he thought nothing too hard or too dangerous for him.

It was well perhaps that he had this feeling, for he had not a moment to waste if he would save himself. As the portcullis struck the ground with a thunderous crash and rebounded, and he turned from the winch to the stairhead, a last warning, cut short in the utterance, reached him, and he saw through the gloom that his companion was already in the grip of a figure which had succeeded in passing out of the staircase. Claude did not hesitate. With a roar of rage he ran like a bull at the enemy, struck him full under the arm with his pike, and drove him doubled up into the stairhead, with such force that the Genevese had much ado to free himself.

The man was struck helpless—dead for aught that appeared at the moment, but the pike coming in contact with the edge of his corselet had not penetrated, and Claude recovered it quickly, and levelled it in waiting for the next comer. At the same time he adjured his comrade to secure the fallen man's weapon. The guard seized it, and the two waited, with suspended breath, for the sally which they were sure must come.

But the stairs were narrow, the fallen body blocked the outlet, and possibly the assailants had expected no resistance. Finding it, they thought better of it. A moment and they could be heard beating a retreat.

"Pardieu! they are going!" the guard exclaimed; and he began to shake.

"Ay, but they will return!" Claude answered, grimly. "Have no fear of that! The portcullis is down, and the only way to raise it, is up these stairs. But it will be hard if, armed as we are now, we cannot baffle them! Has he no pistol?"

Marcadel—that was the soldier's name—felt about the prostrate man, but found none; and bidding him listen and not move for his life—but there was little need of the injunction—Claude passed over to the inner edge of the leads, facing the Corraterie. Here he raised his voice and shouted the alarm with all the force of his lungs, hoping thus to supplement the cries which here and there had been raised by the Savoyards.

"Aux Armes! Armes!" he cried. "The enemy is at the gate! To arms! To arms!"

A man ran out of the gateway at the sound of his shouting, levelled a musket and fired at him. The slugs flew wide, and Claude, lifted above himself, yelled defiance, knowing that the more shots were fired the more quickly and widely would the alarm be spread.

That it was spreading, that it was being taken up, his position on the gateway enabled him to discern; distant as the Porte Neuve lay from the heart of the town. A flare of light at the rear of the Tertasse, and a confused hubbub in that quarter, seemed to show that, though the Savoyards had seized the gate, they had not penetrated beyond it. Away on his extreme left, where the Porte de la Monnaye, hard by his old bastion, overlooked the Rhone and the island, were lights again, and a sound of a commotion as though there too the enemy held the gate, but found farther progress closed against them. On the Treille to his right, the most westerly of the three inner gates, and the nearest to the Town Hall, the enemy seemed to be preparing an attack, for as he ceased to shout, muskets exploded in that direction, and as far as he could judge the shots were aimed outward.

With such alarms at three inner points—to say nothing of the noise at the more distant Porte Neuve—it seemed impossible that any part of the city could remain in ignorance of the attack. In truth, as he stood peering down into the dark Corraterie, and listening to the heavy tramp of unseen feet, now here, now there, and the orders that rose from unseen throats—even then, as he prepared to turn, summoned by a warning cry from Marcadel, the first note of the alarm-bell smote his ear.

One moment and the air hummed with its heavy challenge, and all of Geneva that still slept awoke and stood upright. Men ran half naked from their houses. Boys in their teens snatched arms and sallied forth. White faces looked from barred windows or lofty dormers; and across narrow wynds and under dark Gothic entries men dragged huge chains and hooked them, and hurried on to where the

alarm seemed loudest and the risk most pressing.   In an
instant in pitch-dark alleys lights gleamed and steel clanged
on stone; out of the darkness deep voices shouted questions, or answered or gave orders, and from a thousand
houses, alike in the wealthy Bourg du Four with its three-
storied piles, and in the sordid lanes about the water and
the bridges, went up one wail of horror and despair.   Men
who had dreamed of this night for years, and feared it as
they feared God's day, awoke to find their dream a fact,
and never while they lived forgot that awakening; while
women left alone in their homes bolted and barred and fell
to prayers; or clasped to their breasts babes who prattled,
not understanding the turmoil, or why their mothers
looked strangely on them.

Something of this, something of the horror of that sudden awakening, and of the confusion in the narrow streets,
where voices cried that the enemy were here or there or
in a third place, and the bravest knew not which way to
turn, penetrated to Claude on the roof of the tower; and
at the thought of Anne and the perils that encircled her
—for about the house in the Corraterie the uproar rose
loudest—his face hardened.   But he had not long to dwell
on her danger; not long to dwell on anything.   Before the
great bell had hurled its warning abroad three times he
had to go.   Marcadel's voice, urgent, insistent, summoned
him to the stairhead.

"They are mustering at the bottom!" the man whispered over his shoulder.   He was on his knees, his head
in the hood of the staircase.   The wounded man, breathing stertorously, still cumbered the upper steps.   Marcadel rested one hand on him.

Claude thrust in his head and listened.   He could hear,

above the thick breathing of the Savoyard, the stir of men muttering and moving in the darkness below; and now the stealthy shuffle of feet, and again the faint clang of a weapon against the wall. Doubtless it had dawned on someone in command below, that here on this tower lay the keys of Geneva: that by themselves three hundred men could not take, nor hold if they took, a town manned by five or six thousand; consequently that if Savoy would succeed in the enterprise so boldly begun, she must by hook or crook raise this portcullis and open this gate. As a fact, Brunaulieu, the captain of the forlorn hope, had passed the word that the tower must be taken at any cost; and had come himself from the Porte Tertasse, where a brisk conflict was beginning, to see the thing done.

Claude did not know this, but had he known it, it would not have reduced his courage.

"Yes, I hear them," he whispered, in answer to the soldier's words. "But they have not mounted far yet. And when they come, if two pikes cannot hold this doorway, where they can mount but one at a time, there is no truth in Thermopylæ!"

"I know naught of that," the other answered, rising nervously to his feet. "I don't favour heights. Give me the lee of a wall and fair odds——"

"Odds?" Claude echoed vain-gloriously—but only the stars attended to him. "I would not have another man!"

Marcadel seized him by the sleeve. His voice rose almost to a scream. "But, by Heaven, there is another man!" he cried. "There!" He pointed with a shaking hand to the outer corner of the leads, in the neighbourhood of the place where the winch of the portcullis stood. "We are betrayed! We are dead men!" he babbled.

Claude made out a dim figure, crouching against the battlement; and the thought, which was also in the other's mind, that the enemy had set a ladder against the wall and outflanked them, rendered him desperate. At any rate there was but one on the roof as yet: and quick as thought the young man lowered his pike and charged the figure.

With a shrill scream the man fell on his knees before him. "Mercy!" cried a voice he knew. "Mercy! Don't kill me! Don't kill me!"

It was Louis Gentilis. Claude halted, looked at him in amazement, spurned him with his foot. "Up, coward, and fight for your life then!" he said. "Or others will kill you. How come you here?"

The lad still grovelled. "I was in the guard-room," he whimpered. "I had come with a message—from the Syndic."

"The Syndic Blondel?"

"Yes! To remind the Captain that he was to go the rounds, at eleven exactly. I was there, and they—oh, this dreadful night—they broke in, and I hid on the stairs."

"Well, you can hide no longer. You have got to fight now!" Claude answered grimly. "There are no more stairs for any of us except to heaven! I advise you to find something, and do your worst. Take the winch-bar if you can find nothing else! And——"

He broke off. Marcadel, who had remained at the stairhead, was calling to him in a voice of despair. Claude ran to him. He found him with his head in the stairway, but with his pike shortened to strike. "They are coming!" he muttered over his shoulder. "They are more than half-

way up now. Be ready and keep your eyes open. Be
ready!" he continued after a pause. "They are nearly—
here now!" His breath began to come quickly; at last,
stepping back a pace and bringing his point to the charge.
"They are here!" he cried in a ringing tone. "On guard!"

Claude stooped an inch lower, and with gleaming eyes,
and feet set warily apart, waited the onset; waited with
suspended breath for the charge that must come. He
could hear the gasps of the wounded man who lay on the
uppermost step; and once close to him he caught a sound
of shuffling, moving feet, that sent his heart into his
mouth. But seconds passed, and more seconds, and glare
as he might into the black mouth of the staircase, from
which the hood averted the light of the stars, he could
make out nothing, no movement, no sign of life!

The suspense was growing intolerable. And all the
time behind him the alarm-bell was flinging "Doom!
Doom!" down on the city, and a thousand sounds of fear
and strife clutched at his mind and strove to draw it from
the dark gap at which he waited, as a dog waits for a rat at
the mouth of its hole. His breath began to come quickly,
his knees shook. He heard his companion gasp—human
nerves could stand it no longer. And then, just as he felt
that, come what might, he must plunge his pike into the
darkness, and settle the question, the shuffling sound came
anew and steadied him, and he set his teeth and waited—
waited still.

But nothing happened, nothing moved. Again the seconds, almost the minutes passed, and the deep note of the
alarm-bell swelled louder and heavier, filling all the air, all
the night, all the world, with its iron tongue—setting the
tower reeling, the head swimming. In spite of himself, in

spite of the fact that he knew his life hung on his vigilance, his thoughts wandered; wandered to Anne, alone and defenceless in the hell below him, from which wild sounds were beginning to rise; to his own fate if he and Marcadel got the worst; to the advantage which a light properly shaded would have given them, had they had it. But, alas, they had no light.

And then, while he thought of that, the world was all light. A sheet of flame burst from the hood, dazzled, blinded, scorched him; a crashing report filled his ears, he recoiled. The ball had missed him, had gone between him and Marcadel and struck neither. But for a moment in pure amazement, he stood gaping.

That moment had been his last had the defence lain with him alone, or even with him and Marcadel. It was the senseless form that cumbered the uppermost step which saved them. The man who had fired tripped over it as he sprang out. He fell his length on the roof. The next man, less hasty or less brave, sank down on the obstacle, and blocked the way for others.

Before either could rise, all was over. Claude brought down his pike on the head of the first to issue, and laid him lifeless on the leads. The guard, who was a better man at a pinch than in the anticipation of it, drove the other back —as he tried to rise—with a wound in the face. Then with a yell, assured that in the narrow stairhead the enemy could not use their weapons, the two charged their pikes into the obscurity, and thrust and thrust, and thrust again, in the cruelty of rage and fear.

What they struck, or where they struck, they could not see; but their ears told them that they did not strike in vain. A shrill scream, and the gurgling cry of a dying man proved it, and the wild struggle that ensued on the stairs; where the uppermost, weighed down by the fallen men, turned in a panic on those below and fought with them to force them to descend.

Claude shuddered as he listened, as he waited, his pike still levelled; shuddered at the pitiful groaning that issued from the blackness, shuddered at the blows he had struck, and the scream that still echoed in his ears. He had not trembled when he fought, but he trembled at the thought of it.

"They are beaten," he muttered huskily.

"Ay, they are beaten!" Marcadel—he who had trembled before the fight—answered with exultation. "You were right. We wanted no more men! But it was near. If this rogue had not tripped our throats would have suffered."

"He was a brave man," Claude answered, leaning heavily on his pike. He needed its support.

Marcadel knelt down and felt the man over. "Ay," he said, "he was, to give the devil his due! And that reminds me. We've a skulker here who has escaped so far. He shall play his part now. We must have their arms, but it is dirty work groping in the dark for them; and maybe life enough in one of them to drive a dagger between one's ribs. He shall do it. Where is he?"

Claude was feeling the reaction which ensues upon intense excitement. He did not answer. Nor did he interfere when Marcadel, pouncing on Louis, where he crouched in the darkest corner, forced him forward to the head of the staircase. The lad fell on his knees weeping futilely, wailing prayers. But the guard kicked him forward.

"In!" he said. "You know what you have to do! In,

and strip them! Do you hear? And if you leave so much as a knife——"

"I won't! I daren't!" Louis screamed. And grovelling on his face on the leads he clung to whatever offered itself.

But men who are fresh from a life and death struggle are hard. "You won't?" Marcadel answered, applying his boot brutally, but without effect. "You will! Or you will feel my pike between your ribs! In! In, my lad!"

A scream answered each repetition of the word, and proved that the threat was no empty one. Claude might have intervened, but he remembered Anne and the humiliations she had suffered in this craven's presence.

"In!" Marcadel repeated a third time. "And if you leave so much as a knife upon them I will throw you off the tower. You understand, do you? Then in, and strip them!"

And driven by sheer torture—for the pike had thrice drawn blood from his writhing body—Louis crept, weeping and quaking, into the staircase; and on one of her tormentors Anne was avenged. But Claude was thinking more of her present peril than of this; he had moved from the stairhead. A swell in the volume of sound which rose from the Corraterie had drawn him to that side of the tower, where shaking off the exhaustion which for a time had overcome him, he was straining his eyes to learn what was passing in the babel below.

The sight was a singular one. The Monnaye Gate far to the left, the Tertasse immediately before him, and the Treille on his right, were the centres of separate conflagrations. In one place a house, fired by the petard employed to force the door, was actually alight. In other places so great was the conflux of torches, the flash and gleam of weapons, and the babel of sounds that it wrought on the mind the impression of a fire blazing up in the night. Behind the Porte Tertasse, in the narrow streets of the Tertasse and the Cité—immediately, therefore, behind the Royaumes' house—the conflict seemed to rage most hotly, the shots to be most frequent, the uproar greatest, even the light strongest; for the reflection of the combat below bathed the Tertasse tower in a lurid glow. Claude could distinguish the roof of the Royaumes' house; and to see so much yet to be cut off as completely as if he were a hundred miles away, to be so near yet so hopelessly divided, stung him to a new impatience and a greater daring.

He returned to Marcadel. "Are we going to stay on this tower?" he cried. "Shut up here, while this goes forward and we may be of use?"

"I think we have done our part," the other answered soberly. "If any man has saved Geneva, it is you! There, man, I give you the credit," he continued, in a burst of generosity, "and it is no small thing! For it might make my fortune. But I have done some little too!"

"Ay! But cannot we—"

"What would you have us do more?" the man continued and with reason. "Leave the roof to them? 'Tis all they want! Leave them to raise the old iron gate, and let in—what I hear yonder?" He indicated the dark outer plain below the wall, whence rose the murmur of halted battalions, awaiting baffled, and uncertain, the opening of the gate.

"Ay, but if we descend?"

"May we not win the gate from a score?" Marcadel answered, between contempt and admiration. "Is that what you mean? And when we have won it hold it? No, not if each of us were Gaston of Foix, Bayard, and M. de Crillon rolled into one! But what is this? We are winning or we are losing! Which is it?"

From the Treille Gate had burst a rabble of men; a struggling crowd, illumined by the glare of three or four lights. Pikes and halberds flashed in the heart of the mob as it swirled down the Corraterie in the direction of the gate from which the two men viewed it. Half way thither, in the open, its progress was checked; it hung and paused, swaying this way and that; it even recoiled. But at length, with a roar of triumph, it rolled on again over half a dozen prostrate forms, and in a trice burst about the base of the Porte Neuve, swept, as it seemed to those above, into the gateway, and—in a twinkling broke back, repelled by a crashing volley that shook the tower.

"They are our people!" cried Claude.

"Ay!"

"And now is our time!" The lad waved his weapon. "A diversion in the rear—and 'tis done!"

"In Heaven's name, stop!" cried Marcadel, and he gripped Claude's sleeve. "A diversion, ay!" he continued. "But a moment too soon or a moment too late—and where will we be?"

He spoke in vain. His words were wasted on the air. Claude, not to be restrained, had entered the staircase. Pike in hand, he felt his way over the bodies that choked it. By this time he was half way down the stairs. Marcadel hesitated, waited; then, partly because success begets success, and courage courage, partly because he would not have the triumph taken from him, he too risked all. He snatched from Louis' feeble hands a long pistol, part of the spoils of the staircase; and, staying only to assure himself that a portion of the priming lay in the pan, he hurried after his leader.

By this time Claude was within four stairs of the guardroom. The low door that admitted to it stood open; and toward it a man, hearing the hasty tread of feet, had that moment turned a startled face. Here was no room for anything but audacity, and Claude did not flinch. In two bounds he fell through the door on to the man, . missed him with his pike, but was himself missed. In a flash the two were rolling together on the floor.

In their fall they brought down a third man, who, swearing horribly, made repeated stabs at Claude with a dagger. But the only light in the room came from the fire, the three were interlaced, and Claude was young and agile as an eel: he evaded the first thrust, and the second. The third went home in his shoulder, but desperate with pain he seized the hand that held the poniard, and clung to it; and before the man who had been the first to fall could regain his pike, or a third man who was present, but who was wounded, could drag himself, swearing horribly, to the spot, Marcadel fired from the stairs, and killed the wounded man. The next instant with a yell of "Geneva" he sprang on the others under cover of the smoke that filled the room.

The combat was still but of two to two; and outside the guard-room, almost within arm's length, were a dozen Savoyards, headed by Picot the engineer; any one of whom might, by entering, turn the scale. But the pistol-shot had reached the ears of the attacking party; that instant they rallied and with loud cries returned to the attack. Even while Marcadel, having disposed of one man, stood over the struggling pair on the floor, doubting where to strike, the burghers burst a second time into the gateway, on which the guard-room opened, struck down Picot, and, hacking and hewing, with cries of "Porte Gagnée! Porte Gagnée!" bore the Savoyards back.

For the half of a minute the low-groined archway was a whirl of arms and steel and flame. Half a dozen single combats were in progress at once; with yells and groans, and the clash of a score of weapons. But the burghers, fighting bareheaded for their wives and hearths, were not to be denied; by and by the Savoyards gave back, broke, and saved themselves. One group cut its way out and fled into the darkness of the Corraterie. Four men remained on the ground; two turned and tried to retreat into the guard-room.

But on the threshold they met Claude, vicious and wounded, his eyes in a flame; and he struck and killed the foremost. The other fell under the blows of the pursuing burghers, and across the two bodies Claude and Marcadel met the leaders of the assault. Strange to say, the foremost and the midmost of these was a bandy-legged tailor, with a great two-handed sword, red to the hilt; to such a place can valour on such a night raise a man. On his right stood Blandano, Captain of the Guard, bareheaded and black with powder; on his left Baudichon the Councillor, panting, breathless, his fat face running with sweat and blood—for he bore an ugly wound—but with unquenchable courage in his eyes. A man may be fat and yet a lion.

It was a moment in the lives of the five men who thus met which no one of them ever forgot. "Was it one of you two who lowered the portcullis?" Blandano gasped, as he leaned an instant on his sword.

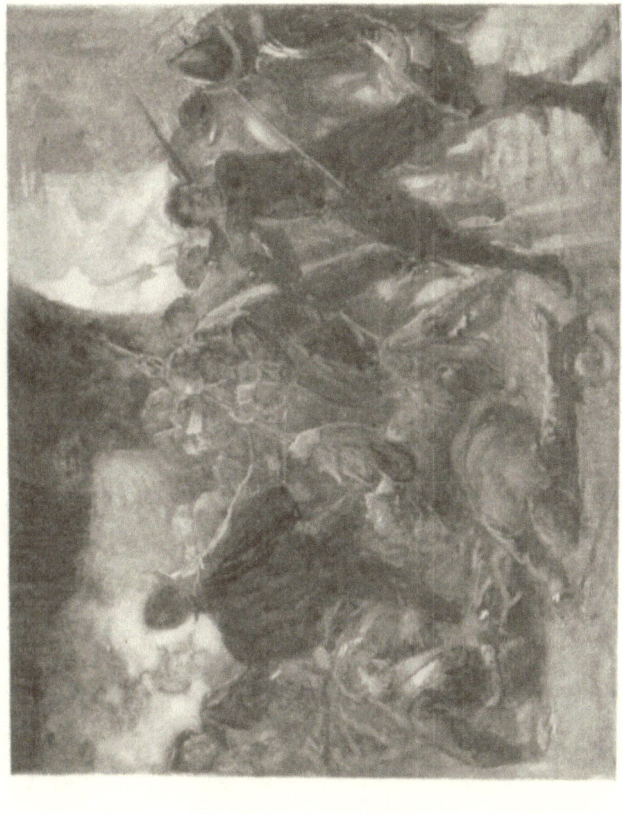

THE DIMLY

LIGHTED

ARCHWAY WAS

A WHIRL OF

LIGHT AND

CONFUSION

"He did," Marcadel answered, laying his hand on Claude's shoulder. "And I helped him."

"Then he has saved Geneva, and you have helped him!" Blandano rejoined bluntly. "Your name, young man."

Claude told him.

"Good!" Blandano answered. "If I live to see the morning light, it shall not be forgotten!"

Baudichon leant across the dead, and shook Claude's hand. "For the women and children!" he said, his fat face shaking like a jelly; though no man had fought that night with a more desperate valour. "If I live to the morning inquire for Baudichon of the Council."

Jehan Brosse, the bandy-legged tailor with the huge sword—he was but five feet high and no one up to that night had known him for a hero—squared his shoulders and looked at Claude, as one who takes another under his protection. "Baudichon the Councillor, whom all men know in Geneva," he said with an affectionate look at the great man—he was proud of the company to which his prowess had raised him. "You will not forget the name! No fear of that! And now on!"

"Ay, on!" Blandano answered looking round on his panting followers, of whom some were stanching their wounds and some, with dark faces and gleaming eyeballs, were loading and priming their arms. "But I think the worst is over and we shall win through now. We have this gate safe, and it is the key, as I told you. If all be well elsewhere, and the main guards be held——"

"Ay, but are they?" Baudichon muttered nervously: he reeled a little, for the loss of blood was beginning to tell upon him. "That is the question!"

CHAPTER XXV

BASTERGA AT ARGOS

THE fear that Blandano might postpone the night-round, to a time which would involve discovery, haunted Blondel, and late on this eventful evening he despatched Louis Gentilis to the Porte Neuve to remind the Captain of his orders. That done—it was all he could do—the Syndic sat down in his great chair, and prepared himself to wait. He knew that he had before him some hours of uncertainty almost intolerable; and a peril, a hundred times more hard to face, because in the pinch of it, he must play two parts; he must run with the hare and hunt with the hounds, and, a traitor standing forward in defence of the city he had betrayed, he must have an eye to his reputation as well as his life.

He had no doubt of the success of Savoy, the walls once passed. Moreover, the genius of Basterga had imposed itself upon him as that of a man unlikely to fail. But some resistance there must be, some bloodshed—for the town held many devoted men; one hour at least of butchery, and that followed, he shuddered to think it, by more than one hour of excess, of cruelty, of rapine. From such things the captured cities of that day rarely escaped. And in all that happened, the resistance and the peril, he must, he knew, show himself; he must take his part and run his risk if he would not be known for what he was, if he would not leave a name that men would spit on!

Strangely enough it was the moment of discovery and his conduct in that moment—it was the anticipation of this, which weighed most heavily on his guilty mind as he sat in his parlour, his hour of retiring long past, his household in bed. The city slept round him; how long would it sleep? And when it awoke, how long dared he, how long would it be natural for him to ignore the first murmur, the succeeding outcry, the rising alarm? It was not his cue to do overmuch, to precipitate discovery, or to assume at once the truth to be the truth. But on the other hand he must not be too backward.

Try as he would he could not divert his thoughts from this. He saw himself skulking in his house, listening with a white face to the rush of armed men along the street. He heard the tumult rising about him, and saw himself stand, guilty and irresolute, between hearth and door, uncertain if the time had come to go forth. Finally, and before he had made up his mind to go out, he fancied himself confronted by an entering face, and in an instant detected. And this it was, this initial difficulty, oddly enough—and not the subsequent hours of horror, confusion and danger, of dying men and wailing women—that rode his mind, dwelt on him and shook his nerves as the crisis approached.

One consolation he had, and one only; but a measureless one. Basterga had kept his word. He was cured. Six hours earlier he had taken the Remedium according to the directions, and with every hour that had elapsed since he had felt new life course through his veins. He had had no return of pain, no paroxysm; but a singular lightness of body, eloquent of the change wrought in him and the youth and strength that were to come, had done what could be done to combat the terrors of the soul, natural in his situation. Pale he was, despite the potion; in spite of it he trembled and sweated. But he knew himself changed, and sick at heart as he was, he could only guess at the depths of nervous despair to which he must have fallen had he not taken the wondrous draught.

There was that to the good. That to the good. He would live. And life was the great thing after all! life and health, and strength. If he had sold his soul, his country, his friends, at least he would live—if naught happened to him to-night. If naught—but ah, the thought pierced him to the heart. He who had proved himself in old days no mean soldier in the field, who had won honour in more than one fight, felt his brow grow damp, his knees grow flaccid, knew himself a coward. For the life which he must risk was not the old life, but the new one which he had bought so dearly; the new one for which he had given his soul, his country, and his friends. And he dared not risk that! He dared not let the winds of heaven blow too roughly on that! If aught befell him this night, the irony of it! The mockery of it! The deadly, deadly folly of it!

He sweated at the thought. He cursed, cursed frantically his folly in omitting to give himself out for worse than he was; in omitting to take to his bed early in the day! Then he might have kept it through the night, through the fight; then he might have avoided risks. Now he felt that every ball discharged at a venture must strike him; that if he showed so much as his face at a window death must find its opportunity. He would not have dared to pass through

a street on a windy day now—for if a tile fell it must
fall on him.   And he must fight!   He must fight!

His manhood shrivelled within him at the thought.   He
shuddered.   He was still shuddering, when on the shutter
which masked the casement came a knock, thrice repeated.
A cautious knock of which the mere sound implied an understanding.

The Syndic remained motionless glaring at the window.
Everything on a night like this, and to an uneasy conscience, menaced danger.   At length it occurred to him
that the applicant might be Louis, whom he had sent with
the message to the Porte Neuve: and he took the lamp and
went to admit him, but with anger and reluctance, for what
did the booby mean by returning?   It was late, and only to
open at this hour, might in the light cast by after events,
raise suspicion.

But it was not Louis.   The lamp flickering in the
draught of the doorway disclosed a bulky form glistening
with metal here and there, that pushed him back, passed
by him, entered.   It was Basterga.   The Syndic shut the
door, and staggered rather than walked after him to the
parlour.   There he set down the lamp, and turned to the
scholar, his face a picture of guilty terror.   "What is it?"
he muttered.   "What has happened?   Is it put off?"

The other's aspect answered his question.   A black
corselet with shoulder pieces, and a feathered steel cap
raised Basterga's huge stature to the gigantic.   Nor did
it need this to render him singular; to draw the eye to
him a second time and a third.   The man himself in this
hour of his success, this moment of conscious daring, of
reliance on his star and his strength, towered in the room
like a demi-god.   "No," he answered, with a ponderous,

exultant smile, slow to come, slow to go. "No, Messer
Blondel. Far from it. It has not been put off."

"Something has been discovered?"

"No. We are here. That is all."

The Syndic supported himself by a hand pressed hard
against the table behind him. "Here?" he gasped. "You
are here? You have the town already? It is impossible."

"We have three hundred men in the Corraterie," Basterga answered. "We hold the Tertasse Gate, and the
Monnaye. The Porte Neuve is cut off, and at our mercy;
it will be taken when we give the signal. Beyond it four
thousand men are waiting to enter. We hold Geneva in
our grip at last—at last!" And in an accent half tragic,
half ironic, he declaimed:

> " ' *Venit summa dies et ineluctabile tempus*
>   *Dardaniæ! Fuimus Troes, fuit Ilium et ingens*
>   *Gloria Teucrorum! Ferus omnia Jupiter Argos*
>   *Transtulit!* ' "

And then more lightly, "If you doubt me, how am I here?"
he asked. And he extended his huge arms in the pride of
his strength. "Exercise your warrant now—if you can,
Messer Syndic. Syndic?" he continued in a tone of mockery. "Where is your warrant now? I have but this
moment," he pointed to wet stains on his corselet—"slain
one of your guards. Do justice, Syndic! I have seized
one of your gates by force. Avenge it, Syndic! Syndic?
ha! ha! Here is an end of Syndics."

The Syndic gasped. He was a hard man, not to say an
arrogant one, little used to opposition; one who, time and
again, had ridden rough-shod over the views of his fellows.

To be jeered at, after this fashion, to be scorned and mocked by this man who in the beginning had talked so silkily, moved so humbly, evinced so much respect, played the poor scholar so well, was a bitter pill. He asked himself if the other spoke truly: if it was for this he had betrayed his city; if it was for this he had sold his friends. And then—then he remembered that it was not for this— not for this, but for life, dear life, warm life, that he had done this thing. And, swallowing the rage that was rising within him, he calmed himself.

"It is better to cease to be Syndic than to cease to live," he said coldly.

But the other had no mind to return to their former relations. "True, oh sage!" he answered contemptuously. "But why not both? Because—shall I tell you?"

"I hear——"

"Yes, and I hear too! The city is rising!" Basterga listened a moment. "Presently they will ring the alarm-bell, and——"

"If you stay here someone may find you!"

"And find me with you?" Basterga rejoined. He knew that he ought to go, for his own sake as well as the Syndic's. He knew that nothing was to be made and much might be lost by the disclosure that was on his tongue. But he was intoxicated with the success which he had gained; with the clang of arms, and the glitter of his armed presence. The true spirit of the man—as happens in intoxication of another kind—rose to the surface, cruel, waggish, insolent; of an insolence long restrained, the insolence of the scholar, who always in secret, now in the light, panted to repay the slights he had suffered, the patronage of leaders, the scoffs of power. "Ay," he continued, "they may find me with you! But if you do not mind, I need not. And I was just asking you—why not both? Life and power, my friend?"

"You know," Blondel answered, breathing quickly. How he hated the man now; how gladly would he have laid him dead at his feet. For if the fool stayed here prating, if he were found here by those who within a few moments might come with the alarm, he was himself a lost man! All would be known!

That was the fear in Blondel's mind; the alarm was growing louder each moment, and drawing nearer. And then in a twinkling, in two or three sentences Basterga put that fear into the second place, and set in its seat emotions that brooded no rival.

"Why not both?" he said, jeering. "Live and be Syndic, both? Because you had the scholar's ill, eh, Messer Blondel? Or because your physician *said* you had it—to whom I paid a good price—for the advice?" The devil seemed to look out of the man's eyes, as he spoke in short sentences, each pointed, each conveying a heart-stab to its hearer.

"To whom—you gave?" Blondel muttered, his eyes dilated.

"A good price—for the advice! A good price to tell you, you had it."

The magistrate's face swelled till it was almost purple, his hands gripped the front of his coat and pressed hard against his breast. "But the pains?" he muttered. "Did you—but no," with a frightful grimace, "you lie! you lie!"

"Did I bribe him—to give you those too?" the other answered, with a ruthless laugh. "You have alighted on it, most grave and reverend sage. You have alighted on the exact fact, so clever are you! That was precisely what

I did some months back, after I heard that you had been to him for some fancied ill, being fearful as rich men are. You had two medicines? You remember? The one gave, the other soothed your trouble. And now that you understand, now that your mind is free from care and you can sleep without fear of the scholar's ill, will you not thank me for your cure, Messer Blondel?"

"Thank you?" the magistrate panted. "Thank you?" He stepped back two paces, groping with his hands, as if he sought to support himself by the table from which he had advanced.

"Ay, thank me!"

"No, but I will pay you!" Blondel cried, and with the word he snatched from the table a pistol that he had laid within his reach an hour earlier. Before the giant, confident in his size, saw the danger, the muzzle was at his breast. It was too late to move then—three paces divided the men; unfortunately in his haste to raise the pistol, Blondel had not shaken from it the handkerchief under which he had hidden it, and the lock fell on a morsel of the stuff. The next moment Basterga's huge hand struck aside the useless weapon, and flung Blondel gasping against the wall.

"Fool!" the scholar cried, towering above the baffled, shrinking man whose attempt had placed him at his mercy. "Think you that Cæsar Basterga was born to perish by your hand? That the gods made me what I am, I who carry to-night the fortunes of a nation and the fate of a king, that I might fall by so pitiful a creature as you! Ay, you are right, 'tis the alarm-bell? And by and by your friends will be here. It is a wonder," he continued, with a cruel look, "that they are not here already; but perhaps they have enough to fill their hands! And come or stay—

if they be like you, poor fool, weak in body as in wit—I care not! I, Cæsar Basterga, this night lord of Geneva, and in the time to come, and thanks to you——"

"Curse you!" Blondel gasped.

"That which I dare be sworn you have dreamt of being!" the scholar continued with a subtle smile. "The Grand Duke's *alter ego*, Mayor of the Palace, Adviser to His Highness! Yes, I hit you there? I touch you there! Oh, vanity of little men, I thought so!" He broke off and listened, as sharp on one another two gunshots rang out at no great distance from the house. A third followed as he hearkened: and on it a swelling wave of sound that rose with each second louder and nearer. "Ay, 'tis known now!" Basterga resumed, in a tone more quiet, but not less confident. "And I must go, my dear friend, who thought a minute ago to speed me for ever. Know that it lies not in hands mean as yours to harm Cæsar Basterga of Padua! And that to-night, of all nights, I bear a charmed life! I carry, Syndic, a kingdom and its fortunes!"

He seemed to swell with the thought; and in comparison of the sickly man scowling darkly on him from the wall, he did indeed look a king, as he turned to the door, flung it wide and passed into the passage. With only the street door between him and the hub-bub that was beginning to fill the night, he could measure the situation. He had stayed late. The beat of many feet hastening one way— toward the Porte Tertasse, the clatter of weapons as here and there a man trailed his pike on the stones, the roar of rising voices, the rattle of metal as someone hauled a chain across the end of the Bourg du Four and hooked it—sounds such as these might have alarmed an ordinary man who knew himself cut off from his party, and isolated among foes.

But Basterga did not quail. His belief in his star was genuine; he was intoxicated with the success which he fancied lay well in his grasp. He carried Cæsar and his fortunes! was it in mean men to harm him? So confident was he, that when he had opened the door he stood an instant on the threshold viewing the strange scene, and quoting with an appreciation as strange—

> " ' *At domus interior gemitu miseroque tumultu*
> *Miscetur, penitusque cavae plangoribus aedes*
> *Femineis ululant ; ferit aurea sidera clamor !* ' "

from his favourite poet. Then he turned without hesitation, and plunged into the stream of passers that was hurrying toward the Porte Tertasse.

He had been right not to quail. In the medley of light and shadow which filled the Bourg du Four and the streets about the Town Hall, in the confusion, in the rush of all in one direction and with one intent, no one paid heed to him, or supposed him to belong to the enemy. Some cried "To the Treille! They are there! To the Treille!" And these wheeled that way. But more, guided by the sounds of conflict, held on to the point, where the short, narrow street of the Tertasse, turned left handed out of the equally narrow Rue de la Cité—the latter leading onward to the Porte de la Monnaye, and the bridges. Here, at the meeting of the two confined lanes, overhung by timbered houses, and old gables of strange shapes, a desperate conflict was being fought. The Savoyards, masters of the gate, had begun to push their way into the town by the Rue Tertasse; not doubting that they would be supported by and by, upon the entrance of their main body through the Porte Neuve.   They had proceeded no farther, however, than the junction with the Rue de la Cité—a point where darkness was made visible by two dim oil lamps—before, the alarm being abroad, they found themselves confronted by a dozen half-clad townsfolk, fresh from their beds; of whom five or six were at once laid low.   The survivors, however, fought with desperation, giving back, foot by foot; and as the alarm flew abroad and the city rose, every moment brought the defenders a reinforcement—some father just roused from sleep, armed with the chance weapon that came to hand, or some youth panting for his first fight.   The assailants, therefore, found themselves stayed.   Slowly they were driven back into the narrow gullet of the Tertasse.   Even there they were put to it to hold their ground against an ever increasing swarm of citizens, whom despair and the knowledge that they were fighting on their hearths, for their wives, and for their children, brought up in renewed strength.

In the Tertasse, however, where it was not possible to outflank them, and no dark side-alley, vomiting now and again a desperate man, gave one to death, a score could hold out against a hundred.   Here then, with the gateway at their backs—whence three or four could fire over their heads—the Savoyards stood stubbornly at bay, awaiting the reinforcements that they were sure would come from the Porte Neuve.   They were picked troops not easily discouraged; and they had no fear that aught serious had happened.   But they asked impatiently why d'Albigny with the main body did not come; why Brunaulieu with the Monnaye in his hands did not see that the time was opportune.   They chafed at the delay.   Give the city time to array itself, let it recover from its first surprise, and all their forces might scarcely avail to crush opposition.

It was at this moment, when the burghers had drawn back a little that they might deliver a decisive attack, that Basterga came up. Fabri the Syndic had taken the command, and had shouted to all who had windows looking on the lane to light them. He had arrayed his men in some sort of order and was on the point of giving the word to charge, when he heard the steps of Basterga and some others coming up; he waited to allow them to join him. The instant they arrived he gave the word, and followed by some thirty burghers armed with half-pikes, halberds, anything the men had been able to snatch up, he charged the Savoyards.

In the narrow lane but four or five could fight abreast, and the Grand Duke's men were clad in steel and well armed. Nevertheless Fabri bore back the first line, pressed on them stoutly, and amid a wild *mêlée* of struggling men and waving weapons, began to drive the troop, in spite of a fierce resistance, into the gate. If he could do this and enter with them, even though he lost half his men, he might save the city.

But the Savoyards, though they gave back, gave back slowly. Within twenty paces of the gate the advance wavered, stopped, hung an instant. Of that instant Basterga took advantage. He had moved on undetected with the rearmost burghers; now he saw his opportunity and seized it. He flung to either side the man to right and left of him. He struck down, almost with the same movement, the man in front. He rushed on Fabri, who in the middle of the first line was supporting, though far from young, a single combat with one of the Savoyard leaders.

On him Basterga's coward weapon alighted without warning, and laid him low. To strike down another, and turning, range himself in the van of the foreigners with a
mighty "Savoy! Savoy!" was Basterga's next action; and
it sufficed. The panic-stricken burghers, apprised of
treason in their ranks, gave back every way. The Savoyards saw their advantage, rallied, and pressed them.
Speedily the Italians regained the ground they had lost,
and with the tall form of their champion fighting in the
van, began to sweep the townsfolk back into the Rue de
la Cité.

But arrived at the meeting of the ways, Basterga's followers paused, hesitating to expose their flank by entering
this second street. The Genevese saw this, rallied in their
turn, and for a moment seemed to be holding their own.
But three or four of their doughtiest fighters lay stark
in the kennel, they had no longer a leader, they were
poorly armed and hastily collected; and devoted as they
were, it needed little to renew the panic and start them
in utter rout. Basterga saw this, and when his men still
hung back, neglecting the golden opportunity, he rushed
forward almost alone, until he stood conspicuous between
the two bands—the one hesitating to come on, the other
hesitating to fly.

"Savoy!" he thundered. "Ville gagnée! The city is
ours! Cowards, come on!" And waving his halberd
above his head, he beckoned to his followers to advance.

Had they done so, had they charged on the instant, they
had changed all for him, and perhaps all for Geneva. But
they hung a moment, and the next, as in shame they drew
themselves together for the charge, their champion stooped
forward with a shrill cry. As he did so, he received full

THEIR CHAMPION SPRANG ASIDE, ONLY TO RECEIVE
THE NEXT MOMENT, FULL ON HIS NECK, A
HEAVY IRON POT

on his nape a heavy iron pot, that descending with tremendous force from a window above him, rolled from him
broken into three pieces.

He went down under the blow as if a sledge-hammer
had struck him; and so sudden, so dramatic was the fall—
his armour clanging about him—that for an instant the
two bands held their hands and stood staring, as indifferent
crowds stand, at gaze in the street. A dozen on the
patriots' side knew the house from which the *marmite* fell,
and marked it; and half as many saw at the small window
whence it came, the grey locks and stern wrinkled face of
an aged woman. The effect on the burghers was magical.
As if the act symbolised not only the loved ones for whom
they fought, but the dire distress to which they were come,
they rushed on the foreign men-at-arms with a spirit and a
fury hitherto unknown. With a ringing shout of "Mère
Royaume! Mère Royaume!"—raised by those who knew
the woman, and taken up by many who did not—they
swept the foe, shaken by the fall of their leader, along the
narrow Tertasse, pressed on them, and, still shouting the
new war-cry, entered the gateway along with them.

"Mère Royaume! Mère Royaume!" The name rang
savagely in the groining of the arch, echoed dully in the
obscurity in which the fierce struggle went on. And men
struck to its rhythm and men died to it. And men who
heard it thus and lived, never forgot it, nor ever went back
in their minds to that night without recalling it.

To one man, flurried already, and a coward at heart, the
name carried a dread assurance of doom. He had
seen Basterga fall—by this woman's hand of all hands in
the world—and he had been the first to flee. But in the
lane he tripped over Fabri, he fell headlong, and only

raised himself in time to gain the gateway a few feet in front of the avenging pikes. Still, he might escape, he hoped to escape, through the gate and into the open Corraterie. But the first to reach them had taken in hand to shut the gates, and so to prevent the townsfolk reaching the Corraterie. One of the great doors, half-closed, blocked his way, and instinctively—ignorant how far behind him the pike-points were—he sprang aside into the guard-room.

His one chance now—for he was cut off, and knew it—lay in reaching the staircase and mounting to the roof. A bound carried him to the door, he grasped the handle. But a fugitive who had only a second before saved himself that way, took him for a pursuer, dragged the door close and held it—held it in spite of his efforts and his imprecations.

Five seconds, ten, perhaps, Grio—for he it was—wasted in struggling vainly with the door. The man on the other side clung to it with a despair equal to his own. Five seconds, ten, perhaps; but in that space of time, short as it was, the man paid smartly for the sins of his life. When the time of grace had elapsed, with a pike-point a few inches from his back and the gleaming eyes of an avenging burgher behind it, he fled shrieking round the table. He might even yet have escaped by a chance; for all was confusion, and though there was a glare there was no light. But he stumbled over the body of the man whom he had slain without pity a few hours before. He fell writhing, and died on the floor, under a dozen blows, as beasts die in the shambles.

"Mère Royaume! Mère Royaume!" The cry—the last cry he heard—swelled louder and louder. It swept through the gate, it passed through to the open; and bore far along the Corraterie, far along the ramparts, ay, and to the open country, the earnest of victory, the earnest of vengeance.

Geneva was saved. He who would have betrayed it, slain like Pyrrhus the Epirote by a woman's hand, lay dead in the dark lane behind the house in which he had lived.

CHAPTER XXVI

THE DAWN

ANNE was but one of some thousands of women, who passed through the trial of that night; who heard the vague sounds of disquiet that roused them at midnight grow to sharp alarms, and these again —to the dull, pulsing music of the tocsin—swell to the uproar of a deadly conflict waged by desperate men in narrow streets. She was but one of thousands who that night heard fate knocking at their hearts; who praying, sick with fear, for the return of their men, showed white faces at barred windows, and by every tossing light that passed along the lane viewed long years of loneliness or widowhood.

But Anne had this burden also; that she had of herself sent her man into danger; her man, who, but for her pleading, but for her bidding, might not have gone. And that thought, though she had done her duty, laid a cold grip upon her heart. Her work it was if he lay at this moment stark in some dark alley, the first victim of the assault; or sorely wounded, cried for water; or waited in pain where none but the stricken heard him. The thought bowed her to the ground, sent her to her prayers, took from her alike all memory of the danger that had menaced her this morning, and all consciousness of that which now threatened her a helpless woman, if the town were taken.

The house, having its back on the Rue de la Cité, at the

point where that street joined the Tertasse, stood in the
heart of the conflict; and almost from the moment of the
first attack on the Porte Neuve, which Claude was in time
to witness, was a centre of fierce and deadly fighting.
Anne dared not leave her mother, who, strange to say, slept
through the early alarms; and it was bowed on the edge of
her mother's bed—that bed beside which she had tasted so
much of happiness and so much of grief—that she passed,
not knowing what the turning page might show, the first
hour of anxiety and suspense.

The report of a shot shook her frame. A scream
stabbed her like a knife. Lower and lower she thrust her
face amid the bed-clothes, striving to shut out sound and
knowledge; or woman-like, she raised her pale, beseeching
face that she might listen, that she might hope. If he fell
would they tell her? And how he fell, and where? Or
would they hold her strange to him? Would she never
hear?

Suddenly her mother opened her eyes, lay awhile, listening, then slowly sat up and looked at her. Anne saw
the awakening alarm in the dear face—that in some
mysterious way recalled its youth; and she fancied that to
her other troubles, the misery of one of the old paroxysms
was going to be added. At such an hour, with such sounds
of terror filling the night, with such a glare dancing on the
ceiling, the first attack had come on—years before. Then
the alarm had been fictitious; to-night the calamity which
the poor woman had imagined was happening with every
circumstance of peril and alarm.

But Madame Royaume's face, though anxious and serious, retained to an astonishing extent its sanity. Whether
the dream which she had had earlier in the night had

prepared her for the state of things to which she awoke, or the weeks and months which had elapsed since that old alarm of fire, dropped in some inexplicable way from her—and as one shock had upset, another restored the balance of her mind—certain it is that Anne, watching her with a painful interest, found her sane. Nor did Madame Royaume's first words dispel the impression.

"They hold out?" she asked, grasping her daughter's hand and pressing it. "They hold out?"

"Yes, yes, they hold out," Anne answered, hoping to soothe her. And she patted the hand that clasped hers. "Have no fear, dear, all will go well."

"If they have faith and hold out," the aged woman replied, listening to the strange medley of sounds that rose to them.

"They will, they will," Anne faltered.

"But there is need of every one!"

"They are gone, dear," the girl answered, repressing a sob with difficulty. "We are alone in the house."

"So it should be," Madame Royaume replied with sternness. "The man to the wall, the maid to the pall! It was ever so!"

A low cry burst from Anne's lips. "God forbid!" she wailed. "God forbid! God have mercy!"

The next moment she could have bitten out her tongue; she knew that such words and such a cry were of all others the most likely to excite her patient. But after some obscure fashion their positions seemed this night to be reversed. It was the mother who in her turn patted her daughter's hand and sought to soothe her.

"Ay, God forbid," she said softly. "But man must do his part. I mind when——" She paused. Her eyes

travelling round the room, fixed their gaze on the fireplace. She seemed to be perplexed by something she saw
there, and Anne, still fearing a recurrence of her illness,
asked her hurriedly what it was. "What is it, mother?"
she said, leaning over her, and following the direction of
her eyes. "Is it the great pot you are looking at?"

"Ay," Madame Royaume answered slowly. "How
comes it here?"

"There was no one below," Anne explained. "I
brought it up this morning. Don't you remember? There
is no fire below."

"No?"

"That is all, mother. You saw me bring it up."

"Ay?" And then, after a pause, "Let it down a hook."

"But——"

"Let it down, child!" And when Anne, to soothe her,
had obeyed and let the great pot down until the fire licked
its sides, "Is it full?" Madame asked.

"Half-full, mother."

"It will do." And for a time the woman in the bed
was silent.

Outside there was noise enough. The windows in the
room looked into the Corraterie, from which side no more
than passing sounds of conflict rose to them; the pounding
of running feet, sharp orders, a shot, and then another.
But the landing without the door looked down by a high-
set window into the narrow Tertasse; and from this,
though the door was shut, rose an inferno of noise; the
clash of steel, the cries of the wounded, the shouts of the
fighters. The townsfolk, rallying from their first alarm,
were driving the enemy out of the Rue de la Cité, penning
him into the Tertasse, and preparing to carry that street.

On a sudden there came, not a cessation of the uproar,
but a change in its character.   It was as if the current of a
river had been momentarily stayed and pent up; and then
with a mighty crashing of timbers and shifting of pebbles,
and a din as of the world's end had begun to run the other
way.   Anne's face turned a shade paler.   So appalling was
the noise, she would fain have stopped her ears.   But her
mother sat up.

"What is it?" she asked eagerly.   "What is it?"

"Dear mother, do not fret!   It must be——"

"Go, and see, child!   Go to the window in the passage,
and see!" Madame Royaume persisted.

Anne had no wish to go, no wish to see.   She pictured
her lover in the *mêlée* whence rose those appalling cries;
and gladly would she have hidden her head in the bed-
clothes and poured out her heart in prayer for him.   But
Madame persisted, and she complied, went into the passage and opened the small window.   With the cold air
entered a fresh volume of sound.   On the walls and
timbered gables opposite her—and so near that she could
wellnigh touch them with her extended arm—strange
lights played luridly; and here and there, at dormers on a
level with her, pale faces showed and vanished by turns.

She looked down.   For a moment, in the confusion, in
the medley of moving forms, she could discern little or
nothing.   Then, as her eyes became more accustomed to
the sight, she made out that the tide of conflict was running inward into the town, a sign that the invaders were
getting the better.

"Well?" Madame Royaume asked, her voice querulous.

Anne strove to say something that would soothe her
mother.   But a sob choked her, and when she regained

her speech she felt herself impelled, she knew not why, to tell the truth. "I fear our people are falling back," she murmured, trembling so violently that she could hardly stand.

"How far? Where are they, child?" Madame's voice was eager. "Where are they?"

"They are almost under the window!" And then withdrawing her head with a shudder, and clinging for support to the frame of the window, "They are fighting underneath me now," she said. "God pity them!"

"And who is—are we still getting the worst of it?"

Forced by a dreadful fascination, Anne looked out again. "Yes, there is one man, a big man, leads them on," she said, in the voice of one who painfully absorbed in a sight, reports it involuntarily. "He is driving our people before him. Ah! he has struck one down this moment. He is almost underneath us now. But his people will not follow him! They are standing. He—he waves them on!"

"He is underneath us?" Madame's voice sounded strangely near, strangely insistent. But Anne, wrapt in what she saw, did not heed it.

"Yes! He is a dozen paces in front of his men—underneath us now. He urges them to follow him! He towers above them! He is——"

She broke off; close to her sounded a heavy breathing, that even above the babel of the street caught her ear. She drew in her head, looked, and, overwrought by that which she had been witnessing, she shrieked aloud.

Beside her, bending under the weight of the great steaming pot, stood her mother! Her mother, who had scarcely left her bedroom twice in a twelvemonth, nor crossed it as many times in a week. But it was her mother; endowed

at this pass, and for the instant, with supernatural strength.
For even as Anne recoiled thunderstruck, the old woman
lifted the huge *marmite,* half-full and steaming as it was,
to the ledge of the window, steadied it there an instant,
and then, with the gleaming eyes and set pale face of an
avenging prophetess, thrust it forth.

A second they gazed at one another with suspended
breath.   Then from the street below rose a wild shriek,
a crash, and lo, the huge pot lay shattered in the kennel
beside the man whom, Heaven directed, it had slain.   As
if the shock of its fall stayed for an instant even the movement of the world, a silence fell on all: then, as the roar of
conflict rose again, louder, more vengeful, with a new note
in it, she caught her mother in her arms.

"Mother!   Mother!" she cried.   "Mother!"

The elder woman was white to the lips.   "Get me to
bed!" she muttered.   "Get me to bed!"   She had lost
the power even to stand.   That she had ever borne, even
for a yard, the great pot which it taxed Anne's utmost
strength to carry upstairs was a miracle.   But a miracle
were all the circumstances connected with the act.

Anne carried her back and laid her on the bed, greatly
fearing for her.   And thenceforth for a while the girl's
horizon, so wide and stormy an instant before, was narrowed to the bed beside which she stood, narrowed to
the dear face on which the lamp-light fell, and disclosed
its death-like pallor.   For the time Anne forgot even her
lover, was deaf to the struggle outside, was unmindful of
the flight of the hours.   For her, Geneva might have lain
at peace, the night been as other nights, the house below
been heavy with the breathing of tired sleepers.   She
looked neither to the right nor the left, until under her

loving hands Madame Royaume revived, opened her eyes and smiled—the smile she had for one face only in the world.

By that time Anne had lost count of the time. It might be hard on morning, it might be a little after midnight. One thing only was clear, the lamp required oil, and to get it she must descend to the ground floor. She opened the door and listened, wondering dully how the conflict had gone. She had lost count of that also.

The small window at the head of the stairs remained open as they had left it; and through it, a ceaseless hum, as of a hive of bees swarming, poured in from the night, and told of multitudes astir. The alarm-bell had ceased to ring, the wilder sounds of conflict had died down; in the parts about the Tertasse the combat appeared to be at an end. But this might be either because resistance had ceased, or because the battle had rolled away to other quarters, or—which she scarcely dared to hope—because the foe had been driven out.

As she stood listening, she shivered in the cold air that came from the window. She felt as if she had been beaten, and knew that it came of the shocks she had suffered and the long strain. She feared for her nerves, and hated to go down into the dark parts of the house as if some danger lurked there. She longed for morning, for the light; and thought of Claude and his fate, and wondered why the thought of his danger did not move her to weeping, as it had moved her a few hours earlier.

In truth she was worn out. The effort to revive her mother had cost her the last remains of strength. Her feet as she descended the stairs were of lead, the brazen notes of the alarm-bell hummed in her ears. When she reached the living-room she set the lamp on one of the tables and sat down wearily, with her eyes on the cold, empty hearth and on the settle where she had sat with his arms about her. And now, if ever, she must weep; but she could not.

The lamp burned low, and cast smoky shadows on the ceiling and the walls. The shuttered windows showed their dead faces. The cheerful soul of the room had passed from it with the fire, leaving the shell gloomy, lifeless, repellant. Anne drowsed a moment in sheer exhaustion, and would have slept, if the lamp on the point of expiring had not emitted a sound and roused her. She rose reluctantly, dragged herself to the great cupboard under the stairs, and, having lighted a rushlight at the dying flame, put out the lamp and refilled it.

She was about to relight it, and had taken the rushlight in her hand for the purpose, when she heard, through the shuttered windows and the barred door, a growing clamour; the tramp of heavy feet, the hum of many voices, the buzz of a crowd that, almost as soon as she awoke to its near presence, came to a stand before the house. The tumult of voices raised all at once in different keys did not entirely drown the clash of arms; and while she stood sullenly regarding the door, resigned to the inevitable, whatever it might be, thin shafts of light pierced the shutters and stabbed the gloom about her.

With that a hail storm of knocks fell on the door and on the shutters. A dozen voices cried "Open! Open!" The jangle of a halberd as someone let its butt drop heavily on the stone steps added force to the summons.

Anne's first impulse was to retreat upstairs, and leave them to do their worst. Her next—she was in a state of collapse in which resistance seemed useless—was to open. She moved to the door, and with cold hands removed the huge bars and let down the chain. It was only when she had done so much, when it remained only to unlock, that she wavered; that she trembled to think on what the crowd might be bent and what might be her fate in their hands. She paused then, with her fingers on the key; but not for long. She remembered that, before she descended, she had heard neither shot nor cry. Resistance, therefore, had ceased, and that of a single house, held by two help-less women, could avail nothing, could but excite to fury and reprisals.

She turned the key and opened. The lights dazzled her. The doorway, as she stood faltering, almost faint-ing, before it, seemed to be full of dancing faces, some swathed in bandages, others powder-blackened, some hot with excitement, others pallid with fatigue. They were such faces, piled one above the other, as are seen in bad dreams.

On the intruders' side, those who pressed in first saw a girl strangely quiet, who held the door wide open for them. "My mother is ill," she said in a voice that strove for composure; if they were the enemy, her only hope, she thought, lay in courage. "And she is old," she con-tinued. "Do not harm her."

"We come to do harm neither to you nor to her," a voice replied. And the foremost of the troop, a thick dwarfish man with a huge two-handed sword, stood aside. "Messer Baudichon," he said to one behind him, "this is the daughter."

She knew the fat, sturdy Councillor—who in Geneva did not?—and through her stupor recognised him, although a great bandage swathed half his head, and he was pale. And, beginning to have an inkling that things were well, she began also to tremble. By his side stood Messer Petitot—she knew him, too, he had been Syndic the year before—and a man in hacked and blood-stained armour with his arm in a sling and his face black with powder. These three, and behind them a dozen others —men whom she had seen on high days robed in velvet, but who now wore, one and all, the ugly marks of that night's work—looked on her with a strange benevolence. And Baudichon took her hand.

"We do not come to harm you," he said. "On the contrary we come to thank you and yours. In the name of the city of Geneva, and of all those here with me——"

"Ay! Ay!" cried Jehan Brosse, the bandy-legged tailor. And he rang his sword on the doorstep. "Ay! Ay!"

"We come to thank you for the blow struck this night from this house! That it rid us of one of our worst foes was a small thing, girl. But that it put heart into our burghers and strength into their arms at a critical moment was another and a greater thing. Which shall not, if Geneva stand—as stand by God's leave she will, the stronger for this night's work—be forgotten! The name of Mère Royaume will at the next meeting of the Greater Council be inscribed among the names of those whom the Free City thanks for their services this night!"

A murmur of stern approval that began with those in the house rolled through the doorway and was echoed by the waiting throng that filled the street.

She was weeping. All it meant, all it might mean, what warranty of powerful friends, what fame beyond the reach of dark stories, or a woman's spite, she could not yet understand, she could not yet appreciate. But something, the city's safety, the city's gratitude, the countenance of these men who came to her door blood-stained, dark with powder, reeling with fatigue—came that they might thank her mother and do her honour—something of this she did grasp as she wept before them.

She had but one thing to ask, one thing to desire; and in a moment it was given her.

"Nor is that all!" The voice that broke in was harsher and blunter than Baudichon's. "If it be true, as I am told, that a young man of the name of Mercier lives here? He does, does he? Ay, he lives, my girl. He is safe, have no fear. For the matter of that he has nine lives, and"— Captain Blandano continued with an oath—"he has had need of all this night, God forgive me for the word! But, as I said, that is not all. For if there is any one man who has saved Geneva, it is he, the man who let down the portcullis. And if the city does not dower you, my girl——"

"The city shall dower her!" The speaker's voice came from somewhere in the neighbourhood of the doorway, and was something tremulous and uncertain. But what it lacked in strength it made up in haste and eagerness. "The city shall dower her! If not, I will!"

"Good, Messer Blondel, and spoken like you!" Blandano answered heartily. And though one or two of the foremost, on hearing Blondel's voice, looked askance at one another, and here and there a whisper passed, of "The Syndic of the Guard? How came——" the majority drowned such murmurings under a chorus of applause.

"We are of one mind, I think!" Baudichon said. And with that he turned to the door. "Now, good friends," he continued, "it wants but little of daylight, and some of us were best in our beds. Let us go. That we lie down in peace and honour"—he went on, solemnly raising his hand over the happy, weeping girl beside him, as if he blessed her—"that our wives and children lie safe within our walls is due, under God, to this roof. And I call all here to witness that while I live the city of Geneva shall never forget the debt that is due to this house and to the name of Royaume!"

"Ay, ay!" cried the tailor. "I too! The small with the great, the rich with the poor, as we have fought this night!"

"Ay! Ay!"

Some shook her by the hand, and some called Heaven to bless her, and some with tears running down their faces —for no man there was his common everyday self—did naught but look on her with kindness. And so, each having done after his fashion, they trooped out again into the street. A moment later, as the winter sun began to colour the distant snows, and the second Sunday in December of the year 1602 broke on Geneva, the voices of the multitude rose in the one hundred and twenty-fourth psalm; to the solemn thunder of which, poured from thankful hearts, the assembly accompanied Baudichon to his home a little farther down the Corraterie.

Anne was about to close the door and secure it after them—with feelings how different from those with which she had opened that door!—when it resisted her shaking hands. She did not on the instant understand the reason or what was the matter. She pushed more strongly, still it came back on her, it opened widely and more widely. And then one who had heard all yet had not shown himself, one who had entered with Baudichon's company but had held himself hidden in the background, pushed in, uninvited.

Uninvited? The rushlight still burned low and smokily, and she had not relighted the lamp. The corners were dark with shadows, the hearth was cold and empty and ugly, the shutters still blinded the windows. But the coming of this uninvited one—love comes ever unexpected and uninvited—how strangely, how marvellously, how beautifully did it change all for her, light all, fill all.

As she felt his arms about her, as she clung to him, and sobbed on his shoulder, as she strove for words and could not utter them for the happiness of her heart, as she felt his kisses rain on her face in joy and safety, who had not left her in sorrow, no, nor in the shadow of death, nor for any fears of what man could do to him—let it be said that her reward was as her trial.

.   .   .   .

Madame Royaume lived four years after that famous attack on the Free City of Geneva which is called the Escalade; and during that time she experienced no return of the mysterious malady that came with one shock, and passed from her with another. Nor, so far as can be ascertained at the distant time at which I write, did the suspicions, which the night of the escalade found in the bud, survive it. Probably the Corraterie and the neighbouring quarter, ay, and the whole city of Geneva had for many a week to come matter for gossip and to spare. It is certain at any rate, that whatever whispers were current in this house or that, no tongue wagged openly against the favour-

ites of the Council, who were also the favourites of the
crowd. For Mère Royaume's act hit marvellously the
public fancy, and, passing from mouth to mouth, and from
generation to generation, is still the first, the best loved,
and the most picturesque of the legends of Geneva.

And Messer Blondel? Did he evade the penalty of
his act? Ask any man in the streets of Geneva, even
to-day, and he will tell you the fate of Philibert Blondel,
Fourth Syndic. He will tell you how the magistrate
triumphed for a time, as he had triumphed in the Council
before, how he closed the mouths of his accusers, how not
once, but twice and thrice, by the sheer force and skill of
a man working in a medium which he understood, he won
his acquittal from his compeers. But though punishment
be slow to overtake, it does overtake at last; nor has the
world witnessed many instances more pertinent or more
famous than that of Messer Blondel. Strive as he might,
tongues would wag within the Council and without. Silence as he might Baudichon and Petitot, smaller men
would talk; and their talk persisted and grew, and was
vigorous when months and even years had passed. What
the great did not know the small knew or guessed, and fixed
greedy eyes on the head of the man who had dared to sell
Geneva. The end came four years after the escalade. To
conceal the old negotiation he committed a further crime,
and being betrayed by the tool he employed, was seized
and convicted. On the 1st of September, 1606, he lost
his head on a scaffold erected before his own house in the
Bourg du Four.

The Merciers had at least one son—probably he was
the eldest, for he bore his father's name—who lived into
middle life, and proved himself their worthy descendant,

for precisely fifty years after the date of these events a poor woman of the name of Michée Chauderon was put to death in Geneva, on a charge of sorcery; and among those—and they were not few—who strove most manfully and most obstinately to save her, we find the name of a physician of great note in the Canton at that time—one Claude Mercier. He did not prevail, though he struggled bravely; the long night of superstition, though nearing its close, still reigned; that woman suffered. But he carried it so far and so boldly that from that day to this —and the city may be proud of the fact—no person has suffered death in Geneva on that dreadful charge.

THE END.